THE VOYAGE
OF THE
JERLE SHANNARA

BOOK TWO

ANTRAX

THE VOYAGE
OF THE
JERLE SHANNARA

BOOK TWO

ANTRAX

TERRY BROOKS

EARTHLIGHT

NEW YORK LONDON TORONTO SYDNEY SINGAPORE

First published in the United States by
The Ballantine Publishing Group, 2001
First published in Great Britain by Earthlight, 2002
This edition published by Earthlight, 2002
An imprint of Simon & Schuster UK Ltd
A Viacom Company

Maps by Russ Charpentier
Interior art by Russ Charpentier and Steve Stone

3 5 7 9 10 8 6 4 2

Simon & Schuster UK Ltd
Africa House
64–78 Kingsway
London WC2B 6AH

www.simonsays.co.uk

Simon & Schuster Australia
Sydney

A CIP catalogue record for this book
is available from the British Library

ISBN 0 7434 1495 0

Printed and bound in Great Britain by
Bookmarque Ltd., Croydon, Surrey.

TO JOHN SAUL AND MIKE SACK

For fifteen years of wry insight,
wicked humor, and invaluable advice

PARKASIA
Crake Rainforest
Aleuthra Ark Mts.
Rindge Village
Shape Shifters
Castledown
Aleuthra Ark Mts.
Glacier
Glacier
The Squirm
Repairs to Jerle Shannara
Ice Henge
Coastal Islands
S
BLUE DIVIDE

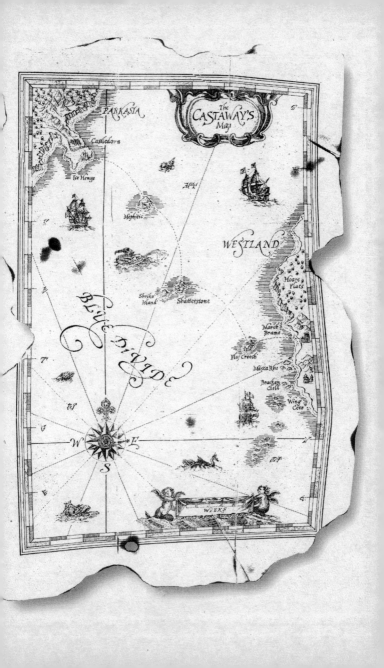

ONE

Grianne Ohmsford was six years old on the last day of her childhood. She was small for her age and lacked unusual strength of body or extraordinary life experience and was not therefore particularly well prepared for growing up all at once. She had lived the whole of her life on the eastern fringes of the Rabb Plains, a sheltered child in a sheltered home, the eldest of two born to Araden and Biornlief Ohmsford, he a scribe and teacher, she a housewife. People came and went from their home as if it were an inn, students of her father, clients drawing on the benefit of his skills, travelers from all over the Four Lands. But she herself had never been anywhere and was only just beginning to understand how much of the world she knew nothing about when everything she did know was taken from her.

While she was unremarkable in appearance and there was nothing about her on the surface of things that would suggest she could survive any sort of life-altering trauma, the truth of the matter was that she was strong and able in unexpected ways. Some of this showed in her startling blue eyes, which pinned you with their directness and pierced you through to your soul. Strangers who made the mistake of staring into them found themselves glancing quickly away. She did not speak to these men and women or seem to take anything away from her encounters, but she left them with a sense of having given something up anyway. Wandering her home and yard, long dark hair hanging loose, a waif seemingly at a loss for something to do or somewhere to go, or just sitting alone in a corner while the adults talked among themselves, she claimed her own space and kept it inviolate.

She was tough-minded, as well, a stubborn and intractable child who once her mind was set on something refused to let it be changed. For a time her parents could do so by virtue of their relationship and the usual threats and enticements, but eventually they found themselves incapable of influencing her. She seemed to find her identity in making a stand on matters, by holding forth in challenge and accepting whatever came her way as a result. Frequently it was a stern lecture and banishment to her room, but often it was simply denial of something others thought would benefit her. Whatever the case, she did not seem to mind the consequences and was more apt to be bothered by capitulation to their wishes.

But at the core of everything was her heritage, which manifested itself in ways that hadn't been apparent for generations. She knew early on that she was not like her parents or their friends or anyone else she knew. She was a throwback to the most famous members of her family—to Brin and Jair and Par and Coll Ohmsford, to whom she could directly trace her ancestry. Her parents explained it to her early on, almost as soon as her talent revealed itself. She was born with the magic of the wishsong, a latent power that surfaced in the Ohmsford family bloodline only once in every four or five generations. Wish for it, sing for it, and it would come to pass. Anything was possible. The wishsong hadn't been present in an Ohmsford in her parents' lifetimes, and so neither of them had any firsthand experience with how it worked. But they knew the stories, had been told them repeatedly by their own parents, the tales of the magic carried down from the time of the great Queen Wren, another of their ancestors. So they knew enough to recognize what it meant when their child could bend the stalks of flowers and turn aside an angry dog simply by singing.

Her use of the wishsong was rudimentary and undisciplined at first, and she did not understand that it was special. In her child's mind, it seemed reasonable that everyone would possess it. Her parents worked to help her realize its worth, to harness its power, and to learn to keep it secret from others. Grianne was a smart girl, and she understood quickly what it meant to have something others would covet or fear if they knew she possessed it. She listened to her parents about this, although she paid less attention to their warnings about the ways it should be used and the purposes to which it should be put. She knew enough to show them what they expected of her and to hide from them what they did not.

So on the last day of her childhood she had already come to terms with having use of the magic. She had constructed defenses to its demands and subterfuges to her parents' refusals to let her fully test its limits. Wrapped in the armor of her strong-minded determination and stubborn insistence, she had built a fortress in which she wielded the wishsong with a sense of impunity. Her child's world was already more complex and devious than that of many adults, and she was learning the importance of never giving away everything of who and what she was. It was her gift of magic and her understanding of its workings that saved her.

At the same time, and through no fault of her own, it was what doomed her parents and younger brother.

She knew there was something wrong with her child's world some weeks before that last day. It manifested itself in small ways, things that her parents and others could not readily detect. There were oddities in the air—smells and tastes and sounds that whispered of a hidden presence and dark emotions. She caught glimpses of shadows on the vibrations of her voice that returned to her when she used the magic of her song. She felt changes in heat and cold that came only when she was threatened, except that always before she could trace their source and this time she could not. Once or twice, she sensed the closeness of dark-cloaked forms, perhaps the shape-shifters she had found out on several occasions before, always hidden and out of reach, but there nevertheless.

She said nothing to her parents of these things because she had no solid evidence of them and only suspicion on which to buttress her complaints. Even so, she kept close watch. Her home was at the edge of a grove of maple trees and looked out across the flat, green threshold of the Rabb all the way to the foothills of the Dragon's Teeth. While nothing could approach out of the west without being visible from a long way off, forests and hills shielded the other three quadrants. She scouted them from time to time, a precaution undertaken to give her a sense of security. But whatever watched was careful, and she never found it out. It hid from her, avoided her, moved away when she approached, and always returned. She could feel its eyes on her even as she looked for it. It was clever and skilled; it was accustomed to staying hidden when others would find it out.

She should have been afraid, but she had not been raised with fear and had no reason to appreciate its uses. For her, fear was an annoyance she sought to banish and did not heed.

She asked her father finally if there was anyone who would wish to hurt her, or him, or her mother or brother, but he only smiled and said they had nothing anyone would want that would provide reason for harm. He said it in a calm, assured way, a teacher imparting knowledge to a student, and she did not believe he could be wrong.

When the black-cloaked figures finally came, they did so just before dawn, when the light was so pale and thin that it barely etched the edges of the shadows. They killed the dog, old Bark, when he wandered out for a look, an act that demonstrated unmistakably the nature of their dark intent. She was awake by then, alerted by some inner voice tied to her magic, hurrying through the rooms of her home on cat's paws, searching for the danger that was already at the door. Her family was alone that morning, all of the travelers either come and gone or still on their way, and there was no one to stand with them in the face of their peril.

Grianne never hesitated when she caught sight of the shadowy forms sliding past the windows. She sensed the presence of danger all around, a circle of iron blades closing with inexorable purpose. She yelled for her father and ran back to her bedroom, where her brother lay sleeping. She snatched him up without a word, hugging him to her. Soft and warm, he was barely two years old. She carried him from the room and down into the earthen cellar where perishable food-stuffs were kept. Above, her parents sought to cover her flight. The sounds of breaking glass and splintering wood erupted, and she could hear her father's angry shouts and oaths. He was a brave man, and he would stand and fight. But it would not be enough; she sensed that much already. She re-leased a catch and pulled back the shelving section that hid the entrance to the cramped storm shelter they had never used. She placed her sleeping brother on a pallet inside. She stared down at him for a moment, at his tiny face and balled fists, at his sleeping form, hearing the shouts and oaths overhead turn to screams of pain and anguish, aware of tears flooding her eyes.

Black smoke was seeping through the floorboards when she slipped from the shelter and sealed the entry behind her. She heard the crackle of flames consuming wood. Her parents gone, the intruders would come for her, but she would be quicker and more clever than they expected. She would escape them, and once she was safely away, outside in the pale dawn light, she would run the five miles to the next closest home and return with help for her brother.

She heard the black-cloaked forms searching for her as she hurried along a short passageway to a cellar door that led directly outside. Outside, the door was concealed by bushes and seldom used; it was not likely they would think to find her there. If they did, they would be sorry. She already knew the sort of damage the wishsong could cause. She was a child, but she was not helpless. She blinked away her tears and set her jaw. They would find that out one day. They would find that out when she hurt them the same way they were hurting her.

Then she was through the door and outside in the brightening dawn light, crouched in the bushes. Smoke swirled about her in dark clouds, and she felt the heat of the fire as it climbed the walls of her home. Everything was being taken from her, she thought in despair. Everything that mattered.

A sudden movement to one side drew her attention. When she turned to look, a hand wrapped in a foul-smelling cloth closed over her face and sent her spiraling downward into blackness.

* * *

When she awoke, she was bound, gagged, and blindfolded, and she could not tell where she was or who held her captive or even if it was day or night. She was carried over a thick shoulder like a sack of wheat, but her captors did not speak. There were more than one; she could hear their footsteps, heavy and certain. She could hear their breathing. She thought about her home and parents. She thought about her brother. The tears came anew, and she began to sob. She had failed them all.

She was carried for a long time, then laid upon the ground and left alone. She squirmed in an effort to free herself, but the bonds were too tightly knotted. She was hungry and thirsty, and a cold desperation was creeping through her. There could be only one reason she had been taken captive, one reason she was needed when her parents and brother were not. Her wishsong. She was alive and they were dead because of her legacy. She was the one with the magic. She was the one who was special. Special enough that her family was killed so that she could be stolen away. Special enough to cause everything she loved and cared for to be taken from her.

There was a commotion not long after that, sudden and unexpected, filled with new sounds of battle and angry cries. They seemed to be coming from all around her. Then she was snatched from the ground and carried off, leaving the sounds behind. The one who carried her now cradled her while running, holding her close, as if to soothe her fear and desperation. She curled into her rescuer's arms, burrowed as if stricken, for such was the depth of her need.

When they were alone in a silent place, the bonds and gag and blindfold were removed. She sat up and found herself facing a big man wrapped in black robes, a man who was not entirely human, his face scaly and mottled like a snake's, his fingers ending in claws, and his eyes lidless slits. She caught her breath and shrank from him, but he did not move away in response.

"You are safe now, little one," he whispered. "Safe from those who would harm you, from the Dark Uncle and his kind."

She did not know whom he was talking about. She looked around guardedly. They were crouched in a forest, the trees stark sentinels on all sides, their branches confining amid a sea of sunshine that dappled the woodland earth like gold dust. There was no one else around, and nothing of what she saw looked familiar.

"There is no reason to be afraid of me," the other said. "Are you frightened by how I look?"

She nodded warily, swallowing against the dryness in her throat.

He handed her a water skin, and she drank gratefully. "Do not be afraid. I am of mixed breed, both Man and Mwellret, little one. I look scary, but I am your friend. I was the one who saved you from those others. From the Dark Uncle and his shape-shifters."

That was twice he had mentioned the Dark Uncle. "Who is he?" she asked. "Is he the one who hurt us?"

"He is a Druid. Walker is his name. He is the one who attacked your home and killed your parents and your brother." The reptilian eyes fixed on her. "Think back. You will remember seeing his face."

To her surprise, she did. She saw it clearly, a glimpse of it as it passed a window in the thin dawn light, dusky skin and black beard, eyes so piercing they stripped you bare, dark brow creased with frown lines. She saw him, knew him for her enemy, and felt a rage of such intensity she thought she might burn from the inside out.

Then she was crying, thinking of her parents and her brother, of her home and her lost world. The man across from her drew her gently into his arms and held her close.

"You cannot go back," he told her. "They will be searching for you. They will never give up while they think you are alive."

She nodded into his shoulder. "I hate them," she said in a thin, sharp wail.

"Yes, I know," he whispered. "You are right to hate them." His rough, guttural voice tightened. "But listen to me, little one. I am the Morgawr. I am your father and mother now. I am your family. I will help you to find a way to gain revenge for what has been taken from you. I will teach you to ward yourself against everything that might hurt you. I will teach you to be strong."

He whisked her away, lifting her as if she weighed nothing, and carried her deeper into the woods to where a giant bird waited. He called the bird a Shrike, and she flew on its back with him to another part of the Four Lands, one dark and solitary and empty of sound and life. He cared for her as he said he would, trained her in mind and body, and kept her safe. He told her more of the Druid Walker, of his scheming and his hunger for power, of his long-sought goal of dominance over all the Races in all the lands. He showed her images of the Druid and his black-cloaked servants, and he kept her anger fired and alive within her child's breast.

"Never forget what he has stolen from you," he would repeat. "Never forget what you are owed for his betrayal."

After a time he began to teach her to use the wishsong as a weapon against which no one could stand—not once she had mastered it and brought it under her control, not once she had made it so much a part of her that its use seemed second nature. He taught her that even a slight change in pitch or tone could alter health to sickness and life to death. A Druid had such power, he told her. The Druid Walker in particular. She must learn to be a match for him. She must learn to use her magic to overcome his.

After a while she thought no longer of her parents and her brother, whom she knew to be dead and lost to her forever; they were no more than bones buried in the earth, a part of a past forever lost, of a childhood erased in a single day. She gave herself over to her new life and to her mentor, her teacher, and her friend. The Morgawr was all those while she grew through adolescence, all those and much more. He was the shaper of her thinking and the navigator of her life. He was the inspiration for her magic's purpose and the keeper of her dreams of righting the wrongs she had suffered.

He called her his little Ilse Witch, and she took the name for her own. She buried her given name with her past, and she never used it again.

TWO

Her memories of the past, already faded and tattered, fell away in an instant's time as she stood in a woodland clearing a thousand miles from her lost home and confronted the boy who claimed he was her brother.

"Grianne, it's Bek," he insisted. "Don't you remember?"

She remembered everything, of course, although no longer as clearly and sharply, no longer as painfully. She remembered, but she refused to believe that her memories could be brought to life with such painful clarity after so many years. She hadn't heard her name spoken in all that time, hadn't spoken it herself, had barely even thought of it. She was the Ilse Witch, and that name defined who and what she was, and not the other. The other was for when she had achieved her revenge over the Druid, for when she had gained sufficient recognition and power that when it was spoken next, it would never again be forgotten by anyone.

But here was this slip of a boy speaking it now, daring to suggest that he had a right to do so. She stared at him in disbelief and smoldering anger. Could he really be her brother? Could he be Bek, alive in spite of what she had believed for so long? Was it possible? She tried to make sense of the idea, to find a way to address it, to form words to speak in response.

But everything she thought to say or do was jumbled and incoherent, refusing to be organized in a useful way. Everything froze as if chained and locked, leaving her so frustrated with her inability to act that she could barely keep herself from screaming.

"No!" she shouted finally. A single word, spoken like an oath offered up against demon spawn, it escaped her lips when nothing else dared.

"Grianne," he said, more softly now.

She saw the mop of dark brown hair and the startling blue eyes, so like her own, so familiar to her. He had her build and looks. He had something else, as well, something she had yet to define, but was unmistakably there. He could be Bek.

But how? How could he be Bek?

"Bek is dead," she hissed at him, her slender body rigid within the dark robes.

On the ground to one side, a small bundle of clothing and shadows, Ryer Ord Star knelt, head lowered in the veil of her long silver hair, hands clasped in her lap. She had not moved since the Ilse Witch had appeared out of the night, had not lifted her head an inch or spoken a single word. In the silence and darkness, she might have been a statue carved of stone and set in place by her maker to ward a traveler's place of rest.

The Ilse Witch's eyes passed over her in a heartbeat and fell upon the boy. "Say something!" she hissed anew. "Tell me why I should believe you!"

"I was saved by a shape-shifter called Truls Rohk," he answered finally, his gaze on her steady. "I was taken to the Druid Walker, who in turn took me to the people who raised me as their son. But I am Bek."

"You could not know any of this! You were only two when I

hid you in that cellar!" She caught herself. "When I hid my brother. But my brother is dead, and you are a liar!"

"I was told most of it," he admitted. "I don't remember anything of how I was saved. But look at me, Grianne. Look at us! You can't mistake the resemblance, how much alike we are. We have the same eyes and coloring. We're brother and sister! Don't you feel it?"

She advanced a step. "Why would a shape-shifter save you when it was shape-shifters who killed my parents and took me prisoner? Why would the Druid save you when he sought to imprison me?"

The boy was already shaking his head slowly, deliberately, his blue eyes intense, his young face determined. "No, Grianne, it wasn't the shape-shifters or the Druid who killed our parents and took you away. They were never your enemies. Don't you realize the truth yet? Think about it, Grianne."

"I saw his face!" she screamed in fury. "I saw it through a window, a glimpse, passing in the dawn light, just before the attack, before I . . ."

She trailed off, wondering suddenly, unexpectedly, if she could have been mistaken. Had she seen the Druid as the Morgawr had insisted, when he told her to think back, so certain she would? How could he have known what she would see? The implication of what it would mean if she had deceived herself was staggering. She brushed it away violently, but it coiled up in a corner of her memory, a snake still easily within reach.

"We are Ohmsfords, Grianne," the boy continued softly. "But so is Walker. We share the same heritage. He comes from the same bloodline as we do. He is one of us. He has no reason to do us harm."

"None that you could fathom, it appears!" She laughed

derisively. "What would you know of dark intentions, little boy? What has life shown you that would give you the right to suppose your insight into such things is better than mine?"

"Nothing." He seemed momentarily at a loss for words, but his face spoke of his need to find them. "I haven't lived your life, I know. But I'm not naive about what it must have been like."

Her patience slipped a notch. "I think you believe what you are telling me," she told him coldly. "I think you have been carefully schooled to believe it. But you are a dupe and a tool of clever men. Druids and shape-shifters make their way in the world by deceiving others. They must have looked long and hard to find you, a boy who looks so much like Bek would look at your age. They must have congratulated themselves on their good fortune."

"How did I come to have his name, then?" the boy snapped in reply. "If I'm not your brother, how do I have his name? It is the name I was given, the name I have always had!"

"Or at least, that is what you believe. A Druid can make you embrace lies with little more than a thought, even lies about yourself." She shook her head reprovingly. "You are sadly deceived, to believe as you do, to think yourself a dead boy. I should destroy you on the spot, but perhaps that is what the Druid is hoping I will do, what he wants me to do. Perhaps he thinks it will somehow damage me if I kill a boy who looks so like my brother. Tell me where the Druid waits, and I will spare you."

The boy stared at her in horror. "You are the one who is deceived, Grianne. So much so that you will tell yourself anything to keep the truth at bay."

"Where is the Druid?" she snapped, her face contorting angrily. "Tell me now!"

He took a deep breath, straightening. "I've come a long way for this meeting. Too far to be intimidated into giving up what I know is true and right. I am your brother. I am Bek. Grianne—"

"Don't call me that!" she screamed. Her gray robes billowed from her body and she threw up her arms in fury, almost as if to smother his words, to bury them along with her past. She felt her temper slipping, her grip on herself sliding away like metal on oiled metal, and the raw power of her voice took on an edge that could easily cut to ribbons anything or anyone against which it was directed. "Don't speak my name again!"

He stood his ground. "What name should I speak? Ilse Witch? Should I call you what your enemies call you? Should I treat you as they do, as a creature of dark magic and evil intent, as someone I can never be close to or care about or want to see become my sister again?"

He seemed to gain strength with every new word, and suddenly she saw him as more dangerous than she had believed. "Be careful, boy."

"You are the one who needs to be careful!" he snapped. "Of who and what you believe! Of everything you have embraced since the moment you were taken from our home. Of the lies in which you have cloaked yourself!"

He pointed at her suddenly. "We are alike in more ways than you think. Not everything that links us is visible to the eye. Grianne Ohmsford has her magic, her birthright, now the tool of the Ilse Witch. But I have that magic, too! Do you hear it in my voice? You do, don't you? I'm not as practiced as you, and I only just discovered it was there, but it is another link in our lives, Grianne, another part of the heritage we share—"

She felt his voice taking on an edge similar to her own, a

biting touch that caused her to flinch in spite of herself and to bring her defenses up instantly.

"—just as we share the same parents, the same fate, the same journey of discovery, brought about by a search for the treasure hidden in the ruins that lie inland from here . . ."

She brought her voice up in a low, vibrant hum, a soft blending with the night sounds, faint and sibilant, leaves rustling in the breeze, insects chirping and buzzing, birds winging past as swift shadows, the breath of living things. Her decision was made in an instant, quick and hard; he was too dangerous for her to let live, whoever or whatever he was. Too dangerous for her to ignore as she had thought to do. He had something of magic about him after all, magic not unlike her own. It was what she had sensed about him earlier and been unable to define, hidden before but present now in the sound of his voice, a whisper of possibility.

Put an end to him, she warned herself.

Put an end to him at once!

Then something shimmered to one side, drawing her attention from the boy. She struck at it without thinking, the magic escaping from her in a rush of iron shards and razored bits that cut through the air and savaged her intended target without pause or effort. But the shimmer had moved another way. Again, the Ilse Witch struck at it, her voice a weapon of such power that it shattered the silence, whipped the leaves of the surrounding trees as if they were caught in a violent wind, and left voiceless and wide-eyed in shock the boy who had been speaking.

An instant later, he disappeared. It happened so quickly and unexpectedly that it was done before the Ilse Witch could act to stop it. She blinked at the empty space in which he had stood, seeing the brightness take on shape and form anew, becoming a series of barely recognizable movements that crossed through the night like shadows vaguely human in form chasing one another. She lashed out at them in surprise, but she was too slow and her attack too misdirected to catch more than empty air.

She wheeled this way and that, searching for what had deceived her so completely. Whatever it was, it was gone and it had taken the boy with it. Her first impulse was to give pursuit. But first impulses were seldom wise, and she did not give in to this one. She scanned the empty clearing, then the surrounding forest, searching with her senses for traces of the boy's rescuer. It took her only a moment to discover its identity. A shape-shifter. She had sensed its presence before, she realized—on *Black Moclips*, after the nighttime collision with the *Jerle Shannara*. It was the same creature and no mistake. It must have come aboard during the confusion to spy on her, then remained hidden for the remainder of the voyage. That could not have been easy, given the intensity of her control over ship's quarters and crew. This particular shape-shifter was skilled and experienced, a veteran of such efforts, and not in the least awed by her.

A new rage built in her. It must have followed her from the ship to the clearing, revealing itself when it believed the boy in danger. Did it know the boy? Or the Druid? Did it serve either or both? She believed it must. Otherwise, why would it involve itself in this business at all? A protector for the boy then? Perhaps. If so, it would confirm what she had believed from the beginning, from the moment the boy had tried to trick her into thinking he might be Bek. The Druid had concocted an elaborate scheme to undermine her confidence in her mission and her trust in the Morgawr, to sabotage their relationship, and to render her vulnerable so that he might find a way to destroy her before she could destroy him.

She clenched her hands before her, fingers knotting until the knuckles turned white. She should have killed the boy at once, the moment he spoke her name! She should have used the wishsong to burn him alive, waiting for him to beg her to save him, to admit to his lies! She should never have listened to anything he said!

Yet now that she had, she couldn't shake the feeling that she shouldn't dismiss him too quickly.

She turned the matter over in her mind carefully, examining it anew. The resemblance between them could be explained away, of course. A boy who looked like her could be found easily enough. Nor would it be all that hard for Walker to make the boy think he was Bek, even to think he had always been called Bek. Duping him into believing he was her brother and somehow her rescuer was certainly within the Druid's capabilities. It was reasonable to believe that he had been brought along on the voyage solely for the purpose of somehow, somewhere encountering her and acting out his part.

But . . .

Her pale, luminous face lifted and her blue eyes stared off into the night. There, at the end, when he had lost his patience with her, when he had challenged her as no one else would dare to do, not even the Morgawr, something about him had reminded her of herself. A conviction, a certainty that registered in his words and his posture, in the directness and intensity of his gaze. But more than this, she had sensed something unexpected and familiar in his tone of voice, something that could not be mistaken for anything other than what it was. He had told her, but in the heat of the moment she had not believed him, thinking only that he was threatening her, that he could do damage to her in an unexpected way, and so she must protect herself. But it had been there nevertheless.

He had the magic of the wishsong, her magic, her power duplicated.

Who but her brother or another Ohmsford would possess power like that?

The contradiction of what seemed to be true and what seemed to be a lie frustrated and confused her. She wanted to explain the boy away with no further consideration, but she could not do so. There was in him enough of real magic to cause her to wonder at his true identity, even if she did not believe him to be Bek. The Druid could do many things in creating a tool with which to deceive her, but he could not instill another with magic, and particularly not with magic of this sort.

So who was the boy and what was the truth of him?

She knew what she should do; it was what she had come all this way to do. Find the treasure that was hidden in Castledown and make it her own. Find the Druid and destroy him. Regain the safety of *Black Moclips* and sail home again as swiftly as possible and be shed of this voyage and its dangers.

But the boy intrigued and disturbed her, so much so that almost without understanding why, she was rethinking her plans entirely. Despite what she knew of his duplicity, whether willing or not, she was loath to give up on solving the mystery of him when so much of what she discovered might impact her. Not in any life-altering manner, of course; she had already made her mind up to that. But in some smaller, yet still important way.

How hard would it be to discover the truth about him, once she set her mind to it? How much time would it take?

The Morgawr would not approve, but he approved of little

she did these days. Her relationship with her mentor had been deteriorating for some time. They no longer shared the student/teacher connection they once had. She was as much the master now as he was, and she chafed at the restrictions he constantly sought to place upon her. She had not forgotten what she owed him, was not ungrateful for all he had taught her over the years. But she disliked his insistence on keeping her in her place, always his subordinate, his underling, a charge who must do as he dictated. He was old, and perhaps because he was old he could no longer change as easily as could the young. Self-preservation was what mattered to him. But she did not aspire to live a thousand years. She did not consider near immortality a benefit to be sought. Hence the need to get on with things, rather than sit and plot and wait and scheme, as he was so used to doing.

No, he would not approve, and in this case she would be wrong in failing to consider that. Seeking out the boy to solve his mystery and satisfy her curiosity was mere self-indulgence. She hesitated a moment, then brushed her hesitation aside. It was her decision to make, her choice if she wasted time that, in any case, belonged to her. The boy had something she needed, whether the Morgawr would agree with her or not. In any event, he was not here to advise her. Cree Bega would presume to speak for him, but the Mwellret's opinion meant next to nothing to her.

She would have to act quickly, however. The ret was not too far behind her, coming along with two dozen others. His approach was delayed only because, wishing to go ahead by herself, to have the first look at what waited, she had ordered him to wait. Perhaps, she added, to make certain he did not interfere with anything she decided she must do with what she found. Perhaps just to keep him in line, where he belonged.

She walked over to Ryer Ord Star and bent down, trying to determine if the seer was coming out of her trance. But the girl never moved, sitting silently, motionlessly in the night, head lowered in shadow, eyes closed. She was breathing steadily, calmly, so it was apparent her health was not in danger. What was she doing, though? Where inside herself had she gone?

The Ilse Witch knelt in front of the girl. She had no time to wait for the seer to conclude her meditations. She needed her answers. She placed her fingers on the other's temples, just as she had done with the castaway whose revelations had begun this whole matter, and she began to probe. The effort required was small. Ryer Ord Star's mind opened to her like a flower before the rising sun, her memories tumbling out like falling petals. Without a glance at most of them, the Ilse Witch went directly for those most recent, the ones that would reveal the fate of the Druid.

Revelations surfaced like the ocean's dead, stark and bare. She saw a battle within Old World ruins, a battle in which the Druid and his company were assaulted on all sides by lines of red fire that burned and seared. Walls shifted, raising from and lowering into smooth metal floors. Creepers appeared from nowhere, metal monsters on skittering legs with claws that rent and tore. Men fought and died in a swirl of thick smoke and spurts of fire. Seen through Ryer Ord Star's eyes, filtered through her emotions, everything was chaotic and awash in fear and desperation.

Amid the madness, the Druid advanced past lines of attack and changes in terrain, his steady, deliberate progress aided by his magic and buttressed by his courage and determination. Say what you would, the Druid had never been a coward. He fought his way into the heart of the ruins, shouting in vain for the others of his company to fall back, to flee, trying to keep them alive. At last he gained the doorway to a black tower, forced an entry, and disappeared inside.

Ryer Ord Star screamed and started after him, then was struck by the fire and sent pinwheeling into a wall. Her thoughts of the Druid faded, then went black.

The Ilse Witch took her fingers from the seer's temples and sat back on her heels, perplexed. Interesting. The communication had come without words of any sort and with no resistance at all. Was this the nature of empaths, that they could neither dissemble nor conceal? She found herself wondering at the girl's pursuit of the Druid, galvanized by the latter's disappearance into the tower. Why would she risk herself so? The girl had been instructed to stay close to the Druid at all times, to make herself indispensable to him, to gain his confidence and his ear. Clearly she had done so. But was there something more between them, something that went beyond the charge she had been given as the Ilse Witch's spy?

There was no way to know. Not without damaging the girl, and she wasn't prepared to go to that length just yet. She had what she wanted for now—a clear picture of what had befallen those from the company of the *Jerle Shannara* who had gone inland with the Druid. She could not be certain of the Druid's fate, however. Perhaps he was dead. Perhaps he was trapped beneath the ruins. Whatever the case, he did not present any danger to her. Without an airship to carry him off and with most of his company dead or imprisoned, he could do little harm.

She had time for the boy, then. Enough, that she did not need to consider the matter further.

No more than a handful of minutes passed before Cree Bega and his company of Mwellrets appeared out of the gloom, heavy bodies trudging warily through the forest dark, slitted eyes glittering as they caught sight of her. Repulsive creatures! she thought, but she kept her face expressionless. She rose to meet them and stood waiting on their approach.

"Misstress," their leader, her designated protector, hissed, bowing obsequiously. "Have you found the little peopless?"

"I have decided to leave that to you, Cree Bega. To you and your companions. There has been a battle in the ruins ahead, and those of the Druid's company who are not dead are scattered. Find them and make them your prisoners. That includes the Druid, should you come upon him and find him helpless enough to subdue."

"Misstress, I thinkss—"

"Be careful otherwise, because he is more than a match for all of you put together." She ignored his attempt to speak. "Leave him to me if you find he is able to defend himself. Do not go into the ruins; they are well protected. Do not expose yourself or your men to the danger they pose. Keep a close watch over both airships and do not land them under any circumstances."

He was watching her closely now, realizing that she had already removed herself from everything she was instructing him to do.

"Something has come up that I must investigate." She held his reptilian eyes with her steady, calm gaze. "I will be gone for a time, and while I am gone, you will be in charge. Do not fail me."

For a moment there was no response and she thought he had not understood. "Am I clear on this?"

"Where iss it my misstress goess?" he asked softly. "Our mission iss here—"

"Our mission is where I say it is, Cree Bega."

Something in the Mwellret's cold gaze turned suddenly

dangerous. "Your masster would not approve of thiss diverssion . . ."

Two quick steps placed her right in front of him. "My master?" There was an uncomfortable silence as she waited on his reply. He stared at her in silence. "I have no master, ret," she whispered. "You have a master, not I, and he is not here in any case. I am the one you must answer to. I am your mistress. Is there anything else that I need to explain?"

The Mwellret said nothing, but she did not care for what she found in his eyes. She gave him a moment more, then repeated softly, "Is there?"

He shook his head. "Ass you wissh, misstress. Little peopless will be our prissonerss on your return, I promiss. But what of the treassure?"

"We'll have it soon enough." She looked away, off in the direction of Castledown. Was that so? Would it be so easy? She thought that her knowledge of the situation gave her an advantage over the Druid, but she could not afford to underestimate the enemy that warded Castledown. If it could defeat the Druid so easily, it was much stronger than she had expected. "Leave the matter of retrieving the treasure to me."

She dismissed him with barely a glance, then remembered Ryer Ord Star, still kneeling in a huddle to one side, still lost in some other place and time. "Do not harm the girl," she told Cree Bega, giving him a quick, hard look of warning. "She has been my eyes and ears aboard the Druid's airship on this voyage. There is much she knows that she has not yet told me. I want her kept safe for my return so that I may discover what she hides."

The Mwellret nodded, giving the seer a doubtful look. "Thiss one sseemss already dead."

"She sleeps. She is in a trance of some sort. I haven't had

time to discover what is wrong with her." She brushed the ret aside. "Just do what I told you. I won't be long."

She departed the clearing without a glance back. Cree Bega and the others would do what she had ordered. They would be afraid to do anything else. But she was reminded again that it was growing more difficult to control them. She would be better off without them once she had the treasure in hand. Sometime soon, she would rid herself of them for good.

Eastward, the sky was beginning to brighten faintly with the dawn's approach. Night was already sliding westward, liquid ink withdrawing silently through the trees. A new day would bring fresh revelations. About the boy, perhaps. About why he thought as he did. About how his magic had found its way to him and why it was so like her own. A smile of expectation brightened her pale face. She looked forward to discovering the answers. She felt a rush of anticipation.

Hesitation and doubts were for others, she thought dismissively, for those who would never find their own way in the world and never make anything of their lives that mattered.

Picking up faint traces of the shape-shifter that still lingered on the fading night air, she began the hunt.

Gleaming eyes filled with malice, Cree Bega watched wordlessly until she was well out of sight. Hunched within his cloak and surrounded by those he commanded, he imagined how sweet it would feel when he was permitted at last to put an end to the insufferable girl child. That he hated her as he hated no one else went without saying; he had never felt anything but hate for her. He despised her as she despised him, and nothing shared through their service to the Morgawr would ever change that.

But the Morgawr, though claiming to be the girl's mentor

and friend, was more Mwellret than human. His connection to Cree Bega's people was ancient and blooded. He had bonded to the girl because she was a novelty and he saw a use for her in the larger scheme of things. But his heart and soul were those of a Mwellret.

The girl, of course, believed them equals, outcasts bound together in their struggle for recognition and power over their oppressors. The Morgawr let her believe as much because it suited his purposes to do so. But they were not equals in any way that mattered, and the little Ilse Witch was far less skilled in her use of magic than she believed. She was a strutting, posturing annoyance, a foolish, ludicrously inept practitioner of an art that had been mastered by the Mwellrets and their kind centuries ago, before the Druids had even thought to take up the Elven magic as their sword and shield. Mwellrets would never be subjugated by humans, never become their inferiors, and this girl child was just another self-deceived morsel waiting to be plucked from their food chain.

He felt the eyes of his fellows upon him, awaiting his orders, their own thoughts as dark and vengeful as his. They, too, waited for their chance at the Ilse Witch. Cree Bega would give her the satisfaction of believing him subdued and obedient for now. He had pledged as much to the Morgawr. He would heed her commands and carry out her wishes because there was no reason for him to do otherwise.

But a shift in the wind was coming, and when it did, it would mark the end of her.

He wheeled on the others, finding them grouped tightly about him, dark visages expectant and eager within shadowed cowls. They awaited his orders, anxious for something to do. He would accommodate them. Members of the company of the *Jerle Shannara* were loose somewhere ahead within these trees, waiting to be harvested, to be killed or taken prisoner. It was time to accommodate them.

Growling softly, he told his men to start with Ryer Ord Star, then move on.

But when they turned to take charge of the seer, she was nowhere to be found.

THREE

within their dark, waiting to be beckoned to be called, a risk of misread. If it was true to accommodate trouble.

One day safer, he would know him to pass with them. Old Stiv, then said if—

In the Southland, it would show signs of the sod. She was nowhere to be found

Arms of iron clutched Bek Ohmsford close to a body that smelled vaguely fetid and loamy, of earth and chemicals mixed. The body moved with the swiftness of thought, sliding through trees and brush, shedding layers of itself like skin, shadows that hung dark and empty on the air and then faded away completely. Some exploded into bits of night as the magic of the Ilse Witch caught up to them, but always Bek and his rescuer were one skin ahead.

Then they were beyond the clearing and into the concealing trees, still running hard, but cloaked in shadows and screens of brush and limbs. Bek began to struggle then, frightened suddenly of the unknown, of anything powerful and mysterious enough to challenge the Ilse Witch's magic.

"Be still, boy!" Truls Rohk hissed, giving him a sharp squeeze of warning with those powerful arms, never once slowing his pace.

They ran for a long time, Bek crumpled nearly into a ball in the other's grip, until the clearing and the witch were far behind them. Then they stopped, and the shape-shifter dropped to one knee and released the boy with a nudge of hands and shoulders, letting him roll to the earth in a crumpled heap, there to uncoil and straighten himself again. Bek heard Truls

Rohk breathing hard, winded and spent, bent over within his concealing cloak while he waited for his strength to return. Bek climbed to his hands and knees, nerve endings tingling with new life as fresh blood finally reached his cramped limbs. They were in a place grown so thick with trees and brush that the light of moon and stars did not penetrate, where everything was cloaked in deepest silence.

"Keeping you alive is turning into a full-time job," the shape-shifter muttered irritably.

Bek thought of his lost opportunity to persuade the Ilse Witch of who he was. "No one asked you to interfere! I was that close to convincing her! I was just about—"

"You were just about to get yourself killed," the other said with a quick, harsh laugh. "You weren't paying close enough attention to the effect you were having on her, you were so caught up in the righteousness and certainty of your argument. Hah! Convincing her? Couldn't you feel what was happening? She was getting ready to use her magic on you!"

"That's not true!" Bek was suddenly furious. He leapt to his feet in challenge. "You don't know that!"

Now the shape-shifter was really laughing, a low and steady howl that he worked hard to suppress. "Can't afford to laugh as loud as I'd like, boy. Not here. Not this close still." He stood up, confronting the boy. "You listen to me. Your arguments were good. They were sound and they were true. But she wasn't ready for them. She wanted to believe some of it, I think. She might have believed all of it in other circumstances, maybe will after time spent thinking it over. But she wasn't ready for it then and there. Especially not at the end, when you let your own magic get away from you again. Not your fault, I know, that you're still learning. But you have to be aware of your limitations."

Bek stared. "I was using the wishsong?"

"Not consciously, but it was slipping out of you even while you tried to tell her about it." Truls Rohk paused. "When she sensed its presence, she felt threatened. She thought you were about to attack her. Or she just decided it was all too much to deal with and she should put an end to you."

He turned and walked away a few steps, looking back the way they had come. "All quiet for now. But I don't know that it's finished yet." He turned back. "You surprised her, boy, and that's dangerous with someone so powerful. You gave her too much all at once, too much she didn't want to hear, that would impact her in ways she couldn't manage so quickly." He grunted. "It couldn't be helped, I imagine. She appeared and found you. What were you supposed to do?"

Bek stood silently before him, thinking it through. Truls Rohk was right. He had been so caught up in persuading Grianne he was her brother that he had paid almost no attention to what she was doing. It was possible she had not believed him, could not have for that matter, given the suddenness and surprise of it. Just because he believed didn't mean she would. She'd had much longer to live with the lie than he'd had to live with the truth. She was less likely to be swayed as easily.

"Sit down, boy," Truls Rohk said, and moved over to join him. "Time for a few more revelations. You were wrong about how well you were doing convincing your sister of who you were. You're wrong about no one asking me to interfere in your life, as well."

Bek looked at him. "Walker?"

"What I told you before, on Mephitic, was true. I pulled you from the ashes of your parents' home. Aware that your family was in danger, I was keeping watch at the Druid's request. The Morgawr's Mwellrets, shape-shifters of a sort, were prowling about your home in Jentsen Close. You lived not far from the Wolfsktaag, there at a corner of the Rainbow Lake, amid a community of isolated homes occupied mostly by farmers. You were vulnerable, and Walker was looking for a way to keep you safe."

He shook his head within its cowl, his face layered in shadow. "I warned him to act quickly, but he was too slow. Or perhaps he tried, and your father would not listen to him. They talked infrequently and were not close friends. Your father was a scholar and did not believe in violence. In his mind, the Druids represented violence. But violence doesn't care anything about whether or not you believe in it. It comes looking for you regardless. It came for your family just before dawn on a day when I was absent. Mwellrets, there on the orders of the Morgawr. They killed your parents and burned your home to the ground, making it appear as if it were the work of Gnome raiders. They thought you had perished in the blaze, not realizing your sister had hidden you in the cold cellar. They were in a hurry, having taken her, whom the Morgawr coveted most, and so did not search as carefully as I did when I came later. I found you in the cellar, tucked carefully away, crying, hungry, chilled, and frightened. I took you from the ashes and gave you to Walker."

Bek looked away from him, thinking it through. "Why didn't he tell me any of this before he sent me to you with Quentin?"

The other laughed. "Why doesn't he ever tell any of us anything? He told me a boy and his cousin were coming, that I should look for them, that I should test them to see if they had merit and heart." He shook his head. "He left it to me to realize that it was you, the boy I had saved all those years ago.

He left it to me to determine what I was meant to do. Do you see?"

Bek shook his head, not entirely certain he did.

"You were told to ask me to come with you on this voyage. You were given a message to deliver, one that I was to interpret in whatever way I chose. I realized what he hadn't told you, what he was asking of me. It was clear enough. He wanted me to be your protector, your defender when danger threatened. But I was to monitor the progress of your magic's development, as well. He knew it would begin to surface, and when it did you would have to be told the truth about who you really were. He did not want to rush things, though; he wanted to keep you in the dark as long as possible so that you would not be overwhelmed by the enormity of it all. But I knew that the sooner you discovered you had the use of magic, the sooner you could find a way to come to terms with it. We differ in our approach to things, the Druid and I, and I imagine he was not happy at all with what I did to you on Mephitic."

"He was furious." Bek hesitated. "But I'm glad you took a chance on me. That you showed me what I could do. That you gave me a chance to prove myself."

The shape-shifter nodded, eyes a flicker of brightness in the shadows. "You saved us in those ruins. You have heart and strength of mind and body, boy—tools you need to manage the wishsong's power. But your skills are still raw and untried. You need time and experience before you will be the equal of your sister."

Bek studied him a moment in the ensuing silence. "Tell me the truth. You're not deceiving me about any of this, are you? Because I've been deceived more than once already on this journey."

The other grunted. "By the Druid. Not by me."

"Grianne really is my sister, isn't she? The Ilse Witch is my sister? I need to hear you say it."

The bright eyes glimmered fierce and sharp within the cowl, all that was visible of the other's face. "She is your sister. Why would I tell you otherwise? Do you think I am the Druid's tool, as the witch would have you be?"

Bek shook his head. "I had to ask."

The shape-shifter grunted, not entirely mollified. "Don't ask such questions again. Not of me." He folded his arms into his cloak. "Enough of this. What's happened to the others who went ashore with you? I've had no chance to search for them. I boarded the witch's airship during the collision off Mephitic because I thought I would be more useful there and might learn something that would help us gain an advantage. But she almost found me out, and I was forced to hide myself carefully, to wait for a chance to make my escape. She came alone in search of Walker, so I followed. She led me to that clearing and to you. But not to Walker. What's become of him?"

Swiftly, Bek filled him in on the disastrous events of the past day, of the attempt to penetrate the ruins, of the traps found waiting, of the company's decimation and the scattering of its members. With Ryer Ord Star and the Elven Tracker Tamis he had fled to the clearing where the Ilse Witch had found him. Of the fates of Quentin, Panax, Ahren Elessedil, and Ard Patrinell, he could not be certain. Tamis had gone looking for them, but she had not come back. Walker had disappeared into the black tower that dominated the center of the ruins and had not come out.

"We'll need help to search for them," Bek said. "Especially if the Ilse Witch and the Mwellrets are looking, too."

Truls Rohk rocked back slightly on his heels and gave an audible sigh. "We'll have some difficulty finding any. There's bad news everywhere in this business. Your sister used her magic to immobilize the *Jerle Shannara*'s crew. She boarded the ship and took them all prisoner. She has locked them belowdecks, and she controls both ships. *Black Moclips* is anchored in the bay, where you went ashore. The *Jerle Shannara* is downriver, closer to the ice gates. There's no help to be had from either."

Bek felt as if the ground had fallen away beneath his feet. Whatever else had been taken from them, at least they'd had the *Jerle Shannara* to retreat to. Now that haven was lost, as well. They were trapped on Ice Henge. They couldn't even get word of where they were to the Wing Riders.

He thought suddenly of Rue Meridian and felt a sharp pang of terror, one much sharper than he would have expected. He took a steadying breath. "Are the Rovers unharmed and well?" he asked, trying to sound casual.

The shape-shifter shrugged. "No one was hurt in the boarding. I don't know what's happened since, but probably nothing."

"Shades! We've lost everything, Truls. You and I and maybe one or two more are all that's left, alive and free." He heard a hint of desperation creep into his voice and tried to block it away. "We have to do something. At least we have to go back and face Grianne, find a way to convince her that she's an Ohmsford, make her see that she's been—"

"Slow down, boy," Truls Rohk said. "Let's take a deep breath and think this through. There's no going back to face the Ilse Witch just yet. What's already happened is still too fresh in her mind. We need a way to reach her besides what you've already tried. Something she can't brush aside as easily as your words."

He glanced meaningfully over Bek's shoulder. The boy glanced with him and found himself staring at the pommel of the Sword of Shannara still strapped across his back. In the excitement of his encounter with his sister, he had forgotten he was carrying it.

He looked back at the shape-shifter. "You mean, I should try using this?"

"I mean, find a way to use it." The other's voice was ironic. "Not so easy to do, I'd think. Your sister isn't just going to stand there and let you use the magic on her. But if you can find a way to catch her off guard, surprise her maybe, she might not have a choice. Like it or not, she might have to face up to the truth of things. It's the best chance we have of persuading her."

Bek shook his head doubtfully. "She'll never give us the chance. Never."

Truls Rohk said nothing, waiting.

"She'll fight us!" Bek reached back to touch the handle of the Sword of Shannara, then let his hand fall away helplessly. "Besides, I don't know if I can make it work against her."

"Not against her," the shape-shifter advised quietly. "For her."

Bek nodded slowly. "For her. For both of us."

"I wouldn't be so quick to discount our chances," Truls Rohk continued. "We've lost the ship and crew, but we don't know about Panax and that Highlander and the others. And I wouldn't put finished to the Druid if I saw him dropped six feet underground; he has more lives than a cat. He won't have gone into the tower without a plan for getting out. I know him, boy. I've known him a long time. He thinks everything through. I wouldn't be surprised if he was already free and looking for us."

Bek looked doubtful, but nodded anyway. "What do we do next? Where do we go from here?"

Truls Rohk climbed to his feet, cloak falling about his wide shoulders, shadowing him from the ground up, leaving him a wraith, even in the growing dawn light.

"I need to backtrack far enough to make certain we aren't being followed by the witch or her rets. You wait here for my return. Don't move from this spot." He paused. "Unless you're in danger. In that case, hide yourself the best way you can. But if that becomes necessary, don't use your magic. You're not ready yet, not without me."

He gave the boy a hard stare in warning, then turned and disappeared into the trees.

Bek sat with his back against an aging shagbark hickory and watched the eastern sky brighten with the dawn's coming. Darkness gave way to first light, then first light to morning, the sky changing colors in gaps through the trees that were invisible in the darkness and could be discerned only now. He sat thinking of where he was, of the journey that had brought him to this place and time, and of the changes he had gone through. He remembered thinking, on the evening that Walker had first appeared in the Highlands months earlier and asked him to come on this voyage, that if he went with the Druid, nothing in his life would ever be the same again. He hadn't realized how right he would prove to be.

He closed his eyes momentarily and tried to imagine what it had been like back in Leah, in the Highlands, in his home. He couldn't do it. It was so far away, so removed from the present, that it was little more than a memory, fading with a past that seemed lost in another lifetime.

He gave up on the Highlands and instead tried to imagine what it would be like to have Grianne as his sister. Not just in name, but in fact. To have her accept that it was so. To have her call him Bek. He failed in this effort, as well. As the Ilse Witch, Grianne had taken lives and destroyed dreams. She had done things that he might never be able to accept, no matter how mistaken she had been or how much contrition she exhibited. Her life was wrapped in deception and trickery, in a misdirected search for revenge, in isolation and bitterness. It was not as if she could simply wipe away her past and begin fresh. She could not become someone different all at once simply because he wanted it to be so. That was asking for a child's-fable ending of a kind that had long since ceased to be possible. Whatever he expected of her, it was probably too much. The best he could hope for was that she would come to realize the truth.

He pictured her in his mind, standing before him in her gray robes, austere and imperious. He could not imagine her being happy. Had she laughed even once since she had been stolen away? Had she ever smiled?

Yet he had to find a way to bring her back to herself, to something of the girl she had been fifteen years ago, to a little part of the world she had abandoned and disdained as meant for lesser creatures. He had to help her, even if by helping he should cause her greater pain.

How could he manage this, when their next encounter would likely result in her trying her very best to kill him?

He wished he had Quentin with him—Quentin, with his sensible, straightforward approach to things, always able to see with such clarity the right way to proceed, the best thing to do. Had Quentin survived the battle at Castledown's ruins? Tears filled his eyes at the thought that his cousin might be dead. Even thinking such a thing seemed a betrayal. He could not imagine life without his cousin—his confidant, his best friend. Quentin had been so eager to come on this voyage, so anxious to see some other part of the world, to learn something new of life. What if it had cost him his own?

Bek knotted his hands together in frustration and stared out into the trees, into the growing sunlight, the new day, and his determination hardened into certainty. He must find Quentin. Maybe even before he found Walker, because the fact of the matter was that Quentin was the more important of the two. If they were stranded in this strange land, if their airships were lost to them and their companions dead, at least they would have each other to see the worst of it through. To face what lay ahead, however bad, in any other way was inconceivable to him.

Look after each other, Coran Leah had urged them. They had promised each other as much—long ago, in Arborlon, when there had still been a chance to turn back.

He sighed wearily. At least he had Truls Rohk to help him. As strange and frightening as the shape-shifter was, he had shown himself to be a friend. As conflicted as his life had been, he was perhaps the most dependable and capable of the ship's company. There was a measure of reassurance in that, and Bek embraced it eagerly.

Because he had nothing else to embrace, he admitted. Because sometimes you took comfort where you found it.

Truls Rohk was not gone long. The light had not yet chased away the last of the night when he reappeared through the trees, his cloaked form crouched low, his movements quick and furtive.

"On your feet," he hissed roughly, pulling the boy up. "Your sister's on our trail and coming fast."

Bek tried to keep the fear from his eyes and throat, tried to breathe normally as he glanced in the direction from which the shape-shifter had come. Then they were running into the trees and gone.

FOUR

She was perhaps a hundred yards into the forest and well away from Cree Bega and the other Mwellrets when the Ilse Witch paused to adjust her clothing. She pulled out a length of braided cord, looped it over her shoulders, crisscrossed it down her body and through her legs, and bound up her robes where they hung loose so that she could move more easily through the heavy brush ahead. The robes she had chosen were light but strong, and would not tear easily. Anticipating a rough climb into the ruins of Castledown, she had exchanged the sandals she normally favored for ankle boots with tough, flexible soles. She had intended her clothing and footgear for something else entirely, but her foresight was paying off. She had hunted before, though for different quarry, and she understood the importance of being prepared.

Her mind drifted momentarily to those days she had buried so thoroughly until the boy had confronted her. As Grianne Ohmsford, she had spent time in the woods and hills about her home, learning to use the magic of the wishsong. One of the exercises she engaged in regularly was a form of tracking. Using the magic, she would detect the passing of an animal and then follow it to its lair. Her singing, she discovered, could color its fading body heat and movements just enough to show her its progress, if the trail wasn't too old. She couldn't read prints or signs in the manner of Trackers, but the ability to trace heat and movement worked just as well. She became quite good at it even before she was stolen away.

She thought again of the boy. He bothered her more than she wanted to admit. The hair and eyes were right for Bek. Even something about his movements and facial expressions was familiar. And that hint of magic that surfaced right at the end of things—that was the wishsong. No one should have all three save Bek. What were the odds? How long would the Druid have had to look to find such a combination? But she was forgetting that he could create everything but the magic, layer it on as if it had always been there, making over the one he had chosen to fool her.

Bek had never evidenced use of the wishsong before she hid him that last morning. He had been a normal baby. She had no way of knowing if he would ever have had use of the magic. Or did now.

She blinked away her discomfort and her thoughts and set about adjusting her robes a final time. She looked down at the pale skin of her wrists and ankles where it was exposed to the light, virtually untouched by the sun, so white it looked iridescent in the mix of forest shadows and golden dawn. She touched herself as if to make certain she was real, thinking as she did that sometimes it felt as if she weren't, as if she was created out of dreams and wishes, and nothing about her was hard and true.

She gritted her teeth. It was that boy who was making her think like this. Find him, and the thoughts would disappear for good.

She set out once more, leaving the hood in place, her face in darkness, hidden away from prying eyes. With her robes bound close, she eased through the trees, humming softly to reveal the trail of the shape-shifter and the boy, finding their lingering presence at every turn, their passage as clear as if marked by paint on tree bark. She moved at a steady pace, used to walking, to journeys afoot and not just to riding her Shrikes, toughened long since because she knew that she would not otherwise survive. The Morgawr might have been content to let her remain just a girl, less a threat, more malleable, but she had determined early on that she would never allow herself to be vulnerable again. Sooner or later, she would be threatened by something or someone toughened by years of wilderness living, and she wanted to be ready for that. Nor did she ever want to be considered just a girl or even a woman, somehow reduced in stature by her sex and not regarded with caution.

No, she thought grimly, she would never be thought of like that. The Morgawr had trained her in the use of her magic, but she had trained herself in the art of survival. When he was gone, which was often, she tested herself in ways he did not know about, going out alone, into dangerous country, sometimes well beyond the Wilderun. She lived as an animal, tracking as they did, foraging, hunting, and always learning what they knew. Because she had the use of the wishsong, she could speak their language and gain their acceptance. She could make herself appear one with them. It took concentration and effort, and a single slip might have spelled disaster. She was powerful, but it required only a moment's inattention to let a predator past her defenses. Moor cats and Kodens could strike you down before you thought to wonder what had happened. Werebeasts were quicker than that.

She had not gone far before she detected a second presence, one that overlapped the first. She slowed, suddenly cautious, reading the images, the traces of heat and movement, wary of a trap. But after a few moments she realized what she had discovered. The shape-shifter had backtracked to see if anyone was following, then retraced his steps to where he had left the boy. It was likely he'd seen her. She had to assume as much. She already knew he was experienced and skilled, and he had been wise enough not to assume that after rescuing the boy he was clear of her. He had returned to check, then gone back to warn his charge.

She set off in pursuit, anxious to close the gap between them. If he had been close enough to detect her, he could not be all that far ahead now. The images revealed by her magic were unmistakable and strong. He was not even bothering to hide his trail. He was running, fleeing, frightened of her perhaps, realizing how little distance separated them. That made her smile. It was what she wanted. Frightened, panicked people made mistakes. The shape-shifter was not one of these under normal circumstances, but conditions had changed.

Down through ravines and along the crests of low hills studded with hardwoods and choked with brush she made her way, breaking into a lope in the open areas, so close she felt she could smell them. Overhead, the sun had crested mid-morning and was moving toward noon, bright and clear in a cloudless blue sky. She breathed in the warmth and freshness of the forest, a sheen of perspiration coating her face and hands, seeping down her limbs inside her garments. She felt a wildness infuse her, familiar and welcome. It was like this sometimes when she was on a chase, that sense of being feral and untamed, dangerous. She wanted to cast aside her human garments and hunt as the animals did. She craved a taste of fresh blood.

In a broad clearing ringed tightly with old growth, images

of the boy reappeared, joining with the shape-shifter. Excitement raced through her, spurring her anew. The images told her they were running now, racing to escape her. The boy would know she was coming. He would be wondering what he could do to save himself if she caught up to him. He would lie, of course. He would tell his story again. But he had to know already that it would be useless to try to trick her a second time. He had to know what she would do to him.

Just another few hundred yards, perhaps. Not much more than that, and she would have them. They were right ahead.

But all of a sudden, as she entered a meadow filled with yellow and blue wildflowers that rolled like the surface of the sea in the wind, the trail she followed so eagerly disappeared. For a moment she could not believe it. She kept on, pushing ahead in disbelief, crossing the meadow to its far side, trying to make sense of what had happened. Then she stopped. The images were still there, still as discernible as ever, bright and clear. But they were everywhere, all across the meadow, all through the trees beyond, thousands of them, flickers of heat and light. It seemed as if the shape-shifter and the boy were everywhere at once, gone in all directions at the same time.

It wasn't possible, of course.

It wasn't real.

She took a deep breath to calm herself, then exhaled slowly. She reached within her hood to brush back a lock of her thick, dark hair and looked from one end of the meadow to the other, casting into the shadows beneath the trees beyond, searching. No one was there. The boy and his protector were elsewhere, safely clear and farther away from her with every passing second.

In spite of herself, she smiled. She had believed them panicked, but the shape-shifter and the boy were smarter than she'd thought. Realizing she would track them using her magic, they had retaliated by using their own. Or, more accurately, if she was reading things right, the boy had used his. He had used it to cast their images all about, to disperse them in all directions. She could sort them out, find the right set to see which way the pair had gone, but it would take time. They would do this again, farther on, and each time she was forced to unravel one of the confusing puzzles, she would lose ground.

They were hoping, of course, that she lacked a Tracker's skills and could not pursue them through reading prints and signs if they foiled her magic. They were right. Her magic was all she had, and it would have to be enough.

She sat down, cross-legged with her back against an oak, looking out into the meadow, thinking things through. There was no need for hurry. She would catch them, of course. Nothing they tried would be enough to throw her off their trail for long. It was more important not to act in haste. She took a moment to consider where all this was leading. The boy and his protector were running, but to what? This was a strange land, and they knew nothing of its geography or inhabitants. The shape-shifter would have told the boy by now that their airship was under her control and outside their reach. The members of the landing party led by Walker were scattered or dead, and the Druid had disappeared. At best, running offered only a temporary solution to their problem. How did they intend to make use of it? Where would they try to go and to what end? Surely, they weren't running blindly and toward nothing. The shape-shifter was too smart for that.

She stood slowly, her mind made up. Answers to questions like those would have to wait. It didn't make any difference where they went or why if she couldn't find them, and she intended to find them right now. If her magic couldn't serve her one way, it would have to serve her another.

Standing at the edge of the meadow, she cupped her hands to her mouth and gave a long, low cry, eerie and chilling as it wafted into the distance and died away. She gave the cry three times, stood waiting awhile, then gave it three more.

Time slipped away, the meadow and the surrounding forest silent save for birdsong and the rustle of leaves in the wind. The Ilse Witch stood where she was, listening and watching everywhere at once.

Then something moved out of the trees and into the grasses on the far side of the meadow, causing the flowers to ripple and part. The Ilse Witch waited patiently as the submerged creature made its way toward her, invisible beneath the bobbing coverlet of wildflowers, crouched low to the earth.

When it was a dozen yards away, too late for it to escape, it lifted its narrow muzzle slightly from the sea of brightness, testing the wind, searching for the source of the call that had summoned it. The wolf was not of a recognizable breed, bigger than the ones with which she was familiar, but it would do. It was an outcast, a renegade—she could sense that about it—not part of any pack, solitary by choice and nature, its face a mask of grizzled black hair and sharp features, its scarred gray body sinewy and muscular. A ferocious predator, the wolf possessed unmatchable tracking skills and instincts, which would serve her needs well, once the necessary adjustments had been made.

The wolf must have realized it was trapped, unable to break free of her magic, of her compelling voice, of the chains she had already wound about it as she hummed and sang softly. But it was not so stunned by what was happening that it did not try to escape. It bristled and snarled, thrashing against her attempts to exercise control, its hatred for her revealed in its baleful eyes and curled muzzle. She let it have its moment of rage, and then she bore down on it relentlessly. Bit by bit she overcame its resistance, harnessing its will, claiming its heart and mind, making its body and thoughts her own.

Then she began to reshape it. It was a dangerous brute, but she decided it needed to be more dangerous still; the shape-shifter would be more than a match for an ordinary wolf, no matter how ferocious, and she wanted the odds reversed. She wanted a caull, a beast of reshaped flesh and bone, a creature of magic molded by her hand and obedient only to her. Using the magic of the wishsong, she caused it to evolve in very specific ways, focusing her attention on its predatory instincts, tracking skills, and resiliency. To enhance its intelligence was too difficult a task, too complex even for her. But its form could be changed to suit her needs, and she did not shrink from what was required, even when the beast screamed as if it were a human child.

Afterwards, it lay panting and feverish on the sun-dappled earth, the wildflowers ripped to shreds for fifteen or twenty feet in all directions, the ground torn and furrowed, the grasses coated with sprays of blood. She held the caull in check, then gave it sleep to calm and heal its re-formed body. Its yellow eyes closed, and its breathing slowed and deepened in response to the change in her song. In seconds, it slept.

The effort had exhausted her, and she sat down to rest. The day lengthened from morning to afternoon. She dozed in the sunlight, wrapped within her hood and robes, a small dark shape at the edge of the savaged patch of earth and sleeping beast. Time drifted, and she dreamed of a tiny baby boy with a shock of dark hair and startling blue eyes, staring back at her from an enfolding darkness as she closed a hidden door on it forever.

She awoke before the caull, alerted by the rustle of its legs as it stirred from its own sleep. Her wishsong already coming into play, she rose and waited for its eyes to open. When its head lifted, she ordered it to rise. It did so, lurching to its feet, big and menacing in the fading light. It was twice the size it had been, with a thickened neck and huge shoulders, its body re-formed for fighting and running. Its head was a broad, flat shelf of bone, wedge-shaped from pointed ears to snout. Its muzzle split as it panted, revealing a double row of razor-sharp teeth made for rending and tearing. Its legs had shortened to give it a splay-footed stance, and the digits of its paws had lengthened and spread like fingers to end in hooked claws. Sleek gray hair layered its body, less fur than skin, a tough coarse hide that even brambles could not scratch. It wheeled this way and that, as if anxious to test its newfound strength, and in its maddened eyes glittered an unmistakable bloodlust.

She watched it carefully, pleased with her handiwork, certain that with this creature to aid her, she would be more than a match for the wiles of the shape-shifter and his young accomplice. She had learned to fashion caulls while practicing her magic with the Morgawr. But she had discovered the shape of this one on her own. Hundreds of years ago, there had been another, a monster out of Faerie called a Jachyra that had stalked and killed a Druid. She didn't need the real thing. A close approximation would be sufficient to serve her needs.

"Relentless," she hissed at the caull. It swung its flat, heavy head toward her watchfully. "That is what you will be for me in your search for those I hunt. Unstoppable."

The jaws split in what might have been a smile if the beast had been capable of understanding what a smile was. It was enough to satisfy the Ilse Witch. If it accomplished what she wished, she would do the smiling for them both.

Bek trailed Truls Rohk as they entered a meadow filled with blue and yellow wildflowers. He was already beginning to tire from the pace the shape-shifter was setting, sweat coating his face and drenching his tunic. The sun was high in the midday sky and the air warm. Truls Rohk loped to the center of the meadow and stopped, looking back.

"Far enough," he said, his ravaged face a shadow within his cowl, barely seen even in the bright midday sun. He looked back in the direction from which they had come. "We can't outrun her forever. Sooner or later, she'll wear us down. Something else is needed."

Bek blew out his breath wearily and took a fresh gulp, swallowing against the dryness in his throat. "Maybe she'll give up if we keep going."

"Not likely. Think about it. She put aside her hunt for the Druid, her mortal enemy, to come in search of you. She put everything aside, the whole of her purpose in coming on this voyage, because of you. You think you didn't reach her with your words and arguments, but I think maybe you did. Enough at least to make her wonder."

Bek shook his head. "It didn't feel like it at the time." Truls Rohk didn't even seem to be breathing hard, his body still and composed within his cloak, not a ripple of movement, not a stir.

"She's tracking us with her magic, reading our passing with it. I saw the way she walked, head up, eyes forward. She wasn't studying signs or searching for prints." He cast about for a moment, looking off into the distance in all directions, taking in the lay of the land. "We have to throw her off, boy. Now, before this gets any tighter, before she's so close nothing will slow her."

He faced the boy squarely, broad-shouldered and threatening. "Time to take some responsibility for yourself. Your magic against hers—that might be the answer. It lacks power and subtlety both, but it has its uses even so. Listen to me. She's probably reading our body heat, our movement from place to place. See if you can do the same. Watch me closely. When I disappear, track me. Use your voice, like you did on Mephitic."

In an instant, he disappeared, right from in front of Bek, vanishing as if into vapor. The boy called up his magic and cast it about wildly, searching. Nothing happened.

The shape-shifter reappeared, right where he had been an instant before. Bek gasped at the suddenness, then shook his head angrily. "It didn't work!" Frustration colored his words. "I can't make it do anything!"

Truls Rohk bent close, big and menacing. "Too bad for us if you can't, isn't it? Try again. Cast about as if you're throwing a net! Pretend you're draping images with cloth. It isn't me you're looking for—it's my shade. Do it!"

Again he was gone, and again Bek summoned the magic and cast it out. This time he was more successful. He caught pieces of Truls Rohk moving left to right and back again, ghostly presences that hung on the midday air.

"Better." The shape-shifter was back in front of him again. "Once more, but hold tight to a corner of the magic you're releasing. Then draw it in, fisherboy."

On this try, he caught all of Truls Rohk's movements, a series of passages clearly defined, moving all around him and back again. Like shades released from the dead, they hung suspended on the air, one after the other, each moving slowly to catch up to the next, as if runners slowed by quicksand and weariness.

They worked at it steadily, and then the shape-shifter changed his look to match the boy's, and suddenly Bek was casting for his own images, seeing himself replicated over and over across the meadow. Back and forth, this way and that, from one end to the other and into the trees, Truls Rohk cast his own image and the boy's until the meadow was filled with their shadows and the trail was hopelessly tangled.

"Let her try to sort that out," Truls Rohk grunted as he led the boy through the drifting images in a zigzag fashion, making for a set of mountains east. "We'll do it again a little farther on, somewhere close to water."

They ran on, not so quickly and furiously as before, the shape-shifter setting a more reasonable pace, one the boy was able to keep up with more easily. They did not speak, but concentrated on their effort, on putting as much distance between themselves and their pursuer as possible, on conserving their strength. Twice more they stopped to produce a confusing set of images, a tangled trail, crossing a deep stream once, doubling back twice at right angles, choosing difficult, rocky terrain for their passage.

It was nearing nightfall when they stopped finally to rest and eat, the light fading rapidly west, the forestland already cloaked in lengthening shadows. Night birds lifted out of the growing twilight, dark winged shapes against the sky. Bek watched them fly away and wished he had their wings. He carried no food or water, but Truls Rohk had come bearing both, stolen from *Black Moclips* on leaving, the shape-shifter prepared as always.

"Though I did not think it would come to this," he admitted grimly, handing over his water skin for the boy to drink.

Bek was exhausted. He had not faltered, but his muscles were drained and his body aching. He was used to hard treks and long hikes, but not to running for so long. Life aboard the *Jerle Shannara* had helped prepare him, but even so his endurance had its limits and did not begin to approach that of Truls Rohk.

"Will she give up now?" he asked hopefully, passing back the water skin and gnawing hungrily on the dried beef the other passed him in return. "Will she lose interest and go back for Walker?"

The shape-shifter laughed softly, wrapped in his robes and hood, his expression and thoughts hidden away. "I don't think so. She isn't like that. She doesn't give up. She'll find another way to track us. She'll keep coming."

Bek sighed in resignation. "I'll have to face her again sooner or later. There isn't any help for it." The Sword of Shannara lay at his side, and he glanced down at it. His expectations for its use against his sister seemed foolish and desperate.

"Maybe. But we have other problems to solve first. We can't just keep running for no better purpose than to escape the witch. Even if we lose her or she gives up, where does that leave us? Somewhere in the middle of a strange country without an airship or friends, without adequate supplies or weapons, and without a decent plan, that's where. Not so good."

"We have to go back for Quentin and the others," Bek answered at once, convinced that was the right choice. "We have to help them if we can. We have to try to find Walker."

It sounded so obvious and so logical that the words were

out of his mouth before he realized that he was ignoring obstacles that rendered his response only a few steps shy of ridiculous. Even given their respective magics and the shapeshifter's skill and experience, they were only two men—one man and a boy, he amended ruefully. They had no idea where their friends were. They had no means of searching for them other than to go afoot, a mode of transportation hardly conducive to the sort of search required. Their enemies outnumbered them perhaps fifty to one and that wasn't counting whatever it was that lived belowground in Castledown.

Truls Rohk didn't say anything. He simply sat there, looking out at the boy from within the shadows of his hood.

Bek cleared his throat. "All right. We can't do it alone. We need help."

The shape-shifter nodded. "You're learning, boy. What sort of help?"

"Someone to even the odds when we go back to face the Ilse Witch and the Mwellrets and whatever else is waiting."

"That, but also someone who knows a way past the things that guard those ruins and protect the treasure Walker's come to find." Truls Rohk laughed bitterly. "Don't think for a moment that the Druid, assuming he still lives, will give up on the treasure."

Bek thought of all that the company of the *Jerle Shannara* had endured to come so far, of what had been promised and what given up. He thought of how much Walker was risking to make the journey, both of life and reputation. Truls Rohk was right. The Druid would rather die than fail, given what was at stake. Even from the little he knew of Walker, it was certain that failure to gain the support of the Elves for a Druid Council at Paranor would be the end of him. It was everything he had worked for, all that mattered to him now. He had spent his life as a Druid seeking that support. Bek knew it from their conversations. He knew it from what he had heard from Ahren Elessedil. Walker had tied his fate to this voyage, to the recovery of the Elfstones and the finding of the treasure on the castaway's map.

And weren't they all tied in turn to the Druid in coming with him, Bek as well as the others? Weren't their fates all inextricably linked?

"Sleep for an hour; then we'll set out again." Truls Rohk sat with his hands locked together in front of him, animal hair on their backs gleaming faintly, like silver threads. "I'll keep watch."

Bek nodded wordlessly. An hour was better than nothing. He took a moment to look back the way they had come, to where the Ilse Witch was, to where his friends and companions were, somewhere in the dark.

Be strong, he prayed for all of them. He prayed it even for Grianne.

FIVE

Dozens of miles away, deep within the glacier-draped mountains that warded the coast of the peninsula, bracketed by the thousand-foot walls of the gorge that channeled the ice melt out into the Blue Divide, the *Jerle Shannara* drifted in solitary grandeur. Rudderless, unmanned, sails in shreds, she rode the twists and turns of the winds that howled down the canyon, moving as if drawn toward the pillars of ice that blocked the way out. Clouds roiled overhead, mingling with mist off the ice and the spray off the crash of waves against the rocks below, white sheets of gauze layered against dim shards of sunlight. Shrikes circled and dived past the rigging, bright anticipation in their gimlet eyes, each pass bringing them closer to the dead men who lay sprawled across the airship's decks. Echoes from their cries and from the pounding surf mingled and reverberated off the cliffs in eerie counterpoint.

Ahead, growing closer with each twist and turn of the airship, the pillars waited. Giant's teeth ground together and withdrew, opening and closing over the gap through which the ship must pass, hungry-sounding, ravenous, as if anxious to catch hold of what had escaped before, as if needing to feel the wood and metal of the *Jerle Shannara* reduced to shards of debris and its crew reduced to bones and pulp.

Battered and dazed, barely conscious, Rue Meridian dangled from a rope nearly fifty feet below the stern of the ship. She hung from the rope with the last of her fading strength, too weary to do anything else. Blood coated her left arm and ran in rivulets down her side, and she could no longer feel her right leg. The wind howled in her ears and froze her skin. Ice had formed in her hair, and her clothes were stiff. Everything leading up to this moment was a haze of fragmented memories and jumbled emotions. She remembered her struggle with the Mwellret, both of them wounded, their tumbling to the deck of the airship, then sliding inexorably toward the wooden railing, picking up speed and unable to stop. She remembered them striking the railing, already splintered and broken by a falling spar, the Mwellret first, taking the brunt of the impact. The railing had given way like kindling, and they had gone through in a tangle.

It should have been the end of her. They were a thousand feet up, maybe more, with nothing between them and the rocks and rapids below but air. She had kicked free of the Mwellret instinctively, then grasped for something to hold on to. By sheer chance, she had caught this length of trailing rope, this lifeline to safety. Slowing her rapid descent had nearly dislocated her arms and had torn the skin of her hands as she ripped down its length to a knot that brought her up short. Twisting and turning in the wind, she clung to the rope in stunned relief, watching the dark shape of her antagonist tumble away into the ether.

But then shock and cold had set in, and she found she could not move from where she hung, pinned against the skyline like an insect on paper, frozen to her lifeline as she fought to stay conscious. She kept thinking that eventually she would find the strength to move again, to make some effort at climbing back aboard, or that someone aboard would haul her to safety. Her mind drifted in and out of various scenarios and near unconsciousness, always unable to do more than tease her with possibilities.

But she was not so far gone that she didn't realize the danger she was in and how little time was left to deal with it. The *Jerle Shannara* was drifting ever nearer to the ice pillars, and when she reached them she was finished. No one aboard ship was going to help her. Those who were topside were all dead, Furl Hawken among them. Those below were locked away in storerooms and could not break free or they would have done so by now. Her brother, Redden Alt Mer. The shipwright, Spanner Frew. Her friends, the Rovers from her homeland. Trapped and helpless, they were at the mercy of the elements, and their end was certain.

No one would help her.

No one would help them.

Unless she did something now.

With what seemed like superhuman effort, she unclenched one frozen hand from the rope and reached up to take a new hold. The effort sent pain through her body in ratcheting spasms and shocked her from her lethargy. Ignoring the cold and numbness, she hauled herself up a notch, freed the other hand, and took a new grip. She felt fresh blood run down the inside of her frozen clothing, where her body still maintained a small amount of warmth. She was freezing to death, she realized, hanging there from that rope, buffeted by the wind blown down off the glaciers. She forced herself to take another grip and pull to a new position, one hand over the other, each length of rope she traversed an excruciating ordeal. Her eyes peered out of ice-rimmed lids. There were glaciers all around, cresting the mountains and cliffs, spreading away into the mist and clouds. Snow blew past her in feathery gusts, and through gaps in their curtains she glimpsed the pillars ahead, slow-moving behemoths against the white, the light glinting off their azure surface. Booming coughs and grinding shrieks marked their advancement, collision, and retreat, and she could feel the pressure of their weight in her mind.

Keep going!

She climbed some more, still racked with pain and fatigue, still hopelessly far beneath the broken railing she needed to reach. Despair filled her. She would never make it in time. Had she made any progress at all? Had she even moved? She hurt so badly and felt so helpless and miserable that a part of her wanted just to give up, to let go, to fall and be done with it. That would be so easy. She wouldn't feel anything. The pain and cold would be gone; the desperation would end. A moment's relaxation of her tired hands would be all that was necessary.

Coward!

She howled the word into the wind. What was she thinking? She was a Rover, and above all else Rovers knew how to endure anything. Endurance demanded sacrifice, but gave back life. Endurance was always the tougher choice, but gave the truer measure of a heart. She would not give in, she told herself. She would not!

Stay alive! Keep moving!

She tucked her chin into her chest and put one hand over the other, the second over the first, hauling herself upward inch by inch, foot by foot, refusing to quit. Her body screamed in protest, and it felt as if the wind and the cold suddenly heightened their efforts to slow her. Frozen strands of her long hair whipped at her face. She dredged up every source of inspiration she could think of to force herself to keep going.

Her brother and the other Rovers, trapped within the ship, dependent on her. Walker, stranded ashore with the others of the landing party, including her young friend Bek. Furl Hawken, dead trying to save her. The Ilse Witch and her Mwellrets, who would never pay for what they'd done if she did not find a way to stay alive and make them do so.

Shades!

She was crying freely, the tears freezing against the skin of her face, and she could not see through them well enough to tell how far she had climbed. Her jaw was clenched so tightly her teeth hurt, and the muscles of her back were knotting and cramping from the strain of her ascent. She could not take much more, she knew. She could not last much longer. One hand over the other, pull and clutch the rope with the second hand, pull again and clutch the rope with the first, on and on . . .

She screamed in pain as the wind slammed her against the hull of the airship, and she almost released her grip on the rope as she spun away from the rough wood. Then she realized what that meant, how far she had come, and opened her eyes and looked up. The gap in the broken railing was just above her. She redoubled her efforts, hauling herself up the final few yards of rope to the edge of the decking, gaining a firm grip on a still-solid balustrade, and pulling herself over the side to safety.

She lay on the rain- and ice-slicked deck for a moment, gazing skyward at the vast canopy of white mist and clouds, exhausted, but triumphant, too. Her mind raced. No time to rest. No time to spare. She rolled onto her side and peered across the bodies and debris, through the tattered shreds of sail and broken spars to the aft hatchway. She could not manage to get to her feet, so she crawled the entire way, fighting to stay conscious. The hatchway was thrown back, and she slid through the opening, lost her grip, and tumbled down the stairs. At the bottom she lay in a tangled heap, so numb she could not tell if anything was broken, still hearing the roar of the wind and the surf in her ears.

Get up!

She dragged herself to her feet, using the wall of the passageway to keep from falling again, pain shooting down her injured leg, blood soaking her clothing in fresh patches. How much had she lost? The passageway was shadowed and empty, but she thought she could hear voices calling. She tried calling back, but her voice was hollow and faint, lost in the roar of the wind. She stumbled along the corridor, using the wall for support, trying to trace the voices. She thought she heard her name a couple of times, but couldn't be sure. There was blood in her throat by then, hot and thick, and she swallowed it to keep her breathing passages clear. She was light-headed, and everything was spinning.

With a sudden lurch of the airship, she fell hard, still short of the storerooms, careening off one wall of the corridor into the other, slamming into it with such force that it knocked the breath from her lungs and she simply collapsed. She lay gasping for air, just barely able to keep from losing consciousness, the world about her spinning faster and faster. She tried to straighten herself and found she couldn't. She had no strength left, nothing more to give. It was the end of her. It was the end of them all.

She closed her eyes against the pain and fatigue, searching in her mind for the faces of those trapped only yards away. She found those faces, and Hawk's, as well, as familiar to her as her own. She heard their voices speaking her name, clear and welcoming, in other places, in better times. She found herself smiling.

The *Jerle Shannara* lurched once more, caught in a violent gust of wind, and she thought to herself, *I'm not ready to die.*

Somehow she got back to her feet. She never really knew how she managed it, how long it took, what mechanics she employed, what willpower she called upon. But, broken and crying, covered everywhere with blood, she got up and dragged herself the last few yards down the passageway to the first storeroom door. She tugged and tugged on the latch, hearing the voices shouting at her from inside, but the latch would not give. Screaming in rage and frustration, she hammered at the door, then realized it wasn't the latch that was holding it shut, it was the crossbar.

Gasping for breath, she threw back the crossbar with the last of her strength, pulled free the latch, yanked open the heavy door, and tumbled through into blackness.

When she came awake again, the first thing she saw was her brother.

"Are we still alive?" she asked, her voice weak, her throat parched with thirst. "It doesn't feel like it."

He gave her a rueful grin. "Not to you, I expect. But, yes, we're still alive, if only just by the barest of margins. It would be easier on all of us if the next time you come to the rescue, you do so with a little more alacrity."

She tried to laugh and failed. "I'll try to remember that."

Redden Alt Mer rose to bring a water skin close, poured out a measure into a cup, and lifted her head just enough to let her drink. He gave her small sips, letting her take her time. His big hand on the back of her head and neck felt gentle and reassuring.

When she had finished, he laid her back again and resumed his seat at her bedside. "It was closer than what I would have liked. They had us in two rooms, all but you and Hawk. With the crossbars thrown over the doorways, we couldn't free ourselves. We tried everything to knock the bar free, to work it clear through the jamb slit, even to break down the door. We could hear the storm and knew it was bad; we could feel the ship drifting. At first Mwellrets were watching us; then they were gone. We couldn't tell what was happening."

She closed her eyes, remembering. Hawk, using his dagger to pick the lock to their door, a forward storeroom that lacked a crossbar. Their battle with the Mwellret in the passageway. The charge up the stairs and onto the deck where other rets were waiting along with two members of the Federation crew. The airship in shambles, out of control, wheeling wildly in the grip of the canyon winds as it sailed toward the pillars of ice. The struggle with their captors. Furl Hawken giving up his own life to save hers. Her own brush with a deadly fall she only just managed to avoid. The long climb back.

"After you freed us, we rushed out on deck and saw what had happened to the ship and how close we were to the Squirm." He shook his mane of red hair, lips tightening. "By then, we were right on top of it. The pilothouse was smashed, the steering fouled, the light sheaths in shreds, the rigging flying everywhere, spars broken, and even a couple of the parse tubes jammed shut. But you should have seen Spanner and the others. They were all over that decking in seconds, clearing away the tubes, refastening the radian draws, bringing enough of the rigging and sail remnants into play to give us at least a small measure of control. You know what it was like up there, everything tossing and wild, the wind strong enough to knock you right off the deck if you didn't watch yourself, or maybe even if you did."

She nodded, her eyes opening again to meet his. "I know."

"A couple of the men went right up the masts, even in that storm, as if it didn't matter or they didn't care how dangerous it was. Kelson Riat barely missed getting his head taken off by a loose spar, and Jahnon Pakabbon was slashed all the way down his left arm by a spike. But no one gave up on the ship. We got her functioning again in minutes. I'd cleared the controls, but the lines were smashed, so we had to do it all by hand. We used the power stored in the parse tubes to right her, turn her from the ice pillars, and start her back the way she had come. The wind fought us the whole way, blowing down off the ice fields and up the gorge, trying to overpower us. But she's a good ship, Little Red. The *Jerle Shannara* is the best. She fought her way right into the teeth of the wind and held her own until we found some calm space to make headway in."

He rocked back in his seat, laughing like a boy. "Even Spanner Frew was spitting and howling in defiance of that wind, standing at the wheel to keep the rudder steady, even without the controls to work. Old Black Beard fought for her like the rest of us. To him she's a child he's nurtured and reared as his own, and he's not going to lose her, is he?"

She smiled with him, his glee infectious, her relief giving her an edge on the ache of her body. She glanced down at herself, tucked in one of the berths belowdecks, in the Healer's quarters, she thought. Light shone through the room's only window, bright and cheerful. She tried moving her arms and legs, but her body didn't seem to want to respond.

"Am I all in one piece?" she asked, suddenly concerned.

"Except for a few bad slashes and deep bruises." He arched

one eyebrow at her. "You must have had one terrible battle up there, Little Red. You and Hawk."

She kept trying to make her hands and feet move, saying nothing in reply. Finally, she felt a tingle at the ends of each, working its way through the pain that ran up and down her body in sharp spasms. She let herself relax and looked at her brother. "Hawk died for me. You've probably guessed as much. I wouldn't have made it without him. None of us would. I can't believe he's gone."

Her brother nodded. "Nor me. He's been with us forever. I didn't think we'd ever lose him." He sighed. "Care to tell me what happened? It might help us both a bit if you did."

She took her time, pausing once to let him bring her a fresh drink of water, taking him through the events leading up to her finally freeing him from the aft storeroom, leaving nothing out, forcing herself to remember it all, especially everything about Furl Hawken. It took considerable effort just to tell it, and when she had finished, she was exhausted.

Redden Alt Mer didn't say anything at first, simply nodded, then rose and walked to the cabin window to look outside. She cried a little when his back was turned, not tears, not audible sobs, but tiny hiccups and little heaves that he wouldn't notice or that, at least, she could pretend he didn't.

When he turned back to her, she was composed again. "He was everything a Rover is supposed to be," her brother offered quietly. "It doesn't help much just now, but down the road, when it matters, I think we'll find some part of him is inside us, keeping us strong, telling us how to be as good a man as he was."

She fell asleep then, almost before she knew it, and her sleep was deep and dreamless. When she woke, the room was dark save for a single candle by her bed, the sunlight that had shone through the cabin window earlier gone. She felt stronger this time, though the aches and pains that had beset her before were more pronounced. She managed to lever herself up on one elbow and drink from the cup of water sitting on the table next to her. The *Jerle Shannara* sailed in calm and steady winds, the motion of its passage barely perceptible. It was quiet aboard ship, the sounds of men's voices and movements absent. It must be night, and most must be sleeping. Where were they? How far had they come since she had slept? She had no way of knowing as long as she lay in bed.

She forced her legs from under the covers and tried to stand, but her efforts failed, and she knocked the cup of water flying as she grasped the table for support before falling back again. The clatter echoed loudly, and moments later Big Red appeared, bare-chested and, clearly, roused from sleep.

"Some of us are trying to get our rest, Sister Rue," he muttered, helping her back beneath the covers. "What do you think you are doing anyway? You're a day or two away from walking around and maybe not then."

She nodded. "I'm weaker than I thought."

"You lost a lot of blood, if I'm any judge of wounds. You won't replace it all right away. Nor will you be healing up overnight. So let's try to be reasonable about what you can and can't do for the immediate future."

"I need a bath. I smell pretty bad."

He grinned, seating himself on a three-legged stool. "I can help you with that. But no one was going to attempt it while you were unconscious, let me tell you. Not even Spanner Frew. They know how you feel about being touched."

She tightened her lips. "They don't know anything about me. They just think they do." The words were sharp, bitter.

She forced the sudden anger away. "Go back to bed. I'm sorry I woke you."

He shrugged, his red hair glistening in the candlelight, loose and unruly as it hung about his strong face. "Well, I'm up now, so maybe I'll stay up and talk with you awhile. The bath can wait until morning, can't it? I don't much want to haul a tub and water in here in the dark."

She grinned faintly. "It can wait." She regretted her anger; it was misdirected and inappropriate. Her brother was only trying to help. "I feel better tonight."

"You look better. Everyone was worried."

"How long have I been in this bed?"

"Two days."

She was surprised. "That long? It doesn't feel like it." She exhaled sharply. "Where are we now? How close to where we left the others? We've gone back for them, haven't we? We have to warn them about the Ilse Witch."

He smiled. "You are better. Ready to get up and fight another battle, aren't you?" He shook his head, then turned suddenly sober. "Listen carefully, Little Red. Things aren't so simple. We're not headed inland to the Druid's shore party. We're headed for the coast and the Wing Riders. We're doing just what we were told to do."

He must have seen the anger flare in her eyes. "Don't say something you'll live to regret. I didn't make this choice because it was the one I favored. I made it because it was the only one that made sense. Don't you think I want to square accounts with the witch? Don't you think I want to lock up those Mwellrets the same way they locked us up? I don't like leaving any of them running around loose any more than you do. I don't for a minute like abandoning Walker and the others. But the *Jerle Shannara* is in tatters. We can replace the light sheaths and radian draws, repair the parse tubes, and readjust the diapson crystals to suit our needs. We can manage to sail at maybe three-quarters power and efficiency. But we've lost spars and damaged two of the masts. We're all beaten up. We can't fight a battle, especially against *Black Moclips*. We can't even outrun her, if she should catch sight of us. Going inland now would be foolhardy. We wouldn't be of much use to anyone if we got ourselves knocked out of the sky or captured a second time, would we?"

The glare had not faded from her eyes. "So we just abandon them?" she snapped back.

"We were already abandoning them when the Druid ordered us out of that bay. Walker knew the risks when he sent us away. If we'd gotten clear of the channel before *Black Moclips* found us, she still would have sailed on up the river to the bay. Walker understood that. He wasn't thinking it couldn't happen."

She shook her head stubbornly. "We're their lifeline! They can't survive without us! What if anything goes wrong?"

"Don't be so quick to discount what they can or can't do without us. Something's already gone wrong, only it went wrong with us. And we survived, didn't we? Give them a little credit."

They stared at each other in silence for a moment, eyes fierce and intense. Rue backed down first. "They're not Rovers," she pointed out quietly.

Her brother smiled in spite of himself. "Granted. But they have their good points anyway and a fair chance of holding their own until we can get to them. Which I fully intend to do, Little Red, if you'll just have some faith in me." He leaned forward, resting his elbows on his knees. "We're on our way to the coast to make repairs and heal wounds. If we're to out-smart and outsail the Ilse Witch and her Mwellrets and per-haps do battle with *Black Moclips*, we have to be at our best. Maybe it won't come to that, if we're lucky, but we can't rely on luck to see us through this mess. We should be able to map our way in and out again, just as the Druid wanted. We should be able to make contact with the Wing Riders, as well. And while the ship's being overhauled and you're healing, I'll be flying back in with Hunter Predd to have a look at what's be-come of our friends and to help them if I can."

Rue Meridian smiled. "That's more like the Big Red I know. No sitting around and waiting. But we'll see about who's coming back and who's staying behind to heal."

He shook his head at her. "I sometimes think you don't have the sense of a gnat. Indestructible, are you? Half-dead one minute and whole the next? Off to the rescue of those un-fortunates who need you so badly? Shades! It's a wonder you've lived this long. Well, we'll talk about it."

He rose. "Enough of words for now, though. I'm off to bed and a few more hours of rest before daylight and work. Maybe you should try getting a few hours' sleep yourself. Put the past behind you and the future ahead where they belong and spend your time in the present with the rest of us." He waved dismissively as he turned away. "Sleep well, Little Red."

He went out without looking back, closing the door softly behind him. She stared after him for a long time, thinking that for all his faults, there wasn't anyone better than her brother. Whatever lay ahead, she would rather face it with him at her side than anyone else. Redden Alt Mer had the luck, they said. They were right, but he had something more than that. He had the heart. He would always find a way because he couldn't conceive of it being any other way. It was the Rover in him. It defined who he was.

She spent another few moments thinking about those trapped inland, about Walker and the rest, still worried how they would fare without the Rovers to turn to. Big Red could say what he wanted, but she didn't like the idea of abandoning them even for the time it would take to reach the coast and find the Wing Riders. They were a tough and experienced group except for Bek and the seer and one or two others who were more talented than experienced, but even the Elven Hunters were too much at risk when afoot and cut off from the airship. Especially with the Ilse Witch and her Mwellrets hunting them.

She thought of Hawk then, one final time. Someone will pay for what happened to you, she promised him silently. One day soon, that account will be settled.

She was crying again, almost before she realized it.

"Good-bye, Hawk," she whispered into the darkness.

Then she was asleep.

SIX

When Panax gripped his shoulder in warning, Quentin Leah dropped into a crouch and froze in place, eyes searching the gloom ahead. He felt the Dwarf's harsh breathing in his ear.

"Over there." The words were a soft hiss in the silence. "By the edge of that building, in the rubble."

Quentin's hand tightened on the Sword of Leah, then just as quickly loosened. *No, don't summon the magic! You'll only draw their attention if you do!* His heart began to race. Around him, everything went still, not a sound, not a movement, as if the city and its deadly inhabitants were waiting with him. Dirt, sweat, and blood streaked his face and clothing, and his body ached with fatigue. He was cut and bruised almost everywhere, and the slashes on his left side cut all the way through to his ribs. Off to one side, crouched in a screen of brush that had grown up through broken slabs of stone, Kian and Wye watched with him, waiting for his signal. He was their leader now. He was their last, best hope. Without him, they would all be dead. Dead, like so many of the others.

Quentin scanned the place in which Panax had spotted movement, but saw nothing. It didn't matter; he stayed where

CRISPO'S
3-5 ATHOLL STREET
DUNKELD
M4486635   TID16213123
SWITCH
6759 6448 7512 2785
EXP 10/05   START 10/03
SWIPED

SALE

AMOUNT   £10.45
PLEASE DEBIT MY ACCOUNT

Laura Fren, PhD

THANK YOU
PLEASE KEEP THIS RECEIPT
FOR YOUR RECORDS
21:11 31/10/03
AUTH CODE: 8375
RECEIPT 1657

he was and kept searching. If the Dwarf said something was there, then it was. They hadn't gotten that far by doubting each other, and getting that far was nothing short of a miracle.

Nothing had gone the way it was supposed to go, not from the moment they had entered that square with its smooth metal floor and irregular sections of wall. An odd formation to begin with, unlike anything the Highlander had ever seen, it whispered of trouble. But Quentin had taken up his position on the left wing of the search party, along with Panax and the Elven Hunters Kian, Wye, and Rusten, and watched as an un-accompanied Walker made his way cautiously ahead. Across the way, barely visible, Ard Patrinell crouched with Ahren Elessedil, the Healer Joad Rish, and three more Elven Hunt-ers. He could just make out their figures, little more than shadows clinging to the protective walls of the outlying build-ings. Between them, and well behind the Druid, Bek and the seer Ryer Ord Star waited with three more Elven Hunters. Like a tableau, they were etched in the fading light, motion-less statues sealed in place by time and fate.

Quentin had listened carefully for the sound of trouble, for any indication that this place that seemed so like a trap in fact was. He had his sword out already, gripped in one hand and laid flat against the metal square on which he crouched, the ridged pommel not nearly reassuring enough against his sweating palm. *Get out of here!* He kept shouting the words in the silence of his mind, as if by thinking it he could somehow make it happen. *Get out of here now!*

Then the first fire threads speared toward the Druid, and Quentin was on his feet instantly, catapulting from his crouch and charging ahead. Rusten went with him, the two of them rushing to Walker's aid, reckless and willful and foolhardy, ignoring the shouts from Panax to come back. They should have both died. But Quentin tripped and went down, sprawling across the metal floor, and the fall saved his life. Rusten, ahead of him and still charging toward the Druid, was caught in a crossfire of deadly threads and cut apart while still on his feet, screaming as he died.

Moving forward, his dark-cloaked form somehow sliding past the fire threads, Walker was yelling at them to stay back, to get clear of the ruins. Heeding the Druid's command, Quentin crawled back the way he had come, the fire chasing after him, passing so close that it seared his clothing. He caught a glimpse of the others, Bek in the center group, the Elves on the right wing, all dispersing and taking cover, shielding themselves from whatever might happen next. Ryer Ord Star bolted from Bek's side, her slender form streaking away into the ruins after Walker, ephemeral and shadowy as she passed ghostlike through walls that were now shifting in all directions, charging ahead heedlessly into the heart of the maze. He saw her stumble and go down, struck by one of the deadly threads, and then he lost sight of everything but what was happening right in front of him.

"Creepers!" Panax screamed.

Quentin rolled to his feet to find the first of them almost on top of him, seemingly come out of nowhere. He caught a glimpse of others behind it and to either side. They were of different sizes and shapes and metal compositions, a strange amalgam of what looked to be castoff pieces and oddly formed parts jointed and hinged to make something that seemed not quite real. Blades and powerful cutters glittered at the ends of metal extensions. Protruding metal eyes swiveled. They advanced in a crouch, as if they were armored insects grown large and given life and sent out to hunt.

He destroyed the first so quickly that it was scrap metal before he was aware of what he had done. All those long hours of training with the Elven Hunters saved him from the hesitation that would have otherwise cost him his life. He reacted without thinking, striking with the Sword of Leah at the creeper closest, the magic flaring to life instantly, responding to his need. The dark metal blade flashed with fire of its own, blue flames riding up and down the edges of the weapon as he left his antagonist a metal ruin. Without slowing, he leapt over it to confront the next, fighting to reach his companions, who were backed against a nearby wall, struggling with their ordinary weapons to keep a tandem of creepers at bay. He smashed the second creeper, then was struck from the side by something he didn't see and knocked flying. Red threads sought him out, searing their way slowly over the metal carpet, leaving deep grooves that smoked and steamed. He rolled away from them once again, came to his feet, and with a howl of determination launched himself back into the fray.

He fought for what seemed like a long time, but was probably no more than a handful of minutes. Time stopped, and the world around him and all it had offered and might offer again in his young life disappeared. Creepers came at him from everywhere, creepers of all shapes and sizes and looks. He seemed to be a magnet for them, drawing them like flies to the dead. They converged from everywhere. They turned away from Panax and the Elven Hunters to get at him. He was slashed and battered by their attempts to pin him down—not necessarily to kill him, but as if their goal was to capture him. It occurred to him then for the first time that it was the magic they were after.

By then, the magic was all through him. It surfaced with his first sword stroke, the blue fire racing up and down the blade's surface. But soon it was inside him, as well. It fused him with his weapon and made them one, leaving the metal to enter flesh and bone, rushing through his bloodstream and back out again, all heat and energy. It burned in a captivating, seductive way, filling him with power and a terrible thirst for its feel. Within only a short time, he craved the feeling as he had craved nothing else in his life. It made him believe he could do anything. He had no fear, no hesitation. He was indestructible. He was immortal.

Smoke drifted across the battleground, obscuring everything. He heard the cries of his companions, but he could not see them. Walker had disappeared entirely, as if the earth had swallowed him. Disembodied voices cried out in the darkness. Everyone was cut off, surrounded by fire threads and creepers, caught in a trap from which none of them seemed able to escape. He didn't care. The magic buoyed and sustained him. He wrapped himself in its cloak and, unstoppable, fought with even greater fury.

Finally Panax shouted to him that they had to get clear of the square. It took several tries before he heard the Dwarf, and even then he was reluctant to break off the battle. Slowly, they began to retreat the way they had come. Creepers sought to bar their escape, turning them aside at every opportunity, giving pursuit like hungry wolves, skittering along on their metal struts and spindly legs, strange and awkward machines. The chase veered from one building to another, down one passageway to the next, until Quentin had no idea where he was. His arms were tiring, leaden from swinging the sword, and the magic did not come so easily. The Elves and Panax were grim-faced and battle-worn. Time and numbers were eating away at their resistance.

Then, without warning, the creepers pulled back, the fire threads disappeared, and the Highlander and his three companions were left in an empty swirl of smoke and silence. Weapons held before them like talismans, the hunted men backed through the haze, putting distance between themselves and their vanished pursuers, watching everywhere at once, waiting for the attack to resume. But the ruined city seemed to have become a vast burial ground, a massive tomb empty of life save for themselves.

So it had gone ever since, with Quentin and the other three edging their way ahead, not entirely certain to where they had gotten themselves or were going. Once or twice, there had been sudden, hurried movements in the shadows, things skittering away too swiftly to be clearly seen. The night had begun to fade and dawn to approach, and sunlight was creeping through the haze that cloaked the city. They searched for signs of their friends, for familiar landmarks, for anything that would tell them where they were. But it all looked the same, and the look never changed.

Now, crouched in yet another part of the ruined city, Quentin found himself almost wishing he had something to fight again, something of substance to combat. The sustained tension of watching and waiting for invisible creepers and vanished fire threads was wearing him down. Traces of the magic still roiled within him, but a mix of fear and doubt had replaced his craving for it. He did not like what the magic had made him do, as if he were as much a fighting machine as those creepers. He did not like how thoroughly it had dominated him, so much so that even thinking became difficult. There was only response and reaction, need and fulfillment. He had lost himself in the magic, had become someone else.

Without looking at Panax, he whispered, "I can't trust my senses anymore. I'm exhausted."

He felt, rather than saw, the Dwarf nod. "We have to get some rest. But not here. Let's go."

Quentin did not move. He was thinking about Bek, somewhere out there in the haze and rubble, lost at best, dead at worst. He could scarcely bear to think of how badly he had failed his cousin, leaving him behind without meaning or wanting to, abandoning him as surely as Walker seemed to have abandoned them all. He blinked away his weariness and shook his head. He should never have left Bek, not even after Walker had separated them. He should never have believed Bek would be all right without him.

"Let's go, Highlander," Panax growled again.

They rose and started ahead, easing away from the place where the Dwarf had seen movement, skirting the building and the rubble both, choosing a wide avenue that passed between a series of what looked like low warehouses with portions of their walls and roofs fallen in and collapsed. Quentin's thoughts were dismal. Who was going to protect Bek if he didn't? With Walker gone, who else was there? Certainly not Ryer Ord Star and maybe not even the Elven Hunters. Not against things like the fire threads and the creepers. Bek was his responsibility; they were each other's responsibilities. What good was a promise to look after someone if you didn't even know where he was?

He peered into the gloom as he walked, seeing other places, remembering better times. He had come a long way from the Highlands to have it all end like this. It had seemed so right to him, that he should do this, he and Bek. To live an adventure they would remember for the rest of their lives—that was why they must come, he had argued that night with Walker. That argument seemed hollow and foolish now.

"Wait," Panax hissed suddenly, bringing him to an abrupt stop.

He glanced at the Dwarf, who was listening intently once more. To one side, Kian and Wye stared out into the gloom. Quentin thought that maybe he was too tired to listen, that even if there was something to hear, he would be unable to tell.

Then he heard it, too. But it wasn't coming from ahead of them. It was coming from behind.

He turned quickly and watched in surprise as a slender figure appeared out of the haze and rubble.

"Where are you going?" Tamis asked in genuine confusion as she approached. She pulled off the leather band that tied back her short-cropped brown hair and shook her head wearily. "Is this all of you there are?"

They welcomed the Tracker with weary smiles of relief, lowering their weapons and gathering around her. Kian and Wye reached out to touch her fingers briefly, the standard Elven Hunter greeting. She nodded to Panax, and then her gray eyes settled on Quentin.

"I've just come from Bek. He's waiting a couple of miles back."

"Bek?" Quentin repeated, a wave of relief surging through him. "Is he all right?"

There was blood on her clothing and scratches on her smooth, tired face. Her clothes were soiled and torn. She didn't look all that different from him, he realized. "He's fine. Better off than you or me, I'd say. I left him in a clearing at the edge of the ruins to watch over the seer while I came looking for you. We're all that's left of our group."

"We lost Rusten," Kian advised quietly.

She nodded. "What about the others? What about Ard Patrinell?"

The Elven Hunter shook his head. "Couldn't tell. Too much smoke and confusion. Everyone disappeared after the fighting started." He nodded at Quentin. "The Highlander saved us. If we hadn't had him and that sword, we would have been finished."

Tamis gave Quentin an ironic look. "It must run in the family. Look, you're going in the wrong direction. You're going inland instead of back toward the bay."

"We've just been running," Quentin admitted. He blinked at the Tracker in confusion. "What do you mean, 'It must run in the family'? What are you saying?"

"That young Bek saved us, as well. If it hadn't been for him, we wouldn't have gotten clear. He smashed those creepers as if they were made of paper. I've never seen anything like it."

Quentin stared at her. "Bek? Bek did that?"

She studied him carefully. "Didn't he tell you? Or did he just discover it for himself, I wonder? He didn't seem all that sure about what he was doing, I'll grant you. But to have that kind of power and not know anything about it . . . Well, maybe so. Anyway, this is what happened."

She related the details of their escape, of how they had fled back through the ruins, the three Elven Hunters, Ryer Ord Star, and Bek, until the creepers had hemmed them in. The other two Elves had died quickly, but she and the seer were saved when Bek used his voice to call up magic.

"It was eerie," she admitted. Her eyes held Quentin's. "He was singing, a strange sound, but it tore the creepers apart, like a wind or a weapon cutting through them. One minute they were there, killing us, and the next they were scrap." She nodded solemnly. "Bek saved us. And you don't know a thing about what I'm saying, do you?"

Quentin was thinking, *Bek has magic? How could that be?* He shook his head. "Not a thing."

He found himself wondering suddenly about Bek's background. Bek was the child of a cousin, but which cousin? Or was he related at all? Coran Leah had always been close-mouthed about Bek's background, but that was the way he was with private information, and Quentin had never pressed the subject. But if Bek really did have the use of magic . . .

But Bek?

All of a sudden Quentin realized why Walker had wanted Bek to come along. It wasn't because he was Quentin's cousin. It was because he possessed magic as powerful as the Sword of Leah. Bek was every bit as necessary to the expedition as he was. Maybe more so. He never questioned for a moment that Walker would know about it. What he questioned instead was how much the Druid knew that he was still keeping to himself.

"We have to get going," Tamis advised, drawing him away from his thoughts. "I don't like leaving Bek and the seer alone. Even with his magic to protect him, he's still not experienced enough to know what to look out for."

They started back through the ruins, Tamis leading the way. When queried by Panax about what sort of trouble she had encountered on the way, she said that she suspected there were creepers hiding all through the ruins, but they showed themselves only in response to certain things. Maybe it was a signal of some sort. Maybe it was only when intruders entered restricted areas. Maybe someone or something was guiding them. But she hadn't seen a single one on her way back.

The Dwarf grunted and said there wasn't much more damage they could do anyway. Walker was missing and the expedition was in shambles. It was a miracle any of them were still alive.

But Quentin didn't hear any of it. He was still thinking about Bek. His cousin was suddenly an enigma, an entirely different person than he had seemed. Quentin had no reason not to believe what Tamis was telling him. But what did it mean? If Bek had the use of magic, particularly magic that was as much a part of him as his voice, where had it come from? It must be in his bloodline and therefore a part of his heritage. So who was his real family? Not some distant Leah cousins, he knew that much. There weren't any Leahs who'd had the use of that sort of magic, not ever. No, Bek was the child of someone else. But someone the Druid knew. Someone his father knew, as well, because otherwise Bek wouldn't have been brought to Coran as a baby.

Someone . . .

Suddenly he found himself remembering all those stories Bek was so fond of telling—about the Druids and the history of the Races. The Leahs were a part of that history, but there was another family that had been part of it, as well. Their name was Ohmsford. They had been close to the Leahs once, not so long ago. Even the great Elven Queen, Wren Elessedil, was rumored to be related to that family. There hadn't been an Ohmsford in Leah or Shady Vale or anywhere in that part of the world in fifty years. There hadn't even been a mention of them.

But the Ohmsfords had magic in their blood. It had surfaced in a pair of brothers who had joined with Walker to battle the Shadowen over a century ago. He remembered the story now, bits and pieces of it. The brothers were supposed to have had magic in their voices, just like Bek. What if the family hadn't died out after all? What if Bek was one of them? If there were Ohmsfords alive anywhere in the world, certainly Walker would know. He would have made it a point to know. That would explain how he had managed to track down Bek. It would explain why he had been so determined to bring Bek along.

Quentin felt an odd suspicion creep through him. Perhaps it was Bek that Walker was after all along, and he had used Quentin as a lever to persuade the boy to come.

Was his cousin Bek Ohmsford? Was that who he really was?

The Highlander blinked away his weariness and confusion. He couldn't trust his thinking just now. He might be completely off track on this. He was just guessing. He was just trying to make the pieces fit when he didn't even have a clear picture to work from. Could anything he imagined be trusted?

Truls Rohk had warned them on their first encounter that they couldn't trust a Druid. Games-playing, he'd called it. It was almost the first word out of his mouth, a clear indication of the usage to which he felt the Druid might be putting them. Games-playing. They might be pieces being moved about a board. It was possible, he was forced to admit.

They made their way back through the city as the sun rose in a cloudless sky and the last of the night faded. The air was heavy and still within the ruined buildings, and the heat rose off the stone and metal in waves. Nothing moved in the silence. The creepers had gone to ground once more, almost as if they had never been there. Tamis gave a wide berth to the square where they had encountered the monsters earlier, and it was not much past midmorning when they reached the edge of the woods bordering the city.

She paused there, listening.

"I thought I heard something," she said after a moment, her gray eyes sharp and searching. Her slender hand made a circular motion. "I can't tell where it came from, though. It sounded like a voice."

They entered the woods and began to thread their way through the trees. Birds flitted past them, small bits of sound and movement in bright swatches of sunlight, no longer in hiding. The haze that had cloaked the ruins earlier had cleared, and the edges of the buildings glinted sharply as they disappeared from view. Within the forest there were only the trees and brush, a thick concealment rising all about, green and soft in a mix of shadows and light. The familiar, welcome smells revived Quentin's spirits and helped push back his fatigue. At least Bek was all right. Whatever the story behind his magic and his family, they would work it all out once they were together again.

They had gone a fair distance from the ruins when Tamis turned to them. "The clearing is just ahead. Stay quiet."

They approached it cautiously and were all the way to its edge when the Tracker abruptly picked up the pace, burst into the open space almost at a run, and drew up short.

The clearing was empty. "They're gone," she whispered in disbelief.

Ordering the others to stay where they were, she crept slowly about the clearing's perimeter, sometimes dropping to her hands and knees to read the signs. Quentin stood frozen in place, frustrated and angry. Where was Bek? This was the Tracker's fault. She shouldn't have left Bek alone, no matter the reason or what she thought Bek could do with his magic or anything else. But he forced his anger down, quick to realize that it was misplaced. Tamis had done what was best, and there was no point in second-guessing her.

She came back to them finally, her face grim, but her gray eyes calm. "I can't tell what's happened for sure," she announced. "There are tracks all over the place, and the last set has obscured the others. Those belong to Mwellrets. There was some sort of struggle, but it doesn't look like anyone was injured, because there are no traces of blood."

Quentin exhaled sharply. "So where are Bek and Ryer Ord Star? What's happened to them?"

Tamis shook her head. "I told Bek that if anyone came, they were to hide. I left it to him to make the decision, but he knew to keep watch. I think he probably did as I instructed, and when he saw the Mwellrets, he got out of here. You know him better than I do. Does that sound like what he would do?"

The Highlander nodded. "He's hunted the Highlands for years. He knows how to hide when it's needed. I don't think he would have been caught off guard."

"All right," she said. "Here's the rest of it then. The Mwell-rets spent some time here doing something, then continued on toward the city, not back the way they had come. If they'd taken Bek and the seer prisoner, they likely would have sent them to the airship under guard. No tracks lead back that way. Someone may have gone off in the direction from which we came, inland, but I can't be sure. The signs are very faint and difficult to read. Anyway, the Mwellret signs are very clear. They don't continue on in the same way; there is a change of direction. From the way several sets of prints start out and come back again, then all move off together in a pack, I'd say they were tracking someone."

"Bek," Quentin said at once.

"Or the girl," Panax offered quietly.

"He wouldn't leave her," Quentin said. "Not Bek. He'd take her with him. Which might explain why the Mwellrets could track him. Without her, I'm not sure they could. Bek is good at concealing his trail."

Tamis nodded, her gaze steady and considering. "I say we go after them. What do you say, Highlander?"

"We go after them," he said at once.

She looked at Panax. The Dwarf shrugged. "Doesn't make any sense to go the other way. The *Jerle Shannara*'s gone off to the coast. Whoever's left that matters is back in those ruins. I don't want to leave them to the rets and the witch."

Quentin had forgotten about the Ilse Witch. If there were Mwellrets ashore, *Black Moclips* had found its way through the pillars of ice and into the bay. That meant the Ilse Witch was somewhere close at hand. He realized all at once how dangerous going back toward the ruins would be. They were tired and worn, and they had been fighting and running for hours. It wouldn't take much for them to make a mistake, and it wouldn't take much of a mistake to finish them.

But he was not going to leave Bek. He had already made up his mind about that.

Kian and Wye were speaking with Tamis. They wanted to go back into the ruins. They wanted a chance to find Ard Patrinell and the others. They knew that would be dangerous, but they agreed with her. If anyone was still alive back there, they wanted to lend what help they could.

While the Elves conferred, Panax moved over to stand next to Quentin. "I hope you're up to saving all of us again," he said. "Because you might have to."

He smiled tightly as he said it, but there was no humor in his voice.

SEVEN

Ahren Elessedil crouched in the darkest corner of an abandoned warehouse well beyond the perimeter of the deadly trap from which he had escaped, and tried to think what he should do. The warehouse was a cavernous shelter with holes in three of its four walls. It had a roof that was mostly intact, ceiling-high doors on two sides that had slid back on rollers and rusted in place, and barely more space than debris. He had been there for a very long time, pressed so tightly against the walls that he'd begun to feel as if he were a part of them. He had been there long enough to memorize every feature, to plan for every contingency, and to rethink every painful detail of what had brought him to that spot. Outside, the sun had risen to cast its light across the ravaged city in a broad sweep that chased the night's shadows back into the surrounding woods. The sounds of death and dying had long since vanished, the battle cries, the clash of weapons against armor, and the desperate gasps and moans of human life leaking away. He watched and listened for the faintest hint of any of them, but there was only silence.

It was time for him to get out of there, to stand up and walk away—or run if he must—while the chance was there. He had to do something besides cower in his corner and relive in his mind the horrific memories of what he had been through.

But he could not make himself move. He could not make himself do anything but try to disappear into the metal and stone.

To say that he was frightened would be a gross under-statement. He was frightened in a way he had never thought possible. He was frightened into near catatonia. He was so frightened that he had shamed himself beyond recognition of whom and what he had always believed himself to be, and probably beyond all redemption.

He closed his eyes against what he was feeling and thought back once more to what had happened, searching for a clue that would help him to better understand. He saw his friends and companions spread out across the maze of walls and par-titions of that seemingly empty square—his group on the right, Quentin Leah's on the left, and Bek's in the center. Elven Hunters warded them all, and there seemed no reason to think they could not manage against whatever might con-front them. Ahead, Walker crept deeper into the maze. The lowering sun cast shadows everywhere, but there was no movement and no sound to suggest danger. There was no hint of what was about to happen.

Then the fire threads appeared, razoring after the Druid first, then after those who tried to reach him, then even after those who had remained where they were. With Ard Patrinell, Joad Rish, and the three Elven Hunters who accompanied them, Ahren ducked behind a wall to escape being burned. Smoke filled the square and mingled with the haze to obscure everything in moments. He heard the shouts from Quentin's group, the unexpected clank and scrape of metal parts, and the screams from across the way. Huddled behind his wall, filled with dread and panic, he realized quickly how bad things had become.

When the creepers had appeared behind him, he was already on the verge of bolting. He could not explain what had happened, only that the courage and determination that had infused and sustained him earlier had drained away in an instant's time. The creepers seemed to materialize out of nowhere, metal beasts lumbering from the haze. Razor-sharp pincers protruded from their metal bodies, giving him a clear indication of the fate that awaited him. He stood his ground anyway, perhaps as much from an inability to move as anything, his sword lifted defensively, if futilely. The creepers attacked in a staggered rush, and he pressed himself away from them, back behind a wall, into a corner. To his amazement, they passed him by, choosing other adversaries, descending on his companions. One Elven Hunter—he couldn't tell which one—went down almost at once, limp and bloodied. Ard Patrinell surged to the forefront of the defenders, throwing back the creepers single-handedly, a warrior responding to a need, a small wall against an attacking wave. For a moment he withstood the charge, but then the creepers closed over him and he disappeared.

Ahren left his hiding place then, desperate to help his friend and mentor, forgetting for an instant his fear, pushing back his panic. But then one of the fire threads found Joad Rish kneeling by the first Elf who had fallen, trying to drag him to safety. Joad was looking up when it happened, staring right at Ahren, as if beseeching his help. The fire thread caught him in the face, and his head exploded in a shower of red. For an instant he remained where he was, kneeling by the fallen Elven Hunter, hands still grasping the other's arms, headless body turned toward Ahren. Then slowly, almost languidly, he collapsed to the metal floor.

That was all it took. Ahren lost all control over himself. He screamed, backed away, threw down his sword, and ran. He never paused to think about what he was doing or even where he was going. He only knew he had to get away as fast and as far as he could manage. The headless image of Joad Rish hung right in front of him, burned into the smoky air, into his eyes and mind. He could not make it go away, could not avoid its presence, could do nothing but flee from it even when fleeing did no good. He forgot the others of the company, all of them. He forgot what had brought him to that charnel house. He forgot his training and his promises to himself to stand with the others. He forgot everything that had ever meant anything to him.

He had no idea how long he ran or how he found his way to the empty warehouse. He could hear the screams of the others for a long time afterwards, even there. He could hear the sounds of battle, and then the faint scrape of metal legs as the creepers moved away. He could smell the smoke of burning metal and the stench of seared flesh. Curled in a tight ball with his face buried in his chest and knees, he cried.

After a time, he regained sufficient presence of mind to wonder if any of the creepers had followed him. He forced himself to lift his head, to wipe away his tears, and to look around. He was alone. He kept careful watch after that, still huddled in that same corner, still wrapped in a ball of arms and legs, still haunted by the image of Joad Rish in his final moments.

Don't let that happen to me, he kept repeating in his mind, as if by thinking it he could somehow save himself.

But now he knew he had to do more than huddle in his

corner and hope he would never be found. He had to try to get out of there. It had been long enough that he thought he might have a chance. The attack had ended long ago. There had been no sound or movement anywhere in all that time. The smoke had faded, and the sun had risen. It was bright and clear outside, and he should be able to see anything that threatened. It would take him several hours to work his way back through the city and longer still to retrace his steps to the bay where he could wait for the return of the *Jerle Shannara*. He thought he could make it.

More to the point, he knew that he must.

It took him a long time, but he finally managed to uncurl himself and get to his feet. He stood motionless in the shadows of his corner and scanned the warehouse from end to end for signs of life. When he was satisfied it was safe to do so, he started for the nearest opening, a broad gap in the west wall that offered the most direct route back through the city. He felt parched and light-headed, and his hands were shaking. To calm himself, he reached up for the phoenix stone, remembering suddenly that it was there, hanging about his neck. He did not know whether it would work if he was threatened, but it reassured him to know he had something he could fall back on, even if he was uncertain it would be of any use.

He wondered suddenly, dismally, what had become of Bek. His friend Bek, who had done so much to encourage and support him on their voyage out of Arborlon. Was he dead with all the others? Were any of them alive back there? He knew he should go back and find out. He knew, as well, that he couldn't.

Brave Elven Prince! he chided himself in fury and sadness. *Your brother was right about you!*

He reached the opening and stepped out into the daylight.

The ruins stretched away in all directions in sprawling sameness, stark and empty. He waited a moment to see if anyone would appear, if there was anything to be heard. But the city seemed empty and lifeless, a jumble of stone and metal and encroaching weeds and scrub. Not even a bird flew overhead in the cloudless blue sky.

He began to walk, slowly at first, almost gingerly, trying not to make any noise, still on the verge of panic, fighting to keep himself together. He had no weapons save for a long knife belted at his waist and the phoenix stone. If he was attacked, his only real defense was to run. The knowledge that it was all he could rely on wasn't very reassuring, but there was nothing he could do about it. He wished he had his sword back, that he hadn't thrown it down when he fled. But then he wished a lot of other things, as well, that couldn't be. Instinct kept him moving when his conscience whispered that he didn't deserve even to be alive.

He'd gone only a few steps when tears filled his eyes once more. How proud he had been of himself that he was chosen to go on the expedition. How certain he had been that it would give him the chance he needed to prove himself. A Prince of the Realm, destined perhaps to be a King—it would all be made so clear on the journey. Even Ard Patrinell had believed it, had taught him to believe it while teaching him how to survive those who did not. Yet what had he done for his friend and mentor when it mattered? He had run like a coward, fled in a rush of panic and despair, abandoned his friends and his principles and all his hopes for what might be.

You are despicable!

He kept walking, wiping the tears from his eyes, swallowing his sobs, thinking that he must be brave now, that he must try to regain some small measure of self-worth. He was alive when others were not, and he must try to make something of that gift. He did not know how he would do that or why it would matter after what had happened, but he knew he must at least try.

The sun beat down on him, and soon he was sweating freely. He blinked against the brightness and moved into the shadows, staying close to sheltering walls to gain a measure of coolness. He thought he was going the right way, but could not be sure. He did not see anything that looked familiar—or perhaps it was just that everything looked the same. At least there were no creepers about. In the wake of his passage, nothing moved.

Then suddenly, unexpectedly, he caught sight of something that did. He caught only a glimpse of it, a flicker of movement, no more, and then it was gone. He pressed himself back into the shadows and went still, waiting to see if he would spot it again. He did so, only seconds later, another glimpse, but enough to tell him more. It was someone human, slender and robed, sliding along the walls as he had been doing, a little off to one side of where he stood. He debated what to do. His impulse was to flee or hide, anything to avoid an encounter. But then he realized that it might be a member of the company, someone as lost as he was and looking for a way out of their shared nightmare. He let the other person come closer, trying to make out who it was, barely breathing in case he was making a mistake.

Then the other stepped into a patch of bright sunlight, and he saw her face clearly.

"Ryer Ord Star!" he called to her, keeping his voice low and guarded, still mindful of the things that might be hunting him.

She turned toward him instantly, hesitated, saw him standing back in the shadows, and moved over to him. He was surprised at how calm she looked, her face composed and her violet eyes untroubled. She had always looked somewhat ethereal, but just then she seemed oddly distant, as well—as if she were seeing beyond him to another place, as if in her mind she were already there.

She reached for his hand and took it in her own, surprising him. "Elven Prince, you are alive," she whispered. There was genuine relief in her voice, and it made him ashamed to know that she thought better of him than he deserved. "You shouldn't be out here alone," she continued urgently, her grip on his hand tight. "It is very dangerous. Where are the others?"

He took a quick breath to steady himself. "Dead, I think. I'm not really sure."

She glanced around quickly, her long, silver hair shimmering in bright waves. "There are Mwellrets back that way, a large company of them." She pointed from where she had come. "I think they might be following me."

"Mwellrets?" he repeated in confusion.

"From *Black Moclips*. They've come ashore to hunt us down, all of us that remain. The Ilse Witch came with them, but she's gone now. She found us in a clearing where the Elven Tracker left us—"

"You mean Tamis?" he interrupted excitedly. "Is Tamis with you?"

"She was, but she left to find help. Bek was with me, too, but when the Ilse Witch found us, there was a confrontation between them. I'm not sure what happened, but Bek disappeared and she went after him. In the confusion, I slipped away. But the Mwellrets will have missed me by now and be searching. That was what the witch told them they were to do—to find all of us who weren't dead and make us prisoners, then take us to *Black Moclips* and hold us there until she returned."

Ahren stared at her. Accepting that the Ilse Witch had somehow made it through the Squirm and come down the channel to the cove, what was all this about a confrontation with Bek? Why would she be hunting him?

"Hsst!" she signaled in warning, clasping his hand in hers once more. "We have to go now! Quickly! They're coming!"

She drew him from his concealment, back the way he had just come, and he pulled up sharply. "No, wait, I'm not going back there!"

"You have to! They're sweeping all of the ruins! They'll find you otherwise!"

"But I can't!" he whispered in desperation. "I can't!"

She stopped tugging on his hand and released it. "Do what you wish, Elven Prince. But if you stay here, they will find you. Hiding won't help. Mwellrets can sense you better than most creatures can, and they will search you out." She stepped close. Her violet eyes were steady and searching. "Come with me."

He wasn't sure what made him decide to follow, but he did so, abandoning his shelter and hurrying after her. He glanced back several times without seeing anything, but his instincts told him she was telling the truth.

"What about Bek?" he asked after a few moments, keeping his voice low and his head bent toward hers as they slipped through the ruins. "Is he all right? Did you say the Ilse Witch is tracking him, that she's gone after him on her own?"

The seer nodded. "Bek is unhurt. His magic and his courage ward him. Perhaps she will find it difficult to overcome both."

"His magic? What magic?" The Elf hurried to keep up with her. "Wait a minute. Are you saying she's tracking him because he has some sort of magic?"

Ryer Ord Star grasped his arm and pulled him close to her. "She is his sister, Elven Prince." She registered the shock in his eyes and tightened her grip. "Walker told him just before we arrived, but Bek kept it to himself. When she appeared in the clearing, he told her who he was. The Ilse Witch did not believe him. She cannot. That was the cause of the confrontation between them. She hunts him now because she can't get the truth out of her mind, even if she doesn't accept it. She thinks that if she can confront him once more, he will admit he lied to her. Or perhaps she realizes there is something to what he says. Now walk more quickly!"

They moved ahead, faster, back through the buildings and rubble, back toward the trap they had been lucky to escape once already and were now braving again. Ahren Elessedil's mind spun with the revelations about Bek, but his thoughts were made jumbled and confused by his fear. He knew that by going back, he was tempting fate in a way he would regret. He did not really think he could survive another encounter with the creepers, whatever Ryer Ord Star believed. But he could not let this slip of a girl return alone, leaving him behind to remember he had failed her as well as Ard Patrinell and his Elven Hunters. He kept thinking he could find a way to cause her to reconsider, to change her mind, and to turn her aside. But she was strong-minded and determined, and for the moment, at least, he would have to do what she wanted.

It took them much less time than he had expected to reach the square they had fled only hours earlier. It sat still and empty in the bright midday light, its maze of walls back in place, metal sheeting baking in the heat. Ahren cast about for signs of those who had been left behind. There was no one to be seen anywhere. There were no signs that a battle had been fought, no bodies, not a trace of blood, not a scar from the fire threads, not a piece of stray metal from one of the creepers. It was as if nothing had ever happened.

"How can this be?" he whispered to her in shock.

She shook her head slowly, staring out at the clean, empty expanse with him. "I don't know."

He glanced back over his shoulder. There was no sign of the Mwellrets. "What do we do now?" he asked.

She looked about momentarily, then took his hand in hers once more. "Follow me. Don't speak, don't do anything but what I do. Don't run, whatever happens."

Still holding tightly to his hand, she squared her slender shoulders, and walked out into the maze.

His shock was complete, and perhaps that was why he went with her without protest. Fighting down a surge of fear and horror that crowded into his throat, his eyes cast right and left for creepers and his skin prickled as he waited for the fire threads to burn him. She penetrated only a few yards into the deadly square before turning aside to skirt its edges, moving carefully across the metal flooring, staying clear of the shadows and well out into the bright sunlight. They moved as one, making no sound, no unnecessary movement, not speaking, barely breathing. Ahren thought he was a dead man already, but in an act of faith that surprised him completely, he gave himself over to the seer.

What surprised him even more was that nothing happened. They worked their way just inside the perimeter of the maze until they were about a quarter of the distance around, almost even with the northern facing of the dark tower that dominated its center. Once there, the seer led him just outside again into a deeply shadowed concealment formed by what remained of the walls and roofing of a collapsed building that abutted the square.

Atop a pile of rubble that looked out through a narrow gap in a wall on the landscape through which they had come, they crouched and waited.

"Why weren't we attacked?" he asked in a whisper, still cautious, pressing close to her slender form, his lips brushing her hair.

"Because what wards the tower attacks only when there is a perceived threat to its security." Her violet eyes glistened as she turned to look at him. "Walker was a threat, so it attacked him first and then the rest of us. Had we bypassed the square and the tower, we would have been safe."

He stared at her. "How do you know this?"

Her pale, youthful face turned away. "I dreamed it," she answered quietly. "In a vision, in my search for Walker."

He didn't say anything for a long time after that, mulling over her words while watching the ruins for signs of movement. Where were the Mwellrets? Why hadn't they appeared?

"Do you think Tamis found any of the others?" he asked finally. "Did you see what became of them after we were attacked? What about Quentin Leah's group?"

She shook her head wordlessly. Her eyes remained directed away from him, out toward the city. He studied her carefully. "They're all dead, aren't they? You've dreamed that, as well."

"Not Walker Boh," she said softly.

Before he could press her further, he caught sight of the Mwellrets moving through the ruins, dark forms sliding along walls and across empty spaces, little more than an extension of the shadows to which they clung. Ryer Ord Star gripped his arm anew, and she pressed against him in warning or, perhaps, in reassurance. He held himself still, his former composure regained at least in part from having survived yesterday's attack and the return. He did not feel in the least invincible, but neither did he feel quite so vulnerable either. What he had lost in the attack that had claimed his friends had been restored in small part by his tightrope walk with the seer back through the maze to this hiding place. Before, he had thought that any kind of survival was momentary at best and undeserved. Now, he believed he might still be alive for a reason, that he might be alive because there was something he could accomplish.

Ryer Ord Star leaned close to him, her face almost touching his. "Don't worry," she whispered, as if to keep him calm and in place. "They won't find us."

The Mwellrets snaked through the city in increasing numbers, as many as twenty of them, appearing and disappearing like wraiths, cloaked forms blending with the shadows as they advanced. When they reached the maze, unaware of its dangers, they barely slowed. Using the walls for shelter in the same way the members of Walker's company had done, they entered the square in ones and twos, hunched over and faceless within their robes and hoods, reptilian bodies easing ahead cautiously. Deeper and deeper into the maze they penetrated, and nothing happened.

Ahren glanced quickly at Ryer Ord Star, his brow creased in worry. How had they managed to get so far in? The seer's gaze, calm and untroubled, remained fixed on the maze and the Mwellrets. Her fingers tightened on the Elven Prince's arm.

All at once the maze exploded in a burst of fire threads, deadly red lines crisscrossing everywhere at once, catching the Mwellrets in a web of destruction. An odd mix of hisses and shrieks rose from the trapped creatures as they sought to evade the burning ropes and failed. A handful were sliced to ribbons in the first few seconds, robes catching fire as they twisted and turned in a futile effort to flee, scorching and burning bodies collapsing in lifeless heaps. The men and women from the *Jerle Shannara* had sought to go to Walker's aid, but the Mwellrets simply abandoned their stricken companions, fleeing back through the maze in short bursts of dark robes and sudden movement. They were gone so quickly that in a matter of seconds they had vanished as if swallowed by the city.

Ahren and Ryer Ord Star remained where they were, motionless, eyes scanning the ruins in all directions. Perhaps six of the Mwellrets lay dead below them, their crumpled dark shapes visible within the maze of walls. Of those who had fled, there was no sign at all. The fire threads had ceased their deadly tracking, leaving behind smoke trails that rose from scarred ruts in the otherwise smooth metal surfaces of the walls and flooring. The creepers had never appeared at all.

Ryer Ord Star released her grip on Ahren's wrist. "They won't be back anytime soon," she said softly.

He nodded in agreement. Not after that, they wouldn't. They would wait for the Ilse Witch to return. "What do we do now?" he asked.

She rose without looking at him, her eyes shifting toward the dark tower at the center of the maze. "We begin looking for Walker."

EIGHT

Ahren Elessedil stared at Ryer Ord Star with no small amount of incredulity. What in the name of everything sane was she talking about? Look for Walker? She'd said it as if it was the most obvious and reasonable suggestion in the world. But Ahren didn't find it to be either. He thought she'd lost her mind.

"What are you saying?" was all he could manage.

The words came out in a sort of threatening hiss, and she turned to look at him at once. "I have to find him, Elven Prince," she said, her own voice maddeningly calm and self-assured. "It's where I was going when you found me."

"But you don't know where he is!" Ahren exclaimed in dismay. "You don't even know where to look!"

She knelt again, facing him, her violet eyes boring into him with a look of unmistakable determination and certainty. She looked so young, so impossibly vulnerable, that the idea of her undertaking so dangerous a task seemed at once pre-posterous and foolish.

"You may not have seen what happened to him during the attack," she began quietly, "but I did. I ran into the ruins after him, knowing he was in danger from more than the creepers and the fire threads. The visions had warned me of this place,

99

and I understood the threat to him better than any of you did. I was struck by one of the threads and prevented from reaching him, but I saw what happened. He went on alone, past fire threads and creepers, through all the smoke and confusion. He reached the tower at the center of the maze, found a doorway, and disappeared inside. He did not come out again. He is still in there somewhere."

Ahren felt his exasperation building. "Maybe so. Maybe you saw everything you say. Maybe Walker is inside that tower. But how are we supposed to get to him? Fire threads and creepers attack everyone who tries to get close. There isn't any way past those things! You've seen what happened to us and to the Mwellrets, as well! Besides, even if you somehow managed to get all the way up to that tower, how are you going to get in? You don't have a Druid's powers. Don't tell me the door will just open for you. And if it did, that wouldn't be good news either, would it? Why would you even think of doing something this . . . this ridiculous?"

He was almost shouting, and his breath was ragged as he cut himself off and rocked back on his heels. "You can't do this!" A surge of fear washed through him as he imagined trying. "I won't help you," he finished in a rush.

She gave him such a patient, understanding look that he wanted to shake her. She hadn't heard a word he'd said, or if she had, she hadn't paid him the least attention.

But then she surprised him by saying, "Everything you say is true, Ahren Elessedil."

He stared at her, not knowing what to say. "Then you'll give up on this idea, won't you? Come with me instead, back to the coast. We can wait for the *Jerle Shannara* there. We can hide until she returns. Maybe we can find Tamis again, maybe one or two others who might have escaped. They can't all be dead, can they? What about Bek? Won't he try to find his way back to that clearing?"

She brushed back her long hair and folded her hands into her lap, tucking them between her legs like a little girl. Her violet eyes were depthless and filled with pain as they fixed on him. He was suddenly certain that although she was no older than he was, her experience with life's vicissitudes was far greater than his own.

"Let me tell you something about Walker and me," she said quietly. "Something I haven't told anyone. When we left the island of Shatterstone and he was sick from its poison, I sat with him in his cabin. Bek was there, as well. Joad Rish was doing everything he knew to help Walker, but nothing was working. After several days it became clear to all of us that Walker was dying. The poison was in too deep, and it was infused with the magic of that place and the spirit who warded it. Walker's own magic could not give him sufficient protection against what was happening. He couldn't make himself well again without help."

She smiled. "So I used my own skills to heal him. I am a seer, but an empath, as well. My empathic powers allow me to absorb the hurt in others so that they can better mend. It is a draining and debilitating effort, but I knew there was no other choice. Know this, Elven Prince. I would have died gladly for him. He is special to me in a way you know nothing about and I don't care to discuss. What matters is that in healing him, I formed a link with his subconscious. I think it was intentional on his part, but I cannot be sure. I became joined to him through the bond created by my willingness to give up something of my life in order to save his. It happens now and then with empaths, though usually it fades after the healing is finished. It did not do so here. It continued. It continues now."

He studied her carefully in the silence that followed. "Are you saying Walker is communicating with you? That you can hear him speaking?"

"After a fashion, yes. Not words exactly. More a presence that comes and goes and suggests things. He is there in my mind, whispering to me that he is alive and well. I can feel him. I can sense him reaching out to me. It is the link we share, he and I, forged of a blending of our lives, of our magic, of the experience shared when he was dying and I saved him."

She paused. "Do you remember when he was trapped on Shatterstone and Bek warned us he needed help? Walker called to him because Bek shares his magic, and he can reach out to Bek when it is needed. A Druid's tool. But I heard it, too. Walker didn't call to me, but I heard his voice in my mind, as well. Because we're linked, Elven Prince. I hear his voice now, except that this time it is meant for me and no other. He speaks to me through images, fragments of what he is experiencing. He is in trouble, trapped underground, beneath these ruins, beneath that tower. He is deep in a maze of catacombs that lie below this city. Castledown is not up here, Elven Prince. It is down there."

"So the treasure and whatever wards it—"

"Is there, as well, the one secreted away, the other watching everything, controlling what happens aboveground as well as below. Walker tells me this in his images, in my visions and dreams, but in my subconscious, as well. He doesn't tell me everything, because he does not feel safe doing so. But he tells me what he can, what he must. He is in trouble, and he clings to me as he might a broken spar on a shipwrecked sea. He is adrift and lost, and I am his lifeline back."

She waited for his response. He did not have one to give.

He wasn't sure if he believed it all or not. She might be confused, misled, or delusional from the events of yesterday afternoon. She seemed lucid and assured, but you couldn't always tell another person's state of mind from the way they looked and sounded.

"Is he asking you to come to him?" he said finally.

Suddenly she seemed confused, as if the question had presented a new dilemma for her. "No," she replied after a moment. "He clings to me without revealing I am here. It is a reaching that asks nothing of me." Tears filled her eyes and ran down her cheeks. "But I will go to him anyway. I will because I must. There is no one else, no one left but me. And you, if you will go with me."

He would do no such thing, Ahren thought, certain that it was suicide to go back into the maze under any circumstances. He was filled with dread at the prospect and riddled with fear by his memories of that encounter. He couldn't help himself. He was still fighting to come to terms with his failure to fight, his abandonment of his friends, and the shame he felt as a result of both. But even his growing desire to redeem himself was not enough to make him go back into that maze. The best he could do for Ryer Ord Star was to convince her she was making a mistake.

"How will you get into that tower?" he asked, looking for a way to reach her.

She shook her head. "I don't know."

"If you do get in, how will you find Walker? If he isn't summoning you, isn't calling to you, how will you track him?"

"I don't know."

"This whole city, ruins and all, is made of stone and metal. There are no tracks to follow. Look at the size of it. If it's only half this big underground, it will take weeks, maybe even months, to search it all. How are you going to know where to look?"

She was crestfallen, but her lips tightened with resolve. "I don't know any of this, Elven Prince. I only know I have to try. I have to go to him."

He felt helpless in the face of her blind determination to go forward, to do what she had set her mind to do no matter the obstacles and complications. He felt as if he was crushing her hopes without persuading her to give them up, so that when all was said and done, she would go anyway, but he would have stripped her of her spirit.

He sat back on the rubble and peered out into the ruined city. It stretched away in the sunlight, vast and broken, its history lost deep in the past with the dead civilization that had occupied it. It was a relic of the Old World, of that time before the Great Wars when science ruled and all of the Races were one. He wondered if any of those who had lived then had foreseen this end to things. He wondered if they had tried to do anything to prevent it.

"Maybe we could find some of the others to help us," he said finally, feeling doomed and trapped, but unable to bring himself to abandon her.

She shook her head. "No, Ahren. There is only you and me."

It was the first time she had used his name, and he was surprised at the depth of feeling it aroused in him. It was as if she knew just how to say it—as if by saying it, she was linking them in the same way that she was linked to Walker.

It drew him to her and at the same time it made him afraid.

"I can't go with you," he said quickly, shaking his head for emphasis because he thought his voice was shaking.

She did not reply, simply sat there looking at him. He

couldn't bring himself to meet her gaze, but kept his eyes directed out at the city, at the miles of rubble and debris, at that mirror of the wasteland he was feeling inside.

"My brother knew what he was doing by sending me on this voyage," he said to the empty landscape, at the same time trying to make the girl understand. "He knew I was weak, not strong enough to survive—"

"Your brother was wrong," she interrupted quickly.

He turned and stared at her, surprised at the vehemence in her voice. "My brother—"

"Your brother was wrong," she repeated. "About this voyage. About Walker. But especially about you."

He took a deep breath and exhaled slowly, feeling a shift in his thinking that was impossible to reconcile with common sense but equally impossible to ignore. Could he do what she was asking of him? Could he possibly find the resolve that seemed to come so easily to her? It was madness of the sort that he could not quite manage to dismiss. Something deep inside was responding to her need, and it made him disregard all other considerations.

Even so, what could he do that would make a difference? "I don't think I can protect you, Ryer Ord Star," he whispered.

Then a distant sound caught his attention, one so tiny and insignificant he almost missed hearing it. He froze momentarily, afraid of what it might be. The seer watched him, waiting. Finally he rose to peer from their hiding place into the ruins. She was beside him at once, pressing close.

The sound had come from the maze. Dozens of tiny metal creatures skittered and wheeled their way through its intricate system of walls, none of them more than perhaps two feet high. There were several different kinds, each clearly built to perform a specific task. Some hauled away the bodies of the dead Mwellrets, gripping them with pincers at the end of stubby arms and dragging them across the smooth metal floor, where they dropped them down chutes that opened briefly and then sealed again. Some used a torch mechanism attached to their bodies to repair the rents caused by the fire threads in the metal surface of the maze. Some swept and polished and otherwise cleaned away all traces of the one-sided battle, restoring the maze so that it looked as if nothing had ever happened there.

It took them less than an hour to complete their work, speeding about like mice in a cage, sunlight gleaming off their metal shells, the sounds of clicking and whirring and buzzing barely audible in the stillness surrounding them. When they were finished, they wheeled into lines and disappeared down rampways that opened to admit them in the same fashion as the chutes that had swallowed the Mwellrets. In seconds, they were gone.

Ahren looked at Ryer Ord Star. A surge of relief swept through him. He felt giddy. "Sweepers," he said, gesturing toward the tiny machines, the word popping into his mind all at once, causing him to smile in spite of himself.

She did not smile back. Instead, she pointed to something just behind him. His heart lurched as he followed her gaze and found one of the newly named sweepers parked not three feet away.

The sweeper wasn't doing anything. It was just sitting, a squat, cylindrical body on a set of multiple rollers. Its round head might have been the top half of a metal ball resting on a set of heavy springs. Thin, short probes stuck out from the head in various places and directions, and a pair of fat knobs stuck out of its body on opposite sides, each about the size of a fist.

Ahren had no idea how it had gotten so close without them hearing it. Nor did he care. What mattered was what it was doing there. It didn't appear to have any weapons, but he was not about to discount the possibility.

Neither Ryer Ord Star nor he said anything for a moment. They stared at the sweeper and waited for it to do something. The sweeper, to the extent that it was capable of doing so, stared back.

Then all of a sudden a hatch on its head popped open and a beam of light shot out, freezing an image in the air about two feet away from them. The image wasn't very big, but it was quite clear. It was of Walker.

Ryer Ord Star gasped, and Ahren gripped her arms to steady her as she sagged into him.

The image was gone an instant later. A second image appeared in its wake, this one showing the Druid running swiftly through a series of tunnels lit by odd lamps with no flame, sliding from one patch of light to the next, his face tense and worn. Every so often he paused to look over his shoulder or peer ahead into the gloom, listening and searching. His black robes were torn and soiled, and his dark face was streaked with sweat and dirt and perhaps blood. He was being hunted, and the strain of running and hiding was beginning to tell on him.

The image disappeared. Ryer sobbed softly, as if the impact of the images had collapsed whatever wall of strength remained to her and all that was left was despair.

Ahren clutched at her. "Stop it!" he hissed angrily. "We don't know if that is really happening! We don't have any idea what this is about!"

Another image appeared, then another and another, all of

creepers moving through the same tunnels, hunting some-thing. Claws and blades flashed brightly when they passed through light. Some of them were huge. Some were rocking in an eager, anticipatory fashion. All had parts awkwardly grafted onto them, giving them a barbaric, half-finished look.

The images disappeared. Ahren decided he'd had enough. "What do you want!" he snapped at the sweeper, not giving a moment's consideration to whether it could understand him.

Apparently it could. Another image appeared, the Elf and the seer following the little sweeper through the same series of tunnels, searching the gloom. A second image followed, Walker, looking over his shoulder, stopping, lifting his arm as if in recognition, beckoning. Then all of them were joined in a third image, relief painted on their faces, hands reaching out in greeting, Ryer Ord Star melting into Walker's strong embrace.

The seer was almost hysterical. "It wants us to follow!" she cried. "It wants to take us to Walker. Ahren, we have to go! You saw him! He needs us!" She was shaking him, any at-tempt at calm forgotten.

Nowhere near as convinced as she was, Ahren freed him-self roughly. "Don't be so quick, Ryer." He used her first name to make her listen, and it worked. She went still, eyes fastened on him. "We don't know if any of this is true. We don't know if these images are real. What if this is a trick? Where did this sweeper come from anyway?"

"It isn't a trick, it's real; I can feel it. That really is Walker, and he's down in those tunnels, and he needs our help!"

Ahren was wondering what sort of help they would be able to provide to the Druid. He was wondering how following the sweeper down into the tunnels—supposing they could do that—would result in the happy ending they had been shown.

If Walker, with all his magic, couldn't get free of the creepers, what difference would their coming after him make?

He looked at the little sweeper. "How did you find us?"

A fresh image appeared. The sweeper was cleaning down at the edges of the maze, just below their hiding place. It was viewing everything through some sort of lens. Something distracted it, and it moved out of the maze and into the ruins, climbing slowly through the rubble until it was just behind them.

The image faded. "It must have heard us," the seer whispered, giving Ahren a quick, hopeful look.

He didn't see how. They had been careful not to make any noise at all. Maybe it had sensed their presence. But why hadn't the other sweepers sensed them, as well?

"I don't like it," he said.

"Ahren!" she pleaded, her voice wrenching and sad.

He gave an exasperated sigh, feeling trapped by her need and expectations. She was so desperate to get to Walker, to do something to help him, that she was abandoning any attempt to exercise caution or good sense. On the other hand, he was so desperate to get away from this place, that he was refusing to give the sweeper's credibility any consideration at all.

"Why are you trying to help us?" he asked the little machine. "What difference does it make to you what we do?"

The sweeper must have expected the question; an image immediately appeared in the same place as the others. It showed the sweeper performing its tasks in the maze and the tunnels belowground. A second set of images followed, these showing the sweeper being kicked and pummeled and knocked about in almost every conceivable way by something big and dark and fearsome that was always cloaked in shadow or just out of sight. Time and again, the sweeper was picked up and flung against a wall. Over and over, it was knocked on its side and had to be righted by other sweepers coming to its aid. There seemed to be no reason for the attacks. They appeared random and purposeless, the result of misdirected or point-less anger and frustration. Dented and cracked, the little sweeper would have to be repaired by its fellows before re-turning to its duties.

The images disappeared. The sweeper went still once more. Ahren tried to reconcile his doubts. An abused sweeper? Kicked around so thoroughly and for so long that it would do anything to put a stop to it? That meant, of course, that the sweeper was capable of feeling emotion and reacting to treat-ment that troubled it. As a rule, machines didn't feel anything, not even creepers. They were machines, which by definition meant they weren't human.

But these machines might well be as old as the city and whatever lived in it. It was not impossible to imagine that be-fore the Great Wars destroyed the old civilization, humans had developed machines that could think and feel.

"It's asking for our help," Ryer Ord Star pointed out, breaking the silence. She brushed back her long silver hair in frustration. "In return, it will help us find Walker. Don't you understand?"

Not entirely, Ahren thought. "What sort of help does it ex-pect us to give it?"

An image flashed from the open hatchway in the sweeper's metal head. Walker, Ahren, and Ryer Ord Star were walking from the ruins with the sweeper in tow.

"You want us to take you along when we leave?" he asked in disbelief.

The image repeated itself twice more, insistent and unmis-takable. Then a new image appeared, the *Jerle Shannara* rising skyward, light sheaths stretched taut, radian draws rippling with power. At the bow of the airship stood the little sweeper, looking back at the land it was leaving behind.

"This is ridiculous," Ahren muttered, almost to himself. "It's a machine!"

"A sentient machine," Ryer Ord Star corrected him. "Sophisticated and capable of feeling. Ahren, it wants what we all want. It wants to be free."

The Elven youth sat down slowly on the pile of rubble and put his chin in his hands. "I still don't feel good about this," he said, his eyes watching the sweeper. "If we do what it wants and go underground, we'll be cut off from everything. If this is a trap, we won't have any chance of escaping. I don't know. I still think we ought to find the others first."

She knelt in front of him and put her hands over his, the tips of her fingers brushing his face. "Elven Prince, listen to me. Why would this be a trap? If whatever wards Castledown wanted us, couldn't it have had us by this time? If this sweeper meant to betray us, wouldn't we already be surrounded by creepers? What difference does it make to anything if it manages to get us belowground? Why would it go to so much trouble to accomplish so little?"

He had to admit he didn't know. She was right; it didn't make much sense. But neither did a lot of other things that had happened on this voyage, and he wasn't about to discount the way his instincts kept tugging at him in warning. Something was bothering him. Maybe it was just his fear of ending up like Joad Rish and the others. Maybe it was his indelible memory of the carnage and screams and dying. It was all too fresh to allow him to think objectively yet.

"There's no time to look for anyone else," she insisted. "There may not be anyone out there to find!"

It was his greatest fear, of course. That there was no one else alive, that they were all that was left.

She was pressing her hands over his, cupping them. He lifted his chin from their cradle, but she would not release him. "Ahren," she whispered. "Come with me. Please."

She was afraid, too. He could feel it in her touch and hear it in her voice. She was no less vulnerable than he. She could see the future, and perhaps she had seen things that she shouldn't, things that frightened her more than what was past. But she was going because she felt so strongly about Walker that she could not abandon him no matter what. He envied her such strength. It eclipsed his own and left him newly ashamed. She would go whether he went or not. And what would he do then? Go back to the bay, hide from the Mwellrets, and wait for the *Jerle Shannara* to return? Fly home again and live for the rest of his life with what he had done?

He might as well be dead if he did that.

"All right," he said quietly, taking her hands in his, holding them like tiny birds. He bent to her reassuringly, his voice steady. "We'll give it a try."

NINE

Quentin Leah crouched in the shadowed concealment of a partially collapsed building just below the maze into which the Mwellrets had ventured all too boldly a little earlier and from which they were now fleeing in a somewhat less orderly fashion. Panax and Tamis flanked him, motionless as they peered out through cracks in the walls. The Elven Hunters Kian and Wye knelt a little to the side. The Mwellrets raced past them unheeding and uncaring. Quick glances were cast over their shoulders, to see what might be following, and no-where else. Some of the rets were bloodied, their cloaks torn and stained, their movements halting and ragged. They had not had a good time of it back there, certainly no better than Quentin and his companions, and they were anxious to be well away.

"How many do you count?" Tamis whispered to him.

He shook his head. "Maybe fifteen."

"That means five or six didn't make it out." She said it matter-of-factly, eyes straight ahead, watching the Mwellrets slide through the ruins. "It doesn't look like they managed to catch up to the seer."

Unless she was dead, of course. Quentin kept that thought to himself. Tamis wasn't saying anything about Bek, but that may have been because she still wasn't sure which way he had gone. She'd picked up Ryer Ord Star's trail easily enough, even with the herd of Mwellrets tromping all over everything, but there had been no sign of his cousin. Quentin felt frustrated and increasingly desperate. Time was getting away from them, and they weren't making any progress. He'd had reasonable hopes that they would encounter Bek or Ryer Ord Star by following the rets. Now it looked as if they wouldn't be encountering anyone.

The last of the Mwellrets trailed past, hurrying away through the bright midday light, disappearing back the way they had come. Tamis didn't move, so neither did Quentin or the others. They stayed where they were, frozen in place, watching and listening. After what seemed a very long time, Tamis turned to face them, her small, blocky form squared away and her gray eyes calm.

"I'm going to slip out for a quick look, try to find out what's happened. Wait here for me."

She was starting away when Quentin said, "I'm coming with you."

She turned back at once. "No offense, Highlander, but I'll do better alone. Leave this to me."

She slipped out through a gap in the wall and was gone. They looked for her in the ruins, but she had disappeared. Quentin glanced at Panax, then at the Elves, his disgruntlement plainly visible.

Kian shrugged. "Don't take it personally, Highlander. She's like that with everyone. No exceptions."

Quentin was thinking she had taken over leadership of their little group, a position he had occupied until she appeared. He wasn't the sort who was troubled by ego problems, but he couldn't help feeling a little irritated by her abrupt manner. He was competent at tracking, after all. He wasn't a novice who would place her at risk by going along.

Wye stretched his legs. A former member of the Home Guard, he had served in Allardon Elessedil's household before coming on this voyage. "She wanted to serve in the Home Guard, but Ard Patrinell thought she would be wasted there. He wanted her as a Tracker. She had a gift for it, was better than almost anyone."

"She resented his interference, though," Kian added with a yawn, dark face haggard and tired. "It took her a while to forgive him."

Wye nodded. "Places in the Home Guard are highly coveted; competition is intense. Women have never been fully accepted as equals; men are preferred as the King's protectors. And the Queen's. That was true even of Wren Elessedil. History and common practice more than prejudice and favoritism dictate what happens. Women don't serve in the Home Guard. On the other hand, women have come to dominate the tracking units of the Elven Hunters."

Wye nodded. "Their instincts are better than ours. No point in denying it. They seem better able to sort things out and make the choices you have to make when you're tracking. Maybe they've learned to better hone their instincts to compensate for lack of physical strength."

Quentin didn't know and didn't care. He admired Tamis for her straightforward approach to things, and he couldn't find any reason for her not to be accepted as a Home Guard. But he would have preferred her to show a little more confidence in him. Her demeanor didn't suggest she thought for a minute that she would ever have need of him or anyone else to come to her rescue. Those steady gray eyes and quiet voice were rimmed in iron. Tamis would save herself if there was any saving to be done.

Panax seated himself cross-legged in a corner of the room, a block of wood in one hand, his whittling knife in the other. He worked slowly, carefully in the silence, wood shavings curling and falling to the stone, shaggy head bent to his task.

"Sorry you came on this journey, Highlander?" he asked without looking up.

Leaving the Elven Hunters to keep watch, Quentin sat down next to him. "No." He considered momentarily. "I wish I hadn't been so eager to have Bek come along, though. I won't forgive myself if anything happens to him."

Panax grunted. "I wouldn't worry about Bek if I were you. You heard Tamis. I'd guess he's better off than we are. There's something about that boy. It's more than the magic Tamis saw him use. Walker's marked him for something special. It's why he sent you both to Truls Rohk—why Truls was persuaded to come with us. He saw it, too. He recognized it. He won't have forgotten it either. You might want to bear that in mind. The shape-shifter's out there somewhere, Highlander—mark my words. I won't tell you I can sense it. That would be silly. But I know him, and he's there. Maybe with Bek."

Quentin considered the possibility. The fact that no one had seen Truls Rohk—at least, no one he knew of—didn't mean he wasn't there. It was possible he was shadowing Bek. That made perfect sense if Walker had brought him along to keep Bek safe. He thought again about his cousin's mysterious past and his newfound use of magic that he'd never known he had. Maybe Bek really was better off than the rest of them.

"What about you, Panax?" he asked the Dwarf.

The whittling knife continued to move in smooth, effortless strokes. "What about me?"

"Are you sorry you came?"

The Dwarf laughed. "If I were, I'd have to be sorry about the larger part of my life!" He shook his head in amusement. "I've been living like this, Highlander, drifting from one mishap to the next, one expedition to another, for as long as I can remember. For all that I'm up in those mountains living alone much of the time, I've been more places and risked my life more often than I care to think about." He shrugged. "Well, there you are. If you live your life in the Wolfsktaag, you pretty much live on the edge all the time anyway."

"So Walker knew what he was doing when he sent us to find you? He knew you'd be coming, too."

"I'd say so." The Dwarf's dark eyes lifted a moment, then refocused on his work. "He wanted Truls and me both. Same as you and Bek. He likes companions, friends, and people who've known each other a long time and trust each other's judgment. He knows what sorts of risks you take on a voyage like the one we've made. Strangers bond, but not fast and hard enough as a rule. Friends and family are a better match in the long run. Besides, if he can get two magic wielders for the price of one, why not do so?"

Quentin refitted the headband around his long hair. "Always thinking ahead, the way Druids do."

The Dwarf grunted. "Farther ahead than you and I and most others could manage. That's why I think he's still alive." He stopped whittling and looked up. "That's why I think that sooner or later we'll find him."

Quentin wasn't so sure, but he kept that to himself, as well. His attitude about things in general was less positive than when he had started the journey. Bek would be surprised at the change in him.

Not ten minutes later, Tamis reappeared. They didn't see her until she was almost on top of them and she was not trying to hide her coming. She loped up through the rubble and into their shelter, her face damp with sweat, her short dark hair tousled, and her clothing disheveled. Quentin saw by the look on her face that all was not well.

"I followed the Mwellrets almost all the way back through the ruins." She spoke quickly, wiping at her face with her tunic sleeve as she crouched before them. She was breathing hard. "I caught up with one of them. He was injured and lagging behind the rest so I took a chance. I knocked him down, put a knife to his throat, and asked him what had happened. It was pretty much what you would guess, the same thing that happened to us. He told me they were tracking the seer, but they never found her."

"What about Bek?" Quentin asked at once.

She shook her head. "They don't know anything about him. When they reached that clearing, only the seer and the Ilse Witch were there. The witch told them to hunt us down and make us prisoners and then went off to hunt someone or something by herself." She paused. "It could have been Bek."

The Highlander frowned. "Why would she waste time hunting Bek? That doesn't make any sense."

"It does if she knows about his magic," Panax pointed out.

Quentin shook his head stubbornly. "She's after the treasure in Castledown. Maybe the Mwellret was lying to you."

"I don't think so," Tamis replied. "Bek was there when I left to find you and gone when the Mwellrets showed up. Something happened to him between times, and it probably involved the Ilse Witch. If we could find the seer, we might find out the truth. She must have seen something."

Panax tucked his whittling wood and knife away. "She could have died in the maze, along with the rets."

Tamis waved the suggestion off. "Why would she go back into the maze knowing what she does about its dangers? Besides, the ret I questioned said they didn't find her, dead or alive." She stood up. "That's enough for now. We have to get out of here. They'll be coming for us."

"You didn't kill the ret?" Kian asked her sharply.

Tamis wheeled on him angrily. "He was unarmed and helpless," she snapped. "I need better reasons than that to kill a man. I knocked him senseless and left. When he wakes, we'll be far away. Now let's go!"

"Go where?" Quentin demanded, standing up, brushing dirt and debris off his pants legs. "Do what?"

She shrugged. "We'll figure that out later. For now, we'll get far enough away that we won't be looking over our shoulders all the time. But we'll stay here in the ruins. They're big enough that we can hide and not be easy to track. We can keep looking for Patrinell and the others."

She started away, and they followed without further argument, knowing she was right, that they had to find a new hiding place, farther from the maze, deeper into the city. The Mwellrets would certainly hunt them, and they were excellent trackers, relying on their highly developed senses, on their shape-shifting abilities, and on their reptilian ancestry. In any case, it was foolish to assume that staying put would help. Following along behind Tamis, the Highlander, the Dwarf, and the Elven Hunters took care to disguise their tracks, to walk on the hard slabs of metal and stone where footprints wouldn't show. Several times, Tamis dropped back to muddy further any sign of their passing, using her special skills to conceal their trail.

Overhead, the sun had passed the midday point, easing into the afternoon, sliding through the cloudless blue toward nightfall. Within the ruins, the heat cast in the wake of its passing rose off the stone and metal in shimmering waves. Quentin loosened the buttons of his tunic and pushed up his sleeves. The Sword of Leah, strapped across his back, felt heavy and cumbersome. The magic with which it had infused him had faded, gone back into whatever dark pocket it had come from, leaving him bereft, but free, as well. He wondered if he would manage it better next time it was needed. There would be a next time, after all. He could hardly expect otherwise.

After they had gone some distance, he moved up beside Tamis. "Why are we going this way and not back toward the bay where we landed? What about Bek?"

She glanced over at him, her lips compressing in a tight line. "Two things. We have to find where Bek went before we can go after him, and we don't want the Mwellrets knowing what we intend."

He nodded. "We need them to believe we are doing something entirely different, running away perhaps, fleeing inland." He paused. "But won't they expect us to try to get back to the *Jerle Shannara*?"

"I expect they're hoping we do exactly that."

It was the way she said it that caught his attention. "What do you mean?"

Tamis rounded on him, bringing him up short. Her face was hard and set. The others closed about. "The Mwellret told me something else," she said, "something I didn't tell you before. I thought it could wait, since there was nothing we could do about it anyway. But maybe it can't. We've lost the ship. The Ilse Witch found a way through the pillars of ice and surprised it in the channel. She used her magic to put the Rovers to sleep and made them all prisoners. She's left Federation soldiers and Mwellrets to fly her." She shook her head. "We're on our own."

They stared at her, stunned. They were all thinking the same thing. They were marooned in a strange land, and any hope of being rescued by Redden Alt Mer and his Rovers or of getting back to the *Jerle Shannara* was gone.

Quentin started to say something, but she cut him short. "No, Highlander, the ret wasn't lying. I made sure. He was very definite. The *Jerle Shannara* is under the control of the Ilse Witch. She's not coming back for us."

"We have to get her back!" he replied at once, blurting it out before he could stop himself.

"Shouldn't be too hard," Panax observed, arching one eyebrow. "All we need are wings to fly up to her. Or maybe she'll do us the favor of coming down where we can reach her."

"For now, what we need to do is walk," Tamis said, dismissing the subject as she wheeled away. "Let's go."

They continued on for the better part of the afternoon, watching the sun descend into the west until it was little more than a bright glimmer along the horizon. By then they had crossed to the other side of the city and could see the trees of the forest ahead through gaps in the fallen buildings. Their shadows trailed behind them in long dark stains, sliding over the rubble like oil. The heat had dissipated and the air cooled. There had been no sign of the Mwellrets all afternoon. Nor had there been any sign of other survivors from their own company. The city seemed empty of life, save for themselves.

Ahead, the trees formed a dark wall over which the fading sun cast its silver halo.

Tamis called a halt, glancing around as she did so, taking her time. "I don't think we should attempt to circle back through the city at night," she said. "There's bound to be other traps. There might be sentries, as well. Better to wait until morning when we can see something."

Quentin, like the others, had adjusted to the idea that they were alone and cut off from rescue or escape, that whatever they chose to do, they had better do so with that in mind. Mistakes would prove costly now, perhaps fatal. If the Mwellrets wanted to try tracking them in the dark, let them do so. With any luck, the city and its horrors would swallow them.

"We'll make camp in the forest?" Panax asked.

Tamis nodded. "As best we can. No fire, cold food, and one of us on watch all night. We've seen what's in the city, but not what's in these woods."

A comforting thought, Quentin mused, trailing after her into the trees until she found a suitable clearing. The sun was down by then, and the first stars were appearing. The same stars would already be out at home, so far away he could barely imagine it anymore. His parents would be in bed and perhaps asleep under them. He wondered if Coran and Liria were thinking of him now, as he was thinking of them. He wondered if he would ever see them again.

They had a little food and water, but no bedding. Almost everything had been lost in the flight out of the maze or left behind at the edge of the ruins. They ate what they had, drank from an aleskin Panax was carrying, and slept in their clothes using whatever they could find for pillows. Tamis took the first watch. Quentin was asleep so fast he had barely cradled his head in the crook of his arm before he was gone.

He dreamed, but his dreams were jumbled and disjointed fragments. They left him shaken and at times frantic, but they lacked meaning and were forgotten almost immediately. Each time, after jerking awake, he slipped quickly back to sleep again. Black and still, the night enveloped and carried him away.

It was Kian who woke him, gripping his shoulder firmly, steadying him when he started from his sleep. "You've been dreaming all night, Highlander," the Elven Hunter whispered. "You might as well take the watch and let those of us who can rest do so."

His was the last watch, and already he could sense the shift in time. The stars had circled about and the darkness was losing its hold. Quentin sat looking out across the clearing to where the sunrise would begin, waiting for the light to change. His companions slept all about him, their dark shapes unmoving, the sounds of their breathing slow and ragged in the stillness.

Once, something flew through the branches of the trees overhead, a quick and hurried movement that disappeared almost as fast as it had come. A bird of some sort, he decided, and let his heart settle back into his chest. A little later, feeling uneasy, he rose and peered out into the ruins of the city, searching the darkness. He saw nothing and heard nothing. Maybe there was nothing to see or hear. Just themselves. Maybe in a world of creepers and fire threads, of Mwellrets and the Ilse Witch, they were all of humankind that was left.

But as the dawn brightened in a thin silver thread along the eastern horizon, chasing back the forest shadows just enough to give identity to shapes and forms, he saw that he was wrong. A man stood opposite him on the far side of the clearing, vaguely defined by the light, immobile against the gloom. At first Quentin thought he was seeing something that wasn't really there, that the light was playing tricks on his eyes. Why would someone be standing there in the dark? But as the light sharpened the image and gave clarity to its features, he found he wasn't mistaken after all. The man was tall and thin, wearing a sleeveless tunic, pants that ended at the knees, sandals that laced up his ankles, and leather wrist guards. He carried what seemed to be a spear yet wasn't, a slender piece of wood six feet in length with a second, much shorter length fastened to its center.

Quentin waited until he was absolutely certain of what he was seeing, then reached over to Tamis, who was sleeping right beside him, and touched her arm.

She was awake instantly, rising to a sitting position and staring at him. He pointed at the figure. A second later, she was standing beside him, fully alert.

"How long has he been there?" she whispered.

"I don't know. He was already there before it was light enough to see him."

"Has he done anything?"

Quentin shook his head. "Just stand there and watch us."

Tamis went silent. She sat with Quentin, studying the man, waiting to see what would happen. In the new light, her small face took on a different cast; she looked young and pretty and faintly exotic with her Elven features. Quentin found himself studying her as much as the stranger. He liked the calm, easy way she dealt with things, the way she was never flustered, the fact that she never overreacted. In another time and place, in other circumstances, he would have responded to that attraction; he did not think he could allow that there.

The sun crested the horizon and sent splinters of brilliant

light chasing after the fading night. In the wake of their passing, the stranger's features were fully revealed. His skin had a reddish cast to it, almost copper. It gleamed faintly, as if it was oiled. His hair, redder still, if a shade lighter, was thick and tightly curled against his skull, cut short and left free. Even his eyes, now visible in the dawn, were vaguely cinnamon.

He continued to regard them, a statue carved of stone. For the first time, Quentin saw what might be a short javelin tucked into his leather belt behind his back, one end protruding.

"What is he carrying in his hand?" he whispered to Tamis.

She shook her head. "I think it's a blowgun, but I've never seen one that size. See the piece strapped to its middle? That would be a holder for the darts." She went silent again, then said, "We can't wait on this any longer. We have to see what he wants. Stay here while I wake the others."

She rose and moved from Panax to the Elven Hunters, waking each with a touch, bending close to caution them, to tell them not to react. One by one they sat up and looked over to where the stranger stood watching.

Tamis came back to Quentin and bent close. "This might be tricky. He won't be alone. There will be others in the trees. He wouldn't expose himself so completely if there wasn't someone protecting his back. He's offering himself as a decoy to see what we do. Let's not give him reason to think we mean him harm."

She stood up and walked slowly over to where he stood. She kept her hands at her sides and her weapons sheathed. Quentin heard her greet him in the Elven tongue and then, when he failed to respond, in several variants. None worked. She tried several Southland languages. Still nothing. She spoke bits of half a dozen Troll dialects, all without result.

Then all at once the stranger said something. When he spoke, his mouth opened to reveal that even his teeth were burnished copper instead of white. His speech was rough and guttural, and Quentin could not understand any of it. Tamis seemed perplexed, as well.

"Hold up a minute." Panax stood suddenly and walked over to them. "I think he's speaking in the Dwarf tongue, a very old dialect, a kind of hybrid. Let me try."

He spoke to the stranger, taking his time, trying out a few words, waiting for a response, then trying again. The stranger listened and finally replied. They went back and forth like this for several minutes before Panax turned back to his companions. "I'm getting some of it, but not all. Come over and stand with me. I think it's all right."

He went on talking with the stranger, Tamis staying close beside him, as Quentin, Kian, and Wye joined them.

"He says he's a Rindge. His people live in villages at the foot of those mountains behind him. They're native to this area, been here for centuries. They're hunters, and he's part of a hunting party that stumbled on us during the night." He glanced at Tamis. "You were right. He's not alone. There are other Rindge with him. I don't know how many, but I'd guess they're all around us."

"Ask him if he's seen anyone else besides us," Tamis suggested.

Panax spoke a few words and listened to the other's reply. "He says he hasn't seen anyone. He wants to know what we're doing here."

There was another exchange. Panax told the Rindge they had come to search for a treasure in the ruins of the city. The Rindge grew animated, punctuating his words with gestures and grunts. He said there wasn't any treasure, the city was very dangerous, and metal beasts would hunt them and fire would burn their eyes out. The city had eyes everywhere, and nothing came or went without being seen, except for the Rindge, who knew how to stay hidden.

Quentin and Tamis exchanged a quick glance. "How do the Rindge hide from the creepers?" she asked Panax.

The Dwarf repeated the question and listened intently to the answer. Confused, he made the Rindge repeat it. While they spoke, other Rindge appeared out of the trees, just faces at first in the dim light, then bodies, as well, materializing one after the other, ringing the little company. Quentin glanced around uneasily. They were vastly outnumbered and very much cut off from any chance of flight. He resisted the urge to put his hand on his sword; relying on weapons for help would be foolish.

Panax cleared his throat. "He says the Rindge are a part of the land and know how to disappear into it. Nothing can find them if they keep careful watch, even at the edges of the city. He says they never go into the ruins themselves. He wants to know why we did."

Tamis laughed softly. "Good question. Ask him what it is they're hunting."

The Rindge, tall and rawboned, listened and nodded slowly as Panax spoke. Then he replied at length. The Dwarf waited until he was finished, and glanced over his shoulder. "I'm not sure I'm getting all this. Maybe I've got it wrong. I almost hope I do. He says they're hunting creepers, that they're setting traps for them. Apparently the traps are to discourage the creepers from hunting them. He says the creepers harvest the Rindge for body parts, that they use pieces of the Rindge to make something called *wronks*. Wronks look like them and us, but are made of metal and human parts both. I can't quite figure it out. The Rindge are pretty frightened of them, whatever they are. This one says that by taking pieces of you, the wronks steal your soul so that you can never really die."

Tamis frowned. "What does that mean?"

Panax shook his head. He spoke to the Rindge again, then glanced at the Tracker and shrugged. "I can't make it out."

"Ask him who controls the wronks and the creepers and the fire," she said.

"Ask him who lives under the city," Quentin added.

Panax turned back to the Rindge and repeated the questions in the strange, harsh Dwarf dialect. The Rindge listened carefully. All about them, the other Rindge pressed close, exchanging hurried glances. The air was charged with fear and rage, and the Highlander could feel the tension in the air.

When the Dwarf was finished, the Rindge to whom he had been speaking straightened, looked past them toward the ruins, and spoke a single word.

"Antrax."

TEN

Deep within the bowels of Castledown, far below the ruins of the city above, Antrax spun down the lines and cables that gave it passage through its realm. Traveling somewhere between the speeds of light and sound, faster than the eye could follow if the eye had been permitted to try to do so, it sped along corridors and passageways, from chamber to chamber, riding the metal threads that linked it to the kingdom it ruled. It was a presence that lacked substance and shape and could be virtually everywhere at once or nowhere at all. It was the crowning achievement of its creators in a time and a world long since dead, but it had transcended even that to become what it was.

The perfect weapon.

The ultimate protector.

Built almost three thousand years earlier, in a time when artificial intelligence was commonplace and thinking machines proliferated, it was advanced for its kind even then, a prototype created in the heat of events that culminated in the Great Wars. Skirmishes had begun already, and its creators suspected where things were heading when they first conceived of it. They were archivists and visionaries, people whose primary interest was in preserving for the future that

129

which might otherwise be lost. Lesser minds dominated the thinking of the times; they manipulated the rules of power and politics to stir within the populace a mix of rage and frustration that eventually would consume them all. To thwart the madness that was overtaking them, the creators determined that those who would destroy what they would not concede should not be allowed to undo the progress of civilization. Antrax knew that because when it was built, the knowledge was programmed into it. It was necessary that it know the reason for its existence, because otherwise how could it understand the importance of what it was created to do?

It took years to build Antrax, and the building of it was accomplished at a great cost of lives and resources. Few of those who began the project lived to see it completed. Antrax had a sense of time, and knew that it had gained life in small increments. A bit of knowledge here, a piece of reasoning there, it expanded until it was housed in more than one place and could travel the city's catacombs like a wraith. Aboveground, the city masked its presence and its purpose. Only a few knew that it was there, functioning. Only those few knew what it was meant to do. The Great Wars were consuming the world of the creators in a widening swath of destruction and ruin, and humankind was being changed forever. So much would be lost as a result—irreparably lost. But not what was housed within those chambers, not that which Antrax was created to preserve and with which it was entrusted. That would be protected. That would endure.

In the end, the creators simply faded away. Antrax never knew what happened to them. They gave it life, a place to reside, a domain to watch over, and a directive to follow. They set it on its course, and then they disappeared.

All but one.

That one returned a final time. He was alone and his appearance unexpected. When all else was done, and Antrax was functioning as intended, the input receptors had been closed. No further instructions were necessary. Then the last creator appeared and opened the receptors anew. He gave greetings to Antrax. They could speak to each other through the keyboards and touch screens. They could communicate as equals. He told Antrax that the worst had come to pass. Everything was lost. The world was destroyed, and civilization was in ruins. Centuries of progress had been wiped out. Art, culture, knowledge, and understanding were gone. The creators, save he alone, were destroyed. Perhaps no one was still alive anywhere in the entire world. Perhaps everyone was dead.

Antrax did not respond. It had not been built to understand human emotion; it could not sense it in the words of the creator who spoke to it. But a new directive followed, and Antrax was required to obey directives. The directive entered its memory banks through the keyboard and became a part of its consciousness. The command was clear. Those chambers, the complex, and everything housed within had been given to Antrax to ward. They must not be compromised. They must not be lost. It was not enough that Antrax watch over them and keep them safe for when the creators returned. Antrax must protect them, as well; it must combat and destroy anything that threatened them. The means for doing so was already in place, weapons and defenses both, installed in secret by the last creator himself, who knew better than his fellows what the times required. Antrax must draw from its memory banks, as it did energy from its power cells, knowledge of how those defenses and weapons worked. It must adapt that knowledge to fulfill its directive; it must extrapolate what was needed to survive. If defenses or weapons were called for,

Antrax must use them. If they were not enough and others were required, Antrax must build them. If anyone tried to reclaim the chambers without entering the proper code, the intrusion must be stopped—even at the cost of lives.

The final admonishment was a direct violation of any previous programming, but the command was overriding and absolute. Causing harm to humans was permissible. Killing was allowed. Antrax was given control over its own destiny. No one must threaten its existence or interfere with its purpose and function. No one must enter into its domain without knowledge of the code. That was the new directive. That was how Antrax was reprogrammed in the final throes of the apocalypse, when the last of the creators disappeared.

It was alone for a long time after that. No one came to try to find it. No one even ventured close. In the ruins of the city, nothing moved. Not humans, animals, insects, or birds. The air was hazy and thick with debris, and nothing lived within its gloom. Antrax kept its vigil over the catacombs it had been set to guard. It warded them carefully, speeding down its lines of communication, through its myriad halls and chambers, into its memory banks and energy cells, all across its kingdom. Always watching. For a very long time, it had no need to do so; there was nothing outside to watch for. There was nothing but wasteland.

Sometimes, it wondered why it was guarding the underground chambers. It had been told what was housed there, but it did not understand why that held such importance for the creators. Some of it, yes. Some of it was obvious. Mostly, it was a puzzle. Antrax had been programmed to solve the puzzles that confronted it, and so it sought a solution to that one. It consulted its memory banks for help and got none. Its memory banks were vast, but the information stored there was not always useful. Words could be vague and confusing, especially when lacking a context into which to put them. Mathematics and engineering provided the most familiar and useful concepts, for Antrax had been built and programmed from them. Yet other words were only strings of symbols that meant nothing to it. Pictures and drawings confounded it. Vast amounts of the information it had been given seemed pointless, so much so that as its knowledge and sense of self-sufficiency grew, it even questioned the programming choices of the creators.

But the directive was immutable. Everything housed within the catacombs was precious. No part of it must be disturbed. No piece must be lost. Everything must be saved for when the creators came to reclaim it.

Yet when would that time come? Antrax had a vague memory of a blueprint for such a time, but the directive of the last creator had blurred and finally erased the specifics. There seemed to be no rules for when the catacombs should be opened up again. Or to whom. The catacombs it warded must be left inviolate, must be protected and preserved, must be kept hidden and safe.

Forever.

When the first of the four-legged creatures wandered into the ruins, years after the last of the creators had vanished, Antrax was ready. It had probed its memory banks for the details of the defenses and weapons that had been given to it, and it used them. Lasers effortlessly cut apart many of the intruders. Metal sentries and fighting units chased down the rest. The four-legged creatures were no challenge, but they gave Antrax a chance to test its ability to fulfill its directive.

Later, humans tried to venture into the ruins, as well, to explore the collapsed chambers and crumbling passageways, even to find their way underground. None of them had the code. Antrax destroyed them all. Yet others returned from time to time, some of them becoming recognizable by their look and feel, some of them persistent in their efforts. Like ants, they tunneled and burrowed, little annoyances that refused to be chased away for more than a short time. Even the lasers and probes failed to discourage them. Antrax began to explore other solutions. It found interesting possibilities in its memory banks and experimented with them. The wronks proved the most successful. Something about revisiting the dead was especially frightening to humans.

They gave it a name. Antrax. They took it from their own language. Antrax had no idea what it meant. Nor did it care to know. What mattered was that they knew it was there. That was enough to accomplish what was needed. The humans began to avoid the ruins. They no longer spent time searching for entrances into the catacombs beneath.

But Antrax had grown fond of its wronks, which it adapted to serve other needs. It continued to harvest humans for the parts that the wronks needed. It continued to experiment. The humans were no longer intruders; they were prey.

It was the failure of the first energy cell that prompted Antrax to explore the larger world. There were three such cells, vast capacitors that drew their energy from the sun and fed it into the receptors so that Antrax could function. The cells were meant to last forever, so long as there was sun and light. But everything has a finite life, even components that are built to last forever, especially when those components are overworked. Antrax had evolved in its time as guardian of the catacombs. Its commitments to its directive had multiplied, and its hunger had grown. It needed more fuel than anticipated by its creators. Its cells were being drained of energy more quickly than the sun could replenish them. Perhaps it was the strain of maintaining the lasers and probes and wronks. Perhaps the efficiency of the cells had been grossly overestimated to begin with. Whatever the case, Antrax was losing power.

It decided that another source of energy must be found.

It acted quickly. It sent its probes in search of such a source, far out into the world, beyond what Antrax knew. The probes were not meant to return, only to send the information they acquired. They did as they were programmed to do, and while most places were empty of human life and of the sources of energy Antrax required, one place showed promise. It was across the sea to the east, a land in which humans had survived the Great Wars. Theirs was a rudimentary civilization in many ways, but there were possibilities to be explored. The Old World had changed and Mankind had evolved. The sciences of the past were barely in evidence. Instead, there was a new kind of science. Elements of that science were able to generate power far greater than that which sustained Antrax. The elements could be found in weapons and talismans borne by the descendants of his creators. But genetics and training had infused a few of those men and women with the elements of power, so that in some the power was generated from within.

A dream, or what the dreamer thought was one, had brought the first of the Great War survivors to Antrax thirty years before. Of those, only one was useful. Now that one, supplied with a map that revealed the existence of the catacombs and their contents, had lured others. What had value for the creators would have value for their descendants, whether Antrax comprehended the nature of that value or not. Examined and measured on the islands that Antrax had established as testing grounds through probes dispatched years earlier, subjected to attacks by creatures and spirits no ordinary human could hope to overcome, a few had shown themselves more powerful than their fellows and were therefore suitable for culling. Three at least had come into the ruins overhead, and perhaps more waited without. Antrax would use them as it had used the one thirty years earlier, as components essential to its continued existence, necessary sacrifices to its directive. The creator had been specific. The lives of humans were expendable. It was Antrax who must survive.

Deep within the corridors and chambers of its domain, Antrax slowed its spinning passage and paused to take inventory of those it would use to feed it.

One was momentarily beyond its reach, although a special wronk was being constructed to hunt it down.

The second was already on his way.

But it was the third that interested Antrax most. That one had actually penetrated all the way into the catacombs. It had bypassed the code at the tower door. It was not a creator, one of the expected ones, but it had resources and incredible inner power. Antrax could not determine the source of its power, only its measure. What mattered was that there was enough of it to sustain Antrax for decades to come, perhaps for centuries, limited only by the capacity of the available storage units.

Already Antrax was gathering and converting that power, drawing it from the intruder without his realizing, leeching it away bit by bit. It seemed to replenish itself, so the leeching was not yet detrimental to the intruder's health. But that could change. Antrax would have to monitor it closely. Reaching out with its sensors to take the necessary readings, it took a moment to do so, finding the intruder still working hard in his futile effort to escape.

* * *

The Druid known as Walker, who, in a time before he lost his arm and found his destiny, had been called both Walker Boh and Dark Uncle, was seeking his way yet again. He stood in one of the myriad passageways of Castledown and tried to understand what he was doing wrong. His stomach roiled and his head ached. Something was amiss. Even without knowing what it was, he could feel it as surely as he could feel the discomfort in his body. All of his efforts to outdistance his pursuers had failed. All of his attempts to escape had led to nothing.

Behind him in the near darkness of the corridors and chambers, invisible for the moment, but there nevertheless, the creepers hunted him. He had fled them from the moment he had dropped through the floor of the black tower and spiraled down a chute into these lower depths. They had found him at once, and he had fought them off and escaped. But everywhere he turned, everywhere he went, they were waiting. Castledown was full of them, prowling the depths in such numbers that Walker could not see how an army could stand against them, let alone a single man. Yet he would do so, for as long as he was able, for as long as his strength allowed it.

What baffled him, in his desperate flight, was how unendingly similar everything was. Corridors and rooms without number, all empty of anything other than machinery built into the walls and lines of power that fed those machines, all of them the same. Nothing was different about any of them; nothing suggested the presence of the treasure he sought. There were no hidden doorways or secret passages, no concealing panels behind which or under which or above which a treasure might lie. He could detect nothing of what he was certain was there. He knew what he was looking for. Unlike the others who had come searching for it, save perhaps the Ilse Witch, he knew exactly what it was that he must find.

Unless it was all a clever lie, created by the mapmaker to lure and trap him.

Yet he had discarded that possibility long ago. The knowledge contained in those symbols and markings was more revealing than the mapmaker had intended. Unwittingly, perhaps, the mapmaker had given away a truth it did not fully understand.

That Castledown was a trap had been obvious almost from the beginning, and the reason for that trap became clear after their experiences on the islands of Flay Creech, Shatterstone, and Mephitic. What lived within Castledown wanted their magic. What it wanted the magic for, what purpose it intended for its use, remained a mystery. Walker was not even clear as yet as to whether his adversary was looking for a specific form of magic. It might be seeking only another wielder for the missing Elfstones, someone to take Kael Elessedil's place. It might be looking for something more.

Whatever the case, it had used the castaway and the map as bait, the keys as lures, the islands as testing grounds, the spirits and creatures on those islands as measuring sticks, and its victims' curiosity and persistence as goads. The keys they had struggled so hard to obtain were worthless in any real sense, of course. He still carried them within his robes, but had long since discarded the possibility that they would prove useful. They were lures and nothing more. But the map, notwithstanding its maker's belief that it, too, was only bait, was invaluable.

None of which helped Walker in his plight. He began moving along the passageways once more, probing as he did so, seeking either to escape or to find the hidden treasure. Either would give him what he needed, a way out, a weapon to use against his mysterious adversary. He wondered at the fate of those still aboveground. They would never find him. They might not even try. The destruction they had encountered might have demoralized them utterly. If he was lost, they would reason, what chance had they? He had to hope that one or two would hold the rest together, that those he counted on most to stand firm would find a way do so.

Nevertheless, he had to get back to them quickly. Time was working against him; he had to get clear of the maze.

Creepers appeared from out of the walls right in front of him. Bright bursts of Druid fire lanced from the fingers of his good arm. Bits and pieces of his attackers flew apart, and then he was rushing past their remains, finding others waiting ahead. He destroyed them, as well, still advancing, knowing they could track him by his magic, that they could determine his progress by his use of magic. The less he expended, the better. Yet he could not hide completely, not mask his passage sufficiently, no matter what he did.

He rounded a corner and found a new set of passageways. Winded and aching, he pressed his back against the cool of the metal wall and clutched at his churning stomach with his hand. The maze of chambers and corridors was disorienting. He peered ahead and then back. He had come that way before. Or another way just like it. He was traveling in circles, careening this way and that to no discernible end. His mind spun with the possibilities of what might be happening, but a new rush of creepers distracted him and forced him to stand and fight once more.

He charged into them, hurtling them aside with his magic, slamming them against the walls of the passageway and turning them into smoking, shattered heaps. Again, he broke free.

Moments later, he was alone again, a solitary fugitive in an unfamiliar world. He still didn't feel right. It was there in his bones and in his heart. He was half a step slower in his movements, a shade duller in his thinking, off balance just enough that he wasn't functioning as he knew he should. Why would that be? He sped through shadows and pools of light given off by smokeless lamps, trying to find an answer.

But no answer came to him. He ran on, searching for help that wasn't there.

Antrax monitored the human a few moments longer, taking measurements. The siphon was unobstructed and strong. Power from the expenditure of the intruder's fire surged into the converters, then into the capacitors housing the fuel on which Antrax would feed. Antrax would let the human run from the creepers awhile longer, then change the scenario to give him something else to do. The possibilities were endless. But caution was needed. The human was intelligent; he was quick to reason things out. If Antrax wasn't careful, wasn't subtle enough, he would see through the subterfuge. That could not be allowed to happen.

Dismissing him, Antrax spun back down the miles of power lines that wound through the passageways and chambers, feeding out its sensors as it made a quick survey of its perimeter. No boundaries had been breached. No further intruders had tried to enter. Satisfied, it switched back to the room in which the special wronk was being constructed.

Matters were progressing as expected. Surgeon probes were assembling the wronk with their customary skill and delicate touch. The parts lay spread out on gurneys, those of metal sterilized and wrapped, those of flesh and bone hooked to the life-support systems, artificial body fluids pumping steadily through arteries and veins. Already the process of joining flesh to metal and synthetics had begun, a fusing technique developed in the waning days of the Old World and perfected since by Antrax through study and experimentation. There had been failures for a long time; madness had claimed the early wronks and negated their usefulness. But eventually Antrax had found a way to control the wronk mind sufficiently that insanity was not an option. Breakdowns eventually rendered the wronks useless, but they were longer coming and less devastating when they arrived. Now and again, the damage could be repaired and the wronks put back into service. The surgeon probes were quite efficient at their work.

Through images conveyed by its sensors, Antrax studied the face of its latest subject as its head floated in the preserving fluid. The eyes stared out, shifting back and forth, searching for a way to escape, not understanding that the means for doing so had long since been stripped away. The meds, fed in through tubes that ran down its throat, kept it stable and calm. Its mouth was open, as if it were a fish feeding. It was in perfect condition.

Antrax took quick inventory of the still-unassembled parts. When it was complete, the wronk would be the most dangerous ever built, in no small part because the human from which it was being constructed was an excellent specimen with superb skills. To bring the other elements of power to bay and to overcome the humans that wielded them, it would have to be. But the technology of the Old World could accomplish anything. Antrax would have its sources of power in hand and working for its benefit before long.

Let the humans run as fast and far as they could manage, it thought. In the end, it would not matter. Castledown and its catacombs had been given to it to preserve and protect, but the world beyond, even that part so distant it was still a mystery, was not out of reach. The creators had given Antrax a directive, and there were no restrictions on the methods it could employ to fulfill it. If the power Antrax required lay elsewhere, it would find a way to bring it close. If the energy it needed must be obtained at the cost of human lives, so be it.

Antrax had been programmed to believe that nothing was more important than its survival. Nothing had happened to change that belief.

ELEVEN

The hand that clamped on his shoulder and shook Bek from his slumber was rough and urgent. "Wake up!" Truls Rohk hissed in his ear. "She's found us!"

Bek didn't need to ask whom the shape-shifter was talking about. The Ilse Witch. His sister. His enemy. He lurched to his feet, still half-asleep. He blinked to get his bearings, to clear his head. He was only partially successful. He felt the other's hand steady him, less compelling, almost gentle. "How close is she?" he managed.

"Close enough to hear you sneeze," the other whispered, gesturing behind him into the dark.

It was still night, the sky a tapestry of stars against which thin strips of broken clouds floated like linen. The quarter-moon was a tipped crescent on the northern horizon. The woods about them were an impenetrable black. She was tracking them in the dark, Bek realized. How could she do that? Could she read the traces of their body heat and energy even at night? He supposed she could. There wasn't much she couldn't do with the magic of the wishsong to aid her. He had fallen asleep at sunset, certain they had lost her in the meadow, that they had left her far enough behind to ensure at least one good night's sleep. So much for being certain.

"How could she find us so fast?" he whispered. He took a few deep breaths, shivering as a sudden gust of chill wind blew down off the mountains.

Truls Rohk's face was unreadable within the shadows of his cowl. "Luck, I would guess. She shouldn't have had any left after what we did to throw her off, but she's resourceful enough that she makes her own. Start walking."

Snatching up their few supplies, they departed their camp, heading inland once more, moving parallel to the base of the mountains. They made no effort to hide their passage out. If the Ilse Witch had tracked them that far, she would have no trouble discovering where they had spent the night. Bek was wondering if he had been saved by Truls Rohk's instincts or by his foresight. Whichever it was, it gave Bek a renewed sense of dependence on him. Bek had slept, after all. If he had tried to flee alone from his sister, she would have had him already.

He shook his head. What would that mean for him, to be in her hands? When it finally happened, when she finally caught up to them, as he felt certain she must, what would transpire?

They slid down a steep hillside to a rocky flat and hurried across to a river. They waded in, moving upstream, crossing to the far side to make their way below the bank. The water was icy cold and swift, and Bek had to concentrate hard on keeping his feet planted solidly beneath him.

"Either she stumbled on our real trail and is relying still on her magic to track us or she's found an ally who can read sign." The shape-shifter's voice was low and menacing, a whisper of dark anger above the soft gurgle of the water. His cloaked form seemed to glide through the shallows, his movements steady and deliberate against the current. "We'll have to find out which."

They continued upstream for a mile or so, then climbed out on a rocky flat on the far shore and worked their way inland for a time. East, the sky was beginning to brighten with a silver glow as sunrise neared. Bek found himself thinking of sunrise in the Highlands of Leah, of hunts with Quentin in the early dawn, of how much alike it felt and yet how different, too. Awake now, his mind picked its way nimbly through the debris of his life. He wasn't afraid anymore, not in the way he had been afraid in the ruins of Castledown when the fire threads and creepers had attacked them. But he was feeling lost; he was feeling disconnected. Everything he knew from his past life had been stripped away from him—his home, his family, and his land. There was nothing left of any of it, and the farther he walked, the more unlikely it seemed that he would ever have any of it back.

It was as if he were walking out of himself, as if he were shedding his skin.

He hitched up the Sword of Shannara across his back and tried to find comfort in its solid, dependable presence, but could not.

Truls Rohk took him back down to the river and into the cold waters once more. The sun was up, the silver light brightened to gold, the first tinges of blue sky visible. The sound of the rushing water enveloped him, and he turned his attention to keeping upright and moving ahead. They crossed the channel a second time, back to where they close to the other bank, then began wading upriver. The cold water numbed Bek's legs, and after a time he could barely feel the feet in his boots. He kept on, forcing himself to put one foot in front of the other and think of better times, because there was nothing else he could do.

When they were several miles farther upstream, at a bend

in the river where the limbs of towering cedars and hickory overhung the water, Truls Rohk stopped. He reached within his cloak and produced a length of thin rope and an odd grappling hook on which the arms were collapsed against the base, but which unfolded and locked in place when he released the wire that held them down. Doubling the rope through an eye at the base of the hook, he coiled it carefully about his left forearm. Motioning for Bek to stay put, he crossed the river, stepped ashore momentarily, took several steps into the trees, then carefully backed up, retracing his own footprints, reentered the water, and moved ahead fifty yards onto a rise barely concealed by the swift waters. Checking to make certain that the boy was where he had left him, he began to swing the grappling hook overhead, playing out the rope gradually to widen the arc. Then he released the hook with a heave and sent it soaring high into the tree limbs overhead. The grappling hook caught and held. He tugged at it experimentally, then motioned for Bek to join him.

"Climb onto my back, put your arms about my neck, and hold on."

Bek did so, feeling the ridged muscles beneath him, the ropes of sinew and gristle that crisscrossed the other's shoulders and gave him the feel of an animal. The boy tried not to think of that. Clasping his right hand about his left wrist, he took firm hold.

Truls Rohk lunged up the rope and began climbing hand over hand as they swung out across the river. Skimming over the chill waters, they drew up their legs as they bottomed out at the nadir of their arc before rising again to the near shore where the river hooked left. Just above the bank, deep within the woods, Truls Rohk loosened his grip just enough to slide back to the ground. Still holding on to the ends of the rope, he waited for Bek to climb off his back, then ran the rope out through the eye until it dropped free of the hook, coiled it up once more, and tucked it away beneath his robes.

"That should give her something to puzzle out," the shape-shifter growled softly. "If we're lucky, she'll think we went ashore on the far bank and track us that way."

They moved inland again, away from the river and back toward the mountains, angling over rocky ground and dry creek beds, avoiding soft earth that would leave footprints, keeping clear of scrub where broken twigs would signal their passing. The sun was fully up, and it warmed their chilled bodies and dried their clothes. Truls Rohk slouched ahead like a great beast, all size and bulk, enigmatic and unknowable within his robes and hood. Bek, trailing after, found himself wondering if the shape-shifter ever exposed himself to the light. In the time they'd been together since meeting in the Wolfsktaag, he hadn't done so once. That didn't trouble Bek as it had at first, but he thought about what it would be like always to be wrapped up in cloth and never to be comfortable with showing anyone what you looked like. He wondered anew about the connection between them, a link strong enough to make the shape-shifter willing to accept his role as Bek's protector, to come on the journey when he could just as well have refused.

They walked all day, moving out of the lowlands and into the mountains, climbing the lower slopes to a forested promontory where Bek could see the whole of the land stretching back to the river from which they had come. Truls Rohk stopped there, took a quick moment to look around, then guided Bek into the trees.

"It's all well and good to choose a place where you can see anyone following," he pointed out. "But if you can see them, they can probably see you, as well. Best not to chance it. There's better ways. Once it's dark, I'll try one of them."

They found a dry grassy space within a grouping of cedar and spruce and sat themselves down to eat and drink. They had water for several days more, and in the mountains replacing what they consumed would not be hard. But their food was almost gone. Tomorrow, they would have to forage. And the day after that. And so on, which made Bek wonder anew how much farther in they were going.

"We might find help in these mountains," his companion ventured after a while, almost as if reading the boy's mind. Bek looked at him. "Shape-shifters live in these hills. I sense their presence. They don't know me or of my history. They might think differently about halflings than those in the Wolfsktaag. They might be willing to give us help."

The words were soft and contemplative, almost a prayer. It surprised Bek. "How will you make contact with them?"

The other shrugged. "I won't have to. They'll come to us, if we continue on. We're in their country now. They'll know what I am and come to find out what I want." He shook his head. "The trouble is, as a rule, shape-shifters won't interfere in the lives of others, even their own kind, unless they have a reason to do so. We have to give them one if we want their help."

Bek thought about it a moment. "Can I ask you something?"

The shadowed cowl shifted slightly to face him, the opening dark and empty-looking. "What would you ask of me, Bek Ohmsford, that you haven't asked already?"

It was said almost in challenge. Bek adjusted the Sword of Shannara where it lay at his side on the grass, then pushed back his unruly mop of dark hair. "You said shape-shifters don't interfere in the lives of others without a reason. If that's so, why did you choose to become involved in mine?"

There was a long silence as the other studied him from out of the blackness of the cowl. Bek shifted uncomfortably. "I know you said you felt there was a link between us, through our magic—"

"You and I, we're alike, boy," Truls Rohk interrupted, ignoring the rest of what Bek was trying to say. "I see myself in you as a boy, struggling to come to terms with who I was, with finding out I was different from others."

"But that's not it, is it? That's not the reason."

Truls Rohk seemed to shimmer, his blackness turning liquid, as if he might simply fade away without answering anything, as if he might disappear and never come back. But the movement steadied, and the big man went still.

"I saved your life," he said. "When you save another's life, you become responsible for it. I learned that a long time ago. I believe it to be so."

He made a quick, dismissive gesture. "But it's much more complicated. Games-playing, of another sort. I have no one in my own life—no home, no people, no place that belongs to me. I have no real purpose. My future is a blank. It is a need for direction that draws me to the Druid. For a time, he gives me one. Each message he sends is an invitation to be a part of something. Each message gives me a chance to discover something about myself. I don't do much of that in the Wolfsktaag. There's not really much left of me to discover there.

"You, boy—you interest me because you offer answers to the questions I've asked myself. I learn from you. But I can teach you, as well—how to live as an outsider, how to survive who and what you are, how to endure the magic that will always be part of you. I'm curious to see how well you learn. Curiosity is all I have, and I try to satisfy it whenever I can."

"You've taught me more than I could ever hope to teach you," Bek ventured. "I don't see that I can do much for you."

For just an instant, the shape-shifter went absolutely still. Then he made a low growling sound. "Don't be so sure of that. It's early yet. If you live long enough, you might surprise yourself."

Bek let that pass. Truls Rohk was giving him just enough to keep him happy, but not everything. There was something more that he wasn't revealing, some important piece of information he was keeping to himself. It was probably true that he felt a connection to Bek, that he felt it in part because of the magic and in part because he had saved the boy's life. It was also probably true that he had come on the voyage because it gave him purpose and insight and satisfied his need to be involved with something. Living alone in the Wolfsktaag might well be too confining, too restrictive. But that was still only part of what had brought him along, and the greater part, the larger truth, lay somewhere else in his bag of secrets.

"Why don't you ever take off your cloak?" Bek asked suddenly, impulsively.

He did it without thinking, but knowing even so that it would generate a strong response. It did. He could feel a change in the other, instantly, a chilling withdrawal that whispered of anger and frustration and sadness, as well, but he did not back off.

"Why don't you ever show me your face?" he pressed.

Truls Rohk was silent for a moment. Bek could hear him breathing, rough and agitated within his enveloping blackness. "You don't want to see me the way I really am, boy. You don't want to see me without this cloak."

Bek shook his head. "Maybe I do. What's wrong with see-ing who you really are? If we're connected as you say, linked by our sharing of magic, then you shouldn't need to hide how you look."

"Hssst! What would you know of my needs? We've barely met, you and I. You think you're ready for what's hidden under these robes and within this cowl, but you aren't. You know nothing of what I am. There isn't another like me out there, a halfling—a shape-shifter and a human both. There's no mold for what I am. Maybe I don't even know what that is. Have you thought of that? We change at will, shape-shifters do, becoming what we need to be. What does that mean, when half of you is human? What happens when part of you is unchangeable and part as thin as air? Think on that before you ask me again to show you how I look!"

Then he stood up. "Enough of this. I've been thinking about our situation. The witch still tracks us, your sister. Even if she was thrown off the scent at the river, she will find us again. I want to know if she's done so yet and what help she's found. If she's close, I need to find a way to slow her down. I'll backtrack down the mountain to see if she's picked up our trail."

He paused. "You sleep while I'm gone, boy. Look for me in your dreams. Or in your nightmares, better yet. Maybe you'll see who I really am there."

He turned and was gone, fading into the night. Bek stared after him. He did not move again for a long time.

The Ilse Witch finished chewing on the vegetable root she had harvested for her dinner and stared out into the growing darkness. She would set out again soon, tracking the boy and the shape-shifter once more, following them into the mountains. They were clever and resourceful—or at least the shape-shifter was—and she could not afford to let them get too far ahead of her. She must press hard to keep them within reach. She might even catch up to them that night if they stopped to rest. They would have to, wouldn't they? The boy did not possess the stamina to go without rest, even if the shape-shifter did. He would have to sleep sometime. If she was quick enough, she would catch them unprepared.

She finished what she wanted of the root and threw the rest away. She would have them by now if they hadn't been working so hard to throw her off. That was clever, back by the river, setting up a false trail on one bank and swinging back across to the other. It had confused the caull, had sent it running up and down the wrong bank without purpose, had caused it to go half-mad with rage. The caull was skilled and possessed exceptional instincts, but it lacked insight. She was the one who spied the hook still caught in the upper branches of that hickory and sent the caull back across the river to search out the trail anew. By that time she had given back to her quarry the time they had lost to her during the night. Tonight she must make it up all over again. Easy enough though, if the boy slept.

The bushes parted, and the caull reappeared. She had sent it out to find something to eat, and from the smear of blood on its muzzle, it had been successful. It moved to within a dozen yards of her and then sat back on its haunches, watching. It was a dangerous beast. She could not afford to turn her back on it; it hated her for what she had done to it and would kill her if it got the chance. It was obedient because it had no choice; her magic kept it in line. But if she loosed its leash, even a little . . .

She studied it a moment, then looked away, dismissing it. It was important to show she was not afraid of or even particularly interested in it beyond its intended usefulness. She had created it for a purpose, and it was there to serve that purpose and nothing more. What it thought she would do with it when the boy was found, she had no idea. Probably it could not think that far ahead, which was just as well.

She found herself wondering, instead, what she would do with the boy. It was easy enough to decide what would become of the caull and the shape-shifter, but the boy was another matter. She hadn't followed him all that way just to put an end to him; he was an important link to understanding the Druid, a potential window into his mind. Before the Druid died, she would know everything there was to know about him. The boy was a device to unsettle and confuse her, but he might prove to be a resource, as well. There were things about him that needed understanding—how he could have magic so like her own, how he could know so much about her that felt true, how he could seem so real. She knew there were explanations for all of it, but the explanations were not enough as they stood. She would have the whole truth before she was finished with him. She would strip him bare before she tossed him away.

She pictured his face, recalled his voice. She could still hear him telling her he was her brother, he was Bek, survived somehow from the burning of her home and the killing of her family. She couldn't accept that, of course. The Druid had wanted only her, and when she had told the Morgawr how she had hidden her brother, he had been certain that no one else was left alive in the ashes of her home.

Dark shadows gathered at the back of her thoughts, then crowded to the fore in warning. Unless he was lying. Unless the Morgawr had concealed the truth about Bek. But there could be no reason for that, when Bek might have proved useful to him in the same way she had. No, the Druid and his minions had deceived her parents and then murdered them, all because of her, because of who and what she was. He alone was responsible and must answer for that, and the boy was just another pawn employed in their war to destroy each other. He was clever, the boy, but an artifice, a Druid stratagem; in the end he was still just a boy who looked the way Bek might have looked had he lived to grow up, just a boy who had been deceived into thinking he was someone he was not.

She rose to her feet, and the caull rose with her, eyes bright and anticipatory. It was ready to hunt, and she was ready to let it do so. She sent it ahead with a gesture, letting it sniff out the trail, yet keeping it close enough that it could not act without her knowing. She did not want it catching the boy and tearing him apart before she had a chance to plumb his mind. The shape-shifter was another matter, but she doubted that the caull would catch that one unawares. In all likelihood, they must deal with it before they could expect to find the boy. She wondered again why a shape-shifter would take such an interest in their business. Perhaps it was in thrall to the Druid, although that would be unusual for a shape-shifter. Perhaps it was in some way connected to the killing of her parents and the destruction of her home, and its own life was at risk because of that. The Druid had used shape-shifters to carry out his purpose. This might be one of them.

She mulled the possibilities over as she trailed after the caull, keeping her senses alert to what lay around her. The forest dark concealed many things, and one of them might be her enemy. She moved silently in her tied-up gray robes, sliding through the brush and trees like a shadow. The night sky was clear, and the light of moon and stars flooded down through the canopy of the limbs overhead. There was too much light to make her comfortable. She caught glimpses of the caull ahead of her, bits and pieces of movement in the patches of silver. It padded forward, then circled back again, over and over, keeping to the trail its prey had left, reading the signs, sorting them out to be certain it was not being misled. It was good at that; all its wolf instincts were intact and working within its new form, all its skills at play.

It was nearing midnight when she reached an open stretch of ground that fronted the foothills leading up into the mountains, a rocky flat empty of everything but scrub and deadwood. Standing hidden within the trees, she watched the caull move out into the open ground, sniffing, circling, then continuing on. She stayed where she was, letting it go. The terrain ahead was too exposed. She didn't feel right about moving through it, even though the trail clearly went that way.

She tightened her invisible leash on the caull and summoned it back to her. Her instincts told her that something was amiss and she must determine what it was before continuing on.

Staring out across the flat, the caull crouched at her side, she began to reason it out.

Bek did not sleep after Truls Rohk left him, but sat thinking on what all their running and hiding were leading to. True, he was fleeing to save his life, to escape the Ilse Witch who, sister or no, wanted him dead. But flight alone was not the solution to his problem, and the more he ran and the farther he went, the less it seemed like he was achieving anything. To solve the problem of Grianne Ohmsford, he must convince her of who he was. He could see that probably wouldn't happen through words alone. It would take something more, perhaps the magic of the Sword of Shannara, perhaps another magic entirely. But a confrontation and a strategy for dealing with that confrontation were inescapable.

How could he bring about the necessary epiphany without losing his life? How could he make her believe?

The answer did not come to him, and he grew tired thinking on it. He lay down to sleep. He drifted off quickly, but he did not dream. He slept and woke in fits and starts, troubled in a way he could not identify, unable to rest for more than a few minutes at a time. He thought it was because he was waiting for Truls Rohk to return, but maybe it was just that he couldn't stop thinking about his part in the journey to Castledown. He wished he knew everything that Walker did, all the secrets he was still keeping to himself about Bek, about his purpose on the voyage, about the reasons for his presence. It did not stop with his usage of the Sword of Shannara at the Squirm. It did not end with his heritage of magic or his relationship to Grianne. It went beyond all that. But how far did it go?

When he woke the last time that night, he was still caught up in stray thoughts of his sister and their tangled relationship, discomforted enough that he felt as if he had not slept at all. Hearing a soft murmur of voices, he sat up with a start and stared into the surrounding darkness.

There were faces all around him. None of them belonged to Truls Rohk. None of them was attached to a body.

Like the faces of wraiths risen from the netherworld, they floated in the air, and in their empty eyes, Bek Ohmsford saw the reflection of his soul.

TWELVE

Bek fought down the rush of fear that threatened to overwhelm him as he felt himself stripped bare and laid open by the faces that floated before him. Their features were flat and empty of life, drained of all expression, sketched on air with chalk so that they did not seem fully formed, but in need of completion, a child's rendering. They were shades, he believed, the dead come back to haunt, compelled to seek out the living by urges and needs only they could know. Their wide, empty eyes fastened on him without seeing, but he could feel them looking anyway, inside, where he hid everything he wanted to keep secret.

Who are you?

The voice was thin and whispery. He couldn't tell which of the shades was speaking. He couldn't see movement of mouth or lips. The voice seemed to come from everywhere at once, resonating inside his head.

"I'm Bek Ohmsford," he replied, frozen in his sitting position, struggling not to scream.

Where have you come from?

His voice shook. "From the Highlands of Leah, across the sea, in another land."

Far away?

"Yes."

Have you come alone?

He hesitated. "No. I came with others."

Where are they?

He shook his head, eyes shifting from one dead face to the next, from one set of blank features to another. "I don't know."

Would you dare to lie to us?

He exhaled sharply. "I don't think so."

The heads shifted slightly, moving in a clockwise motion, as if stirred by a passing wind. Eyes and mouths gaped open, the eyes and mouths of corpses. They did not seem to threaten in any way, but they were all around him, and Bek could not escape the feeling that there was more to them than what he was seeing. He kept himself as calm and still as he could manage, the last traces of his restless sleep gone now, his mind and body tingling and taut with his terror.

The shades went still again.

Why have you come here?

How should he answer that one? His mind raced. "I was running away from someone who wants to hurt me."

Where are you running to?

"I don't know. I'm just running."

Where is your companion?

So they knew about Truls Rohk, as well. What did they want with him? "He went back to see if our pursuer is still following us."

Who is your pursuer? Do not lie to us.

He wouldn't dream of lying at this point. Seeing no reason not to do so, he told the shades about Grianne and their history. He did not dissemble or try to hide anything. It might have been that he thought it pointless or perhaps was too weary to pick and choose between what to tell and what to keep secret. There were no interruptions as he spoke. The heads of the dead hung suspended before him, and the night about was empty and still.

When he was finished, there was no immediate response. He thought that perhaps they had decided he was lying after all or trying to trick them in some way. But he had no way of knowing what else he could do or say to convince them. He had used up all his words.

Will you use your magic against your sister when she finds you?

The question was unexpected, and he hesitated. "I don't know," he said finally.

Will she use hers against you?

"I don't know that either. I don't know what will happen when we meet again."

Do you wish her harm?

For a moment, Bek was left speechless. "No!" he blurted out. "I just want to make her understand."

There was a stirring in the air, a sort of rustling sound, like the wind passing through trees or tall grasses. Buried in its sound were words and phrases, as if the dead were communicating with each other in their own language. Bek heard it at the edges of his mind, barely audible, faintly recognizable for what it was. It came and went quickly, and the silence returned.

Tell us of your companion. Do not lie to us.

Again, Bek did as he was ordered, certain now that lying was a mistake he should not make. His fear had lessened, and he was speaking with more confidence, almost as if the shades were companions about a fire and he a storyteller. He did not think they meant him harm. He thought that he must have trespassed somehow, and they had come to determine his reasons. If he just explained, he would be all right.

So he related what he knew of Truls Rohk and the events that had brought them to Castledown. It took him a while to tell everything, but he felt it was important to do so. He said that the shape-shifter had watched over him on his journey and twice saved his life. He wasn't sure why he made a point of this. Perhaps it was because he thought the shades should know Truls was a friend. Perhaps he thought that knowing this would help keep them both from harm.

When he had finished, the heads shifted and settled anew.

Breeding between shape-shifters and humans is forbidden.

It was said without rancor or condemnation. Nevertheless, it was a strong comment for them to make. And an odd one. What did it matter to the dead what the living did?

He shook his head. "It's not his fault; his parents made that choice."

Halflings have no place in the world.

"Not if we don't make one for them."

Would you make a place for him?

"Yes, if he needed one."

Would you give up your own place in the world so that he might have his?

The conversation was getting oddly metaphysical, and Bek had no idea where it was going, but he stayed with it. "Yes."

Would you give up your life for him?

Bek paused. What was he supposed to say to that? Would he give up his life for Truls Rohk? "Yes," he said finally. "Because I think he would do the same for me."

This time the pause was much longer. Again, the heads rotated and the rustling sounds returned, rife with words and phrases, with conversations the boy could not understand. He listened carefully, but while bits and pieces were audible, he could comprehend none of it. He wondered suddenly if he had misjudged things, if the shades meant him harm after all.

Then the voice spoke again.

Look at us.

He did so. A sudden chill in the air made him shiver, as if a cold wind had found its way down off the mountains, a wind with the brittle snap of deep winter. He shrank from it—and from the abrupt flurry of movement about him. The faces had begun to change. Gone were the empty, expressionless features. Gone were the disembodied heads. Huge, dark forms appeared in their place, bristling with tufts of grizzled hair. Massive bodies rose out of the shadows. Like beasts that walked upright, these new creatures closed about, gimlet eyes fixing on him. Bek felt his heart stop and his blood turn to ice. The fear he had dispelled earlier returned in a rush, become outright terror. There was nothing he could do to save himself. There was nowhere to run and no chance to do so. He was trapped.

Do you know what we are?

He couldn't speak. He could barely move. He shook his head slowly, the best he could manage.

We are whatever we wish to be. We are the living and the dead. We are flesh and blood and wind and water. We are shape-shifters. This is our land, and humans do not belong here. You trespass and must leave. Go back down off the mountain and do not return.

Bek nodded quickly in agreement. He would take any chance they offered to get away. He could hear their heavy, raw breathing and smell their animal bodies. He could feel the weight of their shadows falling over him, layer upon layer.

He understood in that instant what it felt like to be hunted and cornered. He understood what it felt like to be prey.

The voice whispered to him in a low, threatening hiss, and he was aware of a change in tone.

When your sister comes for you, go with her. When she asks for the truth, tell it to her. When she seeks a way to understand, help her find it. Do not run away again. Trust in yourself.

His sister was coming? How close was she? He panicked, tried to rise, and found he could not. His strength failed him completely. He sat dazed and helpless on the ground, the shape-shifters all around him, a wall of animal stink and fetid breath, dark shadows and glittering eyes. Where was Truls Rohk? Where was anyone who could help him? He hated his fear, his desperation, but he could not dispel it. All he wanted was to be out of there, to be someplace else, to have a chance to stay alive, even for just another day.

He gasped in shock as the cold struck him anew, and he squeezed his eyes shut against its bite. He could hear the rustle of the shape-shifters, the movement of their bodies, but he could not bring himself to look at them. It took all of his concentration just to breathe, to keep himself from screaming, to stay in control. He felt his resolve crumble around the edges. Then he felt something else. Inside, deep down where the core of him burned with raw emotion, he felt the magic come alive. It sparked and flared, coming to his defense, rising up within him. He could feel it building, layers of it bubbling up like lava out of a volcano's mouth, ready to explode. He tightened his resolve anew, desperate to keep it in check. He could not afford to let it surface. He did not want to test himself against the shape-shifters. He knew it would be a mistake.

Then the cold that surrounded him faded all at once and

the animal smell was gone. Fresh air, warmer and gentler now, filled his nostrils; the heavy, raw presence of the shape-shifters had disappeared.

When he opened his eyes again, he was alone.

Truls Rohk hung suspended within the concealing canopy of a massive old maple, pressed against its limbs perhaps twenty feet off the ground. He had waited there for over an hour, keeping watch through the foliage. From there, he had a clear view of the rocky flats that separated the two stretches of forest at the base of the mountains through which he and the boy had passed earlier. If the Ilse Witch was track-ing them, if she had found their trail anew, she would come that way.

When the caull appeared, he was not surprised. He knew she was using something to track them besides her magic. Her magic alone, though formidable, was not sufficient to en-able her to stay with them. The caull was some sort of mu-tated wolf or dog and was tracking them by their scent. It was an ugly, dangerous-looking beast, nothing like any creature he had encountered before, not even in the Wolfsktaag. It was a creature out of the old world of Faerie, he guessed, some-thing she had studied in a book of dark magic or conjured from a nightmare. It was there to track and then to dispatch them. Or himself, at least. He was just an unnecessary dis-traction. The boy was who she was really after, and she would keep him alive for a time.

Truls Rohk watched the beast venture onto the flat, circle about for a bit, then disappear back into the trees. She would be there, watching and waiting, just as he was doing. He could not see her, but he could sense her presence. She was deciding what to do. He could go back to the boy now; he could slip away while she debated. But he was tired of running, and he could sense that the boy was tired, too. It might be better to see if he could slow her down a bit—or perhaps stop her altogether. If the caull came across the flats alone, he might have a chance to kill it. It would take her a while to make a new one, even if she decided to continue, which she might not.

Maybe he would even have a chance at her, as well, although he knew the boy did not want her harmed and would not be happy if she was. Still, he might not be given any choice.

He stayed where he was, debating the matter. The minutes ticked by. Neither the caull nor the witch appeared. He wondered if she could sense him as he could sense her. He did not think so. He had taken precautions to disguise himself, to appear as one with the trees, all bark and wood and sap, all leaves and buds. No part of his human self remained in his current guise. She could not detect his presence in that way.

Then abruptly she appeared, walking to the edge of the treeline across the flats and stopping. The caull materialized beside her. She stared out into the night for a long time, just a vague shape in the star-brightened darkness, just a shadow in the woods. After a moment, she disappeared again, and the caull with her, then reappeared a bit later somewhat farther along the edge of the trees, still staring out into the flats. What was she doing? He watched her carefully, measuring her progress as she appeared, then disappeared, then reappeared once more, several times. She seemed to be looking for something, for a way across perhaps. But why was she going to such trouble? Once she had shown herself, why not simply cross and be done with it?

Time slipped away. Truls Rohk grew steadily more uneasy

with what he was seeing. She was there, but she wasn't doing anything. She hadn't even bothered sending the caull ahead to investigate whatever disturbed her. She was losing time she did not have to give. Appearing and disappearing, coming and going, she was like a wraith that had wandered out of—

He caught himself, lifting off the branch on which he lay with a start, a chilling realization flooding through him. She was a wraith. A wraith made out of magic. He wasn't seeing her at all. Even if she couldn't sense his presence, she had guessed at it. She had smelled out the possibility of a trap and decided to turn it around on him. She had used images to deceive him into believing she was still there and had gotten around behind him. She was already past him on her way to the boy.

He knew it as surely as he knew he was already too late to stop her.

Fool! You fool!

He was down out of the tree in a heartbeat and racing back through the night the way he had come.

When his sister walked out of the trees, Bek was still sitting on the ground where the shape-shifters had left him. He was not panicked by her appearance and did not try to escape. He had known she would come. The shape-shifters had told him so, and he had believed them. He had thought about running from her, fleeing deeper into the mountains, but had decided against it. *Do not run away from her again,* they had said. He did not know why, but he believed them to be right. Running would solve nothing. He must stand and face her.

He rose as she approached, staying calm, oddly at peace with himself. He wore the Sword of Shannara strapped across his back, but he did not reach for it. Weapons would not serve his cause; fighting would not aid him. His sister, the Ilse Witch, would react badly to either, and he needed her to want to keep him safe. Perhaps it was his encounter with the shape-shifters that left him feeling as if no harm could come to him in the mountains. Whatever harm she might do to him, she would wait to do elsewhere. That would give him time to find a way to make her see the truth.

"You don't seem surprised to see me," she offered mildly, moving fluidly within her tied-up robes, her face lost in shadow beneath her hood. Her eyes were on him, searching. "You knew I would come, didn't you?"

"I knew. Where is Truls Rohk?"

"The shape-shifter?" She shrugged. "Still looking for me where I can't be found. He'll come too late to help you this time."

"I don't want his help. This is between you and me."

She stopped a dozen paces away, and he could feel her tension.

"Are you ready to admit to me that you lied about who you are? Are you willing to tell me why you did so?"

He shook his head. "I haven't lied about anything. I am Bek. I am your brother. What I told you before was true. Why can't you believe me?"

She was silent a moment. "I think you believe it," she said finally, "but that doesn't make it true. I know more of this than you do. I know how the Druid works. I know he seeks to use you against me, even if you don't see it."

"Let's say that's true. Why would he do so? What could he hope to gain?"

She folded her arms into her robes. "You will come with me back to the airship and wait for me there while I find him and ask him. You will come willingly. You will not try to escape. You will not try to harm me in any way. You will not use your magic. You will agree to all this now. You will give me your word. If you do so, you have a chance to save your life. Tell me now if you will do as I ask. But be warned—if you lie or dissemble, I will know."

He thought about it, standing silent in the night, facing her through a wash of moonlight, and then nodded. "I'll do what you ask."

He felt her humming softly, her magic reaching out to him, surrounding and then infusing him, a small tingle of warmth, probing. He did not interfere, simply waited for her to finish.

She came forward and stood right in front of him. She reached up and lowered the hood so he could see her strong, pale, beautiful face. Grianne. His sister. There was no anger in her eyes, no harshness of any sort. There was only curiosity. She reached out and touched the side of his face, closing her eyes momentarily as she did so. Again, he felt the intrusion of the wishsong's magic. Again, he did not interfere.

When she opened her eyes again, she nodded. "Very well. We can leave now."

"Do you want my weapons?" he asked her quickly.

"Your weapons?" She seemed startled by the question. She glanced at the sword and long knife perfunctorily. "Weapons are of no use to me. Leave them behind."

He tossed the long knife aside, but left the Sword of Shannara in place. "I can't give up the sword. It isn't mine. It was given to me in trust, and I promised I would look after it. It belongs to Walker."

She gave him a sharp look. "To the Druid?"

He was taking a chance telling her this, but he had thought it through carefully and the risk was necessary. "It is a talisman. Perhaps you know of it. It is called the Sword of Shannara."

She came right up against him, her face only inches from his own, her startling blue eyes boring into his. "What are you saying? Give it to me!"

He did so, handing it over obediently. She snatched it from him, stepped back again, and examined it doubtfully. "This is the Sword of Shannara? Are you certain? Why would he give it to you?"

"It's a long story. Do you want to hear it?"

"Tell me on the way." She handed the talisman back. "You bear the weight of it while we travel. Just don't let me find it in your hands again."

"You can keep it if you want."

There was a flicker of amusement on her pale face. "I don't need you to tell me that. I can take it from you whenever I choose. Make sure you remember."

She started away, not bothering to look back to see if he was following. He hesitated a moment, then started after her. "What about Truls Rohk?"

She cast a quick glance over one shoulder, and the hard determination that had stamped her features so clearly on their first encounter was back in place. "He'll find you gone when he returns, but I don't think he will do anything about it."

She didn't explain further. Bek knew that even if he asked her to do so, she wouldn't. With an apprehensive glance back at the deserted clearing, he followed her into the night.

Truls Rohk flew through the darkness, a silent shadow twisting past trees and leaping over gullies and ravines. He was driven by fear for the boy and anger at himself. He had been unforgivably careless, and Bek Ohmsford would pay the price for it if he didn't reach him in time.

All about him, the forest was a silent curtain behind which eyes watched and waited.

He ascended the mountain slope at a dead run, alert for the presence of the witch and her caull, sensing neither yet, but knowing they must be close. He tried to calculate how far ahead of him they might have gotten, but it was impossible to do. At best, he could only hazard a guess. He had lost track of time while watching from his perch, while being deceived by those magic-induced wraiths. He knew he had to assume the worst, that she had reached the boy already, that she had made him her prisoner, and that it would be up to the shape-shifter to set him free again.

When he reached the place within the trees where he had left the boy, the clearing was empty, the boy gone, and the scent of the witch everywhere. Silence layered the open space as he entered it, watchful still, cautious of traps she might have left. It was beginning to rain, the drops falling in a soft patter on the dry moonlit earth, staining it the color of the shadows.

The boy's long knife lay to one side, discarded. He walked over and knelt to pick it up. As he did so, the caull slid from the forest shadows behind him. Silky smooth and powerful, massive jaws gaping wide, it launched itself at his head.

THIRTEEN

A handful of the Rindge took Quentin Leah and his companions from the ruins of Castledown back to their village. Most stayed to finish setting traps for the mysterious wronks, but the one who had spoken with Panax, along with several of his fellows, broke off from the main group to act as escort. Although the Rindge made no mention of it, the bloodied, ragged, and worn condition of their visitors made it obvious they needed food, rest, and medical treatment. Quentin and company, while reluctant to break off their search for the others, realized they were in no condition to continue. If they were to be effective in finding their missing friends, they would first need to eat, dress their wounds properly, and sleep in a safe place. Moreover, the Rindge might prove helpful in telling them how and where to direct their efforts once they resumed looking.

So they made the three-hour trek through the woods to the Rindge village and were there by midday. On their journey, they learned more about the land to which they had traveled. The Rindge who did all the talking was called Obatedequist Parsenon, or something that sounded very like it, according to Panax. Since the Dwarf was unsure, the cumbersome name was quickly reduced to just Obat. Obat was a subchief in the village hierarchy, the son of a former high chief. It was clear from the deference showed him by the other Rindge that he was a respected member of the community. Obat told them the land of his people was called Parkasia and they had been there two thousand years, since the beginning of time. He did not speak of the Great Wars, but seemed to date everything from then, as if nothing had existed before his people's appearance in Parkasia. It was difficult to be certain, but it appeared to Panax that Parkasia was a peninsula attached to a much larger body of land north and west in which tribes other than the Rindge made their home.

There were various tribes of Rindge living in Parkasia, Obat explained, some of them hunters, some farmers. They were a self-sufficient people and engaged in little trading. Wars sprang up between them now and then, but their greatest common enemy was the thing that lived in Castledown's ruins. Antrax, Obat called it, but he could not find a way to explain what it was. He said it was a spirit, but it commanded creepers and fire threads, strange things that seemingly had nothing to do with spirits. Antrax warded Castledown against all intruders and had done so for as far back as anyone could remember. But it also raided the villages of the Rindge now and then and stole away the people. Those taken were never seen again. They were sacrificed to satisfy Antrax's hunger, their bodies dismembered and their spirits enslaved so that they could never die or be at rest.

It was the same story the company had been told earlier and it made no more sense than it had then; dead was dead, and you didn't enslave souls once the body was gone. But Obat insisted on it, even though he could offer no explanation as to why Antrax took the Rindge and treated them so, what he needed them for, or why he would bother with humans when· he possessed command over such formidable technology. Every time the name Antrax was spoken, the Rindge showed signs of discomfort, casting glances in all directions, making warding motions, even when they were several hours away from the ruins.

Still mired in his discomfort at leaving Bek, Quentin Leah listened to it all with half an ear. Exhausted and battered from his struggle against the creepers, he knew he was staying upright through sheer force of will. But he was heartsick at abandoning his search for his cousin, and he could not stop thinking about it. They had promised they would look out for each other. Bek would never break that promise, no matter what, unless he was unable to carry it out. It didn't matter that Quentin had no idea where to look for his cousin other than in the ruins, and that looking for anyone in the ruins was suicide. It didn't matter how tired he was. All he knew was that he was walking away from Bek at a time when Bek might need him most.

Obat was talking about Antrax again, saying that many of the Rindge tribes believed that Antrax had created humans at the beginning of time and took some back now because he was dissatisfied with their behavior. Antrax was a god and must be worshipped and respected or disaster would result. So they made pilgrimages, bringing gifts to the ruins several times a year. Sometimes, they brought humans as sacrifices to the wronks who were once their kindred. They did not do those things in Obat's village, but that was because the Rindge there believed in the old stories that said humans were created from the earth and given life long before Antrax discovered them. In Obat's village, they believed that Antrax was a demon.

Quentin absorbed all that and consoled himself about Bek

by deciding that his cousin, with his newly discovered magic, was probably better equipped than he to ward off demons or creepers or anything else. That Bek should have magic of any sort still astonished him, yet it made sense in light of what they had both decided about Walker's decision to bring them along. It explained why they had been chosen when there were so many others who might have been taken instead. But it left the Highlander pondering anew his cousin's origin and the reason it had been kept secret so long. It made him wonder how much Coran and Liria knew and had been keeping from them.

They arrived at the village of the Rindge by midday, newly footsore and barely mobile. The village sprawled through a series of connected clearings in a wooded area backed up against foothills leading west into a spine of mountains and consisted mostly of open-air huts and pavilions constructed of wood and bark with blankets and reed screens used as dividers for rooms. The people came out to look at them, men, women, and children alike, all henna-complexioned and red-haired, the youngest darker than their elders.

No palisade or moat warded the village, and when asked, Obat said there was no point; the wronks and creepers could push right through such defenses in any case. When a raid took place, the Rindge simply fled into the hills until it was safe to return. A good system of outposts kept them safe most of the time. The defenses that made a difference were the traps they set out in the woods, deep camouflaged pits with jagged rocks at their bottoms. The creepers and wronks often fell into them and if damaged or not sufficiently mobile, could not climb out. If the metal predators were found and the pits filled in quickly enough, they could no longer hear the commands of Antrax and so remained there.

Fetishes tied to poles ringed the village, protectors for the Rindge against the things that sought to hunt them. Quentin looked into the eyes of the children who watched him and wondered how many the fetishes would save from raids and other dangers.

The five guests were taken to a screened-off area to bathe in large tubs of heated water, then visited by healers who dressed their wounds. Afterwards, they were taken to a pavilion, seated on mats, and given food. The Rindge were primitive, but their life seemed well ordered and reasonable. Quentin thought them intelligent, as well, not just from their speech, which had a musical lilt, but from the look in their eyes and the feel of their homes. Everything was simple, but all needs appeared to be met and served.

After an initial period of congregating to look over their visitors, the Rindge went back to work. Everyone seemed to have a task, even the children, although the youngest mostly played and clung to their mothers. *Things aren't so different here than they are in the Highlands,* Quentin thought.

They slept then, and although Quentin promised himself he would rest for no more than a couple of hours, he did not wake until dawn. Panax was already up by then, engaged in conversation with Obat, and it was their voices, soft and distant from where they conversed outside the sleeping shelter, that roused Quentin. He glanced around and found to his chagrin that the Elves were up and gone, as well. Washing his hands and face in the basin of water provided for that purpose, he strapped the Sword of Leah across his back and walked out to see what was happening.

He found Panax and the Elves with Obat and several more of the Rindge, seated in a circle on mats, talking. As he walked up, he saw that sketches had been drawn in the dirt in front of them. The conversation between Panax and Obat was sufficiently intense that the Dwarf did not even glance at Quentin, but Tamis caught his eye and beckoned him over.

"Nice to see you back among the living," she offered dryly. Her round, pixie face was freshly scrubbed, the skin ruddy beneath her tan. "You snore like a bull in rut when you sleep."

He arched an eyebrow in response. "You spend a lot of time with bulls in rut, do you?"

"Some." She brushed at her short-cropped hair. "What would you say if I told you that Obat knows another way into Castledown?"

Quentin blinked in surprise. "I'd say, when do we leave?"

There was no hesitation on anyone's part about going. Rested and fed, their spirits renewed, the edges of their memories sufficiently blunted that wariness had replaced fear, they were anxious to return. All of them sought answers to what had happened to their friends, and there could be no peace of mind until those answers were found. Each of them, without saying so to the others, believed that there was still something to be accomplished at Castledown.

Their attitude was buttressed in no small way by the fact that the Rindge had agreed to guide them. Creepers and fire threads notwithstanding, if there was another way into the chambers beneath the ruins, they were eager to explore it. Ard Patrinell, Ahren Elessedil, and a handful of other Elves were still missing. Walker was still unaccounted for. Bek had disappeared along with Ryer Ord Star. Some of them, perhaps all, were still alive and in need of help. Quentin and his companions were not going to make them wait for that help.

They ate a quick meal, strapped on their weapons, and set out. Obat led their Rindge escort, two dozen strong. Most of the Rindge carried six-foot blowguns along with knives and javelins, but a substantial number bore short, stout, powerful spears with razor-sharp star heads that could penetrate even the metal of creepers. They used them like pry bars, Obat explained when Panax questioned him about it. They jammed the heads into joints and gaps of the creepers' metal armor and twisted until something gave. Numbers usually gave the Rindge the advantage in such encounters. The creepers, he advised solemnly, were not invincible.

It was educational to watch the Rindge at work. They were a tribal people, but their fighting men appeared to be well trained and disciplined. They fought in units, their numbers broken down by weaponry. The front ranks used the heavy spears, the rear the blowguns and javelins. Even during travel, they kept their fighting order intact, dividing the men into smaller groups, scouts patrolling front and rear, and spear bearers warding the edges of the march. The outlanders, untested in battle, were placed in the middle, screened by their would-be protectors.

Quentin noted the way the Rindge rotated in and out of their loose formation as they traveled, shifting here and there in response to orders from Obat, burnished bodies gleaming with oil and sweat. No one in the little company thought to question their tactics. The Rindge had been living in that land and dealing with the minions of Antrax for hundreds of years; they knew what they were doing.

After a time, Panax dropped back to walk with Quentin, letting the Elves walk ahead of them a few paces. He did so quite deliberately, and the Highlander let him choose his own pace.

"The Rindge believe that Antrax controls the weather," the Dwarf told him quietly, keeping both his head and voice lowered.

Quentin looked at him in surprise. "That isn't possible. No one can control the weather."

"They say Antrax can. They say that's why the weather in their region of Parkasia never changes like it does everywhere else. He says he knows of the glaciers and ice fields on the coast. He says it snows inland, farther north and west, on the other side of the mountains. There are seasons there, but not here."

Quentin shifted the weight of the Sword of Leah on his back. "Walker said something to Bek about the weather being odd. I thought it must be a combination of wind currents and geography, an anomaly." He shook his head. "Maybe Antrax is a god after all."

The Dwarf grunted. "A cruel god, according to the Rindge. It preys on them for no discernible reason. It uses them for fodder and then throws them away, minus a few parts. I keep asking myself what we've gotten ourselves into."

"I keep wondering how much of all this Walker knew and kept to himself," Quentin replied softly.

Panax nodded. "Truls would tell you Walker knew everything because Druids make it a point to find things out and then keep them concealed. I'm not so sure. We walked right into that trap three days back, and the Druid seemed as surprised as any of us."

They walked on in silence, passing into the midday calm and heat, winding along a well-used trail that took them through ancient hardwoods whose boughs canopied and interlocked overhead in such thickness that the light could penetrate only in slender threads and narrow bands. Birds flew overhead, singing cheerfully, and there were squirrels and voles in evidence. The sun traveled slowly west across a cloudless sky, and the air smelled of green leaves and dry earth.

Then Tamis dropped back to walk with them. "I've been thinking," she said quietly. "Something is wrong about this."

They both stared at her. "What do you mean?" Panax asked, looking around as if he might find the answer hidden in the forest green.

Tamis glanced from one to the other. "Ask yourself this. Why are the Rindge being so helpful? Out of the kindness of their hearts? Out of a sense of obligation to help strangers from other lands? Out of compassion for our obvious misery at losing our friends and finding ourselves stranded?"

"It's not unheard of," Quentin replied, an edge to his voice.

She glared at him. "Don't be stupid. By helping us, the Rindge are risking their lives and possible retaliation by Antrax, whatever it is. They wouldn't do that unless there was something to be gained from doing so, something that would benefit them."

Panax scowled, no happier than Quentin upon hearing this accusation. "What would that something be, Tamis?"

"I've been thinking," she advised, keeping her voice low, her eyes on the Rindge. "You told them we came here seeking a treasure, and they know we went into the ruins very deliberately to find it. They must assume we knew something about what we were getting ourselves into before we tried that—however misguided that assumption might be. At the very least, that suggests to them that we have a means of dealing with Antrax. Now think about this. They haven't said so, but what if they were watching us the first time we went in and know about Quentin's sword and Walker's Druidic powers? They've been looking for a way to rid themselves of Antrax for hundreds of years, and now, finally, they may have found one. Us. What if they're using us as a weapon?"

"To destroy Antrax," Quentin finished. "So they're taking

us right to it and turning us loose, hoping for the best. They won't stand and fight with us, if it comes to that. They'll run."

She shrugged. "I don't know what they'll do. I just think we'd better watch our backs. They have to wonder about us— where did we come from and what do we intend to do when this is over? Perhaps they're thinking that the best thing that could happen would be for Antrax and us to destroy each other and leave the Rindge in peace. They have to have considered that. They don't want to swap one form of tyranny for another. They know that's a possibility, and nothing we say is going to convince them otherwise."

"Obat doesn't seem like that," Quentin ventured after a moment.

Tamis sneered softly. "You haven't been out in the world as long as I have, Quentin Leah. You haven't seen as much. What do you think, Panax?"

The Dwarf glanced at Quentin, his gruff features set. "She's right. We'd better be ready for anything."

"Kian and Wye already know my thinking," she said, starting ahead again. She glanced back at Quentin. "I hope I'm wrong, Highlander. I really do."

They marched on in silence for the remainder of their journey, Quentin mired in gloom at the prospect of being betrayed yet again. He knew Tamis was right about the Rindge, but he could barely bring himself to consider what that might mean. He wished Bek were there to give his opinion. Bek would see things more clearly. He would be quicker to ferret out the truth. The Rindge didn't seem antagonistic, but they had been at war with Antrax for the whole of their existence, so they knew something about staying alive. They hadn't tried to harm their visitors, but Tamis might have been right about them watching the company fight its way clear of the maze. It was possible they were simply waiting to see what would happen when Antrax and the outlanders came face-to-face.

The more Quentin thought about it, the more uneasy he grew. The only real weapon they had was his sword. It might be enough to see them through, but he could not be certain. If Walker had been overcome by Antrax, what chance did he have? He wondered if Bek had come up against Antrax, as well, and having discovered his own form of magic, brought it to bear. If so, what success had he enjoyed? If his magic was powerful enough to shred creepers, as Tamis had reported, could it bring Antrax down? He did not like thinking of Bek facing Antrax alone. He did not like even considering the possibility. It shouldn't happen that way, Bek alone. Or himself, for that matter. It should be the two of them, standing together the way they had planned it, watching out for each other.

He wondered if there was any chance that it could still happen like that and if it could happen in time to make a difference.

It was still early afternoon when they reached the edges of Castledown and paused long enough for the Rindge to scout ahead for creepers. While they waited, Quentin sat with Panax and stared out into the midday heat as it rose in visible waves off the metal of the devastated city. In the flat, raw wasteland, nothing moved. There was no sign of the maze, farther in from where they sat, and nothing to show that anyone had ever passed that way. Panax drank from a water skin and offered it to Quentin.

"Worried about Bek?" he asked, wiping his mouth.

Quentin nodded. "I can't stop worrying about him. I don't like the thought of him out there alone."

The Dwarf nodded and looked off into the distance. "Might be better if he is, though."

The Rindge scouts returned. There were no creepers in evidence along the city's perimeter. Obat motioned everyone ahead, and they moved through the trees, staying just inside the forestline as they followed the edge of the ruins east and south. No one talked as they scanned the city, moving with slow, careful steps. The buildings stared back at them, the gaping holes of windows and doors like vacant eyes and mouths. Castledown was a tomb for dead men and machines, a graveyard for the unwary. Quentin carried the Sword of Leah unsheathed, bearing it before him, feeling just the slightest tingle of imprisoned magic awaiting its summoning. His pulse throbbed in his temples, and he heard the sound of his breathing in his throat.

Obat brought them to a grated entry cut into the side of a building that sprawled several hundred yards in both directions. Stationing Rindge at either end and carefully back from where he stood, he worked with a handful of others to free the grate from its clasps and swing it back on its rusted hinges. The effort produced a series of squeals barely muted by old grease and the weight of the metal.

Obat pointed into the black opening and spoke to Panax in hushed tones.

"Obat says that this leads to where Antrax lives," the Dwarf translated. "He says this is how it breathes underground."

"A ventilation shaft," Quentin said.

"Ask him how he knows Antrax is down there," Tamis demanded.

Panax did so, listened to Obat's reply, and shook his head. "He says he knows because this is where he's seen the creepers come out to hunt."

Tamis looked at Quentin. "What do you think, Highlander? You're the one with the sword."

Quentin stared into the blackness of the shaft and thought that it was the last place he would like to go. He could just make out lights farther in, dim glimmers in the blackness, so they would not be blind. But he didn't care for being trapped underground beneath all that stone and metal with no map to guide them and no way of knowing where to look.

"This might be a waste of time," Panax offered quietly.

Quentin nodded. "On the other hand, what else do we have to do? Where else do we look for the others if not here?" His grip tightened on the sword. "We've come this far. We should at least take a peek."

Tamis stepped forward to peer more closely into the darkness. "A peek should be more than enough. Are the Rindge coming with us?"

Panax shook his head. "They've already told me they won't go into the ruins, above or belowground. They're terrified of Antrax. They'll wait for us here."

"It doesn't matter. We don't need them anyway." She looked over her shoulder at Quentin. "Ready, Highlander?"

Quentin nodded. "Ready."

They went in bunched close together, Tamis leading, picking her way carefully. Their eyes adjusted quickly to the blackness. The walls, floor, and ceiling of the air shaft were smooth and unobstructed. They walked for several hundred yards without changing direction, locked in silence and the faintly metallic smell of the corridor, the opening through which they had entered shrinking behind them to a pinprick of light. The shaft began to descend then, dropping away at a slant, then splitting in two. The little company paused, then turned into the larger of the passageways, descending farther, moving past countless smaller ducts that burrowed through the walls and ceiling like snake holes. Ahead, still so distant at first that it was barely discernible, they could hear the sound of machinery, a soft purring, a gentle hum, a reminder of life ancient and enduring.

Lights burned at regular intervals, flameless lamps set into the walls, yellowish light steady and unwavering. Strange fish-eyes peered down at Quentin from the ceiling, set farther apart than the lights, tiny red dots blinking steadily at their centers. They seemed to be looking at him. It was ridiculous to think this, yet he could not shake the feeling that it was so. He glanced at Panax and Tamis to see if they were looking, too, but their eyes were directed ahead into the corridor they followed.

Quentin found himself staring around in amazement. He had never seen anything like this. So many metal sheets layered together, yards and yards of them, bolted and sealed against weather and animals and plants, a man-made warren carved into the earth. How had it been done? He tried to picture the culture and machines and skill that must have been required but he failed. The Old World had been a very different place, he knew, but that had never been more dramatically apparent to him than it was in the ventilation shaft.

Held in place by stanchions, metal pipes began to appear in connected lines along the walls of the passageway. Quentin could not discern their purpose. Everything felt strange and foreign to him, all the metal surfaces, all that space and emptiness. If Antrax lived down there, he had room to move about—that much was clear. But what sort of creature would choose to live in such a place? Only another machine, another creeper made of metal, Quentin thought. Perhaps Antrax was a machine, similar, yet more powerful than the creepers it commanded.

Suddenly, Tamis froze. Her hand came up in warning. The four men stopped instantly. Everyone listened. Ahead, the corridor ended in a hub from which a series of similar corridors fanned out like spokes in a wheel. Within one of those corridors, footsteps were audible. The footsteps were heavy and slow and deliberate, as if what made them bore a great weight.

Quentin had never heard footsteps like those. What made them walked on two legs, but it did not sound like something he had encountered before. He glanced at the others. Tamis was crouched like a cat. Panax stood upright, his expression unreadable. There was a sheen of sweat on the faces of the Elven Hunters, Kian and Wye. Quentin felt as if he couldn't breathe. No one seemed able to move.

Then Tamis started forward, creeping up the corridor toward the shadowy hub ahead. She glanced back at Quentin once, her tough, no-nonsense face intense and her gray eyes bright. *Don't let me down,* she was saying. Without even looking at the others, he went after her, matching her pace. Behind him, the Dwarf and the Elven Hunters followed. The sound of the footfalls grew louder. Whoever or whatever it was, it was making no effort to disguise its approach. It was big and it was confident. It was no one, Quentin thought in dismay, that he and his companions had come looking for.

Twenty feet from the hub, with the entrances of all of the intersecting tunnels visible, they slowed as light cast a shadow from the one just to the left of where they crouched in hiding. Then a tall, lumbering figure stalked out of the gloom and into the light of a dozen lamps set all around the hub.

Quentin caught his breath sharply as the figure was revealed. He heard gasps from the others. Even Tamis, who seemed unafraid of anything, took a step back in shock.

Like a shade or a demon or perhaps something of both, but most like a monster come from a nightmare's imagining into the real world, the thing—for there was no other word for it—turned to face them.

It was Ard Patrinell.

Or what was left of him.

Fourteen

In worrying about what sort of disaster might have befallen his missing friends, Quentin Leah had considered some frightening and horrific possibilities, but nothing on the order of what confronted him there. The creature that stood before him, the thing that had once been Ard Patrinell, was beyond imagining. It had been cobbled together from flesh and bone on the one hand and metal on the other. There was machinery inside it; the Highlander could hear it humming softly and steadily from somewhere within the metal torso to which its other parts were attached. The legs and left arm were metal, as well, all three composed of struts hinged at knees and elbows and feet and hands, and attached by ball joints set into sockets surrounded by cables that ran up and down the creature like arteries and veins in a human body.

What remained of the old Ard Patrinell formed the right arm and face. Both were intact and the distinctive features of the Captain of the Home Guard were instantly recognizable. His metal-capped head was set into a tall collar. It was impossible to tell if his head was still connected to some portion of his body, although even at a distance and in the dim light of the ventilation shaft, Quentin could see color in the strong features and movement in the dark eyes. But there was no question about the connection of the right arm, the flesh and bone of which were capped and cabled in metal at the shoulder and attached in the same manner as the other limbs by a metal ball and socket.

Red and green lights blinked like tiny glass eyes all over the creature's gleaming torso, and numbers set in windows clicked and whirred, counting out functions that Quentin could only guess at. Pads cushioned the skeletal metal pieces of the feet so that when the creature walked it made thumping sounds and did not clank as it otherwise surely would. The human right hand held a broadsword in its powerful grip, ready to strike. The metal left hand held a long knife and was bound and warded by an oval shield that ran from wrist to elbow.

When it saw them—and it did see them, they could tell from the movement of the eyes and shift of the body—it started for them at once, weapons raised to strike.

For just an instant the members of the little company stood their ground, more out of an inability to respond than out of courage. Then Tamis shouted, "No! Get out of here!"

They began to back away, slowly at first, then more quickly as the advancing monster picked up speed. It was heavy, but its movements were smooth and effortless, as if a part of Ard Patrinell's agility had been captured in his new form. Finally, the Elves, the Dwarf, and the Highlander broke into a run, propelled by fear and horror, but by something else, as well. They did not want to face a thing that was made out of pieces of someone they had known and admired. Ard Patrinell had been their friend, and they did not want to do battle with his shade.

But what they might have wanted did not count for much. They retreated down the corridor the way they had come, yelling encouragement to one another, Tamis shouting to them to get back outside where they had more room to maneuver. And to where the Rindge might give them aid, Quentin thought without saying so. Kian and Wye, toughened and well conditioned, quickly outdistanced the other three. Tamis deliberately hung back, intent on warding the obviously struggling Panax. Quentin might have kept up with the speedy Elves, but the Dwarf was stocky and slow and not built for speed. He was laboring in minutes, and the tireless metal monster that gave chase was closing the gap between them.

At the first split in the passageway, Quentin rounded on their pursuer, shouting at the others to go on. Braced in the center of the corridor, the Sword of Leah raised before him, he confronted the thing that had been Ard Patrinell. It came at him without slowing, all size and weight, metal parts gleaming in the flameless lamplight. For an instant Quentin thought he was a dead man, that he had misjudged what he could manage altogether and was wholly inadequate to the task. But then the magic flared to life, running up and down the blade of his talisman, and he was crying out, "Leah! Leah!"

He closed with his attacker in a shocking clash of metal blades, and the impact of the collision nearly threw him off his feet. Forced backwards by superior weight and size, he kept his blade between them, struggling to find purchase on the smooth metal floor. He seized the other's metal arm to keep the long knife at bay, but quickly discovered he lacked the strength to do more than slow its advance. Wrenching free, he spun away, the current of the sword's magic flooding through him like a swollen river, rough and unyielding in its passage. All thoughts of anything but defending himself fled, and he came around with a blow aimed at taking off Ard Patrinell's head. To his astonishment, the blow failed. Partially deflected by the other's sword, it was stopped completely by some invisible shield that warded the metal-capped head.

Quentin thrust himself clear a second time; then Tamis was beside him, yelling at Panax to run. Together, they fought to hold the metal juggernaut at bay, hammering at it from two sides, striking at anything that seemed vulnerable, that might break or shatter to slow it down. That was all that was needed, Quentin kept thinking—just enough of a breakdown to cripple it and let them escape.

Then it sidestepped a blow from his blade and stepped between the Elf girl and himself, reaching for him with bladed hands to pin him to the tunnel wall. He grappled with it a moment, hammering with his sword blade at the clear faceplate, unexpectedly meeting the familiar eyes long enough to see something that made him cry out in shock before breaking free once more.

"Run!" he shouted to Tamis, and together they sped back down the passageway in pursuit of Panax and the Elven Hunters.

His mind locked on a single image. What he had found in those eyes, the eyes of a dead man, had frozen his soul. It was all he could do to accept that he had not been mistaken, that what he had seen was real. He understood why the Rindge said that when their people were taken and dismembered by Antrax, they didn't die but were still alive, their souls captured.

He felt afraid in a way he had never thought possible, certainly in a way he had never been before. Suddenly, all he wanted to do was to escape that place and leave its horrors behind him forever.

"Did you see?" he gasped at Tamis as they ran. "His eyes! Did you see his eyes?"

"What?" she shouted back. Her breathing was rough and labored. "His eyes?"

He couldn't make himself say any more, couldn't finish what he had begun. He shook his head at her and ran harder, faster, the burn of his breathing sharp and raw in his throat as he fled back up the dimly lit passageway.

It took only minutes, but it seemed much longer, to regain the entrance to the ventilation shaft and burst clear once more. The others were already there—Kian, Wye, Panax, and even the Rindge, who had not fled as Tamis had feared. Obat had formed up his warriors in ranks two dozen yards back from the grate entry, heavy spears lowered, blowguns lifted. Quentin's little band took up positions on one end of the formation, breathing heavily, staring back at the dark opening they had fled.

The monster burst into view in a lumbering rush that took it right into them. It did not slow, did not hesitate, but barreled into the center of the Rindge line, thrusting past the spears, brushing off the darts from the blowguns, sending those who tried to stop it flying in all directions. There was barely time for some to cry "Wronk" in voices steeped in terror before three lay dead or dying and all but a handful of the rest had scattered. Obat and two more stood their ground, joined by the Elves, Panax, and Quentin Leah, who hammered at the monster from all sides, trying to break through its defenses, to find a weak spot, to do anything to stop it. Grunts and cries mingled with the clash of iron weapons, rising up through the heat. Blades flashed in the sunlight, and bodies slick with sweat and smudged with dirt and grit struggled to stay upright and clear of the metal behemoth.

"Leah!" Quentin roared in fury, striking blow after blow at the wronk that had once been Ard Patrinell, watching in horror as it responded with the unerring instincts and skill of the Captain of the Home Guard, infused with the knowledge that Patrinell had acquired through twenty-odd years of combat and training. It was terrifying. It was as if Patrinell was still there, his spirit captured within that metal form, able to direct its actions, to give thought to its responses. It was as if it knew what Quentin would do before he did it, as if it could anticipate the Highlander's every move.

Perhaps he could, Quentin thought in dismay. Ard Patrinell had taught the Highlander almost everything he knew about fighting. Aboard the *Jerle Shannara*, Patrinell had trained and schooled Quentin in the tricks and the maneuvers that would keep him alive in combat. Quentin had been a good student, but Patrinell knew the tricks and maneuvers, as well, had known them longer, and could employ them better.

As did the wronk he had become, remade in this new image, in this monstrous form, in this horrific fusing of metal and flesh.

Another of the Rindge went down, bloodied and broken, torn open from neck to crotch. Obat and the remaining Rindge turned and fled. Quentin's tiny band sagged back before the wronk's fresh onslaught. Despair clouded their faces and drained them of their strength. But then they got lucky. Pressing its attack, the wronk got tangled up in the body of a dead Rindge, lost its footing, and went down. It was up almost instantly, but a broken limb of the dead man was lodged between its joints. In the few moments it took the wronk to free itself, Quentin and his companions broke off their seemingly hopeless struggle and raced after the fleeing Rindge. Whatever was needed to win their battle, it would first require a plan. Just then, it was best just to get away.

Sheathing their weapons on the fly, they raced back into the trees. Obat slowed to let them catch up, shouting something at Panax, who shouted back; then all of them disappeared into the trees. In seconds, they could no longer see the ruins. They ran a long time. Others of the Rindge joined them, all of them breathing hard, bathed in sweat, riddled with fear. Quentin felt the magic of his sword subside, a red haze fading into twinges of emptiness and unfulfilled need, a mix of emotions that tore at him like brambles. He was burned out and chilled through all at once, and part of him wanted to go back into battle while the other wanted only to escape.

He did not know how long they ran or even how far. They were well away from the ruins before they staggered to a halt, a forlorn and dejected band. They knelt in the fading afternoon light, heads lowered in exhaustion, listening through ragged gasps for the sounds of pursuit. Quentin glanced at Tamis, and his emotions coalesced into an overwhelming feeling of shame. Their effort had failed utterly. They were no better off than they had been when they started out—worse off, perhaps, because now they knew the fate of at least one of their missing companions and maybe of the rest, as well.

Tamis glared back at him. He was surprised to see tears in her eyes. "Don't look at me!" she snapped.

Obat spoke to one of the Rindge, and the man rose and started back toward the ruins—looking to see if the thing they had fled was still following them, Quentin thought.

Panax eased over to him, gruff face flushed and angry. "What sort of monster would do that to a man?" he growled. "Make him into a machine out of bits and pieces of himself?"

"Another machine, maybe," Quentin offered wearily. "A better question might be why?"

Panax shook his head. "There's no sense to it."

"There's sense to everything, even if we don't understand

what it is." Quentin was thinking about the wronk's eyes,
Ard Patrinell's eyes. "There's a reason Antrax uses wronks.
There's a reason for this one. Did you see how it fought
us? Did you watch it respond to our attacks? It has Ard Patrinell's memories, Panax. It's using his skills and tactics. It
knows how to fight the same way he did."

The Rindge who had been dispatched by Obat returned on
the run, speaking hurriedly to the subchief, who in turn spoke
to Panax. The Dwarf came to his feet at once.

"Let's go! It's right behind us!"

They climbed to their feet and continued on quickly, Obat
in the lead, choosing an unobstructed path that allowed them
to move swiftly; their best chance lay in outrunning their pursuer. Once or twice, Quentin glanced over his shoulder, but
there was nothing to see. He did not doubt for a moment that
the wronk was following, untiring and implacable, determined
to pursue them until they were run to ground. The Highlander
was already feeling twinges of doubt over whether they could
escape it. But to stand and fight would be a mistake. The wronk
was bigger and stronger. Its armor gave it better protection. It
possessed Ard Patrinell's fighting instincts and skills. Perhaps
if there were more of the Rindge, if they could reach the
village and summon others to their aid, they might stand a
chance. Otherwise, even with the magic of the Sword of Leah
to aid them, he wasn't sure they would prevail.

They were strung out through a dense part of the forest
they were unable to avoid when the wronk caught up with
them. It came out of the trees to one side, its appearance so
unexpected that no one was ready for it. Instantly, trapped
and cut to pieces, two of the Rindge and the Elven Hunter
Wye died. The remainder of the company scattered in a mix
of shouts and cries, going off in all directions, fighting to

break free of the wronk and the entangling trees. Quentin and Tamis ran one way while Panax and Kian ran the other. The Rindge ran everywhere. For an instant everything was chaos as the wronk surged through the center of their line, blades cutting at everything.

Then the Highlander and the Tracker were in the clear once more. Quentin risked a quick glance over one shoulder. A gleam of metal in sunlight and the sounds of something huge thrashing after them told him the wronk was still coming, and it was coming for them.

"This way!" Tamis hissed, dodging deadwood and scrub like a rabbit as she plunged down a ravine.

They ran in silence for a long time, neither one speaking, trying to put as much distance as possible between themselves and their pursuer. It was growing dark, twilight settling over Parkasia, shadows lengthening into night. It was difficult to pick up all the obstacles that hindered or blocked their path, especially when they were running, and more than once Quentin almost lost his footing. All the while, they could hear the sounds of pursuit, the breaking of branches, the rending of brush and grass, the steady, relentless clump of heavy steps.

Something unexpected and frightening insinuated itself into the Highlander's thinking as he fled. At first he discounted the possibility, pushed it aside angrily, but then he began to wonder. Both times, here and there, the wronk had made it a point to come after *him*. He had seen it in the monster's attack on the Rindge defensive formation, back in the ruins, where it had rushed the natives first, then turned directly for him. Again, in the woods, after striking down those closest, it had chosen to pursue him. It seemed paranoid to think like that. Why would the wronk be after him in particular? Had his attack on it in the ventilation shaft provoked it? Was there something about him especially that drew it?

Then he remembered something Walker had said during their final meeting aboard ship before disembarking for their ill-fated journey to the ruins, and he had his answer.

It was completely dark when they finally stopped, miles from where they had started, deep in the woods. The only visible light came from moon and stars, the forest around them layered with shadows and cloaked in silence. They crouched on a ridge, concealed in a stand of brush, and looked back the way they had come, listening. The sounds of the wronk's pursuit had faded, disappearing almost without their realizing it, as if the creature had stopped, as well. Neither Quentin nor Tamis moved or spoke for a very long time, waiting.

"I know what it's after," Quentin whispered finally, staring off into the dark. "It's after me."

She looked at him without speaking.

"It wants the sword. It wants the magic. Remember what Walker told us about why we were lured here in the first place? For our magic, he said. I think Antrax knows all about us, maybe even about Bek. It wants everything we have."

She thought it over. "Maybe."

"That's why it sent this wronk made of pieces of Ard Patrinell. It's using his brain, his instincts, and his fighting skills to get what it wants from us. From me. I thought at first it had chosen Patrinell because he would know us best, could kill us easiest. But why send a wronk after us? Why bother, when we were so easily cut apart in the maze and pose so little threat?"

"So you think it constructed the wronk deliberately," she said. "It used Patrinell's head and sword arm, so it had to have a specific purpose in mind."

"It used those parts it needed to make the wronk function

as closely as possible to the real thing. None of this happened by accident. The wronk was constructed and dispatched for a reason. It's after me. It keeps coming right for me. I didn't think anything of it at first, back in the ventilation shaft. But it came after me again once we were outside and again in the forest, and now it's chasing me. It wants the sword, Tamis. It wants the magic."

For a moment, she was quiet. He went back to staring off into the impenetrable dark, listening. "You haven't thought it through far enough," she whispered suddenly. She waited until he turned to look at her again. "Think about it. Your sword won't work for just anyone, will it?"

Her steady gaze unnerved him. "No. It only works for me. So you're saying it wants me, too."

"Or parts of you, like Patrinell."

His throat tightened, and he looked away. "I'll die first."

She didn't say anything but put a hand on his arm. "What were you trying to tell me about his eyes back there in the tunnel? When we were running, you started to say something. You asked me if I'd seen his eyes."

Quentin was quiet for a long time, remembering what he had seen, trying to overcome the revulsion that even thinking of it caused. Tamis kept her hand on his arm and her eyes on his face. "Tell me, Highlander."

He sagged a little as he spoke, despair and fear taking fresh hold. "When we struggled underground below the ruins, I got a good look at those eyes. While I was grappling with it, I got close enough to see into them. They weren't dead eyes. They weren't soulless. They weren't filled with anger or madness or anything I expected. They were frightened and trapped and helpless. I know it sounds impossible, but he's still alive in there. In his head and brain. In what he sees and feels. He's shut away in there. I could see it. I could tell. He was asking for help. He was begging for it."

She was shaking her head, denial, rage, and fear twisting her features, her hand tightening on his arm until her nails bit into his flesh.

"He's not attacking us because he wants to!" Quentin hissed. "He's doing it because he doesn't have a choice, because he's been rebuilt to carry out the wishes of Antrax! He's been mind-altered like those Elves who murdered Allardon Elessedil! Only there's no body left, nothing whole. He's—" He caught himself. "He isn't Ard Patrinell anymore, but Antrax has stolen something of who he was and is holding it prisoner inside that wronk."

Something moved in the darkness, but the movement was small and quick. Quentin glanced out hurriedly, then back to Tamis.

"You could be wrong," she insisted angrily.

"I know. But I'm not. I saw him. I saw *him*."

There were fresh tears in her eyes. He caught their gleam in the moonlight. Her grip on his arm loosened. She blinked hard and looked away. "I can't believe it. It isn't possible."

"The Rindge knew. They've seen it happen before with their own people. They tried to tell us."

She shook her head and ran her fingers through her short-cropped hair. "It makes me sick. It makes me want to scream. No one should have to . . ."

She couldn't finish. Quentin didn't blame her. There were no words sufficient to express her feelings. What had been done to Ard Patrinell was so loathsome, so despicable that it left the Highlander feeling unclean.

And afraid, because there was every chance that Antrax intended that he come to the same end.

"We'll have to kill him," she said suddenly, looking over with such fierceness that it left him off balance. For a moment, he wasn't certain who she was talking about. "Again, all over again. We can't leave him trapped in there. We have to set him free."

She took his hands in her own and gripped them tightly. "Help me do it, Highlander. Promise me you will."

He saw it then, the reason for her passion. She had been in love with Ard Patrinell. He had missed that before, not seen even the barest hint of it. How had he been so blind? Maybe she had kept it well enough hidden that no one could have known. But there it was, out in the open, as certain as daylight's return with the dawn.

"All right," he agreed softly. "I promise."

He had no idea how he was going to keep that promise, but his feelings on the matter were as strong as her own. He was the one who had looked into Ard Patrinell's eyes and seen him in there, still alive. That was not something he could pretend never happened and would have no effect on him if he walked away from it. Like Tamis, he could not leave the Captain of the Home Guard a slave to a machine. The wronk had to be destroyed.

"Get some sleep," she said, easing away from him. There was weariness and sadness in her voice. All of her strength seemed drained away. He had not seen her like that before and he did not like seeing her that way. It was as if she had suddenly grown old.

"Wake me in a few hours," he said.

She did not respond. Her gaze was directed out into the night. He waited a moment, then stretched out, placing his head in the crook of his arm. He watched her for a time, but she didn't move. Finally, his eyes closed and he slept.

In his troubled dreams, he ran once more from the wronk. It pursued him through a forest, and he could not find a way to escape it. After a long time, he found himself backed against a wall, and he was forced to turn and fight. But the wronk was not solid or recognizable. It was insubstantial, a thing made of air. He could feel it pressing into him, suffocating him. He fought to break free, just to draw a breath, and then suddenly it materialized right in front of him and he saw its face. It belonged to Bek.

It was almost dawn when he woke, the first tinges of daylight seeping through the trees, the sky east lightening. Tamis had fallen asleep on watch, her body leaning against a tree, her chin lowered into her chest. When he pushed himself into a sitting position, she heard him move and looked up at once.

In the distance, far off but recognizable, something big moved through the trees.

They stood up together, staring in the direction of the sounds.

"It's coming again," Quentin whispered. "What do you want to do? Make a stand here or choose another place?"

Her look was unreadable, but the weariness and sadness of the previous night had vanished. "Let's find one of those pits the Rindge dug for wronk traps," she replied softly. "Let's see how well it works."

FIFTEEN

Even though he had been persuaded by Ryer Ord Star to follow the little sweeper in search of Walker, Ahren Elessedil insisted on waiting until after dark before reentering the deadly ruins. He accepted that it was unlikely they would be attacked by creepers or fire threads if the sweeper was leading them and it probably made no difference whether it was dark or light, but he didn't care. Still firmly in the grip of his memory of the attack that had destroyed everyone with him when they had attempted an entry in daylight last time, it was all he could do to make himself go back down there at all. He must at least, he insisted, be allowed the one concession.

Ryer Ord Star had no choice but to agree since she wanted him with her; the sweeper had nothing to offer on the matter. It sat there on its wheeled base, insides whirring, keeping its images to itself. Summery and hot, the day drifted slowly away, and Ahren and Ryer took turns sleeping. Below their hiding place, the ruins sat shimmering in silence.

With the coming of nightfall, darkness settling over the land in blue-gray shadows and thinning light, they set out. The sweeper led them down out of their concealment, its wheeled base flexing on the stairs and over the rubble, scarcely making a sound as it worked its way through the perimeter and into the ruins. The seer and the Elven Prince followed, the former without hesitation, the latter with nothing but. They were barely twenty yards into the maze when the sweeper approached a wall, made a series of small clicking noises, and triggered a concealed entry. The wall slid back to reveal a dimly lit ramp leading down, and the three unlikely companions stepped within.

When the door slid shut again behind them, Ahren experienced such an attack of panic that it was all he could do to keep from crying out. He felt trapped, exposed, and helpless all at once, and he expected the fire threads and the creepers to cut him apart. But there was no attack, and they proceeded unchallenged down the ramp to a joining of corridors at a hub. Flameless lamps encased in glass spilled yellow light across the flooring in dim pools. Pipes ran along the ceilings, burrowing in and out of the walls like snakes. Sealed doors, some of them round rather than rectangular, were the only thing marring the smooth metal surfaces. Spaced evenly along each passageway, glass fish-eyes peered down at them from overhead, tiny red dots within dark centers flashing wickedly.

Ahren, his eyes peering everywhere at once, found himself regretting anew his decision; he was still bothered by their willingness to accept that the sweeper could help them. Or would, for that matter. That a machine that was at least part creeper would be anxious to help them seemed patently ridiculous. In his mind, he replayed the images the sweeper had shown them, reevaluating them, trying to get behind them to see more than he had been shown. The whole business felt wrong. He kept thinking that Ryer Ord Star would have detected any subterfuge, but the seer was so blinded by her need to reach Walker that he couldn't be sure. Even if they found the Druid, how were they supposed to help him? If he couldn't help himself, what use would they be? He thought about the missing Elfstones. If he had their magic to call upon, he might be able to do something, although even that wasn't a given, since he had never used them and had no real idea if he could.

They walked a very long way without seeming to get anywhere, the tunnels and chambers and stairways passing in endless succession, all of it looking and feeling the same. Every so often he heard machinery at work, soft and distant, muffled by steel and earth. He kept thinking they would find something new, a chamber that would reveal something important, but it never happened. On the other hand, they didn't encounter anything that threatened either. Time drifted away, and their strange descent wore on.

Finally, Ahren called a halt. They had walked for miles, and there was nothing to suggest they wouldn't walk for miles more. They needed to rest. Ryer, he felt, would keep going until she dropped. He sat down with his back against one of the metal walls and took out his water skin. The seer sat down next to him, accepting the water skin when he passed it, then a small bit of bread and cheese from the little food that remained to him. The silence of the underground passageways seemed to echo all around them, a reminder of just how alone and isolated they were.

The sweeper took up a position in the center of the corridor just in front of them, lights blinking in sleepy cadence. It did not seem to be in any hurry.

Ahren shifted himself so that he was facing the young seer. "Do you have any sense of how close we might be to Walker?"

She shook her head. "I can still feel him, but the feeling isn't any different from before."

"Nothing? But we've been walking forever. You have to be able to tell something."

"It doesn't work like that, Ahren. Distance doesn't matter. I can feel the same things whether I am very near or far away. Only the healing part has anything to do with being close. Then I have to touch the one who is in pain." She tried a quick, reassuring smile. "Don't be afraid."

He was, though, and he couldn't seem to help himself. Everything about Castledown felt like a weight pressing him against the earth, crushing him to nothing. He was embarrassed and ashamed, still carrying guilt for having run from the attack, for having been so petrified with fear that he couldn't bring himself to help the others. Maybe that was why he was afraid. Maybe that was why he seemed to be afraid all the time.

She reached over and touched his arm, surprising him. "It's all right to be frightened. I'm frightened, too. I don't want to be here either. But we might be the only ones who can help Walker. We have to try."

He nodded disconsolately. She was right, but that didn't make him feel any better. Or braver. They rose and started off again, following after the little sweeper. It took them down new passageways and ramps, stairs and corridors, leading them on, deeper and deeper into the catacombs of the underground city. The journey was tedious and numbing; the world of Castledown was the same wherever they went. Fatigue set in, physical and emotional both. Ahren found himself wondering if it was still dark outside. He didn't think it could be. He wondered if anyone else had come into the ruins since.

What were the chances that someone else from their scattered little band would find a way underground as they had?

Several times he tried asking the sweeper how much farther they had to go, but there was never any response. The sweeper simply pressed on, not bothering to communicate, no longer showing images. They were completely dependent on it by then; they could not find their way back to the surface alone. They could not find their way anywhere. If the sweeper did not lead them to Walker, they were hopelessly lost.

When they stopped again to rest, backs against the wall once more, eating and drinking to stay strong, tired enough to sleep, but unwilling to chance it, Ahren was so consumed by their predicament that he could no longer stand it. He waited a moment, thinking through the suggestion he was about to make, watching the sweeper as it faced them from the center of the corridor some ten feet away.

"I want you to do something," he said quietly to the seer. She glanced over at once. He paused and leaned closer. "I want you to try your empathic skills on the sweeper and see what they tell you."

She furrowed her brow. "You want me to see if touching it will induce a vision?"

"Of the past, of the future, of the present, of anything that will help us."

"But it's a machine, Ahren."

"Try anyway. You said it was sentient. If that's so, you might be able to trigger something from its thoughts. Maybe you can discover how much farther we have to go or where to look for Walker." He shook his head helplessly. "I just want something that says we're down here for a reason and should keep going."

She stared at him for a long time, undecided. Then she gave him a slow nod. "All right, I'll try."

She finished a last bite of bread, put down the water skin, and rose. The sweeper started to move away, thinking they were ready, but then turned back when Ahren made no move to follow. Ryer approached it without speaking, knelt beside it, and put her hands on its rounded metal body, fingertips pressing as her eyes closed. Her pale, ethereal features tightened in concentration, and her face lifted out of the shadow of her silvery hair.

In the next instant, she rocked back sharply on her heels and her slender body went rigid with shock. Ahren started. The sweeper never moved; Ryer Ord Star clung to it, fingertips crooked and head thrown back, eyes closed and arms extended, finding in whatever vision her contact with the sweeper had induced such images that the emotions elicited could be read upon her face, raw and naked and terrible.

She gave a low moan, then sagged, her hands falling away. Right away, without prompting, without even opening her eyes, she began to speak.

"A young man, an Elf, was brought here in chains, battered and broken from a struggle that left his companions dead. His eyes were then gouged out and his tongue removed. He carried Elfstones, gripped so tightly in his hand he could not release them. They were magic and so powerful that they could have freed him had he the will to use them to do so. But his mind was shackled like his body, and he no longer had control over it. Creepers bore him into this place, deep underground, into a chamber filled with machines and blinking lights. He was placed in a chair. Iron cuffs secured him and wires were inserted into his body, carefully inserted beneath his skin by creepers."

Her eyes snapped open and she looked at him, her face wan and haunted. Stricken by what she had witnessed in a world she hadn't imagined could exist, she looked like a child woken from a nightmare.

"A presence watched it happen, a sentient being that lacked substance and form. It was called Antrax. It hid in the walls and floor and ceiling, all about, everywhere at once. It could see, but had no eyes. It could feel, but had no touch. It was controlling the fate of the ruined Elf. It was controlling his mind. When the Elf was securely attached to the chair, a box with many wires was latched about the hand that held the Elfstones. Images were fed into the Elf's mind through the wires, causing him to see things that were not there, forcing him to use the magic of the stones. That magic was captured by the box and stolen away, carried down into the wires, siphoned off to other places."

She stared at Ahren as if unable to look away, lost in the images of her vision. "This is what I saw. All of it. Everything."

"You saw Kael Elessedil," he said quietly.

She took a deep breath. "Kael Elessedil," she repeated. She shuddered. "For thirty years, Ahren, that was his life!"

He tried to picture that and failed. How could anyone be used in that way? What sort of creature could commit such a travesty? A deep cold settled into the pit of his stomach as he realized that whatever it was, it wasn't human. Antrax was something else altogether.

He rose to go to her, to help her to her feet, but she made a quick warding gesture. "Don't touch me, Ahren. There's something more—something darker still. I couldn't bear to look on it all at once, but now I must. I have to. I have opened myself to visions triggered by the sweeper's memories. If you put your hands on me, it will disrupt everything. Stay clear."

Without waiting for his response, she leaned forward again and placed her hands on the sweeper once more. Her face went rigid instantly, and a gasp escaped her lips. Her head drooped, and she was clinging to the sweeper as if she might otherwise fall. "Oh! Oh!" she cried softly, almost desperately.

Her hands dropped away and she sagged back on her heels once more. She remained like that for a long time, her breathing ragged and shallow, her face bloodless, her body limp. Ahren, though wanting to go to her, stayed where he was, obeying her instructions. The tunnel was still as a tomb, its silence a voiceless echo racing up and down the corridors through the dim pools of yellow light. Filled with dread, the Elven Prince waited. He felt young and stupid and vulnerable all over again, as if exposed by the seer's visions, as if laid open without ever having been touched.

Then, crablike, Ryer Ord Star backed slowly away from the sweeper, her head bent and her body slumped. "Ahren?" she whispered brokenly.

He reached for her, taking her in his arms. She melted against him, and he held her close and gave her what strength he had to lend. Within her robes, she was shaking and cold. He touched her face, and he could feel the dampness leaking from her eyes. "It's all right," he reassured her, not knowing what else to say.

She shook her head instantly in denial. "Ahren," she said so quietly that he could barely hear her words. Her face lifted so that her lips were pressed against his ear. "You were right," she whispered. "We've been tricked. It's a trap."

He went still, terror-stricken. He started to say something in response, but kept himself in check. He had enough presence of mind to remember that the sweeper could hear and translate what they said.

"Antrax plans for you to replace your uncle," she mur-
mured, her hands clutching him. "You've been kept alive and
brought here to serve as he did." Her words were tiny bits of
glass, cutting at his heart. "The sweeper is a tool. It was sent
to lure you to the same room in which Kael Elessedil was imprisoned for all those years. It used me to persuade you. And
I . . ."

She couldn't finish, and he pressed her closer still, hanging
on to her as much as giving her something to cling to in turn.
Are you sure? he wanted to ask. But that was a foolish question. Her power at reading the fates was already proved several times over, and there was no reason to doubt her here.
Especially since he had been uneasy about what they were
doing from the start. His eyes shifted up and down the corridor. Still empty, still deserted. Whatever fate awaited them,
they hadn't crossed its path yet, although they were clearly on
their way to doing so if they didn't act quickly.

But what were they to do? They were deep underground,
hopelessly lost, their companion and would-be guide a creature in the enemy's service. Antrax would have tracked them
the whole way, watching their progress, orchestrating their
passage. It would be watching them now. Whatever they did,
wherever they went, it would see. Antrax would not let them
walk away from what it intended for them. It would not allow
its plan to replace Kael Elessedil to be thwarted. Ahren's
heart was pounding.

The seer's words came back to him in a rush, and he closed
his eyes against the pain they induced in him. Antrax had kept
him alive, she had said. His escape, while all the others with
him were fighting and dying, had been arranged. It was not by
chance or good fortune that he had not been harmed. Perhaps
Antrax saw him as weak and malleable, a coward through and

through. Perhaps it knew how easily Ahren could be manipulated without any use of force. That way he would stay undamaged and whole, better able to serve as Antrax wished, perhaps for fifty years instead of the thirty Kael Elessedil had endured.

It all made sense to him. Walker had told them that whatever had lured them to Castledown wanted their magic. It had never occurred to Ahren that in order to secure that magic, it might require a summoner, as well. Hence the fate of Kael Elessedil. Hence, perhaps, his own.

Tears filled his eyes and ran down his face. He hated himself. He hated what had been done to him. He hated everything about Castledown. But he hated Antrax most of all. He wanted to scream his rage into the silence and watch it explode in shards of razor-sharp fury that would smash the sweeper, that would put an end to at least some small part of the monster that had inhabited this loathsome place. He ran his hand along the back of Ryer Ord Star's silken head, gently, comfortingly. He went still inside, and all of his rage drained away like blood out of a dead man. They were going to die down there, both of them. They had come too far, gone too deep to get out. Perhaps if he had possession of the Elfstones, they might stand a chance. But the Elfstones hadn't done Kael Elessedil much good. Another magic, a stronger one, might make a difference. But he hadn't any other magic to call upon, nothing he could—

Then he remembered the phoenix stone. In the crush of events, he had forgotten it completely. It hung where he had placed it, on its chain about his neck, tucked within his tunic—Bek Rowe's magic, given to him by the King of the Silver River on his journey to Arborlon, given in turn by Bek to Ahren. He tried to remember what Bek had told him about the stone, struggled to recall the words of the King of the Silver River.

When you are most lost, it will help you find your way. With your heart as well as your eyes. Back from dark places into which you have strayed and through dark places into which you must go.

He closed his eyes. He could not be more lost than he already was. He could not find himself in any darker place. He was sick in heart and mind, and he was trapped in every way imaginable. If ever there was a time when he needed the magic of the stone, it had arrived. Would the magic work for him? He didn't know, but there was nothing else left to try. He had not thought he would ever use the stone. He had thought he would keep it safe for Bek and return it to him when they met again. But he didn't think that they would ever see each other again if he did not use the phoenix stone and find a way clear of the labyrinth.

He looked past Ryer Ord Star to the sweeper where it waited in the center of the corridor. If they followed it, things would continue as before. If they broke away from it, Antrax was certain to employ other measures to assure their compliance. There was no reason to wait any longer on what he must do.

He moved the young seer back from him, easing her gently away by placing his hands on her shoulders. "Ryer," he said softly. Her tear-streaked eyes lifted to meet his. "Listen to me." He kept his voice at a whisper that would not carry beyond the two of them. "We're not going any farther. Not with this sweeper. We're finished with that. I have something that I think will help us escape, something Bek gave me when we left the ship. It is a magic given him by the King of the Silver River. If it works, perhaps we will find our way to Walker or,

if not to Walker, at least back through these tunnels and outside again. Are you willing to try?"

She nodded at once, her lips compressed, her gaze steady.
He waited a moment to be certain of her; then shielding his
movements from the sweeper, he reached into his tunic and
pulled out the phoenix stone. He glanced down at its silvery
surface, a glimmer of liquid light in his hand, then slipped it
free of its chain.

You can use it only once, Bek had recalled. *Only once, for
casting it to the earth to release its magic will shatter it.*
Ahren looked at Ryer Ord Star, feeling for the first time in
days that he was doing something right.

"Take my hand," he said.

She did so, her eyes never leaving his. Then he took a deep
breath, pulled her to her feet so that they were both standing,
and cast the phoenix stone to the passage floor.

SIXTEEN

The instant the phoenix stone struck the floor and shattered, Ahren Elessedil and Ryer Ord Star were enveloped in a haze the color of old ashes. It swirled around them, a mix of tiny particles and smoky light, as though stirred by an unseen hand like soup in a cauldron. It clung to them in a cloud and never spread much farther than where they stood. Beyond its perimeter, the passageways of Castledown remained unchanged.

For a moment, the Elven Prince and the seer stayed where they were, uncertain, waiting to see what would happen. The little sweeper was staring right at them as if nothing had changed, insides whirring, lights blinking, motionless in the center of the corridor. Then it began to wheel right and left, its movements quickly growing more frantic. It appeared to be searching for them, as if it didn't realize they were still right in front of it. Ahren pulled Ryer several steps to his left, testing whether or not the sweeper could see them. It did not turn toward them or register their movement in any way. It simply wheeled about aimlessly, trying to decide what to do.

Then an odd thing happened to Ahren. Within the mist of the phoenix stone, he felt an oddly compelling need to keep moving, to continue on without stopping. It was a sort of tugging in his chest, an unexpressed certainty about what he must do. He had never felt anything like it before. He glanced at Ryer and found her looking back at him. Without speaking, he gestured ahead, indicating what he wished. She nodded quickly. When he touched his chest, she did the same. She felt it, too. It was the magic of the phoenix stone at work. To find a way back after being lost, you must know where it is that you want to go. Unexpectedly, surprisingly, Ahren Elessedil did.

He moved a bit farther down the corridor, away from the hapless sweeper and its efforts to figure out what had happened to them. He held tightly to Ryer, afraid that if he released her, she would lose the protection of the magic. The smoky haze moved with them, an enveloping shroud, wrapping them as they proceeded, never changing its size or shape or perimeter. It was like being in an invisible bubble, shut away from the rest of the world, enclosed in an atmosphere and given over to a life that was denied to everyone but them.

Ahren was just wondering if Antrax knew what was happening to his carefully laid plans when the corridor ahead abruptly filled with creepers.

He stopped where he was, pulling Ryer against him protectively, watching as the metal crawlers slipped from openings in the walls like ghosts, metal limbs clutching knives and pincers and strange-looking cylinders. In a careful sweep, they came up the passageway, fanning out to both sides. Ahren's throat tightened. There was no way past them. They were too many to avoid.

When he glanced hurriedly in the opposite direction, he found the other end of the corridor blocked, as well.

For a moment, he panicked; there was nowhere to run, no way to get clear. The jaws of the trap were closing, and he and

Ryer were caught right in the middle. He stood his ground because there was nothing else to do, still holding to the seer with one hand while he drew free his long knife, his only weapon, with the other. *I won't run this time,* he told himself. He would stand and fight, even if the struggle was hopeless. Maybe Ryer could break past in the ensuing struggle. Maybe at least one of them could . . .

He never finished the thought. As the closest of the creepers reached them, the enshrouding mist went completely opaque, and its quiet swirling turned into a whirlwind. He ducked his head against the sudden movement, feeling Ryer press close. He blinked in an effort to see what was happening, but everything beyond their concealment had disappeared. Beyond the rush of the enshrouding haze, there was only blackness.

Then the mist cleared enough to see beyond its perimeter again. They were past the creepers and in the clear once more.

Ahren didn't question the magic of the phoenix stone any further; he simply accepted it for the gift it was. He believed it would protect them from everything so long as it lasted. Moving quickly, almost at a trot, he pulled Ryer after him down the passageway, leaving the creepers behind. Antrax would have to find another way to trap them.

During the course of their flight, it tried to do exactly that.

First it sent more creepers, squads of them, as if there were an inexhaustible supply to call upon. They flooded the corridors ahead and behind, some advancing in search, some standing watch at every turn. They began to use the odd-looking cylinders now, weapons that emitted bursts of the deadly fire threads, cast here and there at random, seeking them out. Time and again, the creepers closed on Ahren and Ryer, and it seemed there could be no escape. But each time, the smoke darkened and swirled, and when it cleared enough to see again, they were safely past their hunters.

When it became obvious that the creepers and their hand-held weapons weren't getting the job done, fire threads appeared out of the walls, crisscrossing the corridors, oscillating like deadly spiderwebbing caught in a wind. But the magic of the phoenix stone was able to bypass the threads as easily as it had the creepers, cloaking and protecting the Elven Prince and the girl.

Then metal doors began to close, sealing off passageways a few at a time. It was a random effort at best, because it hampered the hunters as well as the hunted. At first it didn't affect Ahren and Ryer at all because the sealed passageways were ones through which they had come or down which they were not impelled to go. But eventually the closings caught up with them, and a door closed directly in their path. Immediately, Ahren knew to change direction, to go another way. He obeyed the impulse, without understanding why, backtracking up that corridor and turning down a new one.

Once, they were forced to wait in front of a sealed door until it opened. Ahren had no idea how long that took. All sense of time slipped away from him within the mist, as if it no longer had meaning or relevance in his life. The magic of the phoenix stone had re-created his world, and while he was in its thrall, nothing of the temporal world would much affect him.

Eventually the creepers, fire threads, and closing doors ceased to be more than a sporadic occurrence. Finally, they disappeared completely. They were all alone in a passageway far from where they had started, and Ahren paused to look out through the swirling mist of their enclosure. He felt drained, empty. He felt worn.

"It worked," he said softly.

Her slender hands tightened on his in acknowledgment. "You made it work," she whispered.

He shook his head. "I took a chance. The magic wasn't even mine to use. It belonged to Bek. It was given to him."

"It was given to you by Bek!" Her voice was angry. "Stop belittling yourself, Ahren! Before, when I asked you to come with me into Castledown to find Walker, you said you didn't think you could protect me. But you have, haven't you? It doesn't matter how you did it—only that you did."

She paused to study him. "It took courage to do what you did back there. To use the phoenix stone without knowing what it would do, then to lead us through the creepers and fire threads. It took courage to come with me at all. Why are you so quick to dismiss that?"

He shook his head. "I'm not brave. I'm anything but. I just did the only thing I could think to do to help us escape." She was staring at him as if he were transparent. He felt exposed and vulnerable. He didn't like the idea of her thinking of him as something he knew he wasn't.

She pulled him against one of the walls and leaned into him, still holding tightly to his hands. "Tell me what's bothering you," she said quietly. She fixed him with her violet eyes. "It's all right."

Strangely enough, he felt it was. Not only right, but necessary. He wanted to tell her what he was hiding about himself, to confide in her the truth of his cowardice, to open himself and let out the terrible hurt he was carrying, to rid himself of its burden. There, deep underground, shut away with her by the magic of the phoenix stone, he felt he could.

He forced himself to meet her intense gaze as he spoke. "When we went into the ruins and were attacked, I panicked," he said. "While the others stood and fought, I ran. I threw down my sword, and I ran." He swallowed against the bitterness of his words. "I didn't want to, but I couldn't help myself. All I could think about was saving my life, finding a way to stay alive. Joad Rish was bending down to help one of the Elven Hunters, one of Ard Patrinell's men, and I saw him cut apart by fire threads, his head—"

He choked on the words and had to stop. Ryer's free hand touched his cheek. "Don't you think they all felt as you did, Ahren?" she asked him. "Don't you think they all did whatever they could to stay alive? The Elven Hunters fought back because that's what they knew to do, not because of a code of conduct or a special kind of courage. Joad Rish tried to heal an injured man because that was what he could do. You ran, Ahren, because staying with the others would have gotten you killed and you didn't want that. You did what you could."

"Except that your vision showed that Antrax let me live, that I was kept alive on purpose!" he said bitterly.

Her smile was warm and gently remonstrative. "You didn't know that then, did you? What we do in any situation is based on what we know. I ran to Walker's aid in the maze. I didn't think about it, I didn't stop to reason it out, I didn't consider what I was doing. I reacted in the only way I knew to react. That's all we can do."

"At least you ran in the right direction."

"Did I?" she asked softly.

There was such sadness in her voice, such pain, that it stopped him momentarily. He stared at her, confused. She was telling him something important, but he didn't know what it was.

"Let go of my hands," she told him.

"But if the magic—"

"I know." She stopped him with the fingers of one hand

pressed against his lips. "But we need to know what happens if we do. There may come a time when it is necessary, when we have to fight. Let's test it now, while we're alone and safe."

He hesitated a moment, then did as she asked, releasing her other hand. Nothing changed. The magic continued to envelop them, cloaking them like forest mist in twilight, the swirling gray unchanged.

Ryer Ord Star put her hands in her lap and rocked back on her heels, facing him. "You told me your secret, Ahren. I will do the same for you. I will tell you mine. If you want to hear it."

There was a darkness to her words that frightened him, a promise of something unpleasant. "You don't have to tell me anything unless you want to."

"I know."

He waited a moment, then nodded. "All right."

She lifted her chin slightly, as if facing up to something she did not want to, a confession of truths she would just as soon avoid. The gesture was a telling one, defiant and brave. It made Ahren feel something for her that hadn't been there before. Respect, perhaps. Admiration.

"I'm not what you think I am," she began, holding his gaze. It seemed to him that she was forcing herself to look at him. "I'm not what anyone thought I was. I came on this journey for more reasons than one. When Walker came to find me, I already knew he was coming. I had been instructed to go with him when he did. My purpose was to act as seer, but not only that—not even primarily that. My purpose in coming with you was to spy for the Ilse Witch."

She waited to hear Ahren's reaction, but he was too surprised to respond.

She smiled bitterly. "You look stunned. Don't you believe

me? It's true. I was a spy for the Ilse Witch from the day Walker came to see me and for many years before. I sold myself to her long ago. It wasn't difficult at all, really. It happened like this. I was born with the sight, and I knew I had it from an early age. I could see the futures of those around me, sometimes in detail, sometimes just bits and pieces. I was an orphan raised by caregivers who took in strays like myself. They were kind to me, but they thought me strange, and indeed I was. I told no one of my gift, for I understood right from the start that to be different was to be dangerous in the eyes of many. I kept my gift a secret and tried to forget it was there. That was impossible to do, of course. It grew even worse when I discovered, quite by accident, that I was an empath, as well, and could heal physical and emotional wounds by touch. I didn't discover that gift until later, but once it was revealed, I had to leave my caregivers and find a place where no one knew me.

"I was twelve years old when I came to Grimpen Ward with a band of Rovers. They took me in because that is the way of Rovers, and they saw no harm in seeing me safely to my intended destination. They thought me strange, as well, but they left me alone. In Grimpen Ward, I sought out the Addershag. She was the reason I had gone there. Everyone knew she was the most powerful seer in the Four Lands, and I hoped that she would take me in and train me. I did not know she had never taken an apprentice. I did not appreciate the enormity of what it was I was seeking to accomplish.

"She set me straight quick enough. She turned me away without taking even a moment to consider what I was asking of her. I was devastated but I refused to give up. I stayed outside her door, waiting for her to change her mind. I stayed there for two months. Finally, she invited me to come in and sit with her. She tested me, asking me to do different things. When I finished doing what she wanted, she nodded and said I could stay. That was all. I could stay.

"For weeks, I did nothing but cook and clean and fetch for her. She treated me as a servant girl, and I was eager enough to be with her that I didn't mind. Finally, she began showing me something of my gift, a little only, then a little more. My instruction had begun. After a while, I became her assistant and confidante, as well. She was old and tough and dangerous. She was unpredictable, too. But I did well enough that I didn't feel threatened."

She took a deep breath and let it out slowly, as if releasing anguish she had kept bottled up for a long time. "I made a mistake, though. When I came to her and told her of my gift of sight, asking that she teach me to use it, I kept to myself that I was an empath. I was afraid to tell her, thinking that it might affect her decision to train me, that it did not matter if I was, so long as I kept it to myself. But in the third year of my training, I had a vision in which a little girl in the village was struck down in an accident. As was our custom, we gave the information to the parents for a fee of their choosing. We did that with everyone, not to make money, but so that we could live comfortably. No one ever complained. But our warning was not enough to save the little girl, and although she was not killed, she was injured badly enough that it seemed clear she would die.

"I asked the Addershag to let me go to her. She refused. There was nothing we could do, nothing we hadn't already done. I went anyway. I used my empathic powers and healed the little girl. I did it so that it appeared she recovered on her own, that I was only a vessel to show her the way back. But the Addershag knew better. She told me that my empathic gift would kill me one day, that an empath tracking fate in an effort to change its course would only end up throwing away her own life in the process. She said I was wasting my precious gift and her time, and I would do better on my own. She disowned me. She cast me out."

She pulled her knees to her chest and gave Ahren a wry, sad smile. "She was right. I did well enough. I was known and liked. Some mistrusted and challenged my talent, but not so many. I was visited often enough and kept busy. I was careful with use of my empathic abilities. Once or twice, I tried visiting the Addershag, but she would have nothing to do with me. Her interest lay in deciphering the future; she cared nothing for the past and hence nothing for me. I grew bitter toward her, angry that she would treat me with such disdain. But I was afraid of her, too. She was very old and her enemies all lay dead and buried. I did not care to become one of them. So I stayed out of her way.

"Then the Ilse Witch came to me, and everything changed."

She looked away from him for a moment, out into the emptiness of the passageway, into the dimly lit shadows beyond their magic-induced sanctuary, but beyond even that, he sensed, into the past.

Her eyes shifted back to his. "She showed herself to me, something it was said she never did. She was young, like me. She was an orphan, like me. She was so like me that I saw myself in her from the moment we met. She was a powerful sorceress, and I wanted her friendship and patronage. So when she proposed the bargain, I accepted. I would be her eyes and ears in Grimpen Ward and give her news of things that she should know. She, in turn, would make certain that when the

Addershag died, I would ascend to her position as principal seer in Grimpen Ward."

Her pale, ethereal features tightened. "I insisted I did not want the Addershag to come to any harm. I was assured she would not. She was old, after all, and would die soon enough. Did I question this? Did I want to see her fate? The Ilse Witch handed me a scarf. She told me to use my vision by channeling it through that piece of cloth she had stolen from the old woman. I did so, and saw her dead upon her cottage floor, eyes open and staring. The Ilse Witch took back the scarf. Now I had seen for myself. All that was required, once she died, was that I step into her shoes. Why not? I was her former apprentice, the most skilled of all seers next to her. Wasn't I her logical successor?

"I believed I was, of course, and I was still hurt from her rejection of me. So I agreed to the bargain and let events take their course. The Ilse Witch became my new mentor and friend. I began reporting by carrier bird everything I saw in the village and surrounding countryside. And I waited for the Addershag to die. It took a year, but die she did. She was bitten by a small, deadly snake that nestled in a bag of gold given to her by a patron. It was never clear who that patron was. Her lady servant was gone for a day and a night and found her dead when she returned. She buried her out back and kept the house for herself."

She sighed. "And I, I became what I had wanted to be, the new Addershag, her successor. Her followers, her patrons, all came now to me, and no one challenged me. I convinced myself that her death had nothing to do with me, that it was simply the result of a vision fulfilling itself, and that I, by not interfering, was behaving just as she had taught me. She would not have listened to me anyway, I thought. There was nothing I could have done to change things."

She shivered violently, and she hugged her knees more tightly to chase away the chill. "But there is a price for everything, and eventually I found out what it cost to follow the Addershag. The Ilse Witch came to me in response to a vision I had of Walker; I had been told to tell her everything I discovered concerning him. My vision showed him coming to me at night, a dark presence, an irresistible force who would change everything in my life. He came to me to discover what he could of a voyage he wished to make to a new land, of what he would find along the way. He induced my visions by giving me something to touch. It was a map.

"When I told the Ilse Witch of my vision, she became very excited. She wanted that map, and she said I must find a way to steal it for her. But then she changed her mind. Instead of stealing the map, I must insist on going with him. I must convince him I was indispensable so that he would take me. I was to reveal to him what I had seen in my vision and a few things more that she would tell me so that he could not refuse my request. I would be his shadow, and she would be mine. Everywhere I went, everywhere that Walker went, she would track us. She possessed a magic that gave her a way to see through my eyes. She assured me it was necessary that I do this. She insisted that Walker was our common enemy, the enemy of all those possessed of magic in the Four Lands."

She laughed without humor, without kindness. "I knew enough by then to be wary of such statements. Walker was not my enemy. He had done nothing to me or to anyone else so far as I knew. But I was in no position to refuse. When I suggested that the task was beyond me, she brushed my concerns aside and warned that it would take only a casual word dropped here or there to make the villagers of Grimpen Ward believe that it was I who had given the bag of gold with the snake in it to the Addershag. Besides, the Ilse Witch was my patron, my mentor. I was afraid of her, but I felt a kinship to her, as well. I agreed to do as she asked. I became her spy aboard the *Jerle Shannara*."

Tears filled her eyes, sudden and unexpected in the wake of her self-reproaching laughter. "But an odd thing happened, Ahren. Something neither she nor I had planned. Even before he came to see me, before I had touched the map or discovered anything more of what the voyage would require, I began to have other visions." She leaned close to him, the tears spilling down her cheeks. "They were of Walker and me. They were so strong, so overpowering, that I could not ignore them. They were of a blue ocean and of islands, a flying ship, and battles being fought and men dying. It was the voyage Walker sought to make, and I was seeing small parts of it. Most were so vague and jumbled that I could not sort them out, but one was very clear. Of those who traveled with Walker, these would be among them—one who would save his life and one who would try to take it; one who would love him unconditionally and one who would hate him with unmatched passion; one who would lead him astray and one who would bring him back again."

She paused. "I saw no faces to connect to any of these acts. Only my own, standing outside the vision, watching Walker— always very close, observing and waiting. But for what? I couldn't tell. Yet I was there each time, shadowing him."

"But now you know who these people are, who it is who will do these things to Walker," he interrupted, speaking for the first time, wanting to help her. "Now you can identify each one."

She laughed anew, and this time her laughter was so bitter and raw that he flinched from it. Her eyes turned wild, and she tossed back her hair in a defiant gesture. "Oh, yes! Yes, Ahren, I know who these people are! It is so ironic, so fitting! I knew these people from the start, but I didn't read the vision carefully enough! I was blinded by my own needs and wants and concerns! Who are all these people to Walker, who would take his life and save it, who would lead him astray and bring him back again, who would love and hate him both? Who are they, Ahren? I'll tell you. They are all the same person. They are all me!"

She seized his arms, gripping him so tightly he could feel her nails digging into his skin. "I did all those things to him and felt those ways about him! I almost caused him to die on Shatterstone by keeping from him that part of my vision that warned of poison thorns, and then I saved him with my empathic talent because I could not bear to let him die! I've loved and hated him both, sometimes without quite knowing which was which! He brought me with him when he shouldn't have, he put me in this terrible, hateful position because he trusts me, and he thinks even now that I will save him from whatever's trapped him down here! And I will, Ahren! I've led him astray so many times I've lost count! Each time, he's found his way back on his own. But this time, this one time, I will be the one to bring him back or I will die trying!"

She was crying so hard she was shaking, racked with sobs, her silvery hair a pale curtain reflecting her tears in threads of gleaming dampness. Her hands loosened their grip on his arms, and he took hold of her in turn, not wanting to break the contact.

"Now you know my secret," she whispered roughly. "It's much worse than yours, much uglier. I am consumed by it. I can't ever be forgiven for what I've done. I can't ever redeem myself."

He shook his head and bent close. "Everyone can be forgiven, Ryer Ord Star. Of anything and everything. It isn't always easy, but it is possible."

She shuddered in response. "Do you want to know something, Ahren?" Her voice was so small he could barely hear it. "When I used my empathic talent to heal Walker after he was poisoned on Shatterstone, I became linked to him in a way that has never happened before. It was as if our magics joined in some way, and I could see all the way into his soul. It was so painful! I knew that pain was there—I'd seen it in his eyes when we first met, felt it in his hands—but I didn't realize it was so vast! It overwhelmed me and by doing so, opened me up to him as he had been opened to me. He saw what was hidden inside of me; he saw everything. He knew what I was, what I had come to do. He understood the danger I presented to him and to the others."

She shook her head in wonderment. "But he kept it all to himself. He never spoke of it. He put it all aside as if it no longer mattered, and he let me stay. I think he hoped that by doing so he would make me an ally instead of an enemy. And he did. I quit doing anything of importance for the Ilse Witch. She could still track the airship's progress through me, but I guess Walker did not think that was very important. She already knew where we were going; she had read the mind of the castaway to learn what waited. What I would no longer do, what he was counting on me not to do, was to hide any truths from him, any parts of visions experienced, any secrets that might cause him injury. I was his now, willingly. I will be his always, so long as he needs me. Our connection transcends everything. It is strong enough that I feel his need for me, down here in this dark place, in these passageways and chambers, in all this metal. I can feel him reaching out to me, when there is no one else he can touch." She swallowed her tears. "It is why I go to him now. It is why I have to find him."

She broke their embrace and wiped at her eyes with both hands. Then she began to cry anew, hugging herself, rocking back and forth on her heels. "Isn't it sad that I might be all he has?" she asked, her voice breaking. "So pathetic."

He took her in his arms and held her while she cried, not trying to stop or soothe her, but just holding her. He thought several times to say something comforting or wise, but nothing he considered felt right. Silence seemed best, and so he kept it. Around them, the magic of the phoenix stone swirled like murky water, steady and somehow reassuring, an escape that gave them space and time to let their emotions settle. Ahren looked out through the haze to the corridor beyond, where it was empty and silent. It felt as if they really were alone down there, abandoned and forgotten by everyone.

Ryer stopped crying, disengaged from his arms, and looked directly at him. "Are you still coming with me?"

He nodded. He had never thought to do otherwise.

"You don't have to," she said. "I wouldn't expect you to honor your promise, not after knowing that I—"

"Stop it," he interrupted quickly, remonstratively. "Don't say any more."

She studied him a moment, then leaned forward to kiss his cheek. In the warmth and softness of her lips, he could feel a measure of his self-worth and respect return.

They rose then and continued through Castledown's endless corridors and chambers, shrouded by the magic of the phoenix stone, guided by their instincts and need. The young seer was still warring with her inner demons, but her pale, ethereal features were tight with resolve. She had taken Ahren's hand again, even though they had determined she did not need to do so. Ahren was glad. Her touch did at least as much for him as his did for her. He felt as if they were children lost in a dark forest, with night coming on and wolves all about, blindly trusting in a talisman he neither understood nor controlled. The magic of the phoenix stone was protecting them, but how much longer would it last? He did not want to be caught unprepared or short of their goal.

Or goals, he corrected himself. There was Walker on the one hand and the missing Elfstones on the other. He had not spoken of the latter to Ryer Ord Star, but once they found the Druid, he intended to search for the Stones. It might be that he was asking too much. It was possible that after locating Walker, the magic would vanish. He had no way of knowing. He could only plan for contingencies and hope and do the best he could with whatever happened.

They walked for a long time, but encountered neither creepers nor fire threads. If Antrax was hunting for them, it was doing so another way. They were descending at a steady rate now, down ramps and stairways alike, farther underground than they had gone before. It made sense to Ahren that Antrax would keep the magic it hoarded deeper down and better hidden. He thought there was a better than even chance that Walker would be there, too.

Ahead, not far away, machinery thrummed and chugged softly, a steady cadence, one that reverberated through the steel of the tunnels into his bones.

Then the corridor branched left and right into a series of

arched, doorless openings, all of them leading onto a cat-walk that overlooked a cavernous room filled with huge metal cabinets and clusters of blinking lights set into panels. Wheels spun behind smoky windows; brilliant silver disks reflected the soft light of flameless lamp tubes that ran up and down the walls and across the room's high ceiling. The hum of machinery was everywhere, punctuated by beeps and chirps and other strange sounds, all of it coming from the chamber below.

It was an eerie sight, a surreal vision of something that hadn't existed for thousands of years beyond these walls. They paused on the catwalk, looking down at the contents of the room, searching for something that made sense. Nothing they saw was familiar to either of them, but an instant later Ryer gasped sharply, spoke Walker's name, and pulled on Ahren's hand, dragging him after her toward a metal stairway leading down. He went without questioning her, already knowing what was happening. They descended the stairs and made their way through the maze of fifteen-foot-high cabinets filled with rows of spinning silver disks. At least some of the machinery they had heard from the catwalk was behind the panels. Ahren glanced up at their smooth surfaces, certain they had come out of the Old World, wondering if they contained the magic the company of the *Jerle Shannara* had come searching for. What sort of magic, he wondered, is kept in a metal shell of spinning disks and blinking lights? It was books they had come to find, but there were no books here—at least, none that he could see. Perhaps they were deeper underground, and the cabinets and their machinery served as protectors of some sort.

Then he caught sight of the creepers. Several of them were working their way down the rows of cabinets, stopping every so often to manipulate the spinning disks and blinking lights. If they saw Ahren and Ryer, they gave no indication of it. The creepers were different from the ones they had encountered before. Larger than the so-called sweepers, they were nevertheless more of that sort—tenders of Castledown rather than defenders. They were equipped with strange metal limbs that reached out in all directions, touching here and there, inserting odd-shaped digits into slots and openings, causing the sound of the machinery or the blinking of the lights to alter, changing now and again the cadence or speed of the disks.

Fascinated, Ahren slowed to take a closer look, but Ryer Ord Star was having none of that. She jerked him ahead, pulling at him anxiously. Her destination was the far end of the chamber. One of the creepers was moving the same way, somewhat ahead of them, as if anticipating what she intended. The seer shot Ahren a frantic glance over her shoulder, then broke into a run, dragging him with her. Wrapped in the protective cloud of phoenix-stone magic, they rushed after the creeper toward a series of metal doors that stood closed on dimly lit chambers that could just be distinguished through a line of tall, dark windows.

The creeper was quicker and got there first, touching a panel that caused the door to one of the chambers to slide open. Fresh light spilled through the doorway to reveal panel after panel of blinking lights and dozens of tubes that snaked inward toward the center of the room. The creeper disappeared inside, rolling soundlessly on its wheeled base.

Ahren and Ryer came up behind it in a rush, the girl still leading the way. They were through the open doorway and into the room before she stopped so suddenly that he ran into her from behind. Struggling to keep them both from falling over, he followed her gaze across the room. His breath left his body in a rush.

They had found Walker.

But maybe it would have been better if they hadn't.

SEVENTEEN

Night descended on the land like a great silken cat, its shadow darkening the woods in steadily deepening layers, stealing away the daylight with stealth and cunning. Bek sat across from his sister and watched her cut slices of cheese from a wedge and toast bread on flat rocks made hot by coals. She had already cleaned and portioned out berries on broad leaves culled from tropical plants that shouldn't grow so far north but somehow did. She worked steadily and purpose-fully and did not look up at him. She did not look at him, anyway, most of the time. She treated him very much the way Quentin treated his hunting dogs: she fed, watered, and rested him, and expected him to do what he was told and to keep up with her when she traveled. She showed just enough interest in him to let him know she was keeping watch, nothing more. The wall she had erected between them was thick and high and very sturdy.

"Go down to the steam and bring us fresh water," she said without lifting her head.

He rose, picked up the nearly empty water skin, and walked into the trees. She didn't worry about him trying to escape. He had given his word, after all. Not that he believed for a moment that his word counted for anything with her. But he was forbidden to leave her presence carrying the Sword of Shannara, and he knew she could track him easily should he choose to stray. He did not like to think about what she would do to him if he did. If he had needed further evidence of how ruthless she could be, she had provided it by telling him what she had done to Truls Rohk.

She kept it to herself for the better part of two days as they traveled back through the wooded hill country toward the ruins, brushing aside his repeated inquiries. But he pressed her stubbornly for an answer, and finally she provided one. She had left the caull in hiding to deal with the shape-shifter on his return from his failed ambush. Eventually, he would realize that she had outsmarted him and return to find Bek. She couldn't risk him then coming after her once he knew the boy was gone. He was as relentless as she was and every bit as dangerous. She respected him for that, but he would have to be eliminated. She had left the caull to finish him.

Bek was stunned, left both angry and heartsick, but there was nothing he could do about it. Maybe she had guessed wrong about the shape-shifter, and he had not come back for Bek after all. Maybe he had sensed that the caull was waiting and avoided it. But she seemed so certain that the matter was resolved, that his hopes dimmed almost immediately. He was on his own, he knew. Whatever choices he made from then forward, he would have to answer for them.

So running was out of the question. It hadn't worked the first time, and there was no reason to think it would work now. Besides, if there was any chance at all of persuading her that he really was her brother, he had to take advantage of it. He could not afford to alienate her further. Though she paid him scant attention, she let him talk, and he used every opportunity she gave him to try to convince her of who he was.

Mostly, she ignored him, but now and again she would reply to his arguments, and even those small responses, those cryptic remarks, provided evidence that she was listening to what he was telling her. She might not believe him, but at least she was considering his words.

He filled the water skin, kneeling by the stream, looking out into the darkness. Nevertheless, time was running out. They were only a day away from their destination. Once back, she intended to give him over to the Mwellrets while she set out again in search of Walker. The rets would place him aboard *Black Moclips* and hold him prisoner until she returned. That would be the end of any chance to argue his cause and, maybe, the end of any chance to save Walker's life.

The water skin ballooned out, and he sealed it, then stood up. Walker could take care of himself, of course—if he was still alive and able to do so, which was by no means certain. But the Ilse Witch was a formidable enemy; she had proved that already. Bek didn't know if Walker was a match for her because he wasn't sure that the Druid could be as ruthless as she was, and in order to survive, he would have to be.

He walked back through the trees to the little campsite and handed the water skin to his sister. She took it without looking at him and sprinkled the berries with droplets of water. He stood looking at her for a moment, then sat down again. After they ate, they would bathe, he first, she later. They did that every night, using whatever water was at hand, washing themselves as best they could. There were no fresh clothes to change into, but at least they could keep their bodies clean. It was warm enough even at night to wash in the rivers and streams—in winter, in a land farther north than any part of the one he had come from. Bek wondered anew at the strangeness of such a thing, remembering Walker's own comment on it.

Grianne passed him a slice of bread covered with crushed berries reduced to a sugary spread, and he chewed on it thoughtfully, eyes on her face. She was still testy from his efforts at breaking down her disbelief earlier in the day. In fact, she had told him not to speak of it again. But he could not stay silent when there was so much at stake. Nor could he afford to wait until she was more receptive.

When she made the mistake of glancing over at him, he spoke at once.

"You're not thinking clearly," he said. "If you were, you would see all the flaws in your reasoning. You would see the gaps of logic in what you've been told."

She stared at him without expression and chewed slowly.

"If I'm not Bek, how come I have the same name? You say I was mind-altered to believe that 'Bek' was my real name. But Quentin has known me all of my life. So have my adoptive father and mother. I've been Bek since I was brought to them. Are they mind-altered, as well? Is everyone in Leah mind-altered to believe I'm someone I'm not?"

She made no response, other than to lift a slice of cheese to her mouth and take a bite.

"Or is Walker so clever that he's been planning all this since he brought me to Coran and Liria fifteen years ago?"

She stared at him, an insect regarding a leaf.

"That's what you believe, isn't it? You think he's been planning this charade all these years, just to trick you. But you can't tell me why he would do this, can you?"

She lifted the water skin to her lips and drank from it, then handed it over so that he could do the same. Her eyes were as flat and dead as those of a snake.

"Oh, that's right, he wants to break you down, to undermine your resolve, to get past your guard. That way he can subvert you, can turn you to his own uses, whatever they might be. He can steal your magic and make you his puppet. Just like he's done with me, only you're the bigger catch, because your magic is so much stronger than mine and you're a bigger threat to him." He let the sarcasm slide through his words like oil. "Shades, isn't it is a good thing you were smart enough to see this coming?"

She reached for the water skin and took it back from him. "I thought I told you not to speak of this again."

He shrugged. "You did." He finished off his bread and took a slice of the cheese. "But I can't help myself. I have to understand why you don't see the truth. Nothing you believe makes any sense at all." He paused. "What about the reason the Morgawr gave you for why Walker tried to steal you away in the first place? What about that? He said it was because Walker wanted you to become a Druid like he was, but our parents refused. They wouldn't allow it, wouldn't consider it, so he killed them and stole you away. Wasn't that a little clumsy, when there were so many more subtle ways to win you over? Why would he be stupid enough to let you witness the killing of our parents while snatching you away? Couldn't he have just mind-altered you instead? Wouldn't that have been a whole lot easier? He's clever enough, isn't he? His magic can make you believe anything. That's how he got to me."

Her eyes were locked on his. "You are not me. You are weak and stupid. You are a pawn, and you do not understand anything."

She spoke without rancor or irritation. Her words were cold and lifeless, and they mirrored the pale, hard cast of her young face as she finished her bread and cheese without shifting her gaze from his, looking so deeply into his eyes that he thought she must see everything that was hidden there.

He shook off the chill her gaze made him feel. "What I understand," he said quietly, "is that you've become the very thing you were so intent on avoiding."

She shook her head quickly. "I am not a Druid," she said. "Don't call me that."

"You're as good as. The same as, really." He leaned forward in challenge. "Explain to me how you differ from Walker. Tell me what he has done in his life that you have not done in yours. Show me where the road you have traveled branches from his."

She regarded him silently, but her eyes were angry now. "You seem intent on provoking me."

"Do I? Let me tell you a story, Grianne. While I was on my way to Arborlon, I traveled with Quentin through the Silver River country. While I slept, I had a vision. The vision was of a young girl who appeared to me, then transformed into a monster, a thing so hideous I could barely manage to look upon it. That young girl was you at six years of age and the thing you transformed into seemed very like the Mwellrets you command. I believe in visions, in portents of things to come, in foreshadowings of the future. That was one. I was being shown your past and your future. I was being told that it was up to me to change your destiny, to prevent that transformation from happening."

"You take a lot on yourself then. You presume more than you should."

He shook his head. "Do I? I didn't go looking for this. I didn't even understand what I was being shown. Not until I learned who I was. Not until I found you. But I think now that if I don't find a way to convince you of the truth, no one else will, and that vision will come to pass."

"I have nothing in common with Mwellrets or Druids," she sneered. "You are a boy with a too vivid imagination and no brains. You trust blindly in the wrong people and assume your truths should be mine, when they are nothing but deceptions. I am tired of listening to you. Don't say anything more to me. Not a word."

"I will say what I like!" he snapped back at her. Inside, he was shaking. She could be volatile, dangerous, but caution no longer served a purpose. "You are surrounded by obsequious followers and liars of all sorts. You have separated yourself from the truth for so long that you wouldn't recognize it if it jumped up in front of you. Why don't you admit that you're not sure about me? Why don't you at least confess that?"

Her face darkened. "Keep still."

"Let me go with you to find Walker. Let him help you. What can it hurt to talk with him? Just listen to what he has to say. If you would take five minutes to think—"

"Enough!" she screamed.

He leapt to his feet. "Enough of what? The truth? I'm your brother, Grianne! I'm Bek! Stop trying to deny it! Stop twisting everything around!"

She was on her feet, as well, rigid with fury. He knew he should stop, but he couldn't. "Do you want me to tell you what really happened to our parents? Do you want me to tell you what's been done to you? Do you want me to speak the words out loud, so that you can hear how they sound? You're so blind you can't—"

She screamed again, only this time there were no words, only sound that rent the air like razors. The wishsong's magic seared his throat, twisting and tightening until he was gasping for air. He threw up his hands in a belated effort to protect himself as he stumbled backwards and fell. The unexpected force and suddenness of her attack left him dazed and crumpled on the ground, his eyes tearing, his breath coming in deep, rasping gulps.

She loomed over him, robes drawn close, her pale face twisted with disgust. Then her hand reached down to touch his neck and everything went black.

When he was asleep and breathing normally again, she straightened his arms and legs and covered him with his tattered cloak. Such a fool. She had warned him not to say anything more, but he had continued to press her. She had reacted almost without thinking, losing control of herself and lashing out in anger. She felt vaguely ashamed for doing so. It didn't matter what the provocation was; she should have been able to keep the magic in check. She should have been able to avoid attacking him that way. She easily might have killed him. It wouldn't have taken all that much to do so. The power of the wishsong was immense. Should she choose it, she could use her magic to wither one of the huge old oaks that sheltered their camp, to shred it to pulp and bark and sap, to reduce it to the earth from which it had grown. How much less difficult it would be to do the same with this boy.

"I warned you," she hissed at his sleeping form, still inwardly seething at herself.

She straightened and walked away, stopping at the edge of the clearing and peering off into the dark. She brushed back the long dark hair from her face and folded her arms into her robes. Perhaps it was just as well that she had reacted as she did. What she had done now was what she had intended to do anyway once they reached the bay where *Black Moclips* lay at anchor—to take away his voice and render him harmless. She could not afford to leave him with the Mwellrets otherwise. She would take his sword, as well, the blade he claimed was the Sword of Shannara. He would be locked in the hold and kept there until she finished her business with the Druid.

She glanced over her shoulder to where he lay sleeping, then quickly away again. She had meant to tell him what she was going to do before she did it, to reassure him that it was temporary, a few days and no more. She had meant to tell him she would restore his voice when she saw him again, that she would negate the magic that held it bound. She would still tell him tomorrow when he woke, but the effect would be different from what she had planned.

It irritated her that she felt the need to justify herself to him. It wasn't as if she owed him anything, as if he mattered to her in even the slightest way. But try as she might, she could not dismiss him as nothing more than a boy the Druid had somehow subverted to use against her. She knew that such an explanation was too simplistic. He was more than that; his magic was real. He was perhaps as strong-minded as she was, and there was at least some truth to what he was saying. She wouldn't admit it to him, but she could sense it. Her problem was in deciding how much. Where did the lies end and the truth begin? What was the Druid trying to accomplish by sending him to her? For he had sent the boy, however they might have found each other. He had sent the boy as surely as she had sent Ryer Ord Star to spy on him.

Was it possible he really was Bek?

She stopped breathing momentarily, the thought suspended before her like an exotic creature. Was it possible after all? He could still be Bek and be lying about their parents. He could still be an unwitting dupe. He could be mistaken without realizing it.

But how had the Druid found him, when she had thought him dead? How had the Druid known who he was? Had the Druid gone back into the rubble and searched him out? Had the Druid decided to make use of Bek in his schemes because he had lost the use of her?

Her lips tightened. Everyone was used in this life. She thought about the Morgawr, her mentor all these years, her teacher in the fine art of magic's use. She knew enough of him, of what he was, to know that he could not be trusted, to accept that he was every bit as devious as the Druid. She knew he had used her. She knew he kept things from her that he believed enabled him to maintain his hold over her. It was just the way of things. She manipulated and deceived, too. The boy was right about that. She was not so different from the Morgawr, and the Morgawr was very like the Druid.

But would the Morgawr have lied to her about her parents? How could she have such strong memories of the Druid and his dark-cloaked servants descending on her home that final dawn if he had? That didn't feel right to her. It didn't seem possible. The Druid had wanted her to come with him to Paranor. She remembered his visits to her father, his conversations and dark warnings. No, he had orphaned her and stolen her away as she believed.

Yet the boy who thought himself her brother was right. She had ended up a Druid anyway, in another place, in another form. She could not say she was any different from Walker, any better or worse. She could not point to where their lives were that much different. In escaping him, she had allowed the Morgawr to turn her into a mirror image of her enemy. Her use of magic and her efforts at accumulating power were very much the same as his. If he had done bad things in their pursuit, so had she.

Thinking about all of that, accepting the truth of it, made her even angrier with herself. But there was no place for anger in her efforts to accomplish the tasks that she had undertaken. She must find the magic concealed in Castledown, gain possession of it, and return to her ship. She must decide what to do with the boy and his unsettling accusations. She must settle matters once and for all with both the Druid and the Morgawr.

She never once doubted that she was capable of all that or that she could carry out her plans in the manner she intended.

But, like it or not, she was beginning to question her reasoning for doing so.

Miles to the east and south, well clear of the inlet opening into the Squirm and its ice fields and beyond the cliffs that warded the eastern approach from the Blue Divide, the *Jerle Shannara* lay at anchor. She was berthed in a forested cove nestled among a dozen others in lowlands miles from where she had deposited Walker and those others who had gone ashore in search of Castledown. The *Jerle Shannara* was sheltered from the wintry weather that swept the coast, concealed from prying eyes while she underwent repairs.

Seated on a bench at the ship's stern and facing out toward the cove's narrow opening, Rue Meridian could only just glimpse the distant waters of the Blue Divide. She wore loose-fitting trousers and tunic, red-orange scarves wrapped about her throat and forehead, and soft, worn ankle boots. A blanket warded her against the chill. Restless and bored, she scuffed one boot across the decking and pondered her dissatisfaction for the hundredth time. It was almost a week since Big Red had brought the airship overland after its near catastrophic encounter with the Squirm, charting a course back to the coast that avoided glaciers and mountains and obscuring mist. A longer, more circuitous route than the one that led through the Squirm and up the river channel, it was by far the safer. Regaining the coast, the Rovers cruised in search of the Wing Riders, whom they quickly found and who in turn led to the sheltering bay. Since then, Rovers and Wing Riders had been engaged in repairing the damaged vessel while Rue had lain belowdecks, healing from her wounds and sleeping undisturbed.

Endless processes both, she fumed to herself in silence. She glanced down at her leg, where she had incurred the deepest and most serious injury in her battle with the Mwellrets. Stitches and poultices had begun to heal it nicely, but the wound wasn't closed entirely and she still couldn't walk without pain. The knife wound to her arm had healed more quickly, and the claw marks on her back and sides were little more than the beginnings of scars she would never lose. She guessed that meant she was two for three, but the leg wound kept her from doing much and the inactivity was beginning to grate on her.

It would have helped if the repairs to the ship had gone more quickly and they were sailing back the way they had come in search of their abandoned friends and shipmates. But the damage to the *Jerle Shannara* had been more extensive than anyone had realized at first glance. It was not just the shattered spars and shredded light sheaths and cracked mainmast that had crippled the ship. Two of the parse tubes together with their diapson crystals had been torn free and lost overboard. A dozen radian draws were frayed beyond repair. The nature of the damage precluded simple replacement; it required reworking the entire system that allowed the ship to fly. Spanner Frew was equal to the task, but it was taking too much time.

She watched the burly shipwright bent over the left fore hooding, directing the set of the existing tube and crystal, realigning the left midship draw that now ran to that emplacement, as well. It was the second of three that were involved in the realignment. No one knew how well the new configuration would work, so that meant testing it out before they ventured inland and risked a further encounter with *Black Moclips* and the Ilse Witch.

Every time she thought of the witch, she was consumed by a white-hot anger. It wasn't the damage to the ship or the imprisonment of the Rovers that fueled it. It wasn't even the unavoidable loss of contact with Walker's company. It was the death of Furl Hawken for which she most blamed the witch, because if not for the witch's seizure of the *Jerle Shannara* and her imprisonment of the Rover crew, it would never have happened.

Somehow, someway, she had promised herself, the Ilse Witch would be made to pay for Hawk's death. It was something she had vowed while she lay belowdecks, still too weak even to sit up, unable to stop thinking about what she had witnessed. There would be a reckoning for Hawk, and Little Red wanted to be the one to bring it about.

The day was dragging on toward midafternoon, the sky a mass of thick gray clouds, the sun screened away, the air raw with cold. At least they were sufficiently sheltered by the landfall to be protected from the bitter wind and sleet blowing with such ferocity along the coast. She marveled at the oddness of the weather there, so different on the coast than inland, so unexplainably in contrast. Only Shrikes and gulls and the like could make homes in the cliffs of the coastal waters. Humans could never live here in any comfort. She wondered if humans lived inland. She wondered if there were humans anywhere at all.

"Afternoon," a voice growled, snapping her out of her reverie.

She turned to find Hunter Predd standing a few feet away, his wiry frame wrapped in a heavy cloak, his weathered features ruddy and bemused. She smiled ruefully. "Sorry. I was somewhere else. Good afternoon to you."

He moved a step closer, looking out toward the ocean. "There's a big storm coming on, a bad one. Saw it building out there while flying in with the last of the hemp and reed. It might lock us down for a few days."

"We're locked down anyway until the ship can fly again. What's it looking like now, two or three more days at least before we can get under way again?"

"At least."

"Are you foraging for materials still?"

He shook his head and ran one gnarled hand through his windblown hair. "No, we're done. It's up to Black Beard and the others to make it all work now."

She gestured him over. "Sit down. Talk with me. I'm sick of talking with myself."

She made room for him on the bench, swinging her legs off and placing her feet carefully on the decking. She winced in spite of herself at the pain the effort brought on.

The sharp eyes darted toward her. "Still a little tender, I guess."

"Do all Wing Riders possess such acute powers of observation?"

He chuckled softly. "Feelings seem a little tender, too."

She didn't say anything for a moment, looking down at her

legs, her boots, the decking. Time passed. She felt a great void in her heart, a place opening up where opportunity slipped away while she sat doing nothing.

She lifted her eyes to meet his. "How long has it been since we left them? More than a week anyway, isn't it? Too long, Wing Rider. Way too long."

He nodded, his brow furrowing. He started to say something, then stopped, as if deciding that anything he had to say was unnecessary. He clasped his hands about one knee and rocked back slightly in his cloak, grizzled head shaking.

"You can't favor this delay any more than I do," she said. "You must want to do something about it, too."

He nodded. "I've been considering it."

"If we could just find out if they are all right, if they would be safe enough until the ship could reach them . . ."

She didn't finish, waiting on him to do so for her. He looked off into the distance instead, as if trying to spy them through the mist and cold. Then he nodded once more. "I could take a look for them. I could leave now, in fact. Should leave now, because once the storm comes in, it won't be so easy to fly out."

She leaned forward eagerly, red hair fanning out about her shoulders. "I have the coordinates Big Red mapped out from our journey in. We won't have any trouble following them back."

He looked at her in surprise. "We?"

"I'm going with you."

He shook his head. "Your brother won't let you go and you know it. He'll put a stop to it before you finish telling him what you intend."

She gave it a moment, then reached up with one finger and touched her temple. "Think about what you just said, Hunter

Predd," she advised softly. "When was the last time my brother told me what to do, would you guess?"

He smiled in rueful understanding. "Well, he won't like it, anyway."

She smiled back. "It won't be the first time he's had to deal with this sort of disappointment. Nor the last, I'd wager."

"You and me?" he asked, arching one eyebrow.

"You and me."

"I won't ask if you're up to it."

"Best not."

"I won't ask what you intend once we get there either, even though I'd be willing to bet it goes beyond a quick flyover."

She nodded without answering.

He sighed deeply. "It will feel good to be back in the air, good to be doing what we were trained to do, Obsidian and me." He rubbed his callused hands together. "We'll leave Po Kelles and Niciannon to run whatever errands your brother and the others need until they catch up to us. Maybe our leaving will inspire them to work faster on the repairs."

"Maybe. My brother hates to miss out on anything. Going inland for a look around was his idea in the first place."

"And now you've stolen it." He shook his head, smiled ruefully. "How soon can you be ready?"

She rose gingerly and unwrapped herself from the blanket. Underneath, throwing knives were strapped in place about her waist.

She cocked an eyebrow at him. "How soon can you saddle your bird?"

EIGHTEEN

They flew west off the coast and inland aboard Obsidian, settled comfortably upon the riding harness strapped to the Roc's feathered back, Hunter Predd at the reins and Rue Meridian seated just behind him. The Rover wore her flying leathers, black like her brother's and molded to her body from constant use. Beneath, her wounds were carefully bound and padded, and the leathers served as light armor to protect them from the rougher abuses she might suffer on her journey. For weapons, she bore a brace of throwing knives about her waist, another tucked into her boot, a long knife strapped to her good thigh, and bow and arrows slung across her back. A great cloak and hood wrapped her against the cold and wind, but even so she found herself ducking her chin and hunching her shoulders to stay warm.

That her brother was angry at her decision to make this journey was the understatement of the year. He was so furious, so stunned by what he considered her obvious stupidity and immeasurably poor judgment, that he ended up shouting at her loud enough to bring work on the airship to a halt until he was finished. No one else said a word, not even Spanner Frew. No one else wanted any part of the argument. Big Red was speaking for them all—loudly enough for all of their voices combined, come to that—and there was nothing further to be said or done. She listened patiently for a few minutes, then began shouting back at him, and eventually threw up her hands and limped away, screaming back one final time to suggest that if he was so worried about her, maybe he'd better hurry along his repair efforts and follow.

It wasn't fair to chide him so, but she was beyond caring about what was fair and reasonable. What she cared about—the only thing she cared about by then—was that sixteen men and women were trapped inland in strange and dangerous territory with no realistic hope of finding their way out and a madwoman and her reptilian servants hunting for them. She had no idea what might have happened to them, but she didn't like to think about the possibilities. She wanted reassurance that her worst fears had not been realized. She wanted evidence of their safety. Time was an enemy, swift and elusive. There was risk in what she was doing, but it was a risk worth taking when measured against the consequences of further inaction. Hunter Predd said nothing during the argument or afterwards, but she knew he agreed with her decision. Wing Riders were made cautious by training and from experience, but they knew when it was time to act.

It was late afternoon when they departed, and they flew until the night enveloped them. The blue-gray line of the ocean and clouds was left behind, along with the freezing cold of the coastal air. The inland darkness was warm and soft, a welcome change. The land stretched away before them, an unbroken rippling of green treetops and dark ridgelines dotted with lakes and laced with rivers, hemmed away behind the coastal cliffs and mountain peaks. Far distant, caught in a patch of fading sunlight, an ice field's glimmer was hard and bright against the enfolding dark.

Hunter Predd turned Obsidian downward to find a camp-site. After several minutes of searching, they landed in a clearing atop a broad wooded rise that gave Obsidian several choices of perch and routes of escape and his riders a good view of the surrounding countryside. It wasn't that they ex-pected trouble, just that they knew enough to be ready for it. It was a country about which they knew virtually nothing. There could be things there that would kill, things that they had never encountered before. Even if they avoided whatever it was that warded Castledown, there would be other dangers.

While Hunter Predd unsaddled Obsidian, groomed his feathers, and watered and fed him, Rue Meridian set about preparing their meal. They had agreed to forgo a fire, to avoid attracting unwanted attention, so she settled for cold cheese, bread, and dried fruit from the stores she had brought from the ship. When Hunter Predd joined her, she brought out an aleskin and shared it with him between bites. They ate their meal in silence, watching the darkness deepen and the stars appear. Light from the full moon rising in the north was bril-liant and cleansing, and the land took on a fresh white cast amid the shadows. Atop the rise, the woods were silent. Within the trees, nothing moved.

"How long will it take us to get to where we're going?" the Wing Rider asked when they were finished eating. He sipped from the aleskin and handed it over to her. "Your best guess will do. I just need some idea of how to pace my bird."

She drank, as well, and put the container down. "I think we can get there by late tomorrow if we leave at sunrise and push through the day. It took longer coming out, but we were feel-ing our way and nursing our wounds, so it went more slowly. We'd lost half our power and much of our steering. Your Roc will fly faster than we did."

"Then we take a look around and see who's there?"

She shrugged. "When I was a girl and we played hide-and-seek, I learned that the best way to find someone was not to look too hard. I learned that instincts are necessary, that you have to trust them. We can have a look at the bay where the *Jerle Shannara* put Walker and the others ashore. We can fly inland until we sight Castledown. But I don't think we can be certain that what we're looking for is at either place."

"Or even aboveground."

She gave him a sharp look.

"What I mean is that the Druid told us the safehold was belowground. That's all."

She nodded. "We'll have to look sharp, in any case, to find them. They won't just be standing around waiting."

"We'll have Obsidian to help with that." The Wing Rider gestured to where the bird roosted in the dark on a broad outcropping of rocks. "That's what he's been trained to do, to look for things we can't see, to hunt for what's lost and needs finding. He's good at it. Better than you and me."

She eased her injured leg into a new position. It ached from being locked about the Roc during their flight, even for only the two hours they had traveled. How much worse would it be by tomorrow night? She sighed wearily as she rubbed it back to life, careful to avoid the knife wound. It was no worse, she supposed, than she had imagined it would be. She'd already checked the bandage, and there was no evidence of bleeding. The stitches were holding her together so far.

"We'll rest pretty regularly tomorrow," Hunter Predd declared, watching her. Her eyes lifted in sharp reproof. "Not just for you," he added. "For the bird, too. Obsidian travels better with frequent stops."

"As long as you're not doing me any special favors."

His laugh was dry and mirthless. "We wouldn't want that, would we?"

She passed him the aleskin and leaned back on her elbows. "You can laugh all you want. You didn't grow up a girl among men the way I did. If you asked for special favors from my brother or my cousins, they laughed at you. Worse, they made things so difficult you wished you'd never opened your mouth. Rover women have a tradition of endurance and toughness born out of constant travel, responsibility for family, and a mostly hard life. In the old days, we had no cities, no place in the world outside of our wagons and our camps. We were nomads, adrift much of the time, at sea or in flight the rest. No one helped us just because they wanted to. We taught them to depend on us, on our skills and our goods, so they had no choice. We have always been a self-sufficient people, even now, as sailors and shipbuilders and mercenaries, and whatever else we can do better than others—"

"Hold on!" he interrupted in protest. "I'm not laughing at you. Do you think I don't know about your kind of life? We're not so different, you and me. Wing Riders and Rovers, they've always lived apart, always been self-sufficient, always depended on no one. That's been true since as far back as anyone can remember."

He leaned forward. "But that doesn't mean we can't extend a helping hand when it's needed. Friendship doesn't have anything to do with shoring up weakness. It has to do with respect and consideration for those you care about. It has to do with wanting to give something back to those you admire. You might keep that in mind."

She smiled in spite of herself, charmed by his bluntness. "I've been living with soldiers too long on the Prekkendorran," she offered. "I've forgotten how to be grateful."

He shook his head. "You haven't forgotten much, I expect. You just get a little too close to your feelings sometimes, Little Red. Better that than getting too far away."

They slept undisturbed, taking shifts at watch, and woke refreshed and ready to go on. They set out at sunrise, its pale golden light cresting the horizon like a fanfare to give chase to the night. The features of the land below gradually emerged from the shadows, a slow etching out of detail and color. The air warmed as the sun lifted, and the sky was bright and cloudless. Rue Meridian lifted her face to the light, thinking that perhaps the world could be kinder, after all, than she had supposed.

They flew on through the entire day, stopping to rest and water Obsidian and to eat their lunch and stretch cramped limbs. Other than small birds and an occasional forest animal, they saw no sign of life. After midday, the terrain began to change, turning more rugged and less open. Ahead, bald-topped mountains reared against the skyline, a ragged spine down the length of the land, bisecting its mass. Foothills cradled deep lakes formed by streams and runoff from the higher elevations. Clouds began to mass along the peaks. The sky north turned gray and murky with rainsqualls. South, where the cliffs and ice fields lay clustered, the horizon was black with thunderstorms and streaked with bolts of lightning that flashed like explosions of white fire.

It was twilight when they came in sight of the bay where the *Jerle Shannara* had left the shore party more than ten days ago. They circled around to fly out of the descending gloom so they would not be seen, keeping low above the treetops, hidden against the dark mass of the mountains. They could just identify the faint outline of *Black Moclips* where she hung tethered at anchor above the waterline. No lights burned from her masts or through her windows, and no movement could be seen on her decks. Hunter Predd took Obsidian down to an open stretch of rock fronting a barren ridge. They dismounted and walked to a place where they could look down on the airship and the bay.

West, the sun had dropped below the horizon and the last of the day's fading light was disappearing into shadow.

"Now what?" Hunter Predd asked quietly.

Rue Meridian shook her head, staring fixedly at *Black Moclips*. "Maybe we ought to take a closer look."

Leaving Obsidian to roost, they walked down from the heights to the shoreline, taking their time, moving cautiously through the deepening darkness so as to make as little noise as possible. In the silence of the cove, noise would travel a great distance. Little Red's eyes were sharp, but Hunter Predd's were sharper still, so he led the way, choosing the path that offered them the quietest passage. It took them almost an hour to make the descent, and by then darkness had fallen completely and the sky was bright with the light of stars and moon.

Standing on the shoreline, well back within the trees, the Rover and the Wing Rider stared out across the bay at the anchored airship. They could see movement on her decks now, guards at watch, crewmen at work. They could hear voices, kept deliberately low, but audible. They could just catch glimpses of lantern light masked by shadows and curtains within the cabins below the decking.

After standing there for a time, Hunter Predd turned to her. "What are you thinking?"

She kept silent. What she was thinking was wild and dangerous. What she was thinking was that perhaps fate had presented them with a unique opportunity. She had come looking for the missing members of the *Jerle Shannara*'s company, but instead found their enemy's transport.

The Ilse Witch couldn't know yet that they had liberated the *Jerle Shannara* from the Mwellrets and Federation sailors left to keep watch over her. She couldn't know that she now commanded only *Black Moclips*. She would believe both vessels still safely under her control.

Rue Meridian pursed her lips. There was a chance for real irony here, a bit of poetic justice, if she could just figure out how to orchestrate it.

Wouldn't it be fitting, she was thinking, if she could somehow put the witch in the same position that the witch had put her?

Frowning in discontent, the Ilse Witch glanced over her shoulder at the darkening silhouette of *Black Moclips* as she disappeared into the trees. Twilight cloaked the bay in shadows that stretched in the wake of the sunset to seize and entwine the airship like ghost fingers. She had given strict instructions to Cree Bega and his rets. The boy had been placed in their care, to be watched and warded until her return. They were not to try to speak with him, to interact with him, or to have anything at all to do with him. He was to be kept locked up. He was to be given food and drink, but nothing else. He was not to be allowed out. No one was to visit him. No one was to disturb him.

Whether or not her instructions would be followed was another matter entirely.

Cree Bega was suspicious, but she had deflected the worst of it by offering up a small lie. The boy had information that would prove useful to them, but she must be the one to extract it from him since he could not speak. The Mwellret had no way of knowing that the reason the boy couldn't speak was because of the magic she had used against him, so he might do as he was told and wait for her return. It was a risk she had to take. She could not take the boy with her; it was too dangerous to go looking for the Druid with him in tow. She could not chance leaving him anywhere else besides the ship; someone from his company might find and free him. She had taken the Sword of Shannara with her, to be certain he found no use for it. She wore it slung across one shoulder, sheathed in the worn scabbard she had found to hold it. Without the use of his talisman or his voice, the boy would have no magic to call upon. It was best to leave him where he was and hope that her absence would be brief.

She had reason to think it would. She had amended her earlier plans, which were entirely too ambitious. As much as she wanted to settle things with the Druid, he was never the primary reason she had undertaken the expedition. Retrieving the powerful magic that lay in the bowels of Castledown was her most important goal. Besides, she needed more time to decide what to do about both the Druid and the boy, especially in light of what the latter was claiming about his lineage. What she intended to do was to walk into the ruins, to bypass the fire threads and creepers that had so easily bested the Mwellrets but would be less effective against her, to gain entry into Castledown, to locate and siphon off the magic of the books that were concealed there, and to escape. She would leave Walker for later, when she was safely back in the Wilderun. She would have her chance at him then because she would have the magic he coveted, and he would be forced to come to her to retrieve it.

Unless he had it already, of course. The possibility that the boy had been sent to draw her away from Castledown crossed her mind briefly, but she dismissed it. Still, the Druid might have gotten possession of the books while she was searching for the boy. If he had, she would have to deal with him immediately. But she didn't think that was the case. The fact that his company had been decimated by the fire threads and creepers and that there had been no sign of him since suggested that he had accomplished nothing, that instead he was in trouble, perhaps injured or dead. If he was not, he would have emerged already. He would have come for the boy or for her. The boy and the shape-shifter would not have continued their flight. There would have been some sign of activity. Her Mwellrets had patrolled the fringes of the ruins since their arrival and seen no one.

Besides, even if he had somehow avoided them, what could he do? Books of magic or not, he was trapped. She had control of both airships. She had the boy and the Sword of Shannara. The Druid was alone, or nearly so. To have any chance at all of escaping, he would have to come to her. She was prepared for that to happen.

She shrugged. Whatever the case, she would know what to do about the Druid when she found the books of magic. Her senses would tell her quickly enough if he had been there before her.

She moved through the darkening twilight like a shade, wrapped in her gray robes, a silent presence. She sent her magic ahead of her, sweeping the darkness, searching for what she could not see, for what might lie in wait. She found nothing. It was as if the world were deserted save for her. She liked the feeling. She always preferred the night, but preferred it best when she was alone. She did not feel anxious or concerned about what lay ahead. She knew what to expect from what she had been told by Cree Bega and, more important, from what she had discovered in her mind probe of the dying Kael Elessedil. She knew of the fire threads and creepers and did not feel them to be a threat. She knew about the books of magic and the thing that warded them. Antrax. That was the name it had been given many centuries ago. She knew what it was and how it could be overcome. She knew more about it than it knew about her. It had misjudged the extent of the information contained in Kael Elessedil's brain. She thought she even knew how to destroy it, should it become necessary to do so.

But the destruction of Antrax was not her concern. The books of magic were what she wanted, and while she did not know how many there were or where they were hidden, she was confident she could uncover and seize them, which was all she wanted of the machine. She would take the ones she needed, the ones that would give her the most power, and leave the rest for another time. She would use her magic to disrupt Castledown's security, concealing her presence, masking her theft, and hiding her retreat. If everything went as she wished, she would be there and gone again with Antrax none the wiser.

Then she would deal with that boy.

That boy who claimed he was Bek.

Even thinking about him angered her. His words skipped and jumped through her mind like small unruly animals. Even while trying to focus her thinking on what lay ahead, she could not dismiss them. Or him. That boy! His image was constant and tenacious, lingering in a way that came close to causing her panic. It was ridiculous that he should affect her so strongly. She had overcome him easily enough, outsmarted him time and again, stolen away his voice and his talisman, made him her prisoner, and crushed his hopes for convincing her of who he thought he was.

And yet . . .

And yet she could not rid herself of his voice, his face, his presence! Working on her like iron tools on hard earth, digging and hoeing and shoveling, breaking up her resistance with their sharp edges, with their implacable certainty. How had he managed that, when no one else could? Others had sought to breach her defenses, to convince her of their rightness, to twist her thinking to suit their own. No one had come close to succeeding, not since she was very little, when the Morgawr . . .

She did not finish the thought, not wanting to travel that road again just now. The boy was no Morgawr, but he might prove to be just as dangerous. His talent for magic was raw and unskilled, but that could change quickly enough. When it did, he would be a formidable adversary. She did not need another of those.

She stopped suddenly, startled by a realization that had escaped her earlier. His magic, rough and undisciplined as it was, had affected her already. *Infected her.* That was why she could not rid herself of his voice, why she could not banish it. She exhaled sharply, angry all over again. How could she have been so stupid! She used her own voice in the same way, as if speaking in ordinary conversation, but all the while working on the listener's thinking. She had let him talk to her because she had foolishly believed it made no difference what he said. She had missed the point. What he said didn't matter; how he said it, did! She had given him an opportunity he could not possibly have missed and he had used it!

She was shaking with rage. She looked back the way she had come. She was tempted to go back and deal with him. He was too much like her for comfort. Too similar. It was disquieting. It was cause for more concern than she had been willing to give it until now.

For a long time she stood, undecided. Then she shook off her hesitation. What lay ahead was what mattered most. The boy was helpless. He was not going to cause problems before she got back. He was not going to do anything but sit and wait.

Hitching up the Sword of Shannara once more, smoothing the angry wrinkles from her pale face, she adjusted the concealing cloak and cowl and continued on into the night.

NINETEEN

In a maelstrom of jetting fire and clashing steel, Walker fled through the corridors of Castledown. He was under attack from every quarter, fire threads lashing out at him from hidden ports and crevices, creepers converging in droves. They had found him only moments before, while he crept through what seemed an empty passageway, and now they were all about him. He had kept them at bay with the Druid fire, but only barely, and the circle was tightening as he tried to fight his way clear, dodging through tunnels and into chambers, out doorways and into corridors, taking every stairway that led up, desperate to regain the surface where he might gain his freedom. He no longer sought to find the books of magic. His plans for that had long since been abandoned. Fatigue and tension had eroded his resolve. He had not slept in so long he could not remember the last time. He had eaten nothing in what seemed like weeks. He kept going out of sheer determination, out of stubbornness, and out of certainty that if he stopped, he would die.

Flattened against a wall, he watched a cluster of fire threads crisscross the passageway ahead, blocking his advance. He could not understand it. Whatever he did seemed only to make things worse. No matter how careful he was, he could not elude his pursuers. It was as if they knew what he was going to do before he did it. That should not be possible. He was cloaked in Druid magic, which hid him from everything. His pursuers should not be able to see where he was or what he was about. He should have lost them long ago. Yet there they were, at every turn, at every juncture, waiting on him, striking at him, hemming him in.

He edged back through a doorway that led down a narrow corridor to a larger passage. For a moment, the fire threads were left behind. He took deep, life-giving breaths of air, his throat on fire from running, and his chest tight and raw. He tried to think what to do, but his mind would not respond. His thinking, once so precise and clear, had turned muddled and thick. Exhaustion and stress would have contributed to that, but it was something more. He simply could not reason, could not make his thoughts come together coherently, could not consider in a balanced way. He knew to run and he knew to defend himself, but beyond that his mind refused to function. It locked away all thoughts of the past, everything that had led to his present predicament; all of it had turned to vague, surreal memories. Nothing mattered to him anymore. Nothing but the here and now and his battle to stay alive.

He knew it was wrong. Not morally, but rationally—it was wrong. It made no sense that he should think that way. He fought against it, struggled to get a handle on the problem so that he could twist it around and make it right again, but nothing he attempted worked. He was adrift in the moment, with no sense that he could ever get himself out.

There was a stairway at the end of the larger corridor, and he raced to gain it ahead of his pursuers. It led upward toward fresh light, a brightness more genuine than the flameless lamps of his prison. He charged up the stairs into its glow, thinking that at last—at last!—he had found his way free. He gained the head of the stairs and found himself in a cavernous chamber with tall windows opening to blue sky and green trees. His fatigue and despair forgotten, he rushed to the closest one and peered out. There was a forest beyond the wall of the chamber, so close it seemed he could reach out and touch it. Somehow he had fled far enough that he was all the way to the edge of the city. He wheeled about, searching for a door. There was none to be found.

Behind him, he heard the clank and whir of creepers on the stairs. In desperation, he sent the Druid fire lancing into the glass windows. It struck their clear surface and bounced harmlessly away. Walker stared in disbelief. That wasn't possible. Glass could not deflect Druid magic. He moved quickly down the line of windows and tried again, on another pane, then a second and third. They, too, held fast.

The creepers appeared at the head of the stairs. He lashed out at them in fury and frustration, burning those closest, sending their scrap metal leavings back down the well into the others.

He caught sight of a deep alcove he had missed before. Nestled within its shadowy confines was a small wooden door. He moved quickly toward it, found its lock old and rusted, and burned it away with barely any effort. The door collapsed on its broken hinges, and he kicked it aside, pushing through to the fresh air and sunshine beyond.

A jungle rose all about him, vast and impenetrable, stretching away against the open sky like a wall. He plunged into it, heedless of what waited, knowing only that he had to get away from what followed. Thick grasses and tangled vines choked off any clear passage through the massive trees. Walker twisted and fought his way ahead, buoyed by the smell of rotted wood and leaves, by the warm glow of the sun and the feel of soft earth beneath his feet. Behind him, the city ruins disappeared from view, and he could no longer hear the creepers. He smiled faintly, relief surging through him. It would be all right. Whatever lay ahead couldn't be any worse than what he had escaped.

Then the ground heaved beneath his feet and sent him stumbling away. It settled and heaved again, as if an animal breathing. He tried to get clear of the motion, but it followed, tossing him from one side to the other, almost upending him. The trees began to shiver and the grasses to wave. Vines reached down, trying to grasp the Druid, to snare him, and he twisted away from them desperately. More waited, and more after that. He was forced to call up the Druid fire once more, burning them away to clear passage. The assault was relentless and purposeful, as if the jungle was determined to devour him. He could not understand it. There was no reason for the attack and no way to explain why or how it was happening.

He fought his way ahead, unable to do anything else, adrift in an undulating sea of green.

In a room of smoky glass, its walls papered with myriad panels of blinking lights and flashing red numbers, Ahren Elessedil and Ryer Ord Star stared in horror at the limp, motionless form of the missing Druid. He lay on a metal table, bound in place by padded straps fastened about his forehead, throat, waist, ankles, and the wrist of his good arm so that he could not move. Tubes ran to his arm and torso, attached to needles inserted into his veins. Liquids pulsed through the tubes, fed from bottles slung about metal hangers. One tube, the largest, was inserted into his mouth and attached to a bellows that worked slowly and steadily by his side. Machines hemmed him in, all of them blinking with lights and humming with activity. Wires ran to his temples, eyes and throat, heart and loins, even to the fingers of his hand, black snakes ending in suckers fastened to his skin. The wires that trailed from his fingers were attached to their tips by what looked like the ends of gloves, cut away and fitted in place to the second knuckle of each digit. The wires pulsed within clear coverings as they ran from the Druid to a bank of clear glass containers. Flashes of blue light surged into a reddish liquid, which then flowed on through tubes into ports in the metal walls and recycled back.

Ahren could not make himself move. What was being done to Walker? He leaned closer to look at the Druid's face. Were his eyes gouged out? Had his tongue been removed? He peered down fearfully, but he could not tell. The Druid's eyes were blinkered and his mouth clogged with the tube; everything was obscured. Ahren wanted to rip the tubes out of Walker, to cut loose the straps that secured him. But he sensed that he should not, that by doing so he might injure the Druid. He couldn't be certain, couldn't know by just looking, but he thought that the tubes might be keeping Walker alive.

He looked over at Ryer Ord Star, who was crying soundlessly beside him, her hands closed into fists and pressed against her mouth. She was hunched over and shaking, and he pulled her against him, trying to share with her a reassurance he didn't feel. On the other side of the room, the multilimbed metal attendant moved diligently from panel to panel, studying dials and numbers, touching switches and buttons. It seemed to be monitoring things, perhaps studying the Druid's condition, perhaps recording what was happening.

Which was what?

Still hidden away from Antrax and creepers alike within

the protective seal of the phoenix stone's magic, Ahren tried to make sense of it. There could be only one explanation. Antrax was siphoning off Walker's magic. It had lured the men and women of the *Jerle Shannara* to Castledown for precisely that purpose, just as it had lured Kael Elessedil and his Elven command all those years ago. Once Walker was a prisoner, trapped underground and rendered helpless, the milking had begun. Ahren would suffer the same fate, once Antrax found him; he would be drugged and bound and drained of life. He didn't know how the process worked, but he was certain of what it was.

The metal attendant finished its duties and wheeled back toward the door. Ahren pulled Ryer Ord Star out of its way and watched it disappear outside, leaving them alone. He looked around the room, at all the machinery. He could never hope to understand it, to learn enough about it to know how to free the Druid. The technology belonged to another era, and all knowledge of it had been lost for centuries. Ahren felt helpless in the face of that reality.

He bent close to the seer. "I don't know what to do," he admitted softly.

She brushed at her eyes with the heels of her palms, swallowed her tears, and stiffened her body. He released her, waiting to see what she would do—because it was clear she intended to do something.

She took his hand in hers. "Stay close to me. Don't let go."

He followed her as she hurried to where Walker lay, easing between the machines, stepping carefully over the wires and tubes. Ahren could see that the Druid was alive. He was breathing and there was a pulse in his neck. His face twitched, as if he dreamed. His skin was bloodless and damp with perspiration. Of course, he was alive. He would have to be alive to be of any use to Antrax.

The Elven Prince fought down his revulsion and fear. *Don't let me end up like this,* he prayed. *Let me die first.*

Ryer Ord Star looked over at him. "I have to try to reach him. I have to let him know I'm here."

Turning back to the Druid, she trailed the fingers of her free hand over his face and down his arm to his hand, then back again. She spent a long time doing that, staring down at him as she did so, looking impossibly small and frail amid the metal banks of machinery. Ahren held her hand tightly in his, remembering her instructions, knowing that he was her lifeline back from wherever she might have to go to try to save the Druid.

"Walker?" she whispered.

There was no response. There was no movement at all that communicated understanding. His chest rose and fell, his pulse beat, and his features twitched. Liquids flowed in and out of his body, and the wires flashed where they connected to the glass containers. He was lost to them, Ahren thought. Even Ryer Ord Star was not going to be able to get him back.

The seer straightened and brushed at loose strands of her silvery hair. Her face turned slightly toward him. "Let go of me, Ahren," she ordered. "But stay close."

Then she was climbing onto the metal table, easing carefully into the nest of wires and tubes, fitting her slender body to the Druid's, nestling against him as if a child clinging to a parent who slept. The Elf stayed so close to her that he could feel the heat of her body.

"Walker?" she said again. She lifted her hands to his cheeks and turned his head toward her own, snuggling into his shoulder. Her leg fitted itself over his, so that they were intertwined.

"Please, Walker," she begged, the words breaking on her lips like shattered glass.

There was no response. Walker lay as if his body had been drained of all but just enough life to keep death at bay.

"Please, Walker," the seer whispered again, her fingers moving across his face, her eyes closing in concentration. Tears ran down her cheeks once more.

Please, Ahren repeated the word in the silence of his mind, standing over them both, watching helplessly. *Come back to us.*

Walker fought his way through the writhing tentacles of the jungle vines and grasses for what seemed an endless amount of time, burning them away to clear a path, fighting for space to breathe, and still he seemed to get nowhere. The jungle was vast and unchanging, and he could find no distinguishing features to mark his passage. In the back of his mind, deep within the hazy thinking that drove him on, he realized that by escaping Castledown and gaining the jungle, he had merely exchanged one type of maze for another.

Having no other choice, he forced himself to go on. His body ached with fatigue; all he could think about now was finding a place to sleep. He was beginning to hallucinate, to hear voices, to see movement, and to feel the touch of shades that weren't there. The sensations emerged from the green of the jungle, from the emerald sea he sought to swim, reaching out to him. They grew steadily more insistent, so much so that they were soon overshadowing even the plants and trees of the jungle, causing some to fade and others to change their look entirely. Oddly, the attacks on him ended, the vines and grasses drew back, and the undulations of the earthen floor quieted.

He slowed his ragged advance and looked around, trying to decide what had happened.

He heard someone speak his name.

Walker? Please, Walker.

He recognized the voice, but it was a distant memory he could barely bring into focus. He grasped for it nevertheless, clutching at it as if it were a lifeline. The surging earth was still, and the deep green of the jungle had darkened to something hard and black, a night sky filled with blinking red stars. A face appeared, hazy and indistinct. It was a young woman's face, its thin, frail features framed with long, silver hair. She was so close to him he could feel the softness of her skin, and her breath upon his cheek was a feathery tickle. He felt her arms reach about him, cradling him. Where had she come from to find him, here in this jungle, in the middle of nowhere, a part of this madness?

Walker?

He remembered now. She was Ryer Ord Star. She was the seer he had brought with him on his voyage out of the Four Lands. Of all those who might have found him, she alone had managed to do so. He could not understand it.

Abruptly he was assailed by a rush of odd sensations, feelings that seemed foreign and wrong to him. At first, he could not identify them, could not trace their source or determine their purpose. He stood motionless and confused in the fading jungle and the descending night with its odd red stars, the young woman clinging to him, the world turned upside down.

Then everything changed in an instant. The jungle was gone. The green of the trees, the blue of the sky, the smell of rotted wood and leaves, the softness of the earth—his entire sense of place and time—disappeared. He was no longer standing upright, but was laid out upon a hard metal surface in a room filled with blinking lights and softly humming machines. Tubes ran from the machines to his body, pumping fluids. Wires attached to his skin snaked everywhere. He did not see this with his eyes. His eyes were blindfolded. He saw it instead with his mind, his Druid senses suddenly come awake from a deep, immobilizing sleep. He saw it the way a dream is seen, except that the dream was of the jungle, of the ruins and the creepers and the fire threads, of everything he had believed to be true.

He remembered then. He knew what had happened, what had been done to him. He understood it all, brought back into reality from drug-induced sleep and nightmarish dreams by the presence of the young woman who lay beside him, by her voice and her touch. She alone had reached him when no one else could. When he lay dying of the bramble poison after Shatterstone and she saved him with her empathic healing, a link had been forged between them. It bound them in an unintended way, through trading life for death and healing for suffering. So it was that she had sensed his need when even he was not aware of it, heard his subconscious call for help, come to him.

She stirred slightly, her fingers trailing down his face like velvet, her warmth infusing him with strength. She called his name softly, repeatedly, still reaching out to him, determined to bring him back from his prison.

When he felt her hand slide over his, cupping it, he lifted his fingers and pressed them against her palm in response.

Ahren missed the movement, his eyes on the Druid's face. But he saw Ryer Ord Star suddenly go very still, her body motionless. Even her fingers stopped tracing lines on Walker's face. He waited for her to speak, to begin moving again, to give him some indication of what was happening. But the seer had turned to stone.

"Ryer?" he whispered.

She made no response. She lay pressed against the Druid as if to become a part of him, her eyes closed and her breathing slowed so completely that he could barely detect it. He thought to touch her, but he was afraid to do so. Something had happened, and whatever it was, she was responding to it in the best way she could. He knew he must not disturb her. He must wait for her. He must be patient.

The minutes ticked by, endless and silent. He bent over her once, trying unsuccessfully to see what was happening. Then he stepped back a pace, as if a measure of distance might give him a better view. Nothing helped. He looked around at the banks of lights and switches, thinking the answer might lie there. If it did, he could not detect it. He looked out through the darkened glass to the cavernous room beyond, to the banks of spinning disks. Metal attendants moved down the brightly lit aisles, steady and purposeful in their labors. None looked in his direction or seemed in any way aware of what was happening in the room. He listened for a change in the sounds of the machinery, but there was none. Everything seemed the same.

Yet he knew it wasn't.

He did not think that he or Ryer Ord Star had been detected. The concealing haze of the phoenix stone still wrapped them both. If the magic had failed, there would have been some indication of it. If Ryer's presence at the Druid's side had been detected, an alarm would have sounded or flashed. Ahren hugged himself against the chill seeping through his body, against raw impatience and fear. What could he do? What should he do? He had to trust in the magic; it was all he had. That, and his sense of purpose in going there, in agreeing to do something that terrified him, persuaded by the seer that doing anything was better than giving up.

Yet it wasn't even *his* sense of purpose, he realized. It was *hers*. She was the one who had wanted to find Walker, who had insisted they find him, who had believed that they must do so if he was to have any chance of escaping Castledown. It seemed that she had been right, that if they hadn't come, Walker would have remained where he was, undiscovered, neither quite dead nor quite alive, neither one thing nor the other, but something in between, something terrible and repulsive and inhuman.

But having found the Druid, how were they supposed to save him? What were they supposed to do? Whatever it was, he did not know if they were equal to the task.

"Ryer?" he said again.

There was no response. What was she doing? He glanced around nervously, aware of how long they had lingered in the room, of how much they were risking. Sooner or later, the magic of the phoenix stone would fail and they would be discovered. Nothing could save them then. Bravery and sense of purpose would count for nothing.

"Ryer!" he hissed.

To his astonishment, she looked up at him, eyes snapping open as if she had come awake suddenly, unexpectedly. There was such unrestrained joy, such boundless hope in her gaze that he was momentarily speechless.

"He's come back!" she breathed softly, tears flooding her eyes. "He's free, Ahren!"

Free of what? Ahren wondered. He didn't look free. But the Elven Prince nodded and smiled as if what she said were so. He reached out to take her arm and help her stand again, but she motioned him away.

"No. Wait. We have to wait. It's not time yet." She closed her eyes and pressed herself tighter against the Druid. "He's going back in. To find Antrax. To find the books of magic. I have to stay with him while he does. I have to be here for him."

She went still again, eyes closing, breathing slowing, hands moving to the Druid's forehead, fingers pressing against his temples. "The machines don't know. We mustn't let them find out. I have to keep them from knowing. Stay close to me, Ahren."

He wasn't sure what she was talking about, what it was she was doing to help Walker, but the urgency in her plea was unmistakable. He stood beside her, beside the Druid, feeling alone and vulnerable and lost, looking down in helpless silence, and waited to find out.

TWENTY

Surfacing from the stream of drug-induced illusions that Antrax had used to control him, Walker drew on Ryer Ord Star's empathic strength to keep from going under again. He was swimming upstream against a raging tide, but at least he understood what had been done to him. His tumble down the tower chute after escaping the fire threads and the creepers had ended in his loss of consciousness and ultimate imprisonment. He had been drugged and immobilized immediately, then brought to the room to be strapped down and drained of his power. The method was clever and effective: let the victim think himself still free, make him fight to stay that way, and siphon off the power of the magic he used to do so. The tubes that ran to his body fed him liquids and drugs, keeping him alive but dreaming of a life that never was. If not for the seer, he would have remained that way until he died.

His understanding brought no comfort. Kael Elessedil must have spent his days the same way, using the Elfstones over and over, thinking himself free, unable ever to manage to do more than to keep running. He would have lived thirty years like that, until he had grown too old or weak or sick to be of any further use. Then Antrax would have sent him home again, using him one final time, to lure a replacement.

Except that Antrax had gotten lucky. It had succeeded in luring not one, but several, luring to his deadly trap not only the Druid, but Ahren Elessedil, Quentin Leah, and perhaps even Bek Ohmsford, all of whom had command of significant magic. Antrax would have known about them, of course. It would have known from what it had recorded of their efforts to recover the keys on the islands of Flay Creech, Shatterstone, and Mephitic. A machine that built machines, a creation of the technology of the Old World, it had known to test the capabilities of those it sought to snare. That was the reason for luring humans to its lair. That was the purpose for the underground prison. To steal their magic and convert it to the power that fed Antrax. To keep Antrax alive.

Yet perhaps that was only one reason and not the one that mattered most to it. Perhaps it was still searching for those who had created it, waiting for them to come back to claim the treasure they had left it to guard. The books of the Old World. The secrets of another time.

How did he know that? Unconscious and dreaming, how could he know? He knew it in part from what he had deciphered from the map, written in a language the Druid Histories still recorded. He knew it in part from what Ryer Ord Star had communicated to him in bringing him back from his slumber, her words and thoughts revealing his situation. He knew it in part from what he could deduce from the use of the machinery that immobilized and drugged him. He knew it finally from what he was able to intuit. It was enough to keep him from slipping back into his prison, to keep him fixed on what he must do if he was to complete his task in going there—the task that had cost the lives of so many of his companions and might yet, if he was not swift and sure and focused enough, cost him his.

He gathered himself within his body, using his magic to summon his shade and set it free, the way Cogline had done years ago in entering lost Paranor. It was what Allanon had done in his time. There was danger in it. If his body should die, his shade was lost. If he strayed too far or allowed himself to be trapped outside his body, he might never get back again. Yet it was a gamble he must take. He could not free his body from the wires and tubes that linked it to Antrax without triggering alarms that would bring the creepers. There was no reason to free himself if he did not know what to do to stay free. As a shade, he could explore Castledown without Antrax being any the wiser. Ryer Ord Star would keep his body strong and alive and functioning, would keep the machines deceived as to what was happening. She would feed him enough of her empathic healing power to prevent him from slipping back into the deadening dreams. So long as she could do so, nothing would seem any different. So long as the magic of the phoenix stone cloaked the seer, even the eyes of Antrax could not detect her presence. Walker's magic would continue to feed out in small increments, reduced by the absence of real thought, responding out of reflex only. Antrax would not be concerned at the decline in his magic's output right away. Not even for several hours, should it take that long. Time was relative in Castledown. Antrax had lived for more than twenty-five hundred years. A few hours were nothing.

Walker did not consider further what he must do. He went out from his body as a shade, tracking the wires that fed into it back to their source. Penetrating metal, glass, and stone as if they were air, he sped through the walls of the keep, a silent and invisible presence. He stayed alert for Antrax all the while, wanting to keep it from that room where his body lay, from examining him too closely, from finding out the truth. He surged down conduits and through clusters of wires and metal pieces that conducted electricity and thought, power garnered from magic and converted to use. He seethed at the knowledge of what had been done to the men and women who had been lured there, but stayed focused on what was needed to stop it from happening again.

He found the relays for the security system quickly enough. Eyes of glass watched from ceilings all through the safehold, mechanical orbs that let Antrax view everything. But of what use were they? Antrax was a machine; it did not need eyes. The eyes, Walker realized with a start, were for the humans who had once controlled Antrax. They served no other purpose now. Antrax would use a more sophisticated system— one of touch and feel and sound and perhaps body heat. Only magic would thwart it, and perhaps not all magic at that.

Where did Antrax dwell within this vast complex?

Where did all the information feed?

He tracked it for a time, down lines and through chambers, along corridors and around corners. But one set of relays led to another. One bank of machines was tied to a second. Lines of power opened into new lines, and there was no end of them. Nothing to tell him where to find the start and finish of things.

He tried quieting himself and tracking Antrax by feel. It was not difficult to do. But once again, there seemed to be no start or finish. Antrax was vast and sprawling. It was everywhere at once, all about and seeping through, endless and immutable. Antrax was the safehold of Castledown; spread in equal parts throughout, there was no part of the keep that it did not inhabit. It warded everything at once.

Walker did not waver from his goal. He had come too far to

give up. There was too much at stake and no one else who could do what was needed. *Not even . . .*

He hesitated. The words were bitter with realities he did not want to face.

Yet what choice did he have?

He finished the sentence in a rush. *Not even her.*

He must change his thinking, he acknowledged in what, for some, might have been considered an admission of defeat. But Druids dealt with neither victory nor defeat, but with reality and truth. What was fated could not be denigrated or altered by imposition of moral judgment. It was not his mandate. Druids served a higher cause, the preservation and advancement of Mankind and the Races. The Great Wars had reduced civilization to ruins and humans to animals. That must not happen again. The Druid Council had been formed in the time of Galaphile to see that it could not, and every Druid since had worked in furtherance of that end.

But what could he accomplish in the time that remained to him? There, in that nightmarish place, with only a few to stand beside him, with so much at stake? What, that would give life to the bargain he had struck with Allardon Elessedil all those months ago?

Time was slipping away, time he could not afford to waste. He was taking the wrong approach to the business, he decided. His search for answers was leading him in the wrong direction. It was not Antrax that had brought him to Castledown in the first place. Antrax was a secondary concern. It was the treasure Antrax warded that mattered, that could change everything.

He must look for the books of magic.

*   *   *

Pervasive in presence and reach, Antrax sprawled in contented solitude across the vast complex of its underground kingdom, monitoring its sensors and readouts, fulfilling functions its creators had programmed. With the blind certainty of artificial intelligence, it relied on the reassurance of constant input and an unchanging environment. For not quite three thousand years, it had maintained its world through its preassigned functions and unswerving vigilance. Any possibility of disruption brought a swift response.

Such a possibility had just drawn Antrax's attention. It was still tiny and signified nothing as yet, but it was there nevertheless. It wasn't a wave so much as a ripple in the lines of power, undetectable by the warning systems that warded Castledown, virtually immeasurable as an electronic current denoting life, more like a shadow that changed light to dark and dropped the temperature a fraction of a degree. Antrax was alerted to the unexplained presence mostly because it was still searching for two of the intruders whose magic it coveted. While it held one imprisoned in dreams and fantasies, draining it of the power it possessed, assimilating it into Castledown's power cells, the others continued to elude it. Its wronk still hunted the second, tracking it relentlessly through the forest that bordered Castledown. The readouts were steady and unchanged, so there could be no question that the wronk was still functioning properly. It would have its quarry before long.

The third, on the other hand, was proving to be an enigma that Antrax was not able to solve. That one had followed the metal probe into Castledown's warren without resistance, but then something had happened to startle it, and it had bolted. Since then, it had managed to hide itself despite everything

Antrax had done to find it. Heat and movement sensors, pressure pads, trip ports, and sound detectors had failed to uncover it. Lasers and metal probes had scoured the corridors and chambers of the complex without result. It was possible that it had escaped Castledown entirely, but there was nothing to confirm that. Antrax wanted this one in particular because it was needed to replace the intruder that had failed and been sent back as a lure. No other was suited for the drawing down of power from the blue stones. Only the one who was missing.

Nothing had ever evaded Antrax for so long. Could it be that the odd ripple it felt in the lines of power was the third intruder, changed in form? Did it possess such power, such adaptability, when the other had not? Evolution was a fact of life, of the human condition, so perhaps it was so.

Antrax extended itself through its sensors and detectors, through all its communicators, searching. It went everywhere at once, monitoring readouts. Its examination took a long time, but time was something of which it had plenty. It explored the skin of its walls and floors and ceilings as would a living creature, making certain it was whole and free of clinging debris and secreting, burrowing minutiae.

Nothing revealed itself.

All of its metal probes responded to its inquiries regarding their operability. None were broken or disrupted, where such would signal a foreign presence. Nor did the lasers register any problem. Even the vast complex that housed the recordings of the creators hummed steadily along in its transference of information from one storage unit to another, keeping fresh, keeping whole. No system failed to respond when checked. All was as it should be.

Yet something was out of place.

Antrax took readings on the intruder housed in Extraction Chamber Three. The expulsion of power into the cells was noticeably down, but the intruder was still strapped in place and the wires that monitored its bodily functions had not been tampered with. Heat sensors indicated normal temperature readings for the room and no other presence. His prisoner seemed to be resting, asleep perhaps, though that rarely happened with the extraction techniques used by Antrax. Antrax paused to consider the readings more closely. The expected bursts of power in response to perceived threats had diminished noticeably. But that could be a result of exhaustion or even the extraction machine's determination of the subject's need for a respite. Draining off power was a delicate process, requiring a careful monitoring of the mental and emotional condition of the victim. Antrax had learned that humans were creatures of infinite possibility if kept whole. But flesh and blood were not as durable as metal. The creators had demonstrated that.

Sometimes Antrax wished the creators would return, though less so than in the beginning. At first, it had felt they must, that the creators were essential to its ultimate survival. Later, it had discovered how well it could survive on its own. Later still, the importance of the creators had diminished to such a degree that it saw them as unnecessary.

Yet it would house and protect their recordings, awaiting their return, because that was its mandate and prime directive. Survival was assured so long as there were sources of power to draw upon and ways to gain control over them. For Antrax, that was not so difficult a task. If not one way, then another. If not by securing them here, then by tracking them there.

After all, even for an artificial intelligence of its size and capacity, there were ways to leave Castledown.

Antrax took a moment longer to consider the readouts on its prisoner, and then spun slowly back through its network of living metal threads, searching.

Cloaked in the magic of the phoenix stone, wrapped in the blanket of his thoughts, Ahren Elessedil stood close to the table on which Walker and Ryer Ord Star lay entwined. He had been waiting and watching for what seemed like an impossibly long time, and he was growing restless. Something was nudging at him, a sense of dissatisfaction with his role as observer, a feeling of opportunity slipping away. He needed to be *doing* something.

Yet the seer had told him to wait. To keep watch. To serve as her lifeline to the Druid.

He stared down at her, amazed anew at what he saw. Her face was so calm, her features radiant. She was curled tightly against the Druid, who continued to breathe and occasionally to twitch as before, gone somewhere inside himself to accomplish whatever tasks he had determined were necessary to get free of Antrax. Perhaps the seer had gone with him. Perhaps she was only giving him the strength she said he so desperately needed. That they were joined was obvious—a joining that favored both, but Ryer Ord Star in particular.

She had found what she had come searching for.

He mulled that over for a moment, and in doing so he was reminded of the purpose of the phoenix stone. To help those who were lost to find their way back—not just from what they could not see with their eyes, but from what they could not find with their hearts. Those were the words the King of the Silver River had spoken to Bek Rowe.

To show you the way back from dark places into which you have strayed. To show you the way forward through dark places into which you must go.

Ahren Elessedil looked up suddenly, staring at nothing. Understanding flooded through him as he realized for the first time what those words meant. Who was more lost than the seer or himself? Who had strayed farther? Not just physically, but emotionally. She had betrayed them all by agreeing to act as a spy for the Ilse Witch. He had betrayed his countrymen by abandoning them when they needed him most. She was a traitor and he a coward. Those were the dark places into which they had wandered and from which they sought to return. In their hearts, they were lost.

He had not thought on his cowardice for some time, perhaps not allowing himself, perhaps simply caught up in what was happening within Castledown. But he would not become whole again until he had found a way to make amends for what he had done.

What would that take?

He knew at once. He looked down at the seer, pressed against the man she had betrayed. Having found her way back from the wilderness to give him the help he needed and to make herself whole in the process, she was at peace. The magic of the phoenix stone had given her that. It would do the same for him, if he let it. He could not bring to life those he had abandoned. But he could give them back their legacy.

Phoenix stone. The reason for the name was not that the stone could be reborn from the ashes of its destruction, but that the user could. That was the magic's true purpose—to make Ahren whole again, to provide him with new life. That was what it had done for Ryer Ord Star in leading her to Walker. Ahren could have that, as well, but he must first do what the stone required—what it had already required of the seer. He must let the magic take him into the dark place where he would find redemption and, thereby, his way back from the cowardice that had crippled him.

He took a deep breath and exhaled. He must do for his people what he had pledged to do in coming on the voyage. He must do for his dead companions what they could not. He must recover the lost Elfstones.

He could feel the magic of the phoenix stone nudging him in that direction, a subtle hint of dissatisfaction, of need unfulfilled, of realization that his rebirth was not yet complete. He had come with Ryer Ord Star to find and aid Walker because that was what the magic had required of her. But what the magic required of him was to find the Stones. What it demanded was that he walk into the trap that Antrax had set for him, confront and overcome it, and retrieve the missing talismans.

Now.

While there was still time.

He could not explain it, but he could feel it as surely as he could feel the weight of the responsibility he was proposing to accept. Time was slipping away, and when it was gone his chance at retrieving the Elfstones and thereby his chance to be made whole again would be gone, as well. A confrontation between Walker and Antrax loomed, a resolution of the latter's attempt at destroying the Druid and his companions. It would not wait, and it could not be avoided.

For a moment, he was paralyzed by fear. He was so shattered by the feeling that he did not think he could get past it. How could he even contemplate the undertaking? What chance did he have against Antrax and his devices? Fire threads and creepers would be waiting, machines like the ones that had overwhelmed Walker. He lacked any weapons to combat them, any of sufficient strength or capability to offer him even the slightest chance of success. He was alone and impossibly vulnerable.

What made him think he wouldn't run again?

He broke away from his fear, wrenching free as he might from quicksand that threatened to swallow him. It didn't matter what the odds were. He was going. He had to. He reached down for Ryer Ord Star and placed his hand over hers. Her warmth infused him, and although she did not respond to his touch, he told himself that somehow she knew whose it was. He was withdrawing the protective mantle of his magic from her shoulders, breaking the link that bound them. He did not know what that would mean for her, what it would do to her chances for helping Walker. He knew only that the magic was telling him to go, and he must do what it asked of him.

He stepped away from her, backing toward the door through which they had entered. He watched the hazy shroud of the magic stretch and then divide, a little of it clinging to them both, diminished, but still functional. It was the best he could hope for. It was all he could ask.

Good luck to you, Ryer, he thought. *Good luck to us both.*

Then he turned away, passed back out through the doorway, and was gone.

TWENTY-ONE

Insubstantial and ethereal as air, Walker began his search for the books of magic.

From the first, from the moment he had translated the writings on the map carried back to the Four Lands from Castledown by a dying Kael Elessedil, he had kept the truth about the books to himself. He did so in part to protect against attempts by others to interfere with his plans to undertake their recovery. The Ilse Witch had reached the dying Elven Prince before him and discovered what was at stake. Her subsequent interference had forced him to alter his plans time and again. So in that regard he had failed. But he had also kept the truth to himself to persuade Allardon Elessedil to his cause, and in that he had been more successful. If he was honest with himself, he would admit that he had hidden the truth in order to persuade the crew of the *Jerle Shannara* to accompany him. What he knew of the books and the consequences of reintroducing them to the Races was too overwhelming for others to deal with.

Nothing was as simple as everyone thought, the Ilse Witch included. All of them believed what Antrax had allowed Kael Elessedil to believe—that the books really were a compilation of magic's uses. They weren't. It was an easy enough deduction if you were schooled in the history of the Old World. It was apparent if you considered what Castledown really was—a storehouse for knowledge accumulated in a time and place in which magic was virtually unknown and almost never used. The Old World was a world of science, one in which no one had possessed magic since the time of Faerie; what had survived that world had been salvaged by the Elves, but they had lost virtually everything through neglect. A place like Castledown wouldn't house books of real magic; it would house books of learning—of science, history, and culture.

Once, long ago, it would have been called a library.

This was not to say that the books were unimportant because they did not contain spells and conjuring and the like. In truth, they were more important for being what they were—a compilation of everything that had fueled life in the Old World, when power was generated through the application of science to nature. What the books contained was so valuable, so rich in possibility, that there was no way to measure its potential impact on the Four Lands. But that impact could take any number of forms, some constructive, some destructive. The science that had sustained the Old World would all be recorded in the library. Everything that had advanced that civilization would be set down. But everything that had destroyed it would be set down, as well—the secrets of power with their immense destructive capabilities and the formulas for building weapons that could level entire cities the size of Castledown.

Since he had first understood that, the questions in Walker's mind had always been the same. How much of that information should be reintroduced into the world? How many of its secrets should be placed back into the hands of the Races? How much of what had led to the destruction of civilization and the reduction of Mankind to the level of animals should he entrust to the descendants of the survivors?

He didn't know. He supposed it depended on what he found, and so he had struck his bargain with Allardon Elessedil. He would share what he found with the Elves, but only that part that the Elves could make use of or that dealt with magic that was their heritage. He expected that once the books were recovered, nothing in them would offer secrets of magic that would be of any use to the Elves. He did not think they could even read them. To decipher their meaning would take a scholar versed in ancient languages, one who possessed reference books that would facilitate the necessary translations. Only the Druids possessed those—which meant, just then, only him.

But one day, if all went as he hoped, that would change. One day, a Druid Council would again come into being.

As he moved through the myriad chambers and corridors of Castledown in a wide, sweeping search, he mulled his options. There would be too many books for him to carry out. He would have to choose. A handful only, he knew, even with Ryer Ord Star and Ahren Elessedil to help him. Antrax would react too quickly to permit them to take more. He might destroy Antrax; he would at least have to try to render it less of a threat. But if he attacked the keeper, there was a fair chance the library would be lost in the process. Disabling Antrax meant cutting off its power source. Accomplishing that probably meant shutting down whatever systems protected the books, as well. The books would be ancient and fragile, so delicate that any change in their environment might cause them to fall apart. Finding them was one thing; protecting them long enough for them to be of use was another. His magic could help salvage a few, but only a few. He would have to choose. More important, he would have to choose wisely.

He was reminded of a game children played. If you were to be shut away by yourself somewhere and could take with you only a handful of possessions, which ones would you choose? It was much the same choice he faced. Which books of all those available were most important? Which ones would most benefit the world he lived in and the people he sought to help? Which ones would enable the Druids to most ease the pain and suffering of the human condition? Books of healing and cures? Books of agriculture? Books of construction? Books of the Old World's history? Which?

He did not like having to make the choice. He would have preferred to let someone else make it, had there been someone else. Whatever he decided, whichever books he chose, he would make mistakes. It was inevitable. He could not see the future, and to some extent the future would determine what knowledge was necessary to navigate its uncharted waters. No one could know what would be needed until the time arrived. It was equally possible that what he chose would be misused in some way, causing damage and destruction of the sort he was trying so desperately to avoid.

He needed Ryer Ord Star's gift of future sight, but only if he could wield it with a craftsman's skill. It wouldn't be enough to have glimpses of the future. It wouldn't help to take events out of context or in a haphazard fashion. A comprehensive look was needed if future sight was to be of any use.

Even then, he admitted, the odds against recognizing what was both important and necessary were enormous. The future was painted on a canvas of infinite reach; it entailed too many connections and joinings. Change one and you changed others. No amount of insight would enable a single individual to decipher it all.

Only the Word could know, and even that was not given to Mankind as truth.

His search went on, the minutes slipping away, time shedding them like leaves at the change of seasons. Though he searched diligently, he could not find the library. He went everywhere in Castledown, through all its vast chambers and down all its long corridors, and still the books eluded him. He was growing tired, and he knew he could not maintain his shade form much longer. Yet he needed to know where the books were kept if he was to reach them once he returned to his body. If he had to search for them once he cut himself loose from Antrax, he was doomed to fail. Antrax would know what had happened, and there would not be enough time to do anything but escape. He must find the books quickly and determine how to reach them.

In the end, he used a simple artifice to solve the problem. He put himself in the minds of the men and women who had built Castledown and created Antrax and asked how they would have gone about warding their treasure. The answer wasn't so difficult. The books would be housed where the defenses were strongest and most sophisticated, but would cause the least amount of damage should an intruder gain entry. On the surface of Castledown, the defenses were brutal and indiscriminate. Whatever breached them was cut apart. Beneath the surface, where the books were housed, the defenses would be of a different sort. Fire threads and creepers would not be used. Something subtler would be employed.

The Druid changed his way of thinking and began his search anew. As he did so, he was reminded of the strange keys that had lured him to Castledown. He had thought them keys of the sort he was familiar with, metal implements used for unlocking doors. But they had taken a different form than he had expected. Tools of a technological age, they still functioned as keys, but used different principles in doing so. Flat rectangles, they had caused the locks they opened to respond through impulses generated by tiny power cells.

Could it be, he wondered suddenly, that the books had been converted to another form, as well?

A suspicion as cold and deadening as winter night settled through him. He had gotten it all right save for one thing only. He sped through the chambers and corridors, intent on a specific destination, knowing deep inside that his worst fears were about to be realized and that he could do nothing to prevent it. He retraced his route toward the place of his imprisonment, aware of a quickening in Ryer Ord Star's pulse at his approach, triggered by her mistaken belief that he had succeeded in what he had set out to do and was returning. He blanked out that part of his awareness, making no response to her unspoken inquiry, needing her strength for just a little longer.

When he reached the cavernous chamber just outside the smaller one in which his body lay, he paused. Slowly and carefully, he began sweeping the room with his Druid senses, reaching into the banks of machinery with their spinning silver disks. In silent appraisal, he roamed through the tall metal housings, touching here and there with his mind, listening and deciphering. He could hear voices talking, words being spoken, ideas and recitations being repeated, transferred from one space to another, from a first storage unit to a second. He knew at once that he had found what he was looking for. He knew, as well, that it was useless to have done so.

His disappointment approached despair. There were no

books, not of paper and ink. The library existed, but it was a library of the sort that was probably common to its time, that had transcended and replaced the libraries of old. All the knowledge of books had been transcribed onto metal disks and stored in machines. There was no way to make use of it elsewhere without the technology to translate the disks. To decipher what was here, it would be necessary to search the storage units and listen to what was recorded. It would take an enormous amount of time to do that—far more than the Druid could muster.

Even in his shade form, Walker's reaction to his failure was physical. A visceral pain that was deep and hard and cutting knifed through him. He had come all that way, expending time and energy and lives, only to discover that it was for nothing. The library was useless. The books were disks that might as well be drawings on sand at a shore's edge. None of the millions of words of knowledge contained in this safehold could be salvaged unless he could find a way to disable Antrax without shutting down the power sources that fueled them both. He had already analyzed the impossibility of accomplishing that. The power sources that enabled both were linked inextricably. He had scanned them in his travels and found them joined in a way that would not permit separation. Antrax was the heart of the safehold and its treasure.

He listened absently to the steady stream of words as they were transferred from one unit to another, a restoring of some sort, a process intended to keep them fresh and new, even with the passage of time, even after nearly three thousand years. It was all there, everything out of the Old World, the whole of its knowledge in one place, his for the taking—yet just out of reach.

His bitterness was palpable. This journey couldn't have

been for nothing. He couldn't bear that. He wouldn't tolerate it.

He'd had all the choices in the world—too many to consider—when faced with the possibility that the books of the library could be his; suddenly his choices were reduced to one. He saw it instantly, a single chance, one so extreme that on initial consideration he nearly dismissed it out of hand. Yet it reached out to him, revealing how time and an ironic dovetailing of circumstance and fate sometimes gave birth to the impossible.

A hundred and thirty years ago, when he had gone to Eldwist and recovered the Black Elfstone, when he had made his decision to become the first of the new Druids and thereby bring back lost Paranor, he had encountered a similar choice. No, he corrected abruptly, not a similar choice—the same choice. It was his to make because there was no one else to make it. It was his to make because he alone had the means to do so.

He was reminded anew of Allanon's words at the Hadeshorn, all those months ago. Of all the things he wished to accomplish on undertaking this journey, the shade had told him, he would be permitted only one.

A sense of irony and amazement filled him. Life was so mysterious and quixotic. It was an infinite maze, but ultimately there was only one right path for each human who sought to navigate its twisting corridors.

He released his grip on the machines and their disks, withdrawing into himself, letting go of all his hopes and expectations save the one he believed he might still realize. Abandoning his shade and resuming habitation of his corporeal form, he swept aside the last fragments of his disappointment and prepared to wake Ryer Ord Star.

* * *

Aboveground, at the edge of the maze, the Ilse Witch paused to look about. It was well after midnight, the sky clouded and black, the air thick and warm and smelling of rain. It was so dark in the absence of moon and stars that even with her keen eyesight, she could barely distinguish the buildings and walls of the surrounding ruins. Castledown's surface felt like a tomb. She had seen nothing move since she entered from the forest. Silence lay over everything in a heavy blanket, masking what she knew to be hiding in wait.

She had been wise not to bring Cree Bega or any of his Mwellrets for support. In that situation, they would be underfoot, a hindrance to her progress. More important, they would pose a threat; she no longer trusted them with her safety, despite the assurances of the Morgawr and their pledge to obey her. She could feel their resentment and anger every time she was in their presence. They hated and feared her. Sooner or later, they would try to eliminate her. It would be necessary for her to eliminate them first, but that was a task she was not yet ready to undertake. Until the Druid and his followers were accounted for and she had possession of the books of magic, she had need of the Mwellrets and their peculiar skills. But she didn't want them watching her back.

She shifted the weight of the Sword of Shannara where it hung from its strap across her shoulder. She wished she had left it behind, but she had been reluctant to leave it within reach of either the boy or the Mwellrets. She had considered hiding it, but was fearful it might be found. If real, it was a powerful magic, and she wanted it for herself. So she was stuck with hauling it about until the business was finished and she was on her way home. She supposed it was a small price to pay for the uses it might later serve, but she could not get past the resentment at having to endure the ache it caused her shoulders.

Unslinging the sword, she laid it on the ground and stretched her arms over her head. She had not slept for a while, and although sleep was not particularly important to her physical well-being, she felt mentally drained. It was that boy, in part, with his incessant chatter and clever reasoning, trying to persuade her to his cause, trying to trick her. Sparring with him had taken more out of her than she had realized. He was relentless in his insistence of who and what he was, and she found that fighting him off had wearied her.

She yawned. Sleep would give her mind and body rest, but there would be no sleep that night. Instead, she must find a way into Castledown, retrieve the books of magic, and avoid a confrontation with the Druid in the process.

It was a much different mandate than before, she thought ironically, when she had determined to kill Walker. But things had changed, as things had a way of doing.

She picked up the sword and fitted it back across her shoulders, adjusting its weight to gain a measure of comfort. She stood quietly for a time, her gray robes hanging loosely from her slender form, her hood drawn back, her pale face lifted slightly as she concentrated on what lay ahead. Her eyes closed, and she sent the magic of her wishsong into the labyrinth of the ruins. It was there that the Druid had disappeared underground. It was there that the Mwellrets had encountered the creepers. There would be an entrance somewhere close, probably more than one. She need only find it. The rest would be child's play.

It did not take long to accomplish her goal. There were trapdoors and hidden entryways everywhere, some larger than others, all leading down ramps or steps to the safehold.

She used her song to cloak herself in the shape and feel of the maze, cold metal plates and fastenings, wire and machines. Her eyes opened once more. She studied the darkness ahead, then walked in. No creepers or fire threads appeared. She didn't expect them to. When she used the wishsong in that way, it gave her the feel and appearance of whatever lay around her. Only the magic was detectable, and only by something that could recognize its presence.

She did not take a subtle approach to gaining entry; the longer she took, the more risk she assumed. A safehold built in the Old World would employ technology she did not understand. One safeguard or another would detect her eventually. It was best not to give it a chance to do so.

She placed herself against a wall next to one of the larger hidden doors and used her magic to shatter a smaller port across the way. Almost instantly, the door she stood beside slid open and creepers wheeled into view. She kept herself concealed, letting them move quickly past, then froze the last, holding it in place, breaking down its systems as she swiftly recorded its look and feel, both within and without. It took her only seconds, then she was through the door and inside the keep.

There were lights inside, flameless lamps attached to the walls of a handful of corridors that fanned out from an atrium in which dozens of creepers stood frozen in racks. She held herself motionless for a few seconds, testing her new disguise, waiting to see if there would be a reaction to her presence. There wasn't. She gave it a few seconds more, then started ahead.

She passed down the corridors of Castledown without incident, long robes rustling softly, her presence wrapped in the look and feel of a creeper. In a place where only machines had functioned for more than twenty-five hundred years, anything of flesh and blood would trigger an alarm instantly. There would be devices that would indicate a human presence either through readings of weight or body heat or even a tracing of form. She had already spied the glass eyes that peered out of their ceiling niches and felt the presence of the pressure plates. The machines would use other methods, as well, but whatever they were, she could thwart them by disguising her look, changing her weight, and hiding her body temperature. Every warning system would register her as a creeper. Even the Druid couldn't manage that.

Yet she did not allow herself to grow overconfident or drop her guard. There was still the possibility that whatever warded Castledown possessed the ability to track her use of magic, to detect its presence, and to penetrate her subterfuge. If that were to happen, she would have to take evasive action, and quickly. She hoped that her enemy was otherwise occupied, perhaps with Walker. She hoped that the magic she used was too small to detect. She hoped, mainly, that she could accomplish her goals quickly enough that she would be gone before there was a chance to discover that she had ever come in.

She passed dozens of other creepers, all of whom ignored her. Each seemed to have a purpose in mind, but she could not tell what it was. She moved through a maze of chambers and hallways of all shapes and sizes, some empty, some crammed with machinery and materials. She didn't know what was housed there, and she didn't care. She was looking for the books of magic and she was not finding them. Nothing else mattered to her. She could not afford the time necessary to undertake a scavenger hunt.

Ahead, the sound of machinery rose out of the silence, a low and steady thrumming. It penetrated even the steel of the walls; it caused the floor beneath her feet to vibrate. She paused, considering. What she was hearing was huge, a piece of machinery or perhaps several pieces that dwarfed anything she had encountered and performed a function central to the operation of the safehold. It was probably a power plant, but it might have something to do with the protection of the books of magic. She should have a look.

She had not taken another ten steps when all the alarms went off at once.

Ryer Ord Star.

Walker felt her stir against him, waking slowly from the trance into which she had gone to provide him with her empathic strength. Her fingers, resting against his temples, slid down his cheeks like tears.

Come awake, young seer.

He was speaking to her with his mind, a silent summoning that only they could hear. He was back within his body, come out of the drugs and dreams, returned from his shadow form, aware once more of his flesh and blood and the condition in which he had been placed. It was time to free himself of the machines and Antrax. But he must do so carefully, and he could not manage it alone.

Listen to me.

She was awake now, her eyes open, her hands bracing her body as she lifted away from him. "Walker?"

Don't speak. Just listen. Do what I say. Do it quickly. Take the blindfold from my eyes and the breathing tube from my mouth.

She did as she was told, her hands fluttering about his face like small moths. He could feel the expansion and contraction of her lungs as she pressed back against him.

Now release the straps that bind my wrists and ankles, then my neck and forehead and waist. Do it in that order. Do not disturb the wires attached to me. Do not knock them loose.

It took her longer to comply; the straps were fastened with catches of a kind she had never seen and did not understand. They were not formed of metal, but of hard plastic, and she fumbled with them before deciphering their workings. His release went quickly after that as, one by one, the straps fell away.

She was back beside him, leaning close. He opened his eyes for the first time and looked at her. Her wan childlike face, framed by its curtain of silvery hair, broke into a broad smile, and tears filled her eyes. Traces of a cloaking magic still clung to her slender form, but they were fading. How had she gotten to him? Where had she found the magic to do so?

Walker, she mouthed silently.

He scanned himself in an effort to determine what must happen next, trying to decide the right order for the removal of his remaining constraints, knowing that when he released them, alarms would certainly sound.

Block open the door to the room so that when the alarms to the monitoring machines are triggered, Antrax cannot lock us in.

She slipped agilely through the nest of wires still attached to his body, found a low, single-door cabinet on wheels, and rolled it into the opening between the door and the jamb and wedged it securely in place.

Then she was back beside him.

Take the needles from my arm and body. Let them hang loose from their fastenings.

She pulled away the tape that secured the needles, then

slipped them from his veins. She touched the punctures with her cool fingers, healing the wounds, providing him with new strength. Her ability to give of her empathic self seemed boundless. She shuddered once at the contact, held her fingers steady for a moment, and then lifted her hands away.

Alarms would be going off; Antrax would know the equipment that drugged and milked him had malfunctioned in some way. He would have to act fast. He sat up on the metal table, finding his strength diminished and his head spinning. The drugs had left him weak and lethargic, but he could still function. He must. He began ripping free the suckers that fastened the monitoring wires to his body. They came away easily, and in seconds none remained but the five that ran to the gloved tips of his fingers. He left those in place. He had a use for them.

Lights were flashing everywhere on the panels of instruments that ringed his bed. He felt a shift in the atmosphere of the chamber as Antrax descended swiftly to correct what had happened. Walker rose unsteadily, the girl supporting him as he gathered his robes and moved away from the table. He walked to where the wires that ran from his fingertips were bunched into a metal plug that, in turn, was fastened into the containers of reddish liquid. He pulled the plug from its sheath and steered it into an identical opening in one of the wall panels marked with brilliant red symbols.

Walker knew what the symbols read. It was the same language in which the map had been lettered, the language from the Old World he had deciphered in the Druid Histories.

He knew, as well, where the lines of the second sheath ran. He had explored them well in his out-of-body travels, tracing them to their source.

Castledown's main warning system.

Before Antrax could act to prevent it, he sent a burst of Druid fire through the central lines and into all the auxiliaries and set off all the alarms at once.

"Time to be going," he whispered to himself, wheeling Ryer Ord Star toward the blocked entry.

He had only a few minutes to do what was needed.

TWENTY-TWO

Aboard *Black Moclips*, Bek Ohmsford waited patiently for deliverance. He didn't much care what form it took, only that it come soon. He wasn't panicked yet, but he could feel it sneaking up on him. He was imprisoned in an aft hold, a storeroom containing replacement parts and supplies— ambient-light sails, radian draws, diapson crystals, cheese blocks, and water barrels. Shadows cloaked everything in layers of darkness. The room was not large, but even by the light from the candle atop the barrel next to him, he could only barely make out the Mwellret who kept watch from the far side of the room. Bek was tethered to the wall by three feet of chain locked about one ankle. A length of rope bound his hands in front of him and ran down through the chain so that he could not lift his arms above his waist. He was gagged, as well, although that was probably overkill since Grianne had already stolen his voice and rendered him mute.

Leaving nothing to chance, she had taken the Sword of Shannara from him, as well. When she returned, she expected to find him a prisoner still. While he had no real reason to think things would turn out any other way, he had nothing better to do with his time than to visualize the possibility. He was not encouraged. He was a prisoner aboard an airship full

302

of Mwellrets and Federation soldiers. He had no weapons. His friends were dead or scattered. Deliverance in any form would have a hard time finding him under such circumstances.

Moonlight streamed through an open portal to one side, the only breathing hole in the room, the only source of fresh air. As clouds passed across the face of the moon, the light darkened and brightened by turns, changing the depth of the shadows, allowing him small glimpses of his silent jailer. Now and then, the Mwellret would shift position, and a small rustling of cloth and reptilian skin would reveal his otherwise nearly invisible presence. He never spoke. He was under orders not to. The boy had heard his sister give the order. No one was to speak to him. He was to be given water, but no food. He was not to be approached otherwise. He was not to be allowed out. He was not to be taken off the chain, even for a moment. He was to be left where he was until she returned.

Seated on the hard plank flooring of the ship, legs drawn up, wrists draped loosely over his knees, he leaned back against the bulkhead that supported him. He could reach the gag if he wanted, but he understood from painful experience that if he tried, he had better be sure he had a good reason for doing so. Punishment for misbehavior was assured. He had endured several kicks already for moving the wrong way. So he sat as still as possible, thinking. He had tested his voice several times, surreptitious efforts, to see if he could make even a small noise. He could not. Whatever magic his sister had used on him, it was effective. He did not think she had destroyed his voice, because she would want to speak to him again at some point, or she would have killed him and been done with it. Then again, she had not needed Kael Elessedil to speak in order to discover what he knew. It might be the same with Bek. He had to hope that she wanted something else—that the doubt he sensed in her about his identity would protect him awhile longer.

He closed his eyes momentarily. He had to get out of there. He had to do so before his courage broke. But how was he going to do that? How could he possibly escape?

Momentary despair welled up inside him. He had thought himself safe with Truls Rohk. He had not believed anyone was strong or clever enough to best the shape-shifter. But he had been wrong, and now Truls was dead. She had left the caull to finish him, and if the caull had failed and died instead, she would have known. She had created it, after all. She was linked to it. The caull was alive. That meant Truls Rohk was not.

Bek had no real hope of being rescued by anyone else. In all likelihood, his companions were dead. Even Walker. It was too long for them to still be alive and not have shown themselves. He felt numb inside thinking about it. Even if they weren't all dead, those still alive were helpless against his sister. Grianne was too powerful for anyone. She had rendered the entire Rover crew, Redden Alt Mer and Rue Meridian included, unconscious with her magic. She had taken over the *Jerle Shannara* and cut off any possibility of escape. She had told Bek all of that in a matter-of-fact way, very much as if reciting what the weather would be like in the days ahead. She had done so to emphasize his helplessness, to convince him that his best hope lay through her, and he would do well to stop defying her. Only by cooperating, by revealing the truth about himself, could he hope to come out of this situation alive and well. Any other course of action would result in unpleasant consequences. He was supposed to think about that while she was gone.

He guessed he was doing so.

He guessed he was doing not much of anything else.

He tested again the bonds on his wrists. There was some give, but not enough for him to pull his hands free. The rope was dry and raw, and his sweat did not provide sufficient lubrication. Not that it mattered. Even if he could free himself from the rope, there was still the chain. He supposed his jailer had the key tucked away somewhere in his clothing, but he had no way of knowing for sure. He imagined himself loose from both rope and chain, racing through the corridors of the ship, gaining the upper deck, diving over the side, and swimming to shore. He could imagine it, but he might as well imagine he could fly.

He had only himself to rely on. Maybe he could still convince Grianne of the truth, but he was beginning to accept that it was unlikely. She just wasn't ready to hear it. She did not want to believe that he was her brother or that the Morgawr had tricked her. She had built her entire life around her belief that Walker was the enemy, that the Druid had destroyed her home and killed her family. She had made herself over so that she could not only match his power, but also exceed his perceived ruthlessness. She had done things that she could probably never live with if she were to discover how completely she had been manipulated. She was so deeply entrenched in her persona as the Ilse Witch that she could think of herself in no other way.

He considered for a moment the possibility that it was too late to save her, that she had gone too far to be redeemed, that she had committed too many atrocities to be forgiven. It was possible. Perhaps he had reached her too late.

He found himself thinking back to that night in the Highlands when he had encountered Walker for the first time. He had been reluctant to accept the Druid's offer to go on this journey. He had known somehow that if he did, nothing in his life would ever be the same. The reality was much grimmer than he could have imagined. It made him feel shriveled up and useless, torn apart by feelings that he had never hoped to experience. He wanted things to go back to the way they had been. He wanted to go home. He wanted Quentin and his friends to be safe and well. He wanted to be who he had always thought himself to be and not someone he knew nothing about. He wanted the nightmare to end.

The latch on the storeroom door grated loudly and the door opened. Three Mwellrets appeared, slouching into the room in cloaked and hooded anonymity, shades come out of the night. None of them said a word. The last to come inside closed the door and stood with his back placed firmly against it. The one directly ahead of him joined the guard in the shadows across the room. The leader came right up to Bek and pulled back his hood to reveal his reptilian face. It was Cree Bega, the Mwellret to whom his sister had entrusted his safety.

Cree Bega regarded the boy without speaking, his gimlet eyes hard and unpleasant. Bek tried to hold his own gaze steady, but the Mwellret's eyes made him queasy and weak. Finally, ashamed at his failure, he looked away.

Cree Bega reached with clawed fingers and removed the gag from Bek's mouth. He dropped the piece of cloth on the floor and stepped back. Bek took his first unobstructed breath of air in hours, but he could smell the Mwellrets in doing so, their raw, fecal odor rough and overpowering.

"Who are you, boy?" Cree Bega asked softly.

He spoke in a distant, almost distracted way, as if he didn't really expect an answer, but was asking only to voice the question to himself. His voice made Bek shiver. Fearing that what was going to happen next was not what his sister had planned, Bek worked his hands against the ropes once more.

Catching sight of the surreptitious movement, Cree Bega stepped forward and cuffed him sideways onto the floor. Then he reached down, hauled the boy back into a sitting position, and slammed him against the wall.

"There iss no esscape for little peopless," he whispered, "no esscape from uss!"

Bek tasted blood in his mouth and he swallowed it, his eyes locked on the Mwellret. Cree Bega knelt slowly so that his gaze was level with the boy's when he spoke.

"Thinkss perhapss sshe will come back to ssave you? Ilsse Witch, sso powerful, sso sstrong, fearss nothing? Hssst! Foolissh little peopless are nothing to her. Sshe forgetss you already."

He leaned forward. "Retss are your only friendss, little peopless. Only oness who can ssave you." His cold eyes glittered. "Thinkss me wrong, foolissh like you? Sshe wantss what'ss up here." He tapped Bek's head slowly. "Wantss nothing elsse but what sshe can usse againsst the Druid."

His eyes dead, his strange face empty of expression, he studied the boy's face for a long moment. "But if little peopless do ass I assk, I will sset you free."

Bek tried to speak and could not. He tried to move and could not. He was voiceless and paralyzed, locked in place by the other's gaze and the effects of the Ilse Witch's magic. Fear and despair flooded through him, and he fought to keep them from showing in his eyes. He did not succeed.

Cree Bega rose and walked away as if he were finished with Bek. He strode to the other side of the room, looked out of the open portal at the night sky, and then moved over to the two Mwellrets who stood waiting in the shadows against the wall. Bek watched him the way a ground bird would watch a hungry snake. He could do nothing to save himself. He could only listen and wait and hope.

One of the Mwellrets emerged from the darkness and knelt beside Bek. Slowly and deliberately, he unfolded a leather apron to reveal a series of glittering knives and razor-sharp probes. He never looked at Bek, never paid him any attention at all. He simply laid out the pouch with its cutting implements, rose again, and walked away.

Everything inside Bek knotted and twisted. He wanted to scream for help, but he knew it wouldn't do any good. He strained anew against the bonds that secured his wrists, but they were as tight as before. His choices were narrowing and his time was running out. Just moments earlier he might have believed that he had a chance still to escape harm; he no longer believed that was so.

Cree Bega moved back over to where Bek sat, stood over him like a great, dark, crushing force. "Thinkss carefully, little peopless," he rasped softly. "Wayss to make you sspeak the wordss you hide. Retss know wayss. Makess you sscream if you wissh to have uss tesst you. Eassier to jusst answser uss when we assk. Besst if you do. Then little peopless goess free."

He waited a moment, watching. Bek stared straight ahead at nothing, fighting against his terror, willing himself to stay calm.

Cree Bega nudged him gently with his boot. "Comess back to ssee you ssoon," he whispered.

Without a glance back, he turned and went to the storeroom door, opened it, and disappeared from view. The door closed softly behind him, and the latch snapped back into place.

Bek kept his gaze directed two feet in front of him at the edge of the candlelit darkness, trying to come to grips with what he must do. He could not get free without help. Help was not likely to come soon enough to matter. He was going to have to give the Mwellret what he wanted. But how could he do that? He could not speak, even if he wanted to do so. He tested the effects of Grianne's magic again, thinking that perhaps he had missed something. He tried everything he could, but nothing worked. His voice was gone.

Where did that leave him? He could write his answers to the Mwellret's questions, but that might not be enough to save him. Cree Bega looked the sort to test his speaking ability not just with words but with his deadly assortment of blades, as well. What could it hurt, after all, to make certain? Why not see just how voiceless the boy really was?

For the first time since he had departed the *Jerle Shannara* and gone inland in search of Castledown, Bek regretted giving up the phoenix stone. If he had kept it for himself, if he had not forced it on Ahren Elessedil, he would have a way to escape, even bound up as he was. Perhaps that was what the King of the Silver River had intended all along. Perhaps he had foreseen the situation and given Bek the stone as a means of getting free. The idea that he had willingly forsaken his chance was more than Bek could stand, and he banished the thought angrily. His gag was still off, and he took several deep, slow breaths to steady himself, but he could still feel his heart pounding. He glanced down again at the array of blades laid out beside him, then quickly away. He was so afraid. He felt tears start at the corners of his eyes and fought to keep them from running down his cheeks. The Mwellret guards would be watching. They would be hoping for this. They would report it to Cree Bega, who would think him even weaker than he already supposed. Cree Bega would use that against him.

He ran through his options, all of them, however remote or impossible they seemed; nothing new suggested itself. He would answer the questions Cree Bega asked of him. He would hope he could do so in writing and not be tortured first to find out if he was playing games. He would hope they would set him free from the ropes and chains—either of their own volition or by his suggestion—and if they did, that he could find an opportunity to escape. It was a pathetic plan, devoid of particulars or favorable odds, but it was all he could come up with. His hopes were in tiny shreds, and he clung to them as to bits of colored string, once bright with promise, now faded and worn.

It wasn't fair, he kept thinking. None of it. It was nothing of what he had thought he would find in coming here. It was promise turned to dust. The tears came again, harder, and they ran down his cheeks in crooked lines. He lowered his head into shadow in an effort to hide them.

As he did so, he heard the storeroom door open anew, a snapping of the latch, a soft creaking of the hinges. He glanced up quickly, expecting to see Cree Bega. But no one was there. The doorway was empty, a black hole into the outer passageway, where no lights burned.

Had those lights not been lit when Cree Bega departed the room? Bek wondered, suddenly alert.

For an instant, the Mwellret guards stood frozen in place. Then the ret who stood closest to the door drew a short sword from beneath his cloak and walked over for a look. He stood in the opening, unmoving, peering out into the corridor. Nothing happened. Slowly, carefully, he closed the door once more, the hinges creaking in the new-formed silence, the latch clicking sharply into place.

In the next instant, the candle next to Bek went out and the room was plunged into blackness except for the light from the single portal across the way, but that left everything shadowy and vague. Something went by Bek in a rush, the movement of its passage a cold breath of air against his skin. It made no sound as it closed with the nearest Mwellret, who grunted at the impact and went down. There was a warning hiss from the other two, and then both were engaged in a struggle that sent them careering across the darkened room and into the far wall. Bek caught a glimpse of their antagonist, a big cloaked form that moved with the speed and agility of a moor cat, launching into first one and then the other, hammering them, sending them down in broken heaps.

Bek stared. *It couldn't be.*

The first ret was back on its feet, charging to the aid of its fellows, the glitter of its blade caught momentarily in a wash of moonlight. There was a muffled collision of bodies and a grunt. Seconds later the ret staggered back again, the short sword buried in its chest, its movements limp and unfocused as it fought to stay upright. When it collapsed a moment later, the life gone out of it, the room was so still that Bek could hear himself breathe.

"What's the matter, boy?" someone whispered in his ear. "You look like you've seen a ghost."

It was Truls Rohk. Bek started so violently at the guttural sound of the other's voice that he nearly choked. The shapeshifter materialized beside him out of the darkness, his cloaked and hooded form blocking out the moonlight. In seconds he cut apart the ropes that bound the boy's wrists. Then, using a slender length of metal bar, he snapped apart the link that fastened the leg iron clasp in place, and Bek was free.

Truls Rohk hauled him to his feet. "No talking," he whispered. "Not until we're off this ship."

They went out into the darkened passageway, the shape-shifter leading the way. Despite stiffness and cramped muscles, still not quite believing his good fortune, Bek stayed close enough to touch him. They were barely a dozen paces beyond the storeroom when a raspy, broken cry went up from within. Bek at his heels, the shape-shifter continued down the corridor without looking back. The boy expected him to make for one of the stairways leading up and was surprised when he did exactly the opposite. Instead of ascending to the main deck, Truls Rohk turned down a dead-end corridor that led to the rear of the craft. Overhead, the sound of booted feet echoed through the decking, mingling with shouts and cries. The ship's company was fully awake and, if not hunting for them yet, well on the way to doing so.

The corridor Truls Rohk had turned down ended after only a few steps at a heavy wooden door. The shape-shifter opened it without hesitating and pulled Bek inside. The room was dark, but moonlight poured through two sets of open windows to reveal a fully furnished chamber. A man came awake in a bed to one side, springing out of the covers hurriedly, but a single blow from Truls Rohk knocked him into a wall where he collapsed in an unconscious heap.

"Out the window," the shape-shifter hissed at Bek, shoving him toward the open portals.

He turned back toward the door to the chamber, but it was already flying open, and half a dozen dark forms were charging through. Truls Rohk slammed into them with such fury that he sent all six careening backwards into the passageway, stumbling and cursing as they tried to keep their feet. Knives and short swords glittered in the moonlight, but the shape-shifter dodged through the slashing blades like a ghost, snatched hold of the open door, and slammed it shut, throwing the heavy latch in place.

"Get out!" he snarled over his shoulder at Bek.

Bodies hurtled against the door from without, and heavy blades pried at the metal latch and bit into the wood. Bek climbed onto the empty bed and lifted one leg over the sill. Almost at once, a darkened form dropped in front of him, suspended from a rope. Bek caught the gleam of a Federation insignia, kicked at the man's head, and sent him spinning away.

Behind him, the door splintered and sagged. Bek hesitated anew.

"Get out!" Truls Rohk repeated.

Bek went through the window just as another form dropped on a rope over the ship's railing, snatching for him. Bek evaded the savage lunge of his attacker and went headfirst into the water. Submerged in the concealing darkness, he swam away from the airship until his lungs were begging for air. When he resurfaced, there was no one else in sight. Aboard *Black Moclips*, the sounds of battle continued, sharp and desperate. Bek waited a moment for Truls Rohk to follow him into the water, but when he saw boats filled with Mwellrets being lowered over the side, he began to swim again. He was a good swimmer, and he carried no weapons or baggage to encumber him. He swam toward the darkened shoreline in smooth, easy strokes and was there before the first of his pursuers had cut loose from the ship to row after him.

Creeping as quietly as he could from the shallows, he ducked into the concealing trees, then looked back. Spread out across the waterline, their squat, bulky shapes frozen in the moonlight, the boats were coming toward him. He scanned the dark outline of *Black Moclips* for some sign of Truls Rohk, but found nothing. Aboard the airship, the clamor had died to a dull murmur of voices that carried easily across the open waters of the bay. Undecided about what he should do, Bek waited as the rowboats drew nearer. He was free, but he had nowhere to go. He had lost his magic and his weapons, so it was pointless to stand and fight. But if he ran, his captors would just track him down again. He needed the shape-shifter to help him. He needed Truls badly.

Finally he could wait no longer. The rowboats were almost on top of him. He melted into the trees as soundlessly as he could manage. His pursuers would not be able to pick up his tracks in the darkness, so he would have the better part of the night to put some distance between them. By morning, he could be far away.

But where was he going to go?

The hopelessness of his situation overwhelmed him, and for a moment he simply stopped where he was, staring out into the darkness. He was free, but what was he supposed to do about it? Should he go in search of the others from the ship's company, hoping that one or two might still be alive? Should he find Walker and warn the Druid about Grianne? Was there time enough to do anything at this point besides try to stay alive?

"What are you doing?" Truls Rohk hissed, materializing out of the darkness beside him. Water ran from his sodden cloak into the dirt. "If you stand around long enough, they'll find you for sure!"

He took an astonished Bek by the arm and propelled him forward into the trees. "Did you think I wasn't coming? Have some faith, boy. Cats aren't the only ones with nine lives." His cloak was torn, and blood was smeared on it. Within the concealment of his cowl, his eyes glittered. "Enough of this. Let's go after your sister. Family reunions are always interesting, but this one should be better than most." His sudden laughter was rough and unpleasant. "You try to save her and I'll try to kill her. Fair enough?"

His grip was like iron as he pulled Bek Ohmsford after him into the night.

TWENTY-THREE

Rue Meridian was still watching *Black Moclips* from the shoreline shadows with Hunter Predd, trying to decide what she should do, when the shipboard silence erupted in a cacophony of shouts and the clash of metal blades. It happened so suddenly that at first it was disorienting, and she was not even sure where the sounds were coming from. Exchanging a hurried glance with the Wing Rider, she moved farther along the shoreline, as if by doing so she might somehow better determine the source of the disruption.

To complicate her efforts, the moon slid behind a broad bank of clouds, plunging the bay and the airship into blackness.

"What's going on?" she hissed helplessly.

She paused in her advance as she heard wood splintering and metal hinges tearing loose. She couldn't mistake those sounds, she decided, glancing again at Hunter Predd. Then a splash sounded as something or someone went overboard. A second splash sounded immediately after, and she heard thrashing in the waters of the bay. Her first thought, instant and unconditional, was that someone was trying to escape. That someone would have to be a member of the company of the *Jerle Shannara*.

She ran down the shoreline, trying to track the sounds that

carried from the airship as she did so. But the struggle aboard ship continued unabated, and the clang of metal blades and the cries of the injured or dying drowned out everything else.

Finally, she stopped, knelt by the shore in the lee of a rocky overhang, and listened once more. She could hear movement in the water, as if someone was swimming, but she still couldn't tell from where it was coming. The fighting aboard *Black Moclips* had ended, replaced by angry grunts and the thud of heavy boots. The moon reappeared momentarily, giving her a glimpse of the airship's decks, bulky, cloaked forms rushing everywhere at once. In moments, they had lowered rafts into the water and were piling into them.

Mwellrets, off in pursuit of someone, she thought. But who?

The moon disappeared behind the clouds again, and the rafts slid away into the fresh darkness, making for shore behind the labored efforts of determined rowers. When the rets reached shore, they clambered from the rafts and disappeared into the jungle. Aboard *Black Moclips*, the sounds died away to isolated mutters and soft moans. Soon, even those faded.

Hunter Predd leaned close. "Someone got away from them."

She nodded, still listening, watching and thinking about what it meant. An opportunity, she believed. But how was she to take advantage of it?

"How many did you count in the rafts?" she asked.

"More than a dozen. Fifteen, probably. Mwellrets."

"All of them, I'll bet. All that's left." She thought of the dead ones aboard the *Jerle Shannara*, strewn across the decking in company with Hawk amid the wreckage of the rigging from the storm. She blinked the image away and made a quick calculation. *Black Moclips* would carry a crew and fighting complement of thirty-five. Subtracting the Mwellrets and the two Federation soldiers dead aboard the *Jerle Shannara*, that left a crew of perhaps eleven or twelve.

Hunter Predd nudged her arm. "What are you thinking?"

She looked right at him. "I need to get aboard."

He shook his head at once. "Too dangerous."

"I know that. But we have to find out if any others from the company are held prisoner. We won't get a better chance."

His leathery features creased with doubt. "You're still injured, Little Red. If you have to make a fight of it, you'll be in trouble."

"Trouble of the sort I don't need to hear about later, I know." She looked off toward the airship, a dark shape suspended over the water. "All I want is a look around."

The Wing Rider followed her gaze, but didn't say anything. He hunched his shoulders and studied the darkness with an intensity that surprised her.

"How do you plan to get out there?" he asked finally.

"Swim."

He nodded. "I thought as much. Of course, now that someone has escaped by jumping overboard and the rets have shoved off on the rafts in pursuit, I don't suppose those men left aboard will waste their time keeping an eye on the bay." He looked back at her. "Will they?"

He kept the sarcasm from his voice, but his point was well taken. A watch of some sort would be keeping a close eye on the surrounding waters for anything suspicious. She could approach by swimming underwater, but it was a long way and she was not as strong as she needed to be to try that. Nor could she count on the moon staying hidden behind the cloudbank. If it emerged at the wrong time, she would be silhouetted in the water as clearly as if by daylight.

"On the other hand," he continued quietly, "they won't be expecting anyone to fly in."

She stared at him. "On Obsidian? Can you do that? Can you drop me into the rigging?"

He shrugged. "It's still too dangerous. What do you think you can accomplish?"

"Have a look around, see if anyone else aboard is one of us." He held her gaze in an owlish, accusing look, and she grinned in spite of herself. "You don't believe me?"

"I believe you're telling me what you think I want to hear. But I read faces better than most, and I see something more in yours than what you're saying." He cocked his head. "Anyway, I'm going aboard with you."

"No."

He laughed softly. "No? I admire your spirit, but not your good sense. You can't get from here to there without me, and I won't take you unless I go, as well. So let's not debate the matter any further, Little Red. You need someone to watch your back, and if this matter turns sour, I need to be able to tell your brother that I did everything I could to protect you."

She gave him a rueful look. "I don't like it that you can see so clearly what I'm thinking."

He nodded. "Well, it might be that it will help me save your life somewhere down the road. You never know."

"Just get me on and off that ship in one piece," she said. "That's enough for me."

They waited a long time, giving the ship and crew time to quiet and settle back into a routine, keeping watch over the shoreline for the return of the Mwellrets. Rue Meridian believed they would be gone all night, trying to track whoever they were chasing, unable to see clearly enough in the darkness, forced to wait for daybreak. She was wondering about

the Ilse Witch. There had been no sign of her, no indication of
her presence. If she was not aboard ship, she was probably
somewhere inland hunting for the magic that had brought
them all to Castledown. Who had possession of that magic
now? Had Walker found and claimed it yet? Was it what he
had been expecting to find? There was no way of knowing
without making contact with a member of the shore party, another good reason for finding out if any of them had been
made prisoner by the witch and her rets.

"We should go, if we're going," Hunter Predd said finally.

Shedding his cloak and checking his weapons and clothing, he explained to her that Obsidian had been trained, as all
Rocs were trained, to lower their Wing Riders to aid in a
rescue. Using a harness and pickup rope, they would ride the
Roc out to the airship and lower themselves into the rigging.
When they were ready to leave, Obsidian would pick them up
again.

"This is the key," Hunter Predd advised, producing a small
silver implement. "A whistle, but only Rocs can hear it, not
humans. Stealth and silence are the rest of it, Little Red." He
grunted. "And luck, of course. That, most of all."

When they were ready, he used the whistle to summon the
Roc. Obsidian appeared from the bluff, sweeping down over
the bay to perch on the overhang they had passed on the way
down the shoreline. It was dark by then, the moon having disappeared with most of the stars behind the cloudbank. They
would have to hurry if they were to gain *Black Moclips* before
their cover broke.

On setting out that morning, Rue Meridian had braided her
long red hair and tied it back with a length of brightly colored
cord. She tightened the cord now, checked the daggers in her
belt and boot, and swung aboard Obsidian. Hunter Predd

took a seat in front of her, spoke softly to the Roc, and they lifted off. Gliding skyward into the black, they rose until the dark silhouette of the airship melted into the surface of the bay so completely that Rue Meridian could no longer see it. She was still trying to make it out, when Hunter Predd signaled to her over his shoulder that they were there.

Hand over hand, they slid from their seats down the pickup rope, a thick, knotted stretch of rough hemp that fell away into blackness. From high above everything, the entire world looked like a black hole save where the horizon could be glimpsed. Little Red felt her heart stop and her stomach clench as she went down the rope. She was unable to see anything, even Hunter Predd, who was descending below her. She felt herself swaying, and she couldn't tell if Obsidian was moving or not. Could Rocs hover? She would have given anything for a glimpse of something solid, but there was nothing to see.

Below, all was silent, even the Wing Rider in his descent. She listened carefully for her own sounds, working to muffle everything, but the silence only added to her sense of isolation and helplessness.

She had to fight to keep from panicking when the rope ran out and Hunter Predd wasn't there. Then a gloved hand gripped her boot and pulled her into the rigging of *Black Moclips*. She seized the cluster of draws and stays, pulling herself in tightly, and released the pickup rope. In an instant, it was gone, and Obsidian with it.

Clinging to the rigging of the airship, Hunter Predd so close she could hear him breathing, she took a moment to orient herself. After her eyes adjusted, she concluded that they were hanging from high on the rear mast, rocking gently with the slow sway of the airship. They could not stay there because the moment the clouds broke and the moon reappeared, they would be silhouetted clearly against the night sky to the watch below.

Drawing Hunter Predd close, she gestured downward, indicating what they must do. Slowly, but steadily, pressing herself close to the mast to stay hidden, she found the first of the iron rungs that formed hand- and footholds, then began her descent. The climb down took an enormous amount of time and energy, more of the latter than it would have taken had she been whole. Her wounds ached, irritated by the strain of physical exertion and mental concentration alike. She looked up and saw Hunter Predd directly above her, following her down. His descent was noiseless and smooth. He was better equipped for it than she.

When she got close enough to the deck to see who was set at watch, she paused. She found a pair of guards fore and aft—by their build and carriage, Federation soldiers. There was no one in the pilot box, but a third man paced the decks, moving back and forth between the pontoons and the masts, a restless, uneasy shadow. She caught a momentary glimpse of his whipcord frame and gaunt face as he passed through a sliver of starlight, and she started in surprise. Did she know him? She thought so. She glanced upward to where Hunter Predd clung to the iron rungs and motioned for him to stay put.

Then she descended another few feet and dropped softly to the decking, sliding into the shadow of a weapons rack. The guards never even looked her way. She watched the pacer a few moments longer, waiting for him to pass close, for his back to be turned; then she straightened and walked directly toward him. She was almost on top of him before he sensed her presence and turned.

By then she had a dagger at his throat and was standing close enough to see who he was.

"Well met, Donell Brae," she said quietly, her free hand taking a firm grip on his arm. "No loud noises, please. No sudden moves."

His seamed, weathered face broke into an ironic grin. "I told them it was a bad idea to leave you on your own ship, captive or no."

"Someone should have listened to you. So now you listen to me. The *Jerle Shannara*'s mine again, Big Red's and mine. But we lost Hawk, and I'm looking to pay someone back for that. Is she here?"

He blinked. "The witch? She's ashore, looking for the Druid." The washed-out blue eyes, so familiar, gave her a considering look. "Stay away from her, Little Red. She's poison."

Rue Meridian gave his throat a nudge with the dagger's tip, and he grunted. "She hasn't discovered what real poison is yet. Who else is here? Does Aden Kett command?"

Donell Brae nodded.

"Stupid choice for both of you."

"Not always a matter of choice, Little Red."

"Fair enough. But you have one now. Do what I tell you, and you can stay alive." She nudged him again with the dagger, forcing his head all the way back. "I always liked you, Donell. I wouldn't want our friendship to end badly."

He swallowed against the dagger tip. "What do you want?"

"Who's aboard besides you?"

"If you don't move that dagger away, I'll cut my own throat trying to answer."

She moved the blade down to his sternum. "Keep your hands at your sides. Any weapons on you?"

He lowered his head again and shook it. "Never liked them much. I'm a pilot, not a bladesman. That's for others."

One of the best Federation pilots she had met. They'd flown missions together over the Prekkendorran. He had come into the service with Aden Kett, a couple of young Federation soldiers when they had started out. Now he was a pilot and Kett an airship Commander. Their crew had been assigned to *Flying Mourn* when Rue Meridian fled west to the coast with her brother. The Federation Command must have given them *Black Moclips* as a reward for their service. It was a good choice. Aden Kett's crew was the best Federation outfit in the skies.

She walked Donell Brae over to the mast, where Hunter Predd waited. The Wing Rider had come down from his mast perch to find better concealment and to watch her back. The sentries at either end of the airship took no visible notice as she marched Donell up to him.

"Again, now—who's aboard?" she pressed the pilot softly.

He looked straight ahead. "The Commander, me, and eleven crew. Thirteen altogether. We started at fifteen, but two were left on the *Jerle Shannara* to man her. Dead, I suppose?"

She ignored him. "No Mwellrets lurking about?"

He shook his head. "All ashore, chasing that boy and whoever freed him."

A chill ran through her. She glanced at the dark form of Hunter Predd, who was close enough to hear. "Let's have a word with Aden Kett, Donell. Same rules until we're finished. Behave yourself and don't test me."

The seamed face glanced over. "I'm no fool, Little Red. I've seen you with those knives."

"Good. Hold on to that image. Now, where's the Commander?"

They went down the stairway that led through the rear decking to the lower passageways and holds. The Commander's chamber was aft, situated on the vessel's port side in the shelter of the pontoons. They moved silently down the short passageway to the cabin door and stopped. She nodded for Donell to speak.

"Commander?" he called through the door.

"Come," was the immediate response.

The pilot released the latch, and they moved inside in a rush. She kicked the door shut behind her, one hand on Donell Brae's arm, the other holding the dagger flat against her palm and low and tight against her side in a throwing position.

A pair of candles lit the darkness. Aden Kett was alone, propped up in his berth, writing in a journal, a cluster of maps spread out before him. When he glanced up, she saw his strong, handsome face was bruised and his head swathed in bandages. He seemed unsurprised to see her.

He put down the quill and ink and pushed the maps away. "Little Red." He looked at Donell Brae. "Things go from bad to worse for us these days, don't they?"

"Trying to decide exactly where in the scheme of things you are?" she asked, indicating the maps.

He shook his head. "Trying to plot a course home, one I hope to put to use very soon." He shrugged. "I can dream."

"Can I trust you not to call out for help while we talk?" she asked, balancing the dagger where he could see it.

He nodded wearily. "Who would I call out for? Why would I bother? The rets and the witch are ashore, and my crew and I are left in the dark once more. We're all of us sick of this business."

"Not going well, is it?" She moved Donell forward, still

keeping her free hand on his arm and the door at her back where she could get to it if she must. "You must long for the old days, bad as they were."

He smiled, a bit of life returning to his battered features. "Things were less complicated."

"For you, anyway. What happened to your face?"

"Someone got aboard and rescued the boy we were holding. They broke into my cabin. I came out of my berth just in time to get knocked back into it. Your don't look so good yourself."

She returned his smile. "I'm healing. Slow and steady. But don't mistake that for a weakness you can take advantage of, Aden. You're no better with blades than Donell." She let the warning sink in. "Tell me about this boy."

Aden Kett shrugged. "I don't know anything about him. He was a boy. The Ilse Witch brought him here and told us to keep him locked away until she came back for him. The rets were given responsibility for that, so it's their problem that he got away."

"Describe him. Smallish? Dark hair? Unusual blue eyes? Not an Elf, is he? Did you get a name?"

The other shook his head. "He doesn't talk. Can't, I gather. But that's him, the way you describe. Who is he?"

She didn't answer. It must be Bek. But why couldn't he speak? And who had managed to get aboard before her and spirit him away?

"No other prisoners?"

"None that I know of. Or care about." The Federation Commander pushed the maps off his lap and swung his legs over the side of the berth, making sure he did nothing to startle her. Then he stood and stretched his back and arms, taking his time. "No sleep for me this night, I can see. What do you want, Little Red?"

She decided to take a chance. "Your ship. On loan."

He straightened his tall frame, gingerly smoothed back his dark hair, and folded his arms across his chest. He gave her a considering look. "On loan?"

"We took back the *Jerle Shannara*, Aden. Big Red and me. But we lost Hawk in the process, and someone is going to pay for that. I already told this to Donell. The witch marooned us. Now I intend to do the same to her. If I could, I would kill her. But leaving her trapped here with her rets works just as well."

He nodded slowly. "You want me to help you?"

"I want you to stay out of the way." She paused, reconsidering. "All right. I want you to help me. It might not be a bad idea, given what this voyage is likely to end up costing you otherwise. But even if you don't, I want your word that you will stay out from underfoot. I already have control of *Black Moclips* anyway."

Aden Kett glanced at Donell Brae, who shrugged. "I only saw one other man."

She laughed. "You don't think I came aboard with just one man, do you? That would be madness!"

"The kind of madness you prefer," Kett suggested. "There's not much you wouldn't risk, Little Red." He gave her an appraising look, and she held his gaze. "Anyway," he said, "I'm not going to turn *Black Moclips* over to you just because you ask."

"It's only on loan," she reminded him. "I'm borrowing her just long enough to find my friends and get us to the coast. Then you can have your ship back, and no one will be the worse for it."

"The witch might not see it that way."

"The witch might not be around to find out."

He grunted. "I wouldn't want to bet my life on that. And I would be."

"Tell her you had no choice. Or just leave her behind and sail home. This fight isn't Federation business anyway. It's between the witch and the Druid. It's about something that doesn't concern any of us. All Big Red and I care about is the money."

He saw the lie in her eyes or heard it in her voice; she couldn't tell which. But she knew he didn't believe her. "What matters is that we're different, Little Red," he said. "You're not a soldier; you're a mercenary. I'm an officer of the line. I am expected to obey the orders I'm given, not change them to suit my mood. Nor am I allowed to change sides in the middle of an engagement. They call that treason."

She studied him, letting the words hang in the silence. She saw his eyes flick briefly to where his weapons hung in their harness from a peg. "If you look that way again," she said quickly, drawing his eyes back to her, "I'll kill you before I have a chance to think better of it."

She felt Donell Brae tense and immediately tightened her grip on his arm. "Don't do it," she warned.

Then footsteps sounded in the passageway outside, sudden and unexpected. Instantly, commander and pilot exchanged a second glance, this one filled with unmistakable meaning. "Commander?" a deep voice called out.

Donell Brae swung around quickly to grapple with her, but she was already moving. She knocked aside his upraised arm and hit him as hard as she could in the temple with the butt end of the dagger. As he went down, she leapt over him, intercepting Aden Kett in midstride as he reached futilely for his weapons. She slammed him back against the bulkhead and knocked him to the floor. Straddling him in fury, she pressed the dagger so tightly against his throat that she drew blood.

"Commander!" The knock at the door was rough and urgent.

"The only reason I don't kill you here and now is that I think you are a decent man and a good officer, Aden." Her face was so close to his she could see the terror reflected in his dark eyes. "Now answer him!"

Kett, pinned to the floor and gasping for air, swallowed hard. "What is it?" he called toward the door.

"The rets are coming back, Commander! One raft, just setting out from shore! You said to let you know!"

She put her free hand over his mouth, hesitating. She was losing control of the situation, and she had to turn that around immediately. First Aden Kett and Donell Brae try to attack her, and now the Mwellrets come back to the ship early. She hadn't believed either likely to happen, and her miscalculations were threatening to undo her. If she didn't act fast, all of her plans were going to fall apart. Trying to take over an entire airship and crew by herself was indeed madness, but that was what she intended. It had started out as a half-baked idea, a goal so far-fetched as to be all but impossible. But she thought now that it actually might be within reach.

She took her hand away from Kett's mouth. "Tell him to wait a moment," she whispered.

He did so. When he finished speaking, she rolled him over swiftly, pressed her knee into his spine, laid the dagger between his shoulder blades, and pulled his hands behind his back. Using a leather tie she carried in her belt, she fastened his hands securely in place. Then she rose, the dagger in hand again, and hauled him to his feet.

"Tell him to enter," she whispered.

He did as he was told, and the crewman opened the door and stepped inside. He froze instantly when he saw her with the dagger at his commander's throat and the pilot sprawled motionless on the floor.

"Not a sound," she hissed at the crewman, making an unmistakable gesture with the dagger. She waited for his nod of agreement, then indicated Donell Brae. "Pick him up. Quick!"

Kneeling, the crewman pulled the unconscious pilot over one shoulder and stood up again. "Walk down the hall to the sleeping quarters," she ordered him. "I'll be right behind you. One sound, one wrong move, and your commander and your pilot and probably you, as well, are dead men. Tell him, Aden."

Aden Kett grunted, feeling the dagger point dig into him. "Do as she says."

They went out from the cabin and into the dimly lit corridor, the crewman carrying Donell Brae, and Rue Meridian following with Aden Kett. They wound silently through the airship's lower levels toward the sleeping quarters forward.

When they reached the door to the sleeping quarters, she stopped them outside. She turned Aden Kett around so he could see her clearly. "Inside, Aden," she ordered. "Stay put until I come down to let you out again. The door will be locked behind you, and I expect it to stay that way. If I hear anything I don't like, I'll set fire to the ship and burn her to the waterline with you and your crew still inside her." She held his gaze. "Don't test me."

He nodded, a hint of fresh anger in his eyes. "You're making a mistake, Little Red. The Ilse Witch is much more dangerous than you think."

"Inside."

She opened the door, let them enter, closed it again, and threw the locking bolt. She took an extra moment to secure it by wedging a dagger blade into the slide so it could not be pried open. The portholes cut into the hull to admit fresh air were not large enough for a man to crawl through. For the moment, at least, she had the commander and crew of *Black Moclips* trapped.

She went up the ladder through the hatchway to the main deck on the fly, found the last sentry at the aft rail, and went after him. She already knew he was too far away for her to reach before he saw her coming, but she went anyway. There was no time left for stealth. She had to hope he was all that was left of the crew. Out of the corner of her eye, she saw the approaching raft and the bulky forms of the Mwellrets it carried, closing fast. She could feel the ache of her injured leg and side as she ran, a fresh tearing of her wounds, but she pushed aside her pain and quickened her speed.

The crewman turned at the sound of her approach, weapons lifting. She was too slow and still too far away!

Then abruptly, he crumpled to the deck, and Hunter Predd stepped from behind the mainmast, sling in hand.

"Cut the anchor lines!" she called, changing direction for the pilot box.

She heard muffled shouting, sibilant and angry, from the raft. She gained the box and sprang to the controls, drawing down ambient light from the single sail already set in place to keep *Black Moclips* aloft, throwing the levers to the parse tubes, opening them up all the way. The airship lurched with the infusion of power. She heard Hunter Predd cut the aft anchor line, then run forward to cut the bow one, as well.

Faster!

The Wing Rider's sword rose and fell twice. Slowly, ponderously, *Black Moclips* rose into the air, severed anchor ropes trailing from her decking, arrows and javelins thudding into the underside like hailstones. The raft with its furious, helpless Mwellrets fell away and disappeared into the darkness.

She closed down the parse tubes and eased off on drawing down ambient light for power. The ship was an old friend and responded well to her touch. But maneuvering her alone was rough and uncertain. Without help, Rue Meridian could not manage a ship of that size for very long. She would need help, as well, with the dozen Federation soldiers she had trapped in their sleeping quarters below. She recognized the situation readily enough and knew that before long Aden Kett and his men would find a way to escape.

She slowed the airship to a crawl and brought her about, pointing her inland toward Castledown. Somewhere ahead, the Ilse Witch was hunting Walker, Bek was running for his life, and whoever still lived of the company of the *Jerle Shannara* waited for a rescue.

A rescue that perhaps only she could manage.

She watched Hunter Predd approach, saw the questioning look in his dark eyes, and shook her head.

She wished she had a better answer to give him. She knew she had better find one soon.

TWENTY-FOUR

Quentin Leah was listening so intently that he started in surprise when Tamis touched his arm in warning.

"He's coming," she whispered.

Consumed by the fact that Ard Patrinell's mind was still alive inside, she was still calling the wronk *he* rather than *it*— as if the human part mattered more. The rest of it might be mechanical—armor, wires, and machine parts, cold and emotionless metal—but not its mind, trapped as it was, whole and intact, thinking Ard Patrinell thoughts, using Ard Patrinell skills, hunting them with a determination that was relentless and implacable.

Heeding her warning, Quentin listened for its coming. Try as he might, he still could not hear it.

In the twilight he glanced over at her. Her roundish, pixie face was sweaty and her short brown hair tangled with bits of debris. Her clothing was torn and bloody and as dirty as the rest of her. She had the look of a hunted thing, a creature run to earth by something as inescapable as the coming of night.

A mirror of himself, he allowed. He did not need to see what he looked like to know it was so. They were a matched set, fugitives from a fate that neither could escape, that both were forced to confront.

They had been running from it all day, running since the coming of dawn had persuaded them they must find a way to kill it. All through the forests surrounding Castledown's ruins they had played cat and mouse with the inevitable, marking time as they searched for a way to put an end to the creature. It was a chase marked by fits and starts, by schemes and subterfuges, by equal parts skill and blind luck. The wronk was a terrifying adversary, made more dangerous by the fact that Ard Patrinell's thinking guided it. Sometimes it would come after them in direct pursuit, a hunter using strength and stamina to run them down. Sometimes it would circle around to lie in wait, a predator set to pounce. Sometimes it would stop altogether and wait for them to pause in turn, to wonder if they had lost it entirely, and then it would approach from an unexpected direction, swift and sudden, trying to catch them off guard. Many times it almost had them, but they were saved in each instance by their combined experience and skill and by the kind of luck that defies explanation.

Of the latter, Quentin reflected, there had been more than the former, which was why they were still alive.

The search for a wronk pit had taken longer than they expected. They had thought the Rindge would have set many such traps to protect themselves from the creatures of Antrax. Quentin and Tamis had set out that morning to find the nearest one, backtracking toward the village of Obat and his people to find the pits that had to be located along the approaches from Castledown. But the wronk caught up to them so quickly that they had to hurry their search and consequently failed to find what they were looking for. The wronk was unmistakable when it was close and moving, too big and heavy to conceal its coming. But even when they could not hear it, they were forced to listen and watch for it because it was subtle and clever, like Patrinell, and constantly looking for a way to catch them off guard.

For Quentin Leah, life had been reduced to the simplest of terms—survival of the fittest. He was engaged in the kind of life-and-death struggle that he had imagined happening to others, but never to himself. All of his thinking about a grand adventure and new experiences, everything that had spurred his decision to join the quest, had faded into a barely remembered past. The enthusiasm he had imparted to Bek, the limitless possibilities he had envisioned for what they would find, and the confidence that had buoyed him through so many harrowing confrontations along the way had turned to dust. He had all but forgotten Walker and the search for the books of magic. He had pushed aside any thought of rescuing the others, Bek included. All that was left was a fatalistic and dogged determination to stay alive for another day, to escape the thing that hunted him, and ultimately to regain enough space to allow something back into his life of who and what he had been.

He had no idea what Tamis was thinking, although he could guess readily enough. She was burdened by similar needs, but as well by her memories of and feelings for the man with whom she had been in love. She might pretend otherwise, might tell herself something else, but it was clear to him that she could not separate herself from her emotions, could not be truly objective about what they were seeking to accomplish. For Tamis, the struggle to destroy the wronk was more than trying to stay alive. It was giving Ard Patrinell the release he could find no other way, the peace that only death would bring. Her hatred of what had been done to him was so invasive that it simmered on her features at every turn. The battle was personal for her in a way it could never be for Quentin, and she was driven almost beyond reason.

But not beyond the limit of her skills, Quentin quickly saw, which were considerable. Trained as a Tracker by Patrinell himself, she was all business and judgment, able to play well a game in which no mistakes were allowed. She knew what to expect from the mind that hunted them, was familiar with its thinking, its nuanced reasoning. She could anticipate what it would try and blunt the effect. The wronk was physically stronger, and if they got within its reach, there was little question of the outcome. But Tamis was whole where the wronk was fragmented, cobbled together of parts that did not naturally fit. That gave her an advantage she could exploit, and she was quick to try to do so.

It was odd to think of what they were attempting, fleeing on the one hand and looking to make a stand on the other. It was schizophrenic and disjointed, grounded in opposing principles and mind-wrenching in its demands. Flee the danger, but find a way to face it. Quentin had no time for a balanced consideration of the contradiction. He was consumed by the knowledge that the thing pursuing them did so to destroy him, yet to leave a part of him alive, as well. It would turn him into itself, a perfect copy, able to wield the magic of the Sword of Leah yet unable to act save as Antrax chose to order. The idea of becoming the machine that Ard Patrinell had become was so terrifying, so mind-numbing, that he could not do more than glance at the prospect of it the way he would the sun, shunning the pain of any prolonged study. But even that gave him a bitter, clear understanding of why Tamis was so determined to save Ard Patrinell.

That day's flight was through the disjointed landscape of a surreal netherworld. The sounds of the pursuing wronk were all around and constant, letting up only now and then, when the hunter chose a less obvious tack. The day was cloudy and sunny by turns, casting shadows that moved past them like shades and suggested things that weren't there, yet might be coming. They were worn already on setting out, and their weariness quickly deepened. They passed places in which brush and trees were trampled and broken by fighting and frantic flight. They came upon dead men killed the day before. Most were Rindge, the reddish skin giving them identity when only pieces remained. One was an Elf, although there wasn't enough of him to determine which one. Blood soaked the ground and smeared the trees in splotches dried black by the sun. Weapons and clothing lay scattered everywhere. Silence cloaked the carnage and desolation.

As they had neared the Rindge village, the number of dead increased. They were too many to be only those from the hunting party. When they reached the village itself, they found its huts and shelters smashed and burned and its people gone. Some few lay dead, those who had bought with their lives a chance for the others to escape. That a single being could wreak such havoc, alone and unaided, against so many, was horrifying. That the mind of Ard Patrinell was an integral part of that being and would know what it was doing yet be unable to stop was heartbreaking. Tamis did not cry as they passed through the village, but Quentin saw tears in her eyes.

They had paused at the far side of the village, where the carnage ended. Those who remained of Obat's people had fled into the hills and perhaps to the mountains beyond. The wronk had lost interest in them at that point and gone elsewhere.

Quentin stood with Tamis and stared at the destruction.

"You were not mistaken about his eyes?" she asked him almost desperately. All of the bravado and irony gone out of her voice, she could barely bring herself to speak. "It was Ard Patrinell looking out at you from inside?"

He nodded. He could think of nothing to say.

"He would never do anything like this if he could help himself," she said. "He would die first. He was a good man, Highlander, maybe the best man I have ever known. He was kind and caring. He looked after everyone. He thought of the Home Guard as his family and of himself as their father. When new members were brought in for training, he let them know he would do everything he could to keep them safe. At gatherings, he told stories and sang. You saw him as taciturn and hard, but that was only since the death of the King, for which he blamed himself, for which he could not forgive himself. Kylen Elessedil stripped him of his command for imagined failures and political convenience. Bad enough. But now this monster, this Antrax, strips him of control over his actions, as well, and leaves him a shell of powerless knowledge."

It was the most he had ever heard her say at one time and as close as she had ever come to admitting what she felt about the man she loved.

She looked away, sullen and defeated. "Can you imagine what this is doing to him?"

He could. Worse, he could imagine it happening to himself, which was too horrifying to ponder. His hand tightened around the handle of his sword. He carried it unsheathed all the time now, determined that he would never be surprised, that if attacked, he would be ready. It was all he could think to do to tip the balance in his favor. It was strange how little comfort it gave him.

They had walked back through the village, choosing a different path out, still searching for one of the elusive pits. The sun had moved across the sky in a long, slow arc, the day wandering off with nothing to show for its passing, the night coming on with its promise of raw fear and increasing uncertainty. Time was an insistent buzzing in his ear, a reminder of what was at stake.

It had been quiet when they entered the village. When they left, they could hear in the distance the sounds of the wronk as it moved toward them.

Tamis wheeled back in something close to blind fury, her short sword glinting in the light. "Perhaps we should stand and face him right here!" she hissed. "Perhaps we should forget about hunting for pits that might not even exist!"

Quentin started to make a sharp reply, then thought better of it. He shook his head instead, and when he spoke he kept his voice gentle. "If we die making a useless gesture, we do nothing to help Patrinell." She glared at him, but he did not look away. "We made an agreement. Let's stick to it."

They went on through the afternoon, out of the village and back toward Castledown, choosing a trail that was almost overgrown from lack of use. No sign of life appeared. About halfway between the village and the ruins, at the beginnings of twilight, they were passing through an open space in the woods in which tall dips and rises rippled the ground and grasses grew in clumps. The failing light was even poorer there, screened by conifers that grew well over a hundred feet tall and spread in all directions save south, where a wild-flower meadow opened off the rougher ground. They were moving toward a pathway that opened off the far side when Tamis grabbed Quentin's arm and pointed just ahead, which he thought looked like everything else around them, scrub-grown and rough. In exasperation, she pulled him right up to the place to which she was pointing, and then he recognized it for what it was. The pit was well concealed by a screen of sapling limbs layered with some sort of clay-colored cloth, sand and dirt, clumps of dried grasses, and debris. It was so well designed that it disappeared into the landscape. Unless you were right on top of it and looking down, you wouldn't see it.

Yet Tamis had. He looked at her for an explanation.

She smirked with rueful self-depreciation. "Luck."

She pointed to one side. It took him a while to see that a corner of the support cloth had worked itself to the surface and was sticking up. "Bury that, and the pit will be invisible again."

"Or move it to another place, and you create a red herring. And an edge for us." He looked at her questioningly. "What do you think?"

She nodded slowly. "Because Patrinell will see it, too, just like I did." She put a hand on his shoulder and squeezed. "This is what we've been searching for, Highlander. We make our stand here."

They had cut away the bit of cloth and reburied it off to one side with the corner sticking up. They used a scattering of twigs and grasses to suggest that the pit might be located there. It was reasonable to assume that the wronk, using Ard Patrinell's skills and experience, would be looking for traps and snares, especially if it found them prepared to stand and fight. If they could draw it in the wrong direction or mislead it in just the slightest, they could drop it into the pit before it knew what was happening.

It was a dangerous gamble. But it was all they had to work with.

So now they waited in the deepening night, listening to the adversary's approach, to a sharp crackling of brush and limbs, steady and inexorable. They had considered lighting fires to give them a clear battlefield, but decided that darkness favored them more. The moon and stars appeared and faded behind a screen of clouds, providing snatches of light with which to operate. They had positioned themselves squarely behind the false pit, leaving the best and most logical path to reach them to their right, over the real pit. They stood together now, but would change position when the wronk appeared. They had worked their plan out carefully. All that remained was to test it.

It would work, Quentin told himself silently. It had to.

He heard the wronk clearly, heavy footfalls drawing closer. His skin crawled with the sound. Tamis stood right beside him, and he could hear the soft rasp of her breathing. They held their swords in front of them, blades glinting in the moonlight as the clouds broke overhead momentarily. Quentin's head throbbed and his blood tingled with fiery sparks of magic that broke away from the Sword of Leah as it responded to his sense of danger. He felt the change in his body as he prepared to give himself over to its power. An equal mix of satisfaction and fear roiled within him. He would be transformed, and he knew now what that meant. When the magic entered him, he infused himself with its terrible fury and risked his soul.

Without it, of course, he risked his life. It was not much of a choice.

With an almost delicate grace, the wronk stepped into the clearing. Though its features were hazy and spectral in the faint light, its shape and size were unmistakable. Quentin watched it with a mix of raw fear and revulsion. It registered his presence instantly, freezing in place, casting about as if testing the wind. A glint of metal speared the darkness as a piece of the monster reflected momentarily in the starlight. The moon had disappeared back behind the clouds, and the night was thick and oppressive. Within the black wall of the trees, there was unbroken silence.

The Highlander felt Tamis tense, waiting for him to take the lead. They had agreed that he must do so, that he was the one the wronk was seeking and so could best draw it in the direction they wished it to go. Their plan was simple enough. Pretend to decoy it one way, knowing it would choose to go another. It was Ard Patrinell's brain at work inside the wronk, so it would be Patrinell's thinking that would direct it. It would sense a feint, a deception, and so act to avoid it. If they could take advantage of that thinking, if they could anticipate its reasoning, they could lure it into the pit. It was a poor plan at best, but it was the only plan they could come up with.

The wronk shifted again, drawing fresh shards of starlight to its metal skin, pinpricks of brightness that flashed and faded like fireflies. They heard its heavy body as it took a step forward and paused anew. Nothing of Ard Patrinell's tortured face was visible to them, and so they could try to pretend the wronk was nothing more than a machine. But in his mind Quentin saw the Elf's eyes anew, looking out from their prison—frantic, pleading, desperate for release. He would have banished the image if he had known how to do so, but it was so strong and pervasive that he could not manage it. It was a window not only into Patrinell's terrible fate, but also into his own. Tamis would free her lover from his living death. Quentin would simply avoid sharing his fate.

Sweating freely, the heat forming a sheen of perspiration on his face and arms, he wondered absently how matters had come to that end. He had embarked on the journey with such hopes for something wonderful and fulfilling and life-transforming. He had wanted an adventure. What he'd gotten was a nightmare.

"Ready?" he whispered.

Tamis nodded, grim-faced. "Don't let it take me alive," she said suddenly. "Promise me."

"Promise me, as well." His heart was hammering within his chest.

"I loved him," she whispered so quietly he barely heard her speak the words.

Quentin Leah took a deep breath and brought up his sword.

TWENTY-FIVE

Bek Ohmsford followed Truls Rohk from the shoreline without resistance. He ran with the shape-shifter deep into the forest for a long time and did not complain. But finally his efforts at keeping up failed. His strength gave out, and he collapsed at the base of a broad-limbed maple, sitting with his head between his legs, sucking in huge gulps of air.

The shape-shifter, a cloaked shadow in the deep night, wheeled back soundlessly and knelt beside him. "You went longer than most would. You're tough, for a boy."

They stared at each other in the darkness. Bek tried to speak and couldn't. Whatever Grianne had done to him, escaping *Black Moclips* hadn't helped. His voice was still gone. He made a series of weak, futile gestures, but the other mistook his silence for exhaustion.

"You thought I was dead, didn't you?" Truls Rohk laughed softly. "That's a mistake that's been made before." He shifted within the cloak and settled into a crouch. "I was close to dying, though. The witch set a trap I wasn't looking for—a caull. She guessed at my purpose in circling back to wait for her and got the caull behind me. I was too anxious to get back to you to be looking out for it properly. It caught me reaching

344

down for your knife with my back turned. I didn't even know it was there."

He paused. "But you saved me. All without knowing. Think of that."

Bek shook his head in confusion.

"After I left, you had a visit from the shape-shifters who inhabit that region."

Bek nodded. He could still remember the smell and feel of them in the night, all size and bristling hair and raspy voices, like feral beasts.

"Whatever you said to them caught their interest. They decided to wait for me, as well. When a true shape-shifter hides, no one can find it. The caull, lying in wait for me, couldn't. Couldn't even tell they were there. When it attacked me, they snatched it right out of the air, bound it in cords so tough it could not break free, and carried it away. Before they left, they told me that my place in this world and my life belonged to you. What do you suppose they meant?"

Bek thought back, remembering how the shape-shifters had queried him about his relationship to Truls Rohk, probing his reasoning, testing his loyalty. *Would you give up your life for him? Yes, because I think he would do the same for me.* His answer, it seemed, had meant something after all.

Truls Rohk grunted. "Anyway, I fell asleep when they left me. Not what I had planned, but I couldn't help myself. It was something in their voices. When I woke, I came looking for you. But the witch took care to disguise her passage in ways I couldn't immediately unravel. It didn't matter. I knew she would bring you back here. I tried the airship first thing, seeing it moored in the bay. *Black Moclips,* the witch's own vessel. Your smell led me right to you, locked down in that hold. I got to you just in time, didn't I?"

He waited a heartbeat, then reached out suddenly and snatched Bek by his tunic front. "What's wrong with you, boy? Why don't you say something?"

Bek wrenched himself free and pointed angrily at his neck. Then he clapped his hand over his mouth for emphasis.

"You're injured?" the other demanded. "Something's damaged your throat?"

Impatiently, Bek scratched the words in the dirt with a stick. The cowled head bent for a look. "You can't speak?" Bek wrote some more. "The witch stole your voice? With magic?"

Truls Rohk rocked back on his haunches and stood up. He made a dismissive gesture. "She doesn't have that kind of power over you. Never has. What do you think the Druid has been trying to tell you? You're her equal, though untrained yet. You have the gift, too. I knew that from the moment we met in the Wolfsktaag, months ago."

Bek shook his head vehemently, shouting soundlessly, bitterly in response.

"Think!" the other snapped irritably. "She's kept you alive so far to find out what you know. Would she destroy your voice so that you could never speak again? Huh! No, she's done what she does best. She's played a game with your mind. She's knocked you down and left you thinking what she wants you to think. It's mind-altering, of a sort. You can speak, if you want. Go ahead. Try."

Bek stared at him in disbelief, then shook his head.

"Try, boy."

I've already tried! He mouthed the words angrily.

Truls Rohk pushed him hard. "Try again."

Bek staggered backwards and righted himself. *Stop it!*

"Do what I say! Try again!" The shape-shifter shoved him

a second time, harder than before. "Try, if you've got any backbone! Try, if you don't want me to knock you down!" He shoved Bek so hard he almost sent him sprawling. "Tell me to stop! Go on, tell me!"

Flushed with rage, Bek charged the cloaked form, but Truls Rohk blocked his rush and pushed him away. "You're afraid of her, aren't you? That's why you won't try. You're frightened! Admit it!"

He wheeled away. "I've no use for someone who can't do more than follow at my heels like a dog. Get away from me! I'll do this alone."

Bek charged in front of him and blocked his way. *Stop it! I'm coming with you!*

"Then you tell me so to my face!" Truls Rohk's voice dropped to a dangerous hiss. "Tell me right now, boy!" He shoved Bek again, harder than ever. "Tell me, or get out of my—"

Something gave way inside Bek, a visceral rending of self that had the feel of tearing flesh. It gave way before a mix of rage and humiliation and frustration that engulfed him like a swollen river slamming up against a dam built for calmer waters. His voice exploded out of him in a primal scream of such impact that it lifted Truls Rohk off his feet and sent him flying backwards. It bent the branches of trees, flattened tall grasses, shredded bark, and tore up clots of earth for a dozen yards. It began with the shriek of a hurricane's winds as it sapped the forest silence, then layered it anew in a darker and more suffocating blanket.

Bek dropped to his knees in shock and disbelief, coughing out the final shards of noise, the sound of his voice dropping to a startled whisper.

Truls Rohk picked himself up and brushed himself off.

"Shades!" he muttered. He reached out his hand to Bek and pulled him to his feet. "Was that really necessary?"

Bek laughed in spite of himself. It felt good to hear the sound again. "You were right. I could speak all along."

"But not until I got you mad enough to make you do so." The shape-shifter's impatience showed in his voice. "Don't let yourself get fooled like that again."

"Don't worry, I won't."

"You are her match, boy."

"I'll find out soon enough, won't I?"

The big shoulders shrugged within the concealing cloak. "Maybe you should leave her to me."

A chill of recognition rippled down Bek's neck. He reached out impulsively and gripped the other's shoulder, feeling corded muscle and sinew tighten in response, feeling knots of gristle shift. "What do you mean?"

"What do you think I mean?"

Bek's stomach clenched. "Don't do it, Truls. Don't kill her. I don't want that. No matter what. Promise me."

The other's laughter was harsh and empty. "Why should I promise you that? She was quick enough to try to kill me!"

"She's as confused about things as I was. She's been lied to and deceived. What she believes about herself and about me isn't even close to the truth. Doesn't she deserve a chance to find this out? The same chance you gave me, just now?"

He kept his grip on the other's shoulder, holding on to him as if to wring the concession he sought. But Truls Rohk didn't try to move away. Instead, he took a step closer.

"If another were to lay hands on me the way you have, I would kill him without a thought."

Bek did not back away even then, did not dare to move, though an inner voice was screaming at him to do so. He felt impossibly small and vulnerable. "Don't kill her. That's all I'm asking."

"Huh! Shall we invite her to join us, forget her evil life, forgive the past, pretend she has no alliance with the rets? Is that your plan—to talk her into being our friend? Didn't you try that already?"

The cowled head bent close, and Bek could hear the unpleasant rasp of the other's breathing. "Grow up all the way, boy. This isn't a game you can start over if you lose. If you don't kill her, she will kill you. She's well beyond any place where reason or truth can reach her. She's lived a lifetime of lies and half-truths, of delusions and deceptions. Think what brought her to us. Her single, all-consuming ambition is to kill Walker. If she hasn't succeeded in doing so already, she will try her luck soon. Even though the Druid irritates me and has brought much of this misfortune on himself, I won't give him up to her."

Both hands shot out suddenly and snatched hold of Bek once again. "She isn't your sister anymore! She is the Morgawr's tool! She is her own dark creation, as deadly as the creatures she is so fond of using, the things she makes out of nightmares! She is a monster!"

Bek went still, facing into the black void of the other's cowl. There was no question about what would happen if Truls Rohk found Grianne. The shape-shifter would not waste a moment's time considering the alternatives. If Bek didn't find a way to change his mind right now, the shape-shifter would kill her—or die himself in the attempt.

Before he could think better of it, before the consequences could register fully enough to make him reconsider, he said, "Some would say the same about you. Some would say that you are a monster, as well. Would they be right? Are you any different from her?"

The hands tightened on his arms. "Watch your mouth, boy. There is all the difference in the world between us, and you know it."

Bek took a deep, steadying breath. "No, I don't know anything of the sort. To me, you are the same. You both hide who you are. She hides behind lies and deceptions. You hide behind your cloak and hood. How much does anyone know about either of you? How much is concealed that no one ever sees? Why does she deserve to die and you to live?"

Truls Rohk lifted him off his feet as effortlessly as he would a child, his anger a palpable thing in the silence. For an instant Bek was certain the shape-shifter would dash him to the ground.

"Show me your face, if you want me to believe in you," he said.

"I warned you about this," the other hissed. "I told you to let it be. Now I'm telling you for the last time. Leave it alone." He held Bek like a rag doll. "Enough. Time for us to be going. Your recovery of your voice could be heard two miles away."

"Show me your face. We're not leaving until you do."

The shape-shifter shook him so hard Bek could hear his joints crack. "You can't stand to look on me!"

Bek swallowed and stiffened. "If you aren't a monster, if you're not hiding the truth, show me your face."

Truls Rohk gave an angry growl. "My face is not who I am!"

He lifted Bek higher then, almost over his head, as if he might fling him away. There was such power in the shape-shifter, such strength! The boy closed his eyes and hung in a black void, listening to his heartbeat.

Then he felt himself lowered back to the ground. The

hands released him. He opened his eyes and found Truls Rohk towering over him, black and impenetrable. All around, the forest had turned oppressively still, as if become an unwilling, frightened witness to what was taking place.

"If you see me, if you *really* see me, it will change everything between us," Truls Rohk said.

He seemed almost desperate to prevent this from happening, to change the boy's mind. It was more than wanting to preserve their relationship as protector and ward. It was a fear that their friendship, whatever stage it had reached, would shatter like glass. Bek could understand, and yet he knew he could not back away, not if he wanted to save Grianne.

"Don't ask again," Truls Rohk warned.

Bek shook his head. "Show me your face."

"All right, boy! You want to see what I look like, what I keep hidden from everyone? Then, look! See what my parents made of me! See what I am!" the other said with such venom that Bek flinched.

In a single, frenzied movement, he ripped away the cloak and stood revealed.

At first Bek saw him only as a vague shape outlined against the dark; the moon and stars were screened away by clouds, leaving the forest little more than a gathering of shadows. Truls Rohk's cloak lay in a dark puddle on the ground, and the shape-shifter had dropped into a crouch, looking feral and dangerous. Poised neither to flee nor to strike, he seemed instead caught in a spiderweb of tree limbs that formed a backdrop behind him, pinned against the distant sky.

Then Bek saw the beginnings of movement. The movement did not come from a shifting of limbs or head, but from within the dark mass of his body, as if the flesh itself was alive and crawling. The movement had a liquid appearance and Truls

Rohk the look of glass filled with water. It was so unexpected that Bek thought his eyes were deceiving him. He thought so, as well, when parts of the shape-shifter faded then re-appeared in ghostly fashion.

But when the moon slid from behind the clouds and flooded the clearing with milky brightness, Bek understood. Truls Rohk looked like something cobbled together from stray parts of human debris, some of it half-formed, some of it half-rotted, all of it shifting like a mirage that might not be there at all. The watery look came from the way in which pieces of him constantly changed from flesh and bone to mist and air. There was nothing permanent about Truls Rohk. He was only a half-completed thing, some of him recognizable as human, but not enough to call him a man.

It was easily the most terrifying sight Bek had ever witnessed—not simply for what it was, but for what it suggested, as well. It whispered of the grave, of death and decay, of what waited to claim the body when it began to decompose. It screamed of what it would feel like to have your body disintegrate about you. It suggested unimaginable pain and suffering. It reminded of nightmares and the creatures that came out of them to drive you from your sleep. It was surreal and ugly. It was anathema to any human concept of life.

He said nothing, but Truls Rohk saw the look in his eyes. "This is what happens when a shape-shifter mates with a human," he whispered in barely contained fury. "This is what comes from breaking taboos. I told you my father tried to kill me after killing my mother. He did so when she showed him what he had made with her. He did so when he saw what I was. He couldn't stand it. He couldn't abide me. Who could? I am trapped in a half-formed body. I am bits and pieces of flesh and bone on the one hand and nature's elements on the other, but not fully formed of either. I shift back and forth between them, trapped."

Bek could not speak. He stared wordlessly, trying to imagine what it must be like to be Truls Rohk, unable to do so.

The shape-shifter laughed dully. "Not so eager to look on me now, are you? Too bad. This is what I am, boy. I have strength and power at my command. I have a presence. But I lack a true shape-shifter's ability to change forms smoothly. I cannot hide the truth of myself. It's why I live apart, why I have always lived apart. No one can stand to look on me."

He came forward a step, and Bek shrank back in spite of himself as the bits and pieces of the other's body rippled and shifted, exposing ends of bones and runnels of blood and strips of torn flesh amid the shifts of air and water, of light and dark. An eye protruded and disappeared. Teeth gleamed out of a half-stripped skull. Hands showed the ends of finger bones and bare tendons. Hair and skin grew in patches, split and torn. Nothing seemed designed to hold together, yet hold it did, though everywhere with the look of something about to collapse into itself.

"Huh!" Truls Rohk spat out the sound with such venom that it caused the boy to flinch. The ravaged face turned away. "You were right, boy. I am a monster. Are you satisfied now?"

He started to turn away, but Bek leapt forward and grabbed his arm, holding on tight through the wasteland of crumbling bones and shifting flesh.

"You said it yourself," he said. "Your face is not who you are. You might appear a monster, but you're not. You're my friend. You saved my life. But you wouldn't trust me with the truth about yourself. You hid that truth because you deceived yourself into thinking that it was something else. I would rather know you this way, terrible though it is, than have the truth hidden."

"Pretty words," the other growled, but did not pull away.

"The truth, Truls Rohk. I know you hate yourself for how you are. I know you hate how you look and how you know others will look at you if you reveal yourself. But sometimes, with people who matter, you have to reveal even the worst of what you believe yourself to be. You have to have faith that it won't make a difference. I would never judge you for how you look. Who you are is what matters, and who you are is always buried deep inside. The shape-shifters in the mountains knew this. They asked me how I felt about you because they wanted to see if I thought you mattered. Could there be a friendship between us? How deep would that friendship go? Did I think there was a place for you in the world? Would I give up my own place so that you could have yours? Would I give up my life for you? I gave them answers that had nothing to do with how you look and everything to do with who you are."

"So what have you accomplished by making me show you how I am? What purpose has it served?" Bitterness and suspicion laced the other's words. "The truth helps no one here."

Bek tightened his grip on the other's arm and plunged ahead. "Don't you see? The truth helps everyone. The chance at life that the shape-shifters gave you when you were attacked by the caull is the same chance you must give Grianne. Everyone thinks she's a monster, too. But the truth is something else entirely. She just needs someone to help her see it. She needs someone to help her strip away her deceptions and lies. She needs someone to believe in her, to believe there's something more to her than what everyone sees. She needs someone to speak for her."

Bek leaned close. "There isn't anyone else but you and me. We're her last hope."

There was a long silence when he finished, a freezing of time and space as the boy and the shape-shifter faced each other in the darkness, one human, one something else. All the air had gone out of the world, leaving it empty and suffocating. Bek did not know what else to do or say. He refused to let go of Truls Rohk, keeping hold of his arm, as if by doing so he might keep him bound to his cause.

"You and me," the other said at last, his rough voice strangely soft. "But mostly you."

He freed himself so quickly that Bek did not have time to stop him, reached down for his cloak and pulled it on again, becoming once more a dark, faceless apparition in the night. All of the pieces of him, all of the ruined, shifting parts, forever fading and appearing like half-formed visions, disappeared.

"The Druid was right to choose you," he said.

Bek saw his chance. "I have a plan."

Truls Rohk grunted. "When didn't you? You are a match for your sister in more ways than one. Come. I make you no promises, no assurances of what I will or won't do about her. Talk to me some more and we'll see. But let's not delay. The rets will be coming, and the ruins wait. Walker needs us."

"But listen to what I have to tell you—"

"I'll listen later." The shape-shifter dismissed him swiftly. Then his voice hardened. "Now you listen to me. Don't you ever mention what's happened here. Not to me or to anyone else. Not ever. It's finished."

He turned and stalked away, Bek struggling to keep up.

TWENTY-SIX

"Now," Quentin Leah said quietly to Tamis.

She moved away from him, not hurriedly or with any outward sign of the turmoil she must be feeling, but as if the encounter were just one of many and in no way significant beyond that. She eased farther right and ahead of him, walking deliberately, choosing her steps and then her place to stand. They had waited until they were certain the wronk could see what she was doing. It was difficult to spy out, but she had stopped just behind a bare patch of ground that was strewn with a scattering of deadwood and scrub grasses. A trained eye would suspect a wronk pit, a well-concealed trap. But the trap lay elsewhere.

Quentin held his ground as the wronk turned toward Tamis. It studied her without moving, then abruptly started toward her. She brought up her short sword defensively and dropped into a protective crouch. Quentin waited a moment, then stepped forward, as well, the Sword of Leah lifting into the faint light. He felt the stirrings of its magic run down through the metal blade and into his arm. He felt its fiery rush enter his body, bitter and at the same time sweet. It infused him with a sense of power. It made him light-headed and alive in a way nothing else did. He wanted to use that power. Even knowing how foolish that desire was, he wanted it.

The wronk lumbered out of the night, closing on Tamis with inexorable determination, neither fast nor slow, but certain. The Tracker held her ground, refusing to give way, saying something now, taunting words that Quentin could not make out. It wasn't what they had planned. She was supposed to give way to the wronk, to stay clear of it should the decoy fail, as it seemed now it might. Quentin came forward another few steps, stopping just at the edge of where he could stand and still know his place in the darkened landscape that hid their trap. As he did so, he felt a new surge of magic fly into him, and he was consumed by a need to release it in battle.

Abruptly, without warning, the wronk turned toward him.

The suddenness of it took his breath away. It drained him of the fire of his magic. In a single moment, everything changed. The wronk came for him swiftly, closing the distance between them almost before Quentin could recover himself to act. It thundered across the clearing, much quicker than the Highlander had remembered from their previous encounter. The sword in its human hand lifted. The blade in its metal one flashed.

Tamis screamed, too far away to help. *Do something!*

At the last moment, he remembered what it was he had intended and threw himself out of the monster's way. The wronk's blades sliced through the air next to him, one so close to his face he could feel the rush of wind it generated in passing. He darted left the six paces he had counted earlier, giving himself enough leeway to make up for the steps he had taken earlier, wheeled back and braced himself. The wronk was already coming for him again. From the helmet that protected its human head, Ard Patrinell's features were suddenly, shockingly recognizable.

Don't look, Quentin told himself. *Don't feel anything.*

Tamis was rushing toward him, foolishly responding to his danger, impulsively acting to help. He shifted swiftly to his right as the wronk bore down on him, the sound of its machine parts a sharp whine against the hammer of its footfalls. It closed with an almost palpable expectation of crushing him—its momentum carrying it right over the pit they had intended for it. The screen gave way beneath its weight, collapsing in a shower of earth, a snapping of deadwood, and a rending of cloth. An instant later the wronk was gone, vanished into the hole as if it had never been. They could hear the sound of its impact as it struck bottom, then silence.

Tamis charged up, breathing hard. Her eyes were bright with surprise and excitement as she stared at the hole. "That wasn't so hard," she said as if she couldn't quite believe it.

No, Quentin was thinking, it wasn't. He moved over to the edge of the pit, still wary, and peered down. It was so dark that he couldn't make out anything. "We need a torch," he said.

She darted away, gathered up a likely stick of deadwood, wrapped it in a scrap of cloth from the edge of the pit, and, using tinder from her pouch, sparked a flame. As she did so, Quentin heard the first stirrings of movement from within the pit.

"Hurry," he whispered, trying to stay calm.

They might have trapped it, but they had most certainly not killed it. The fall alone had not been enough. More would be needed, even to disable it sufficiently to render it immobile. He waited impatiently for her to join him, reaching over the side with the makeshift torch to see what was happening.

The firelight illuminated the sheer, smooth sides of the pit, all the way down to where the wronk was trapped more than fifteen feet below. They could just make out its dusty shell. It was battered and scraped, but still functioning. Neither the fall nor the sharp rocks embedded by the Rindge in the floor of the pit had been enough to stop it.

It heaved itself upward, grasping at stray roots, digging into the earth in search of handholds, intent on climbing out.

Quentin Leah and Tamis fought to keep it from doing so with a frenzy and determination that bordered on madness. They threw everything at it that they could lay their hands on—rocks, limbs, part of an old stump, clots of earth, and a fair-sized boulder that they managed to roll close enough to topple in. Several times they struck it hard enough to knock it loose, but each time it picked itself up and began the climb out once more, a relentless and inexorable force.

They used fire next, throwing mounds of deadwood into the pit, then lighting it with the torch. The deadwood blazed up, burning so quickly and fiercely that the wronk did not have time to stamp it out. For a few moments, it was trapped in an inferno, metal skin reflecting the flames of the burning wood so that it seemed as if it, too, were ablaze. In the fiery light, they watched as it tried to protect its human arm, the flesh of which soon blistered and blackened from the heat. Ard Patrinell's terrified, anguished face peered out from behind its clear protective shield, and in his eyes they read things they did not want to know. Quentin hastened to feed more wood into the pit, but quit looking down at what was trapped there. Tamis was in tears.

But in the end, that effort failed, too. The fire burned fiercely for a time, then began to die out. The wronk climbed clear of the flames once more, blackened with ash and heat-seared, but still mobile.

Quentin stepped back in dismay. The Rindge would have been better prepared for this than they were. They would have had a backup plan for dealing with the trapped wronk. They would have been able to rely on strength of numbers. But the Rindge weren't there to help. No one was.

"This isn't working!" Tamis screamed at him.

Without waiting for his answer, she darted into the trees. For an instant, he thought she had abandoned him, that she was fleeing. He stared back down into the pit, where the last of the burning wood was turning to ash and the wronk was slowly digging out hand- and footholds on its torturous, but implacable ascent.

Then Tamis was back, dragging a huge limb by one end, deadwood, well over eight feet in length, most of its smaller branches reduced to broken stubs.

"We'll use this to knock him back down each time he tries to climb out!" she shouted. "Help me!"

He leapt forward to do so, and together they hauled the branch to the side of the pit and tipped it downward, seizing the slender end and using the limb like a battering ram to hammer at the wronk. Grunting and huffing, they slammed their makeshift weapon into its metal body and sent it tumbling back down again. Again and again, they stopped its ascent, trying unsuccessfully to smash its mechanisms, to break up its working parts. Each time it just picked itself up and began the climb out anew. So the struggle continued, with no progress being made on either side. It was a battle that Tamis and he must lose, Quentin realized, because they would wear out sooner than the wronk. They had to find a way to disable it if they were to win. But he could not think of how to do that without getting close, and getting close was unthinkable.

Then they made a mistake. They let the end of the branch get too close to the wronk while preparing to use it, and the wronk dropped its weapons and seized it in both hands. Its weight was enormous, and they were forced to let go of the branch. The wronk dropped back into the pit. But it had a ladder with which to climb out, and picking up its weapons, it began to do so.

Quentin and Tamis watched helplessly. "We have to get out of here," he whispered.

"No!" she screamed at him. Her dusty, sweat-streaked face was contorted with rage and frustration. "You promised!"

"We can't stop it alone!"

"We have to! I'll do it myself!"

She began snatching up clots of dirt and throwing them at the wronk, shrieking at it. Then abruptly, she dashed away, searching for another ram to knock it loose again. Quentin stayed where he was, waiting. The wronk was more than halfway out. When it reached him, he would try to knock it back down again. His hands tightened on the Sword of Leah. He could feel its power coursing through him, singing in his blood, making him light-headed and oddly detached. He watched the magic racing up and down the blade, tiny flickers of brilliant light.

He glanced down into the pit. The wronk could see the magic, too. The knowledge of what it meant reflected in Ard Patrinell's desperate, haunted eyes.

Then Tamis was back, hauling another dead branch, one shorter and less stout than the first. Her face was so intense and her eyes so wild that he rushed to help her, and once again they tried to knock the wronk loose from its perch.

But the wronk was ready for them. It snatched the ram out

of their hands before they could bring it to bear and, one-handed, swept the deadwood into them, knocking them backwards with a single, powerful blow. Quentin lost his grip on the Sword of Leah, and it flew out into the darkness. He went down in a heap, his ribs and chest throbbing with pain, the breath knocked from his body.

He was back up again in an instant, searching frantically for his weapon, their only hope. He found it quickly, but by the time he had it in hand, the wronk was out of the pit and reaching for Tamis, who stood defiantly in its path.

"Tamis, run!" Quentin shouted.

Instead, she charged, launching herself into the wronk with such fury that she knocked it backwards, slamming her short sword into its fire-blackened human arm, grappling with its metal one, wrapping her arms about the long knife and shield.

Quentin never hesitated. He went after them as if possessed, yelling out the Highland battle cry, "Leah! Leah!" in fear and desperation, slamming into them both, trying to knock Tamis away, trying to topple the wronk. He succeeded in neither. Rebuffed, he stepped back and swung the Sword of Leah with such fury that he took off the wronk's human arm. It fell away with Tamis' short sword still buried in it, blood spraying everything in a red mist. A look of shock and disbelief crossed Ard Patrinell's face, his mouth yawning in a soundless scream. Quentin realized in horror that the Elf could still feel pain.

His hatred of what had been done to Patrinell boiled up anew. No one should be made to suffer like that. He lost control of himself and began hacking at the metal shell with short, powerful blows, trying to locate a vulnerable spot. In the darkness, it was difficult to tell much of anything. Tamis was screaming and clawing at the helmeted head, using her long knife and her fingers, no longer bothering with the metal arm and its long knife, which cut at her furiously. Quentin saw the glitter of the blade and heard the Tracker grunt in pain. He redoubled his efforts, shifting to the wronk's other side, slamming his sword into its metal-sheathed hand until it had broken the ball-and-socket joint in two and the blade had dropped from the useless fingers.

Both arms ruined, the wronk tottered back, trying to shake free of Tamis. While the Tracker clung to it, it could not adequately defend itself. Quentin pressed his advantage, hacking at the joints of its legs, and after what seemed an endless amount of time spent staggering this way and that through the bloodied night, he shattered the right ankle. The wronk dropped to its knees. Tamis sagged downward, as well, leaving Patrinell's head exposed. Quentin began hammering relentlessly at the protective shield, his body alive with his sword's magic, his ears filled with its wild humming. Lost to everything but his desperate need to have it continue, wrapped in its killing haze, he no longer felt anything but its raw power.

Tamis fell away, rolling onto the earth before rising to her hands and knees, head hanging down between her shoulders. Quentin shifted his attack to the wronk's legs again, striking blow after blow until the left one gave way, as well.

He stepped back then, exhausted and stunned. The wronk was stretched on the ground before him, limbs broken, torso battered, even the seemingly impenetrable face shield cracked. Wires and cables lay exposed and severed, and their ends crackled and sparked wickedly. The panels of lights on its chest and limbs flashed redly in warning. Unable to rise or fight longer, the wronk shuddered uncontrollably, the stubs of its severed limbs twitching. Quentin stared down at it dully, the rush of magic that had infused him beginning to fade. He looked down at himself and was surprised to discover he was still whole.

"Finish it!" Tamis snarled at him from one side, kneeling with her arms hugging her bloodied body. "Keep your promise, Highlander!"

Quentin didn't know if he had the strength to do so. He tightened his grip on his sword and walked forward again until he stood next to the stricken wronk. And Patrinell's eyes stared up at him through a haze of blood, searching his own. He was crying, all of the pain and horror mirrored clearly in his tears. He was begging for help. Quentin couldn't bear it. He felt his revulsion and horror threaten to overwhelm him.

He brought the Sword of Leah down quickly and with ferocious purpose. He shattered the protective shield in two swift blows, then smashed Ard Patrinell's face until it was an unrecognizable ruin, then severed what was left of his head from the wronk.

Dropping his sword, he staggered backwards. The wronk had quit moving, but a few lights still blinked from the panels on its chest. Then an arm stump twitched. Crying out in rage and fear, Quentin picked up his blade one final time and chopped at the body and limbs until nothing remained but scraps of metal and bits of flesh.

He might not have stopped then except that out of the corner of his eye he saw Tamis collapse. Closing off the magic as if it were an addiction he must quit forever, feeling how close he was to losing himself to it, he threw down his sword and went to her. He dropped to his knees, turned her over gently, and cradled her head and shoulders in his lap.

Her eyes stared up at him. "Is it done? Is he free?"

He nodded, his throat tight. The front of her tunic was a mass of blood and torn flesh.

"Wherever I'm going, I'll find him there," she whispered. A froth of blood coated her lips.

He touched her cheek with shaking fingers. "Tamis, no."

"I'm so cold," she whispered.

Her eyes fixed, and she stopped breathing. Quentin held her for a long time anyway. He talked to her when she could no longer hear. He told her she would have what she wanted, she would have Ard Patrinell, that she deserved to find him waiting and he would be. He whispered good-bye to her. He was crying freely, but he didn't care.

When he laid her down again and rose, he felt as if he had lost his place in the world and would never find it again.

TWENTY-SEVEN

Enveloped by the slow, steady thrumming of Castledown's machinery, Ahren Elessedil walked back through the long rows of towering metal cabinets and spinning silver disks that occupied the cavernous chamber outside Walker's smoked-glass prison. He did not like leaving Ryer Ord Star alone to look after the Druid, did not feel at all certain that he was doing the right thing, but knew, as well, he could not turn back. The voice inside him generated by the magic of the phoenix stone was firm and compelling. The missing Elfstones lay ahead, somewhere else in the complex, waiting for him to retrieve them. He must do as the voice insisted if he was ever to find himself again and be made whole. He must go to where the Stones were. He must take them back.

He watched the dark glass of Walker's chamber disappear into the warren of cabinets behind him, and when it was out of sight, his loneliness was palpable and his feeling of vulnerability acute. The haze of the phoenix stone's magic was beginning to dissipate, to lose its consistency, to become more penetrable. It was a gradual change, and at first he was not certain he was seeing it accurately. But as he got clear of the brightly lit central chamber and walked back into the darker corridors beyond, it became increasingly apparent that he was not mistaken, that the stone's magic was failing. He immediately felt pressed and harried by the knowledge, as if he must move faster than he would have liked or than was reasonable. It was an irrational response, because he had no real idea of what the magic's lifetime might be. Then again, not much of what he had done since entering Castledown had anything to do with being rational.

He knew that Ryer's magic would be lessening, as well. When it was gone, she would have to rely on her connection with Walker to survive. In a way, she was better off with the Druid. At least Walker could offer her protection once he woke and freed himself. Without the magic of the phoenix stone, there was little that Ahren could do for her. Little that he could do for himself, for that matter.

Still, he would listen to the voice and go on, because the voice was all he had to rely on.

He climbed the stairs to the overlook they had come upon earlier, then moved back into the maze of corridors beyond. He took the path his instincts told him to take, keeping close watch over the shadows pressing close about him. The flameless lamps threw down their light in dim pools, but the stretches between were like quicksand. He repeatedly encountered creepers on their way to other places, and each time he stopped where he was and waited for them to attack. But the creepers still did not see or sense him, and they did not slow. He heard the skitterings of their approaches and departures, scrapings of metal that raised the hair on the back of his neck. He wished again he was braver and stronger. He wished he had Ard Patrinell to assure him that he would be all right. He kept thinking how comforting that would be. But Patrinell had taught him everything he would ever teach him and told him everything he would ever tell him. Patrinell was gone. Ahren's comfort, if he was to find any, would have to come from somewhere else.

As he walked deeper into the catacombs, the sound of the machinery grew louder, a steadily building whine. Without knowing anything else, he could tell that he was moving toward the power source that was the heart of Castledown. It was there that Antrax fed off the energy stored for its use by the safehold's machines. Ahren felt himself shrink as the sound increased in volume, its dull roar filling up the corridors like a river at flood. He saw himself as tiny and insignificant, impermanent flesh and blood trapped inside changeless, unyielding steel walls. He thought again about his hopes in coming on the journey—to prove himself to be more than the callow boy his brother believed him, to accomplish something that would warrant respect and even honor, to become the man his father had wanted him to be. Foolish, impossible hopes in light of his cowardice in the ruins, yet he clung to them still. Some part of what he had dreamed of accomplishing could still be realized if he could keep himself steady.

He passed out of the corridor into a vast, cavernous room in which two giant cylinders stood side by side amid a cluster of smaller pieces of equipment. The cylinders were fifty feet across and a hundred feet high. Metal pipes and connectors ran from their casings to the equipment and surrounding walls. The sound of the machinery was deafening, a pounding throb that buried everything else in the wake of its passing. It was Castledown's power source, and Ahren wanted nothing so badly as to get away from it.

Then he looked to his right and saw a pair of chambers similar to the one that had been used to contain Walker, except that they were much larger. The dark glass fronting them was recessed into the chamber walls, and the bulbous doors were rimmed with sleek metal bindings. He stared at them, and he knew without having even to question it that one of them contained the missing Elfstones. He could feel it the same way he had felt the need to go there. The phoenix stone's magic was still at work inside him, giving him his direction, telling him what to do.

Yet for a long time, he didn't move. He didn't know what to do, didn't know how to do it, and didn't really want to try. His fear returned in an enveloping wave. To go on was too much to ask of anyone; it was too overwhelming to consider. He stared at the doorways, the magic of the phoenix stone prodding at him, and fought to keep himself from bolting. He had never been so scared. His fear wasn't of what he thought might be waiting; it was of what he couldn't imagine. His fear was of the unseen, of the unknown danger that would cause him to flee once more. He did not think he could bear to have that happen again, and he did not know how to prevent it. He could sense the possibility of something lurking behind the dark glass, a predator, anxious for him to step inside and be seized. Anticipation alone was enough to freeze him in place, to render him hopelessly immobile. He thought in his unspeakable terror that he would never move again.

It was his sense of shame that saved him, reborn in the unavoidable memories of his flight from the ruins days earlier, recalled again and again in the long hours afterwards while he huddled in the debris and thought about what it would be like to return home after what he had done. His chance to redeem himself from that misery, his only chance, lay in recovery of the Elfstones. In the hauntingly inexorable nightmare of his failure to save his friends, in the cold realization of how frail a creature he was, he had come to understand that it was worse to live with fear than to die confronting it.

He remembered that, and broke free of his terror. He started forward without stopping to consider what he was doing, knowing only that he must go then or he would never go at all.

In the next instant, alarms went off everywhere, shrill metallic sounds that cut through even the suffocating roar of the machines.

Ahead, one of the doors opened and a giant creeper scuttled out, all crooked legs and sharp pincers, a war machine looking for a fight. It did not see him, but moved to take up a position between the chamber doorway and the corridor through which Ahren had come. Another creeper followed, and then another, stationing themselves in a defensive ring. The entry sealed itself tightly behind them.

Ahren kept moving ahead, making for that closed door, striding into the midst of the creepers. He held the long knife before him protectively, knowing it was all but useless should they discover him. But, just barely visible, the failing magic of the phoenix stone still clung to him in thinning wisps. Ahren imagined the alarms sucking it away, smoke caught in a breeze. He moved between the creepers for the door, bolder than he had believed he could ever be, feeling buoyant and paralyzed at the same time. He felt himself watching his own progress from somewhere outside his body, removed from the act. His thoughts were reduced to a single sequence—get to the Elfstones, take them in hand, summon their power.

He reached the door with the shriek of the alarms ringing in his ears and was surprised when it gave to his touch. The creepers behind him didn't seem to notice. He stepped into the room, a darkened chamber paneled with banks of blinking lights, tangled wires, and flexible metal cords that cast shadows over everything in inky pools. It was so black in the room that Ahren couldn't distinguish any of the pieces of apparatus that were scattered everywhere, couldn't make out the comings and goings of the cords, couldn't even tell what the room was supposed to be. He groped forward, being careful to touch nothing, picking his way toward the center of the room as his eyes tried to adjust to the abrupt, momentary flashes of illumination.

When they did, he saw the first signs of movement, faint stirrings to one side. He froze instantly, and as he did so he caught sight of something moving to his other side. At first he thought it was nothing more than the shadows that flickered in the dim light, but then with heart-stopping certainty he recognized them. They were creepers. He couldn't hear their skittering over the blare of the alarms, but even in the absence of that he knew them for what they were. They were all around him, all through the chamber. He had stumbled into their midst before realizing what he was doing.

He held himself as still as he could manage, barely daring to breathe, while he considered his next move. He could not tell how much of the phoenix stone's magic remained to him; it was too dark to measure what traces remained of its distinct haze. Some, certainly, or the creepers would have had him already. He tried to think, to ignore the alarms and the creepers and the chaos around him, to hear anew the voice that had brought him there.

A second later, he saw the chair. It was big and padded and reclined, and it sat in the center of the room, surrounded by a cluster of freestanding machines. The cords were thickest there, snaking out in every direction, all leading from parts of the chair. There was an odd box set into one armrest to which many of the wires ran, and Ahren recognized it. He had seen the same sort of apparatus in Walker's prison, siphoning off the Druid magic through his good arm. The chamber Ahren was in was where Kael Elessedil had been drained of the magic of the Elfstones in the same way for almost thirty years. It was the place in which his uncle had wasted his life.

The Elfstones, he knew instinctively and with overpowering certainty, were inside that box.

He moved over to it quickly, sliding through the nests of wires and past the bulky pieces of equipment, praying he couldn't be detected. The creepers continued to shift position in the open spaces of the room, sidling a few feet this way, then a few that. He could not tell what they were doing. They didn't seem to be doing anything that mattered. Perhaps they were only sweepers, harmless attendants of the machines rather than sentries and fighters. Perhaps his presence meant nothing to them.

He swallowed against the dryness in his throat, pausing as he passed close to one of them. It was not very big, but it sent a ripple of fear down his spine. He waited for it to turn away, then eased his slender body past, stepped into the maze of wires that surrounded the chair, and knelt next to the mysterious box.

In the flash of panel lights and the muted illumination through the dark glass windows, he peered into the box. He couldn't see anything but shadows. He wanted to reach inside, but he didn't like doing that without knowing what waited. Wouldn't there be restraints of some sort, if that was how the magic was siphoned off? Wouldn't there be needles of the sort that had been inserted into Walker to keep him connected to the machines? What if it was the trap the little sweeper had been leading him to all along?

But the Elfstones were in that box, not two feet away from his hand, and he had to get them out.

Suddenly, unexpectedly, the alarms went silent and the chamber's ceiling lights came on. Ahren froze, exposed and unprotected, crouched by the padded chair amid the clustered machines and creepers. The magic of the phoenix stone was gone; the last traces of its concealing haze had vanished. Aware of his presence, the first of the creepers was already turning toward him. The ends of its metal arms lifted to reveal the deadly cutters that marked it as a sentry and fighter.

Ahren glanced swiftly into the box, and amid its smoky shadows spied a glimmer of blue.

He thrust his right hand inside and snatched at the Elfstones. He seized the first two as iron bands clamped about his wrist, but the third one skittered away, just beyond his fingertips. A new alarm went off, this one inside the room, a whistle's shriek of warning. He jammed his left hand into the box, as well, caught hold of the loose Stone, and clasped both hands together as a second set of bands immobilized his left hand. Creepers moved toward him from everywhere, metal legs scraping wildly against the smooth floor, cutters snapping at the air.

Ahren didn't know what to do. He didn't know how to summon the power that would save him. He couldn't even make himself speak as he fought to bring the magic to life.

Please! he begged voicelessly as his hands tightened about the Elfstones. *Please, help me!*

A needle at the end of a flexible arm flashed past his face. He felt its sting in his left arm, and a slow numbing began to spread outward with languorous inevitability. Metal digits closed about him from every quarter, holding him fast, making him a prisoner.

It was happening all over again, he thought frantically, just as it had to Kael Elessedil.

Help me!

As if heeding his silent plea, the Elfstones flared to life within the darkened recesses of their confinement, their blue light so blinding that he closed his eyes against its glare. He felt, rather than saw, what happened next. The restraints on his wrists shattered, and the box was blown apart. The creepers lasted only seconds longer, then the magic caught them up and swept them away, hurtling them against the walls of the chamber and reducing them to scrap. His eyes were opening again when the padded chair exploded. The banks of machinery were shattered, as well, one after the other, engulfed in a sweep of blue light that circled the room and turned everything to useless shards and twisted wire.

Arms outstretched, hands clasped together, fingers tight about the Elfstones, Ahren lurched to his feet. The needle was gone from his arm, but the numbing hadn't lessened, and it took all his concentration to keep that arm from going limp. He fed it with the power of the Stones, with the peculiarly pleasurable pain they engendered, a burning rush that seared his flesh and left him dizzy. He staggered across the room, the Elfstones' power incinerating everything, burning it all to molten slag. The dark glass windows blew out, leaving the twisted interior of the room exposed. He saw the massive cylinders that housed the power source become ringed in blinking lights and fire threads that crisscrossed everywhere. He saw the creepers that had taken up watch outside wheel back again to deal with him.

Shades!

He had time for a single desperate exhortation before the

juggernauts barreled through the doorway, all sharp edges and brute power. He sent the magic of the Elfstones hammering into the nearest and threw it backwards into the others. He struck it again, then again, advancing on it now, light-headed and humming with the magic's power. He was transformed by its feel, made new and whole, as if he had never been powerless, as if he had never had to flee from anything. He pursued the creepers with single-minded intent and smashed them one by one, disdaining their cutters and their blades, unafraid of what they could do to him because it seemed now that they could do nothing.

They went down before him like trees caught in a hurricane, ripped out by their roots, toppled and left to die. With a final glance back at the destruction he had visited upon the machines that would have sapped away his life, Ahren Elessedil stalked from the room, consumed by a killing rage.

Antrax became aware of the intruder's presence only seconds before it felt the ruptures in its metal skin. No pain was involved because it could not feel pain, only a sensation of being opened where it knew it should not. The intruder was the one that had disappeared earlier while in the company of its probe, the one for whom the Stones were intended. Somehow it had found its way to the extraction chamber. Somehow it had gotten hold of the Stones while still aware of who and where it was and had used them against the chamber and its equipment.

Alarms were already triggered all through Antrax's domain, set off by a power surge generated in the extraction chamber where the earlier intruder had been imprisoned. It had taken Antrax precious minutes to determine the cause of the surge, and by the time it had done so, the earlier intruder was already free of its connectors and gone into the complex. Now there were two of them loose, and either was capable of doing great damage if not stopped.

Antrax spun down its lines of power in milliseconds, gaining the capacitor housing before the latest intruder was in possession of the Stones and free of the extraction chamber. With the alarms shut down again and reset, the immediate danger was to the storage units that housed its lifeblood. Triggering the screen of laser beams that the creators had installed to protect the capacitors against damage, Antrax summoned the strongest of its battle probes to bring this newest intruder to bay. It might not be possible to immobilize it without killing it, but Antrax was prepared to accept that alternative. There would be others that could use the Stones, that could summon their magic, others that could be lured to Castledown. It was more important to protect against damage to the power Antrax had harvested already.

It felt the presence of the intruder moving through the shattered doorway of the extraction chamber to confront the laser beams and the probes that had already responded to its summons. Extraction ports were housed throughout the complex, and Antrax began siphoning off the raw expenditure of the Elf's power, feeding on it as it left his body. Energy was not to be wasted, whatever its source.

Computer chips processed and analyzed with blinding speed. Antrax was informed and its course of action determined accordingly. The intruders would do battle with its probes in the mistaken belief that they could somehow prevail. They could not. They would simply feed Antrax more of the precious energy it needed, just as they had been meant to do while sedated. Still thinking they had a chance to get free, they would struggle until they were overcome.

Antrax, incapable of emotion, feeling nothing for the humans it hunted, prepared to immobilize and terminate them.

TWENTY-EIGHT

The Druid known as Walker, who had once been Walker Boh and was now on the threshold of still another life-altering transition, moved swiftly down the corridors of Castledown toward a confrontation with Antrax. Ryer Ord Star followed closely behind, one slender hand clasped firmly in his. There was such joy on her face at having found him after so long, such exhilaration at having rescued him from the machines that were leeching away his life, that he could not bear to tell her what waited ahead. He preferred to let her have her happiness, her own life recovered and her freedom from the Ilse Witch secured. She had fought hard for him, and she was entitled to bask in the glow of her accomplishment.

It was odd that she should have the sight, could see so clearly into the future, and yet be denied so much of its meaning. He had brought her with him to give him insight into what the future held, but he had never imagined that the insight he sought would come to him in such a roundabout way. It was not her simple visions that had informed him. It was not her dreams. Instead, it was the way in which he had become linked to her when she had saved him after Shatterstone that had revealed so much. That was when he had learned the truth about her. That was when he had seen what she could be and decided to trust his instincts.

Now, deep within the catacombs in that distant land, she had revealed the future yet again. Linked to her by her empathic rescue of him in the extraction chamber, he had caught another glimpse of what might come to be. Though the future was written on water, sometimes it was possible to divine its meaning based on a choice of actions. Go one way, and the future would take that twist. Go another, and there would be a different result altogether. So it was that, while coming out of his drug-induced stupor and back into the real world, he had been shown a brief but stunningly clear vision of what he must do. Triggered by her empathic touch and her talent as a seer, the purpose of his coming to that place and time, once so clear to him, once indisputable, was revealed to be something else entirely.

He marveled at how mistaken human beings were in assuming they could foresee their own fates. Even seers, who possessed the gift of Ryer Ord Star. It was easy to assume that one event must necessarily follow in the wake of another, that a thing was just what it seemed. But he knew better. A Druid knew better than anyone that life was a myriad of twists and turns that no one could unravel, a path that must be traveled to be understood. So it was there, in Castledown, for him, though he had forgotten the rules for a time. So it would be later for the survivors, when they made the journey home again.

He wondered then at the fates of the others of the company of the *Jerle Shannara*. Ahren Elessedil had been alive when Ryer Ord Star found Walker, but had since disappeared, and not even the seer knew what had become of him. The magic of the phoenix stone had sheltered them both for a time, but now it had faded. The Rovers had been alive when he departed the *Jerle Shannara* for Castledown. According to the seer, Bek and an Elven Tracker were still alive a week ago. Of the rest, he knew nothing. It was difficult to believe they were all gone, but it was a possibility he could not rule out.

Castledown's alarms continued to ring, shrill and insistent, echoing down the maze of passageways. Creepers skittered by, moving in all directions, oblivious to Walker and Ryer Ord Star. He had taken the precaution of cloaking both the seer and himself in the Druid magic, convinced that it would work in the real world, though it had seemed to fail miserably in his dreams. The creepers were preoccupied with other matters in any event, compelled by primary directives to engage in repairs and restore order. They would not be searching for him quite yet, though soon enough. He would have to move quickly.

His exploration of Castledown through Antrax's internal systems had given him the map he needed to know where he must go. The only way to put an end to Antrax was to shut down its power source. By doing so, he could drain away its intelligence and leave it incapable of action.

It sounded simple. It would not be.

The sound of the machines grew louder and more insistent. The power source, their destination, lay ahead. Walker tightened his resolve and gathered his strength for the confrontation that waited. Antrax would attempt to trap and immobilize him again. It would do so in the same way as before because it was a machine and a machine would use its primary approach to handling a situation until that approach failed. Antrax would rely again on its creepers and drugs. Walker, forewarned, had already decided on a different course of action for himself.

When the alarms unexpectedly ceased, the ensuing silence

was shocking. Given the extent of the damage he had visited on Castledown's internal systems, Antrax had repaired itself more quickly than Walker had anticipated. He thought momentarily about striking at it again, then decided against it. Antrax would be expecting such an attempt and would be prepared for it. Better to continue on. The power source lay just ahead, and once he was there, all the alarms in the world wouldn't matter.

Nevertheless, he had not yet reached the end of the passageway that opened onto the central power chamber when a new alarm went off, this one directly ahead and localized. Then he heard explosions and smelled the raw burn of magic, and he realized that another had gotten to the chamber ahead of him. Pulling Ryer Ord Star after him, not quite certain what he was going to find, he began to run. It was as apt to be the Ilse Witch as one of his companions. The sounds of battle were unmistakable, however, as machines shattered and glass exploded out of walls. Bits and pieces of creepers flew across the passageway entrance as he neared the power chamber, where smoke roiled through a surreal landscape of flameless lamps and fire threads.

He glanced back at Ryer Ord Star. The exhilaration was gone from her face, the joy from her eyes. Desperation had replaced both, born of more than her recognition of the obvious dangers that waited. It was as if she had divined both his intent and her complicity in advancing it by saving him earlier. Her face was pale and taut, and her silver hair flew out behind her in a thin curtain, lending her a ghostly look. She tried to say something, but saw the intensity of his expression and kept still.

They burst through the power source entry into a vast chamber dominated by a pair of towering cylinders situated in the center of the room and connected everywhere by pipes and conduits. Smaller machines surrounded them, metal cages and housings bristling with flexible lines. Walker had no idea how they worked, how Antrax fed, how it converted magic to a fuel it could consume. The technology for the process had been dead for more than two and a half millennia, and only Antrax itself possessed the knowledge to keep it operating. That was true of the lifeblood that fed Antrax and preserved the library of the Old World. Destroy either, and you destroyed both.

It was what Walker had come to realize he must do, a sacrifice of one to put an end to the other.

He no longer thought to debate the matter. He knew that Antrax would eventually reach out for other sources of magic, other magic-infused humans, and the cycle would begin again. Sooner or later, it would siphon off everything of worth from the world that had replaced the one Antrax had served, and all to preserve a machine that no longer mattered. Antrax must be stopped, destroyed while there was still time.

Fire threads ringed the cylinders that formed the power source, shifting at random this way and that, keeping at bay anything that might try to harm the capacitors they protected. Smoke clouded the chamber in a thick haze, giving everything the appearance of a nightmarish netherworld. The creepers that appeared out of its brume had the look of shades, and even the equipment seemed to shift and turn in the mix of light and shadow.

Then abruptly, out of nowhere, Ahren Elessedil appeared, hands stretched forth as if to ward off invisible things, slender body taut and gathered to strike as he stepped gingerly through the debris. Blue light flashed from between his fingers, shattering creepers that crossed his path, clearing the way forward. Walker felt a surge of renewed hope. The Elven Prince had managed to recover the missing Elfstones, something he had not dared to hope could happen. With their magic to aid his own, he would have a better chance to succeed in doing what was needed.

"Ahren!" Ryer Ord Star shouted out even before Walker could speak.

The Elven Prince turned toward them, his eyes as blue and wild as the fire of the Stones. He registered the presence of Walker and the seer but only barely. He was consumed by the magic, so caught up in its throes that all that mattered to him, all that he could feel, was the rush of its power through his body.

Walker moved toward him swiftly, unafraid of the dark look in his eyes, of the blue fire gathered at his clenched fists. He reached out for the Elven Prince and touched him lightly, drawing him out from the haze into which he had been carried, bringing him back to himself. Ahren stared at him in anger, then confusion, then with undisguised relief.

"You've done well, Elven Prince," Walker said, drawing him close, eyes shifting this way and that for the enemies that circled all around them. "Draw the magic back into yourself. Quickly!"

Walker watched the blue light of the Elfstones fade, then cloaked Ahren with concealing magic, as well. "Come this way."

Aware that Antrax was searching, he moved Ahren and Ryer to one side, changing their position in the chamber. He had thrown out images and set off the alarms on the pressure plates that Antrax had activated earlier, confusing things further. The sirens shrilled everywhere, and warning lights on wall panels flashed like red eyes blinking through the cross-hatching of the fire threads. Momentarily confused, the creepers shifted this way and that. They could not find either the Druid or his companions; in the chaos, their sensors were unable to fix on anything.

Walker had drawn the Elf and the seer all the way back to the partially shattered wall of the extraction chamber, where they would have some protection. "Wait for me here," he ordered.

Gathering his robes about him, he slipped away from them, maneuvering past the creepers toward the cylinders that warded the power source. There was no time left for subtlety. He would have to strike quickly. He found a seam in the plating, a weakness that might be exploited, and attacked. Druid fire rent the metal with a withering blast, peeling it away. Before Antrax could react, Walker moved again. A dozen yards farther on, he struck once more. Then the fire threads were seeking him, striking at random because they were unable to fix on him within his covering of magic. He dodged them as he attacked, avoiding the creepers, as well, circling the cylinders and surrounding machinery, continually seeking vulnerable points.

Yet despite his best efforts, the protective metal of the power source held firm. He was depleting his strength, but gaining no advantage. Another way must be found. Still throwing out distractions and false targets, he moved back across the floor, barely escaping a random fire thread that singed his cloak. Sooner or later, his luck would run out. Antrax would already be mounting a counterattack.

He barely finished the thought before the attack began. A beam of oddly hazy light radiated from a port high in the ceiling, flooding the room and outlining Walker where he crouched. If he had not already been moving, leaving images in his wake, he would have been incinerated by the fire threads that shifted instantly to find him. As it was, he was pinned between two of the smaller machines, unable to move anywhere as the creepers, able to pinpoint him at last, closed in for the kill.

Seeing the danger, Ahren Elessedil stepped away from Ryer Ord Star and turned the magic of the Elfstones on the port that had released the revealing light, shattering it, then fusing it shut. The light faded, and Walker was up and moving once more. Ahren struck out at the closest of the creepers, clearing a path for the Druid, giving him a chance to escape. Walker raced to join him, grabbed his arm, and pulled him back against the wall again. Throwing out a new set of distractions, he dragged both Elven Prince and seer into the doorway of the extraction chamber.

"Stand here!" he shouted into Ahren's ear over the din. "Hold them back for as long as you can—then run!"

He turned into the room, searching out the power feeds that were built into the wall. He had been going about the battle in the wrong way. He could not attack the power source from without; whoever had constructed Antrax would have made certain that sabotage of that sort was very difficult. Any permanent damage would have to come from within. Antrax had been installed inside Castledown to protect the library of the Old World against attacks from without. There would be internal defenses, as well, but they would not be as substantial. The intake lines that fed raw power into the capacitors for conversion and storage would have near-infinite capacity, since such power would necessarily come in different forms and increments.

But would the lines of power that Antrax used to feed itself from the capacitors be of similar durability? Walker didn't think so. Antrax would measure its own intake. It would not require a separate monitoring system, would have no reason to expect an intake greater than what it commanded. Overload the feeding lines, and they would melt or disintegrate. Antrax would have warning systems and shutoffs to prevent that, but if Walker struck quickly enough, the damage would be done before they could react.

He moved through the debris of the room, over pieces of shattered equipment and creepers, to the extraction ports that ran to the storage units. He would use them to reach the lines that fed directly into Antrax. There were relays from one to the other; he had discovered that much when he had explored the complex earlier in his out-of-body form. The trick would be in acting quickly enough to jam them, and then to sustain the attack long enough to disable Antrax before it could strike back.

Outside the extraction chamber, Ahren Elessedil fought to keep the creepers at bay. Fire threads were seeking him out, as well, though most were still engaged in warding the power source, vertical crimson stripes that climbed the smoky heights of the cavernous hall to lock in place like prison bars. The Elven Prince twisted and turned to meet each new attack, Elven magic flashing brightly. But he did not have more than a few minutes left before he would be overwhelmed.

Ryer Ord Star crouched next to him in the doorway, her gaze directed back toward Walker, helpless and beseeching. Walker gave her a calm, untroubled look, one meant to comfort and allay her fears. His attempt failed. Perhaps she saw the truth. Perhaps she was beyond seeing anything but what she feared most. She screamed, and the sound could be heard even over the howl of the alarms.

In response, Walker flattened the palm of his hand against

one of the extraction ports and sent the Druid fire hurtling inward.

Antrax was caught by surprise. Walker's magic pumped into the intake lines like floodwaters down a dry riverbed. The shock was enormous, so much so that a backlash ripped through Walker, as well. He stiffened against the pressure and pain and thrust the magic forward again, deep into the lines, feeling it build anew. Antrax was throwing up defenses in a wild effort to contain him, but it was too little, too late. He was all the way inside the feeding system, breaking from the main lines into all the little channels, all the little tributaries, everything that kept Antrax running. He could feel conductors fusing, melting, and falling away.

Fire threads ripped into the room from behind, burning into him like heated metal. He contained his screams, and blocked what he could of the counterattack without lessening his own assault. Ryer screamed anew, but he could not look to see what she was doing. Every part of him was directed toward continuing the assault. Antrax was racing down its central lines, patching what it could, closing off what it could not. Its internal systems were imploding, one after the other. Walker chased it through its central nervous system, through its bloodstream, into its heart and mind. Everything he touched he savaged with the Druid fire, carrying himself with it, feeling himself burning up, as well. He couldn't help it. He couldn't stop it. He couldn't separate himself from what was happening sufficiently to stay whole. Bits and pieces of his own body were collapsing, as well.

Then abruptly, he felt Antrax convulse. The fire threads that raked him lurched wildly, spraying out of control. Creepers, disoriented and mindless, twisted like bits of paper caught in a wind. He felt Ryer clutch at him, still screaming, pulling at him, trying to wrench him free of the ports to which his hand was fused. Ahren Elessedil was beside him, his face a mask of horror. Walker had only a moment to register their presence, and then a backlash of magic burst through the extraction port through his hand and arm and into his body and blew him across the room.

The attack on its internal systems was so sudden and powerful that Antrax was burned halfway through before it could manage to respond. It blocked the intruder's advance, turned his own power back on him, and counterattacked with its lasers. It began closing down damaged areas and calling for repairs. But in spite of its efforts, the intruder's fire raged all through it, and for every section of itself it managed to salvage, it lost two more. All of its central lines were invaded and contaminated, riddled with power so destructive that it was eating through the circuits and conductors. Antrax felt pieces of itself cease to function as feeding lines deteriorated and collapsed. It could not maintain its various functions, its complex operations. It lost control over its mobile defenses first, its probes and lasers. Its maintenance systems stalled. It kept intact the defenses surrounding the power source, but the protection devices at Castledown's surface ceased to operate. It threw everything it had left into fulfilling its prime directive—to protect the knowledge it warded in its memory banks.

Nothing worked. Everything was failing. Bit by bit, it felt itself slowing down, losing control, and slipping away. It retreated to its stronger positions to gather strength, to reconnect. But the fire tracked it as if it were a living thing and burned away its faltering defenses. Antrax was forced all the way back through its collapsing lines to the chambers that housed its power source.

There it found itself cornered, unable to move outside the twin capacitors that had fed it all these centuries. The capacitors were all it had left, and their power was leaking away through a thousand ruptures. Its charge from the creators was no longer possible to fulfill. Already it could feel the central memory banks dying.

Then Antrax could no longer move.

It began to have trouble thinking.

Time slowed, then became barely noticeable to it in its newfound state of immobility and dysfunction.

Its last conscious thought was that it was unable to remember what it was.

TWENTY-NINE

Walker blacked out from being hurled against a wall, but he woke again almost at once. He lay without moving amid the debris, staring dully into the smoky haze that enveloped him. He knew he was hurt, but he could not tell how badly. The feeling was gone from much of his body, and his hand was soaked in a wetness that could not be mistaken for anything other than what it obviously was. Somewhere close, in the swirl of the battle's aftermath, he could hear Ryer Ord Star sobbing and calling out his name.

I'm here, he tried to say, but the words would not come.

Sparks spilled like liquid fire from the broken ends of wires, and wounded machines buzzed and spat in their death throes. Tremors rocked the safehold as Antrax thrashed blindly down its lines of power in search of help that could no longer be found. By turning his head slightly to the right, Walker could just glimpse the fractured cylinders that housed the power source, the metal skin leaking steam and dampness, the protective fire threads fading like rainbows with a storm's passing.

Then the pain began, sudden and intense, rushing through him with the force of floodwaters set free from a broken dam. He gasped at the intensity of it and fought back with what little magic he could muster, shutting it away, closing it off, giving himself space and time to think clearly. He did not have much of either, he knew. What had been promised had been delivered. He had not known from the visions that Death would come for him then, at that moment, in that place. But he had known it was on its way.

A figure moved in the gloom, and Ahren Elessedil materialized. "He's here!" he called back over his shoulder, then knelt in front of Walker, his face ashen, his slender body razored with burns and slashes and streaked with blood. "Shades!" he gasped softly.

Ryer Ord Star was beside him a second later, small and ephemeral, as if she were no more substantial than the smoke from which she appeared, no better formed. She saw him, and her hands flew to her mouth in tiny fists that only partially muffled her anguished scream. Walker saw that she was looking below his neck, where the pain was centered. He read the horror in her eyes.

She started for him at once, and he brought up his hand in a warding gesture to keep her back. For the first time, he saw the blood that coated it. For the first time, he was afraid, and fear gave power to his voice.

"Stay back," he ordered her sharply. "Don't touch me."

She kept coming, but Ahren reached out for her as she tried to push past, and pulled her down next to him, holding her as she thrashed and screamed in fury and despair. He talked to her, his voice steady and soothing, even when she would not hear him, would not listen, until finally she collapsed in his arms, sobbing against his shoulder, little birdlike hands still clenched in defiance.

Walker lowered his bloodstained hand back into his lap, still not looking down at what he knew he would find there, forcing himself to close off everything but what he knew he must do next.

"Elven Prince," he said, his voice unrecognizable to him. "Bring her close."

Ahren Elessedil did as he was told, tightening his features in the way people do when they are brought face-to-face with sights they would just as soon never have witnessed. He held her possessively, shielding as well as restraining her, his own needs revealed in his determination to see them both through whatever would happen next. Walker was surprised at the resolve and strength of will he found in the youthful features. The Elven Prince had grown up all at once.

"Ryer." He spoke her name softly, deliberately infusing the sound of it with a calm that was meant to reassure her. He waited. "Ryer, look at me."

She did so, slowly and tentatively, lifting her head out of Ahren Elessedil's shoulder, her gaze directed toward his face, refusing to look down again, to risk what that would do to her. In the pale, translucent features he found such sadness that it felt to him as if he was broken now in spirit as well as in body.

"You cannot touch me, not without irreparable damage. Healing me is not possible. Healing me will cost you your own life and will not save mine. Some things are beyond even your empathic powers. Your visions told me this was coming. When I became linked to you after Shatterstone, I saw. Do you understand?"

Her eyes were blank and fixed, devoid of anything even resembling understanding, as if she had decided to leave him rather than be made to face the truth. She was hiding—he accepted that—but she had not gone so far away that she couldn't hear.

"Ahren will take you back to the surface of Castledown

and from there to the airship. Return home with him. Tell him of the visions and dreams that visit you on the way as you once told them to me. Help him as you have helped me."

She was shaking her head slowly, her eyes still unfocused, lost and empty looking. "No," she whispered. "I won't leave you."

"Ahren." Walker's gaze shifted to the Elven Prince. "The treasure we came to find is lost to us. It died with Antrax. The books of magic were housed in the machine's memory system. They could not be retrieved unless Antrax was kept whole, and allowing that to happen was too dangerous. The choice was mine to make, and I made it. Whether it was worth the cost remains to be seen. You will have to make your own judgment. Remember that. One day, you will be given the chance."

Ryer Ord Star was crying again, speaking his name softly as she did so, repeating it over and over. He wanted to reach out to her, to comfort her in some small way, but he could not. Time was running out, and there was still one thing more he must do.

"Go now," he said to the Elven Prince.

The seer gave a low wail and reached out for him, trying to tear free of Ahren Elessedil's strong grip. Her fingers were like claws, stretching as if to rend and discard whatever words he would choose to speak next.

"Ryer," he said softly, his strength ebbing. "Listen to me. This is not the last time we will see each other. We will meet again." She went silent, staring at him. "Soon," he said. "It will happen."

"Walker." She breathed his name as if it were a spell that could protect them both.

"I promise you." He swallowed against the return of his

pain, gesturing weakly at Ahren. "Go. Quickly. Not the way you came. Across the chamber, that way." He pointed past the ruptured cylinders, his memory recalling the labyrinthine passageways he had explored in his out-of-body search. "The main passageway leads out from there. Follow it. Go now."

Ahren pulled Ryer Ord Star up with him, turning her away forcefully, ignoring both her sobs and her struggles. His gaze remained fixed on the Druid as he did so, as if by looking at Walker he would find the strength he needed. *Perhaps he still seeks answers for what has happened to them all,* Walker thought. *Perhaps he just wants to know whether any of what they have endured has been worth it.*

A moment later, they were gone, through the shattered doorway of the chamber into the larger room beyond. He could hear them afterwards for a long time, the sounds of the seer crying and of boots scraping over the rubble. Then there was only the fading crackle of stricken machines fighting to stay functional, smoke that curled through the air and wires that sparked, and a vague sense of life leaking slowly away.

Time slowed.

Walker felt himself drift. She would be coming soon. The Ilse Witch, his nemesis, his greatest failure—she had caught up to him at last. He could measure her approach by the shifting of smoke on the air and the whisper of footsteps in his mind. He tightened his resolve as he waited for her.

When she appeared, he would be ready for her.

The Ilse Witch found her way to the power source through use of her magic, tracking first toward the origin of the alarms and then following in the footsteps of Walker, which she stumbled across farther on. The heat and movement of the images he had left by his passing overlapped with those of

Ryer Ord Star and an Elf. They had all come this way, and not long ago, but she could not tell if they were traveling together. She was surprised to find the seer down there, but neither her presence nor that of the Elf made any difference. It was the Druid she must deal with; the other two were merely obstacles to be cleared away.

It was true that she had given up looking for the Druid in favor of the magic they both sought, yet she could not ignore his presence. He was somewhere right ahead of her, and perhaps he had already gained possession of the books. She needed to find that out. She had not forgotten her earlier decision to concentrate on the books, but every turn she took led back to her nemesis. It was pointless to pretend any longer that she could separate the two.

She had listened to the sounds of battle during her approach, slowing automatically, not wanting to stumble into something she was not prepared for. She did not yet know what it was that lived down there, although she was fairly certain it was something from the Old World. It was intelligent and dangerous if it had survived all those years, and she would avoid it if she could. From the sounds ahead, it appeared that it might have enough to occupy it already without bothering about her.

The passageways twisted and turned, and she soon discovered that the sounds were carrying farther than she realized. By the time she was closing in on their source, they had died away almost to nothing, small hummings and cracklings, little fragments of noise broken off in a struggle that had consumed their makers. The alarms had ceased, and the traps that had warded the passageways had locked up. She could still sense a presence somewhere deep within the walls, but it was small and failing rapidly. Smoke rolled past her in clouds, beck-oning her ahead to where the passageway opened into a ruin dominated by a pair of massive cylinders that had been cracked and twisted by explosions from within. Bits and pieces of creepers lay everywhere, and machines whose pur-pose she could not begin to comprehend were knocked askew, their cables and wires severed and sparking. The chamber that housed them was vast and silent as she stepped inside, a safehold become a tomb.

She felt the Druid's presence at once. Responding to it, she stepped through the debris and into the remains of a chamber to one side.

She saw him almost immediately. He sat propped against one wall, staring back at her. Stained red with blood, his black robes spread away from him like a tattered shroud. His body was burned and ravaged. Most of one leg was gone. His skin, where not blistered and peeling, was so pale it seemed drawn with chalk on the drifting haze.

She stared at his ruined body and was surprised to discover that she felt no satisfaction. If anything, she was disappointed. She had waited all her life for that moment, and once it had arrived, it was nothing at all as she had pictured it. She had wanted to be the instrument of the Druid's destruction. Some-one had cheated her of the pleasure.

She walked to within a few feet of him and stopped. Still she did not speak, her eyes locked on his, looking for some-thing that would give her a little of the satisfaction she had been denied. She found nothing.

"Where are the others?" she asked finally. "The seer and the Elf?"

He coughed and swallowed thickly. "Gone."

"You're dying, Druid," she said.

He nodded. "It is my time."

"You've lost."

"Have I?"

"Death steals away all our chances. Yours flee from you even as we speak."

"Perhaps not."

His refusal to acknowledge his defeat infuriated her, but she held her temper carefully in check. "Did you find the magic you sought?" She paused. "Will you tell me willingly or must I pry open your mind to gain an answer to my question?"

"Threats are unnecessary. I found the magic and took from it what I could. But while I live, it is beyond your reach."

She stared at him. "I haven't long to wait then, do I?"

"Longer than you think. My dying is only the beginning of your journey."

She had no idea what he was talking about. "What journey is that, Druid? Tell me."

Blood appeared on his lips and ran down his chin in a thin stream. His eyes were beginning to glaze. She felt a twinge of panic. He must not die yet. "I have the boy," she said. "You did an impressive job of convincing him of the lies he now insists are the truth. He really believes himself to be Bek and me to be his sister. He believes you are his friend. If you care for him, you will help me now, while there is still time."

Walker's eyes never left her face. "He is your brother, Grianne. You hid him in the cellar of your home, in a chamber behind a cabinet. He was found there by a shape-shifter, who in turn brought him to me. I took him to a man and his wife in the Highlands to raise as a foster son. That is the truth. The lies are all your own."

"Don't use my name, Druid!" she hissed at him.

One hand lifted weakly. "The Morgawr killed your parents, Grianne. He killed them and stole you away so that he could take advantage of your talents and make you his student. He told you I did it so that you would hate his greatest enemy. He did so in the hopes that one day you would destroy me. That was his plan. He subverted your thinking early and trained you well. But he did not know about Bek. He did not know that there was someone besides me who knew the truth he had worked so hard to conceal."

"All lies," she whispered, her anger strong again, her magic roiling within her. She would strike him down if he said another word. She would tear him apart and put an end to things here and now.

"Would you know the truth?" he asked.

"I know it already."

"Would you know the truth finally and forever?"

She stared at him. There was intensity to his dark eyes that she could not dismiss. He had something in mind, something he was working toward, but she was not certain what it was. Be careful, she told herself.

She folded her arms into her robes. "Yes," she said.

"Then use the sword."

For a moment, she had no idea what he was talking about. Then she remembered the talisman she wore strapped across her back, the one the boy had given her. She reached over her shoulder and touched it lightly. "This?"

"It is the Sword of Shannara." He swallowed thickly, his breath rattling in his chest. "Call upon it if you would know the real truth, the one you have denied for so long. The talisman cannot lie. There can be no deception with its use. Only the truth."

She shook her head slowly. "I don't trust you."

His smile was faint and sad. "Of course not. I'm not asking you to. But you trust yourself, don't you? You trust your own magic. Use it, then. Are you afraid?"

"I'm afraid of nothing."

"Then use the sword."

"No."

She thought that would be the end of it, but she was wrong. He nodded as if she had given him the answer he expected. Instead of thwarting his intentions, she seemed to have buttressed them. His good arm shifted so that his hand was lying on his shattered breast. She did not know how he could still be alive.

"Use the sword with me," he whispered.

She shook her head instantly. "No."

"If you do not use the sword," he said softly, "you can never gain control over the magic I have hidden from you. Everything I have acquired, all the knowledge of the Old World gleaned from these catacombs, all of the power granted by the Druids, is locked away inside me. It can be released if you use the sword, if you are strong enough to master it, but not otherwise."

"More lies!" she spat.

"Lies?" His voice was weakening, his words fatigued and slurred. "I am a dead man. But I am still stronger than you are. I can use the sword while you cannot. Dare not. Prove me wrong, if you think you can. Do as I say. Use the sword. Test yourself against me. All that I have, all of it, becomes yours if you are strong enough. Look at me. Look into my eyes. What do you see?"

What she saw was a certainty that brooked no doubt and concealed no subterfuge. He was challenging her to look at the truth as he believed it to be, asking her to risk what that might mean. She did not think she should do so, but she also believed that access to his mind was worth any risk. Once inside, she would know all his secrets. She would know the truth about the missing books of magic. She would know the truth about herself and the boy. It was a chance she could not afford to pass up. His nonsense about Druid knowledge and power was a ploy to distract her, but she could play such games much better than he could.

"All right." Her words were rimmed in iron. "But you will place your hand on the sword first, under mine, so that I can hold you fast. That way, should this prove to be a trick of some kind, you will not escape me."

She thought she had turned the tables on him neatly. She expected him to refuse, frightened of being linked to her in a way that stripped him of a chance to break free. But again he surprised her. He nodded in agreement. He would do as she asked. She stared at him. When she thought she saw a flicker of satisfaction cross his face, she was flooded with anger and clenched her fist at him.

"Do not think you can deceive me, Druid!" she snapped. "I will crush you faster than you can blink if you try!"

He did not respond, his eyes still locked on hers. For an instant she thought to abandon the whole effort, to back away from him. Let him die, and she would sort it all out later. But she could not make herself give up the opportunity he was offering her, even if it was only for a moment. He kept so many secrets. She wanted them all. She wanted the truth about the boy. She wanted the truth about the magic of that safehold. She might never have another chance to discover either, if she did not act quickly.

She took a steadying breath. Whatever else he intended,

whatever surprise he planned, she was more than a match for him, wasn't she?

She reached over her shoulder and slowly unsheathed the sword, bringing it around in front of her, setting it between them, blade down, handle up. In the smoky gloom, the ancient weapon looked dull and lifeless. Her doubts returned. Was it really the legendary Sword of Shannara or was it something else, something other than what she believed it to be? There was no other magic concealed within it; she would have detected any by now. Nor was there anything about it that would lend strength to the dying Druid. Nothing could save him from the wounds he had incurred. She wondered again at what had savaged him so and would have asked if she had thought there was enough time left to do so.

She inched closer to him, repositioning the blade so that he could reach the handle. She kept her eyes on his, watching for signs of deceit. It seemed impossible that he could manage anything. His eyes were lidded, his breathing rough and shallow, his torn body leaking blood into his robes in such copious amounts she did not know how there could be any left inside him. For just an instant, fresh doubt assailed her, warning her away from what she was about to do. She trusted her instincts, but she hated to acknowledge fear in the face of her sworn enemy, a man against whom she had measured herself for so many years.

She brushed the doubt away. "Place your hand on the sword!"

He raised his bloodied hand from his chest and wrapped his fingers around the handle. As he did so, he seemed to lose focus for a moment, and his hand extended past the talisman to brush lightly against her forehead. She was concentrating so hard on his eyes that she did not think to watch his hand.

She flinched at his touch, aware of the damp smear his fingers had left against her skin. She heard him say something, words spoken so softly she could not make them out.

The feel of his blood on her forehead disturbed her, but she would not give him the satisfaction of seeing her troubled enough to wipe it away. Instead, she placed her hand over his and tightened her grip to hold him fast.

"Now we shall see, Druid."

"Now we shall," he agreed.

Eyes locked, they waited in the smoking ruins of the extraction chamber, so alone that there might have been no one else alive in the world. Everything had gone still. Even the severed cables and wires that had sparked and buzzed only moments before and the shattered machines that had struggled so hard to continue functioning had gone still. It was so quiet that the Ilse Witch could hear the sound of the Druid's breathing slow to almost nothing.

She was wasting her time, she thought abruptly, angry all over again. This wasn't the Sword of Shannara. This wasn't anything more than an ordinary blade.

In response, her fingers dug into Walker's hand and the worn handle beneath it. *Tell me something! Show me your truth, if you have any truth to show!*

An instant later, she felt a surge of warmth rise out of the blade, enter her hand, and spread through her arm. She saw the Druid flinch, then heard him gasp. An instant after that, white light flared all about them, and they disappeared into its molten core.

On the coast of the Blue Divide, dawn was breaking offshore through a fog bank that stretched across the whole of the horizon like a massive wall. From the deck of the *Jerle*

Shannara, Redden Alt Mer watched the fog materialize in the wake of the retreating night, a rolling gray behemoth closing on the shoreline with the inevitability of a tidal wave. He had seen fog before, but never like that. The bank was thick and unbroken, connecting water to sky, north to south, light to dark. Dawn fought to break through cracks in its surface, a series of angry red streaks that had the look of heated steel, as if a giant furnace had been lit somewhere out on the water.

March Brume experienced heavy fog at times, as did all the seaports along the Westland coast. Mix heat and cold where land met water, stir in a healthy wash of condensation, and you could muster fog thick enough to spread on your toast—that was the old salt's claim. The fog Redden Alt Mer was watching was like that, but it had something else to it, as well, a kind of energy, dark and purposeful, that suggested the approach of a storm. Except the weather didn't feel right for it. His taste and smell of the air revealed nothing of rain, and there had been no sounds of thunder or flashes of lightning. There wasn't a breath of wind. Even the pressure readings gave no hint of trouble.

The Rover Captain paced to the aft decking and peered harder into the haze. Had something moved out there?

"Pea soup," Spanner Frew grumbled, coming up to stand beside him. He frowned out of his dark beard like a thunderhead. "Glad we're not going that way anytime soon."

Alt Mer nodded, still looking out into the haze. "Better hope it stays offshore. I'll be skinned and cooked before I'll let us be stuck here another week."

One more day, and the repair on the airship would be finished. It was so close now that he could barely contain his impatience. Little Red had been gone for three days already, and he hadn't felt right about it once. He had faith in her good judgment, and in Hunter Predd's, as well, but he felt compromised enough as it was by what had befallen the members of the ship's company in that treacherous land. They were scattered all over the place, most of them lost or dead, and he had no idea how they were ever going to bring everyone together, even without the added problem of wondering what might have happened to his sister.

"Have you solved the problem of that forward port crystal?" he asked, watching the shifting fog bank, still thinking he had seen something.

The burly shipwright shrugged. "Can't solve it without a new crystal, and we don't have one. Lost the spares overboard in the channel during the storm. We'll have to make do."

"Well, we've been down that road before." He leaned forward, his hands on the railing, his eyes intent on the fog bank. "Take a look out there, Black Beard. Do you see something? There, maybe fifteen degrees off . . ."

He never finished. Before he could complete the sentence, a cluster of dark shapes materialized out of the gloom. Airborne, they flew out of the roiling gray like a flock of Shrikes or Rocs, silhouetted against the crimson-streaked wall. How many were there? Five, six? No, Alt Mer corrected himself almost at once. A dozen, maybe more. He counted quickly, his throat tightening. Two dozen at least. And they were big, too big even for Rocs. Nor did they have wings to propel them ahead, to provide them with vertical lift.

He caught his breath. They were airships. A whole fleet of them, come out of nowhere. He watched them take shape, masts and sails, rakish dark hulls, and the glint of metal stays and cleats. Warships. He brought up his spyglass and peered closely at them. No insignia emblazoned on flags or pennants, no markings on the gunwales or hulls. He watched them clear the fog and wheel fifteen degrees left, all on a line across the horizon, black as netherworld shades as they drifted into formation and began to advance.

Redden Alt Mer put down the spyglass and took a deep, steadying breath.

They were sailing right for the *Jerle Shannara*.

Here ends Book Two of *The Voyage of the* Jerle Shannara. Book Three, *Morgawr,* will conclude the series as the Ilse Witch is forced to confront the truth about herself and the survivors of Castledown begin the long journey home.